I0593697

Charles Gavan Duffy

Thomas Davis

The Memoirs of an Irish Patriot, 1840-1846

Charles Gavan Duffy

Thomas Davis
The Memoirs of an Irish Patriot, 1840-1846

ISBN/EAN: 9783744717120

Printed in Europe, USA, Canada, Australia, Japan

Cover: Foto ©Raphael Reischuk / pixelio.de

More available books at **www.hansebooks.com**

THOMAS DAVIS

THE MEMOIRS OF AN IRISH PATRIOT

1840—1846

BY

SIR CHARLES GAVAN DUFFY
K.C.M.G.

"Those who live as models for the mass
Are singly of more value than they all.
Keep but the model safe, new men will rise
To take its mould, and other days to prove
How great a good was Luria's having lived"
BROWNING

LONDON
KEGAN PAUL, TRENCH, TRÜBNER & CO., Lt?.
1890

DEDICATION.

I DEDICATE this memoir to Englishmen and Irishmen who honestly doubt the desire or the capacity of Ireland for self-government.

They will judge whether the man depicted in the memoir and his associates did not seek a worthy and practicable end by honourable and commensurate means.

CONTENTS.

MEMOIR OF THOMAS DAVIS.

CHAPTER I.

THERE are readers to whom the name of Thomas Davis will sound strange, but to the wide circle to whom it is familiar it represents a unique type of patriotism and integrity. If the educated Irishmen of to-day, of all classes and parties, were required to name the man who came nearest their ideal of an Irish patriot, no one born in the century now drawing to a close would combine so many suffrages as Davis.

He has been dead nearly half a century, and no memoir of him has hitherto been published. To write his life was a task which more than one of his early friends desired to undertake. But when he died they were engaged for the most part in exhausting public labours, and before he was half a dozen years in his grave many of those who knew him best were scattered to the ends of the earth by political disaster. When they rallied, some years later, the design was not forgotten, but his family were of opinion that the time had not yet come when his posthumous papers might properly be

B

published. Now, at length, when all the necessary materials are available, only two or three of his comrades survive; and with their cordial encouragement and assistance I hasten to take up the long-deferred work, lest death should deprive me, too, of the happiness of depicting the best man I have ever known.

Thomas Davis was born in Mallow, county Cork, on the 14th of October, 1814. When he came into the world Ireland was a garrison, in the same sense that Calcutta or Gibraltar is a garrison to-day. The native population, who were universally Catholics, amounted to between six and seven millions, but none of them under the existing law could occupy any office of authority in their native country. The town where he was born was a type of a system which existed, slightly modified by local circumstances, in every town in the island. There was some form of municipal government, but the administrators were· exclusively Protestants. There· was an Established Church, maintained at the common cost of the whole population, for a minority of less than one in a dozen, and more profusely endowed than any establishment in Christendom. The only schools supported or recognized by the state were under exclusively Protestant management. Justice was administered in courts in which the entire official staff were of the favoured creed. And the recognized test of what was called "loyalty" was the determination to perpetuate this system, to support Protestant ascendancy in the Church, the executive government, the magistracy and the municipalities. Ireland was represented by a hundred members in the parliament of London, but only Protestants could be

chosen, and, though votes had been conferred upon
Catholics twenty years earlier, the rural electors
were tenants at will, who voted under orders of
their landlord or his agent. The Irish nobility with
half a dozen exceptions lived in England, and the
resident gentry and professional classes led gay
convivial lives, with little thought of politics beyond
the necessary precautions to keep the populace quiet.
A few prosperous Catholics, in the mercantile or
professional classes in Dublin, demanded civil and
religious liberty from time to time; but the Protestants who sympathized with them were scarcely
more numerous than the Indian officials to-day who
would manumit the Hindoo.

Davis belonged by birth to the minority who
enjoyed the monopoly of property and power. His
father, James Thomas Davis, was a surgeon in the
Royal Artillery, and served in the Peninsular War,
with the rank of Inspector of Hospitals. His mother,
Mary Atkins, descended from a good Anglo-Irish
family, which traced back its line to the great
Norman House of Howard, and—what Davis loved
better, to remember—to the great Celtic House of
O'Sullivan Beare. I found among his papers this
fragment of a letter, in his own handwriting, which
probably tells all the reader will care to know on the
subject :—

"My father was a gentleman of Welsh blood, but his family
had been so long settled in England that they were, and considered themselves, English. He held a commission in the English
army. I am descended on my mother's side from a Cromwellian
settler whose descendants, though they occasionally intermarried
with Irish families, continued Protestants, and in the English
interest, and suffered for it in 1688. I myself was brought up
High Tory and an Episcopalian Protestant, and if I am no longer

a Tory it is from conviction, for all those nearest and dearest to me are so still. Forgive this bit of biography. It cannot arise from egotism in an anonymous writer, but I want you [to understand my position]." *

This mixture of Celtic and Norman blood is an amalgam which has nourished noble fruit. Nearly a hundred years earlier, a father of Anglo-Norman descent and a mother of pure Celtic strain reared a son who ranks with Bacon and Milton in the intellectual hierarchy of these islands, and a majority of the most noted Irishmen are of the same mixed race as Edmund Burke.

Davis was born after his father's death, the youngest of four children, of whom a brother and sister survive. When he was four years of age the family removed to Dublin, living at Warrington Place till 1830, and afterwards at 61 (now 67), Lower Bagot Street, where the survivors still reside. His birthplace was a garden of traditional and historical romance, but he left Mallow so early that it would be fanciful to speak of boyish impressions at an age when he was scarcely breeched. He was educated at the noted school of Mr. Mongan, Lower Mount Street, and in 1831 entered Trinity College. As a

---

* "He was, genealogists affirm, a man of old and honourable descent, both on the maternal and paternal side. His mother's family was a branch of the Atkins of Firville, in the county Cork, sharing also the blood of the O'Sullivans. His great grandfather, Sir Jonathan Atkins, of Givensdale, in Yorkshire, was Governor of Guernsey in the seventeenth century, and left, by his first wife, Mary (daughter of Sir Richard Howard, of Neworth Castle, Cumberland, the sister of the first Earl of Carlisle), three sons, the second of whom settled at Fountainville, county Cork, and was the maternal ancestor of Davis. His father, James Thomas Davis, was the representative of a Buckinghamshire family originally from Wales" ("Young Ireland," chap. iii.).

From a family genealogy I learn that Richard Atkins married Anne, only daughter of the O'Sullivan Beare (she was born in 1712 and died in 1756), and by her left John Atkins, who married Mary, second daughter of Robert Atkins of Fountainville, and had two sons and four daughters, the fourth of whom was mother of Thomas Davis.

child he was feeble and delicate, for which the
anxiety his mother suffered at his father's premature
death will probably account; and in youth.he was
subject to frequent fits of despondency—less an individual trait, I fancy, than an ordinary result of the
poetic temperament. But when he became a student
of Trinity all symptoms of debility had disappeared;
he was fond of long walking excursions, and entered
almost immediately on the systematic study which
needs a solid reserve of vigour to sustain. His boyhood passed as the boyhood of poets and thinkers
is apt to pass. He was silent, thoughtful, and self-
absorbed. We hear, without surprise, that the
boisterous spirits of schoolboys oppressed him, and
that he took slight pleasure in their sports; for that
is the common lot of his class. So little is known
with certainty of that period, that I must borrow
from a former book the few particulars I was able
to gather from his contemporaries:—

"One of his kinswomen, then resident in Melbourne, who
judged him as the good people judged who mistook the young
swan for an ugly duck, assured me that he was a dull child. He
could scarcely be taught his letters, and she often heard the schoolboy stuttering through 'My Name is Norval' in a way that was
pitiable to see. When he had grown up, if you asked him the day
of the month, the odds were he could not tell you. He never was
any good at handball or hurling, and knew no more than a fool
how to take care of the little money his father left him. She saw
him more than once in tears listening to a common country fellow
playing old airs on a fiddle, or sitting in a drawing-room as if he
were in a dream when other young people were enjoying themselves; which facts I doubt not are authentic, though the narrator
somewhat mistook their significance. Milton, in painting his own
inspired youth, has left a picture which will be true for ever of
the class of which he was a chief:—

    "'When I was yet a child, no childish play
      To me was pleasing; all my mind was set

> Serious to learn and know; and thence to do
> What might be public good: myself I thought
> Born to that end—born to promote all truth,
> All righteous things.'" *

" He was not a precocious boy," said another contemporary; " he did not speak often or willingly, but an observer who marked how readily the beads of perspiration gathered on his brow would understand that there were forces at work under the surface."

He lived a life of day-dreams, for the most part,—the first and most subtle discipline of a boy of genius. He has told us himself the subject of his reveries.

> " What thoughts were mine in early youth!
>   Like some old Irish song,
> Brimful of love, and life, and truth,
>   My spirit gushed along.
>
> " I hoped to right my native isle,
>   I hoped a soldier's fame,
> I hoped to rest in woman's smile,
>   And win a minstrel's name."

When he entered college, in his seventeenth year, we do not pass at once from obscurity to light; many of his fellow-students and some of his teachers are still living, but they have nothing to tell of that era, except that he was habitually self-absorbed and a prodigious reader. For four or five years he hibernated among his books, slowly gathering knowledge and silently framing opinions. From his casual talk he was regarded as a Benthamite, a dumb questioner of authority, discontented with many things established, but not likely to prove a formidable opponent. In 1836, when he was keeping his last term as a law student in London, one of his early friends saw with amazement silent tears fall down his cheeks at some

* " Young Ireland," chap. iii.

generous allusion to the Irish character on the stage
—a sensibility he was far from expecting in the
supposed Utilitarian.

Though Trinity College was a fortress of Protestant
ascendancy, the amphitheatre where young athletes
were trained to defend the Established Church, the
land code, and the exclusive magistracy and municipalities, it has always reared passionate Nationalists.
There is scarcely a man distinguished as an opponent
of British supremacy, from Jonathan Swift to Isaac
Butt, who was not educated in that institution. In
1793 two of its graduates, Thomas Emmet and
Wolfe Tone, first taught nakedly the doctrine, that
the essential basis of Irish liberty was peace and
brotherhood among Protestants and Catholics. Since
Catholic emancipation was conceded, Charles Boy-
ton, a fellow of the University, with a remarkable
gift of popular eloquence, made some discursive
attempts to revive the impossible nationality of Flood
and Charlemont—a nationality from which the bulk
of the nation was excluded. And when Davis matri-
culated, there was a little knot of generous Protestants
in college who talked to each other the old doctrine
of Tone and Emmet—Ireland, not for a sect or
a social caste, but for the whole Irish people. Thomas
Wallis, a college tutor, Torrens McCullagh, a young
barrister of great colloquial powers, and Francis
Kearney, a student, who died before he was called to
the Bar, were the leading spirits in this connection.
For a time these young men barely knew Davis, and
I learned from the survivors that they misunderstood
him so completely that one of the set fixed upon him
a nickname implying contented mediocrity. They
always insisted that his nature had not then

awakened; that he was still slow, laborious, and tame; and that there was no hint in his conversation of the fountain of thought and passion soon to overflow, or of the indomitable will masked under habitual silence.

That his fellow-students misjudged Davis's natural endowments became plain enough to themselves in the end; but I think they misjudged as seriously the condition of his mind when they knew him first. His writings, when he came to write, furnish evidence difficult to resist that his voluminous studies were guided by a purpose from an early period. While the young men about him were dreaming, as the goal of life, to win the great seal or episcopal lawn, this silent student had a rarer and more daring ambition. He resolved to be the servant of his country, as the great men of old who touched his heart had been. If he devoured history, and the historical romance and drama which light up the past, and pondered on the codes, annals, and memoirs, the speculations of economists and moralists, who disclose the laws which govern human conduct, it was that he might not be an unprofitable servant. The foundations of character are laid in boyhood and youth; and in his verses, where we may most confidently seek the secrets of a poet's heart, he tells us how early the hope of serving Ireland began: "when boyhood's fire was in his blood" he read of Leonidas and Thermopylæ, and how Horatius and his comrades held the Sublician Bridge, and prayed that he too might be worthy to do some gallant deed for his country.

> "And from that time, through wildest woe,
> *That hope* has shone, a far light;

Nor could love's brightest summer glow.
Outshine that solemn starlight:

"It seemed to watch above my head
   In forum, field, and fane;
Its angel voice sang round my bed,
  'A NATION ONCE AGAIN.'"

He sat down before the chaos of Irish annals
confused by honest ignorance and distorted by industrious malice, determined to understand the story
of his native country. So far as we know there was
no friendly hand to lead him through this pathless
thicket. Fortunate is the youth who has a guide fit
to make plain the difficult and to light the obscure
places of his study. But is he not stronger and
more sure-footed in the end who has made his way
over the impediments and through the darkness by
his native force? This silent arduous labour was a
discipline for life, and laid the foundations of a consummate man. In his little den in college, apart
from the babble of local politics, he studied the Irish
problem in the abstract. He saw in the island all
the natural capacity and resources for self-government. Nature had furnished the first conditions and
essential equipments for a great emporium of commercial enterprise to this land of multitudinous rivers
and harbours, lying between two continents. The
native race had proved their capacity in early civilization and early commerce, and by workmanship of
marvellous beauty, before the base jealousy of a
stronger neighbour had brought them to ruin. Their
exiles in later times had won distinction in war,
diplomacy, and the art of government, and there was
no reason to fear that the native sap had dried up.
The people were generous, pious and romantic, vigilant

husbandmen and skilled artisans, and would be fortified by the mettle of harder races; for the Ireland he dreamed of restoring was one in which native-born men, of whatever origin, should unite as Irishmen; as the Briton, the Angle, the Dane, the Norman, and the Netherlander had united in England. It was in this spirit he approached the Irish Tory :—

> " We have no curse for you or yours,
>   But Friendship's ready grasp,
> And Faith to stand by you and yours
>   Unto our latest gasp—
> To stand by you against all foes,
>   Howe'er, or whence they come,
> With traitor arts, or bribes, or blows,
>   From England, France, or Rome.

> " What matter that at different shrines
>   We pray unto one God—
> What matter that at different times
>   Your fathers won this sod—
> In fortune and in name we're bound
>   By stronger links than steel ;
> And neither can be safe nor sound
>   But in the other's weal."

A man of genius commonly attributes an inordinate importance to the mind which gave his own the first impulse towards action at a critical period of development. Very often it is a mind inferior to his own, but he is slow to perceive and loth to acknowledge this fact. Coleridge had such a feeling towards Bowles and Landor towards Southey, and Davis had certainly such a feeling towards Wallis. Wallis's position among his associates bore a not remote resemblance to that of Coleridge among the Lake Poets. He projected on a prodigious scale, but he made no attempt to perform what he projected. A thinker who does not work is not necessarily a wasted force.

His talk was full of new, startling, and often audacious truths; he had the gift of inspiring thought and awakening feeling, and, like his great exemplar, he considered his function exhausted when he had exhorted a man to do some good work, without any intention of setting him the example. One of his half-scoffing admirers used to say that if you could work miracles or were willing to try, and ready to be bullied for having failed, Wallis had a fascinating series of prodigies at your service. But to the serious mind of Davis these wild coruscations were like the electric current smiting the dusky coil of wire. They kindled his faculties for action, and inflamed his slumbering imagination. The apparently impossible did not frighten him; he felt within himself the will and capacity to perform what were prodigies and miracles to scoffing men of the world. In Cardinal Newman's fascinating confessions there is nothing more touching than his admission of important truths learned, or salutary impressions received, from some friends in the work which he was born and appointed to perform. And Davis rejoiced to exaggerate his obligations to Wallis. Wallis frankly accepted the hypothesis that he was the firebearer. Long after Davis's death, he wrote to me—

"You must consider all the experience I have had for the ten years or so that I was 'Professor of Things in general and Patriotism in particular,' in a garret in T.C.D. If I, and surely it was I that did it (his exorbitantly extravagant praise of me showed it), if I loosed the tenacious phlegm that clogged Davis's nature and hid his powers from himself and the world—if I kept Torrens McCullagh for several years from deflecting into the Whig parabola, which was his natural tendency—and if I changed John Dillon from a Whig and Utilitarian to a Nationalist and a popular leader—I must have expended rather a serious amount of magnetic force in the task, to say nothing of the scores of others that I mesmerized with less success, or less remarkable results. Don't think I am boasting, for I am rather ashamed than otherwise, both of the plentiful nonsense I used to talk, and of the foibles of human nature that make dreams and illusions more potent over it than the daylight of mature reason."

Torrens McCullagh was at this time the model of a handsome accomplished young Irishman. He had just begun to practise at the Bar, but posed as the jocund, good-humoured cynic who despised any success which might be won in that prosaic pursuit; a man destined, one might surmise, to go triumphantly to the world's end, but whose career has been considerably shorter. He had established a *Dublin University Review*, which had a brief existence; and, somewhat later, the *Citizen*, a monthly magazine in which he and his friends taught an enlightened national Whiggery such as they considered befitting the citizens of a free state.

In the society of these young men and their friends the knowledge Davis had gathered got classified by friendly discussion, and opinions which were in solution became crystallized. But he had as yet done nothing by which he could be estimated.

"Truth to say," says Wallis, "much of the early misconception of his character was his own fault. He learned much; suffered much, I have no doubt; felt and sympathized much; and hoped and enjoyed abundantly; but he had not yet learned to rely on himself. His powers were like the nucleus of an embryo star, uncompressed, unpurified, flickering and indistinct. . . . The result was, that during his college course, and for some years after, while he was very generally liked, he had, unless perhaps with some who knew him intimately, but a moderate reputation for high ability of any kind. In his twenty-fifth year, as I remember—that is, in the spring of 1839—he first began to break out of this. His opinions began to have weight, and his character and influence to unfold themselves in a variety of ways."

A debating society is the natural training school

of ambitious students, but at this time there was no
such society in the University, and an extern Historical Society, composed chiefly of college students,
which had done good service in its day had recently
ceased to meet. The first College Historical Society
had been founded in 1770, when Edmund Burke was
a student, and had met within the walls for nearly
a generation. Lord Avonmore, Temple Emmet,
Thomas Addis Emmet, and Wolfe Tone were among
the members. It had troubles with the authorities,
which never looked with much favour on these
unlicensed seminaries, but in 1792, after an interval
of sluggishness, it was remodelled under a new name.
Plunket, Bushe, John Shears, Peter Burrows, and,
later, Robert Emmet were among the members; but
new troubles with the authorities on political questions arose, and the society had to quit the college, and meet in the city. With the disasters of
1798 it disappeared altogether. In the memoir of
Richard Sheil, he speaks of a College Historical
Society in which Magee and North were his competitors, but there are no records of it. In 1829–1830,
when the Catholic contest and the Reform movement
kindled public spirit anew, there was a new society
meeting outside the college, in which Isaac Butt and
Torrens McCullagh were leaders, and Joseph Lefanu,
William Keogh, Wilson Gray, James O'Hea, Thomas
Wallis, Thomas MacNevin and Joseph Pollock, son of
a notable anti-Union pamphleteer, and John Lalor,
afterwards known in London as a writer in the *Morning Chronicle* and author of " Money and Morals,"
were distinguished members. In the beginning of
1839 a new society was projected, and it was understood that the provost and fellows were disposed to

sanction its establishment on the original basis. But
the most thoughtful of the students were of opinion
that it would be more useful and independent as an
extern society. The sanction of the authorities
would involve them in a certain responsibility which
might be exercised so jealously as to create ill will
between the teachers and the pupils. Contemporary
politics could not be effectually excluded by any
statute, for to debate the past in Irish history was to
debate the cause of the present. And a debating
society without freedom of speech would be not only
useless but injurious. At a meeting at Francis
Kearney's chambers, 27 College, on the 29th of
March, 1839, a new College Historical Society was
founded. The original members consisted of ten
Conservatives and ten Liberals; there was as yet no
talk of Nationalists. The third name in the list was
that of Thomas Davis, the preceding ones being
John Thomas Ball, since Lord Chancellor of Ireland,
and Joseph Lefanu, afterwards distinguished as a
popular novelist.*

Addresses were delivered at the opening of the
society's session in November, and at the close in
June. And Davis who became auditor, equivalent
to president, delivered the closing address in June,
1840.

It was in the Historical Society that he made the
acquaintance of a man to whom, in later years, he
was accustomed to open his whole mind and heart.
Daniel Owen Maddyn was then a law student pre-

---

* "You have been appointed, by mutual nomination of Conservatives
and Liberals, an original member of the new Historical Society. The preliminary meeting will be held to-morrow (Thursday), at Mr. Kearney's
chambers, 27 College, at three o'clock p.m. precisely" (Wallis to Davis,
March 13, 1839).

paring for a call to the Bar, but more disposed to philosophical and literary studies, into which he got finally drawn as the business of his life. He knew Davis while he was still undervalued by his associates, and understood him better than the majority. Forty years ago, when I first meditated writing this memoir, Maddyn sent me as a contribution to it his recollections of Davis at this period, and his impression of the young men among whom he lived. And since his death, his kinsman, Denny Lane, has given me the correspondence which, during the entire period of his public career, Davis maintained with Maddyn.*

"I first knew Thomas Davis in the early part of the year 1838. I had been just then made a member of the King's Inns, and Davis had been a short time previously called to the Bar.

"Though not entitled to be admitted a member of the College Historical Society, by the kindness of Messrs. Lawson† (then auditor) and Hodder I was enrolled amongst its members, a circumstance which led to my acquaintance with Davis. He had, a short time previously, published a hasty, but in many respects an ably written pamphlet on 'The Reform of the House of Lords'—a subject which, in those palmy days of Whig-Radicalism, attracted much attention. I remember buying the pamphlet in Westmorland Street, and feeling curious to know who the author was. I was told by one of the collegians that it was by Davis. 'And who was Davis?' 'Oh! he was an odd sort of man, of immense reading.' I heard him alluded to in the Historical Society, and I found that he had a confirmed reputation for most extensive and varied reading. One evening, seated by the side of Thomas MacNevin, I saw a short thickset young man, wrapped in a fearnought coat, shamble into the room, and speak in a tone between jest and earnest to several of the members. 'That,' said Mac-

* Author of the "Age of Pitt and Fox," "Leaders of Opinion," and some other notable books. He spelt his name originally Madden, but in later years adopted the other form in his books and correspondence. The paper is dated Fermoy, March 3, 1847, and has for title "Recollections of Thomas Davis, by his friend, Daniel Owen Madden," and for mottoes "Hæc miminisse juvabit," "Of him you know his merits such, I cannot say—you hear —too much" (Elegy on Sidney).

† The late Judge Lawson.

Nevin, 'is Davis.' 'What! was it he wrote the pamphlet on Peerage Reform?' 'Ay, yonder you behold the cataract that is to sweep away the House of Lords.' There was something about Davis which I liked at first sight. There was a frank honesty about his face, and I liked his large well-opened eyes.

"The Historical Society was at that time tolerably well sustained. It had undergone so many changes since its foundation, that it had been a different kind of institution at various periods. In 1838 it used to assemble at Radley's Hotel, in a large room upstairs. A temporary bar was placed across the room, inside of which were the members, who used to muster to the number of thirty or thereabouts, and have an audience of visitors double that number. The only members that had obtained decided reputation as good ready speakers and effective debaters were Messrs. Butt and James O'Hea, the former of whom had ceased to attend the society at this period. Amongst other prominent speakers in those days were Messrs. Torrens McCullagh,* Joseph Pollock,† James Anthony Lawson; ‡ John Thomas Ball, Thomas Wallis,‖ William Keogh, W. Conway Dobbs, the Messrs. Roberts, F.T.C.D., Jellett, now F.T.C.D., and various other members of the University. The style of speaking was vicious in the extreme, showy, declamatory, and vehement. The arts of elocution were little studied. Fluency and vehemence were the objects aimed at. To astound, not to persuade, the audience, was the aim of nine-tenths of the speakers. It was necessarily, therefore, a bad school of eloquence, and was suited to produce only platform speakers.§

* Author of "The Use and Study of History," and other works.
† Now of the English Bar, the son of the eminent barrister of the same name, who wrote the letters signed Owen Roe O'Neill, which at the close of the last century were much read in Ireland (1847).
‡ Ex-Professor of Political Economy, T.C.D. (1847).
‖ Editor of Davis's " Poems," and author of several essays in the *Citizen* and *Nation* (1847).
§ " The vituperative propensities of the members were shocking. Mr. Walsh, of the Conservative party, one night attacked the character of O'Connell ; Mr. Keogh, of the Liberal side, replied and denounced Mr. Walsh, commenting on his personal appearance in the following words :—
" 'The grim and grisly skeleton, howling in death-bed agony, and lifting its plague-tainted countenance to heaven,—*that*, too, may be eloquent.'
" This sentence contained what Sheridan would have called ' a very formidable likeness ' to Mr. Walsh, who was a tall meagre man, who spoke with upturned eyes, and whose face was blotched with nasty eruptions. When Mr. Keogh uttered the sentence, Walsh burst into tears; all were indignant; there was a strong feeling roused against Keogh. Afterwards, when MacNevin was appointed auditor, he named Keogh as his secretary, and a vote of censure was proposed on MacNevin—' that the officers of the society had not the confidence of the members.' This produced a row. It became the talk

THE STUDENT.

"There were other, and perhaps more serious, defects in the society; there was a fondness for invective, and a propensity to altercation and personality which got it the character of a 'scolding club.' Many of the young declaimers revelled in composing speeches against each other, in which epigrammatic impudence and elaborate personality formed the chief ingredients. Many of the more learned and able members took no part, save that of spectators, in the society, which in those days was a declaiming rather than a debating club.

"But there was much about the society which was attractive. There was much in its proceedings to amuse and excite; several of its members were men of wit and pleasantry. Cloistered students rubbed off within its walls their rust and pedantry. College rivals became friends within its social circle; men of opposite sentiments became acquainted; and friendly intercourse was promoted amongst those who were afterwards to meet in scenes of real competition. After the violent speeches there were excellent suppers, and members forgot over broiled bones the belabouring they had inflicted upon each other. Thus there was a great play of character amongst the members, and a young man learned in a pleasant way a good deal of life. The evils were in some respects counterbalanced by its advantages. They who derived most advantage from the institution were probably those who never spoke at all, but quietly looked on while others were making fools of themselves, and reserved their jaws for the suppers.

"Sometimes there was genuine eloquence. I remember particularly a debate on the Ballot, in which Messrs. Ball and MacNevin made each a most brilliant and ably reasoned speech on that question. In the subsequent year I heard the same subject discussed in the House of Commons, on the night (June 16, 1839) when Mr. Macaulay made his reappearance in Parliament after his residence in India, and I felt that if, upon either side, such speeches as those of Messrs. Ball and MacNevin had been delivered, they would have been heard with attention and greeted with applause.

of Dublin. Keogh's friends rallied, and made every effort to save him from the disgrace of being turned out of the office. By getting up a party cry, and by practising on the nerves of Mr. ——, the leader of the Conservatives at that time, Mr. Keogh was saved from the vote of censure.

"Poor MacNevin! 'Alas! how full of burs this weary working-day world is!' He was far the wittiest man in the society, he was a favourite of all parties, and he was an admirable elocutionist. He was a pupil of Vandenhoff—Mr. Keogh once told me so; he had great power of artistic assumption of a *rôle* in speaking. He was then in the tide of spirits, buoyant with hope. His sarcasm was poignant, and clean cutting."

c

"Davis made no figure in this society. For its mock contests and unreal encounters the earnestness of his character unsuited him. His solid massive talents were not adapted for the light clever fencing of the wordy disputants. But he liked the society on the principle that anything amongst young men was better than total intellectual stagnation. The names of Grattan, Plunket, Burke, and other great men who were associated with the institution in its earlier and better days, invested it with natural interest in his eyes. Being of a very social turn, he liked to mingle with his youthful contemporaries, and enjoyed their company very much. He was elected Auditor of the society, whose office was to manage its affairs and keep the members together.

"He had no 'name' as a speaker, but he was respected as a man of talents. His moral qualities, however, were not appreciated, chiefly because, up to that time (his twenty-fourth year), he had not openly developed all his character. It certainly did not redound much to the discrimination of his associates that his merits were not earlier recognized. The general opinion of him was that he was 'a book in breeches.' His varied knowledge, extending over a very wide surface, and deep upon many questions, was perceived by all who approached him.

"I remember his coming one morning to me while I lived in William Street. My table was strewed with books, which he took up one after another. Some of them he had read, and rapidly characterized them in his vigorous manner. He made no pretensions, after the fashion of literary coxcombs, to omniscience. When he did not know a thing, he said so very humbly. I was much pleased with the evident simplicity, manliness, and unaffected candour of his nature. They were qualities so strongly marked in his character that a person in his society would be apt to forget the high intellectual powers which, with the force of true genius, were blended and interwoven with his nature. Indeed I can say that, in the early part of my acquaintance, I forgot his abilities, and liked the man solely for himself.

"In college he read for honours, solely for the sake of exercising his mind and training it to intellectual discipline. . . . *
The Rev. Samuel Butcher, F.T.C.D., was the examiner, and he said that he never heard better answering. The candidates were men of great talents, and were laboriously prepared by 'grinders.' Davis, however, read by himself, and had no recourse to professional assistants in preparing himself for the

* I have omitted a sentence in which Mr. Maddyn assumes that Davis obtained a gold medal in Ethics, but he never competed for honours.

examination. It is right to add that he read more thoughtfully than the other students. He weighed the opinions of the philosophers whom he perused, and reflected deeply upon the tendency of their peculiar principles. That earnest moralizing spirit which pervaded his mind then took possession of him. Few things were more effective in forming his high-toned character than his ethical studies. They made him a strong thinker, and gave him large and noble views of mankind. Of all the moral philosophers Bishop Butler was his favourite. He placed him above all the others for originality and grandeur of views. It is not too much to say that the thoughts of Butler were a creed to him. If my memory does not deceive me, he once called Butler 'the Newton of Ethics.'

"I recollect his admiring Paley very much at that time; but at a subsequent period he used rather to disparage that most plausible and moderate of the Utilitarians. I remember him dwelling, with hearty appreciation, on the strong common sense and delightfully racy style of Paley. In his common sense and rationality, Davis found an able ally against a certain class of the religious world prone to a gloomy mysticism. Davis, like many others, was often brought into contact with men of harsh and fanatical prejudices upon sacred subjects. He met in the ministry not a few men of dark gloomy views, and uncharitable sentiments towards their fellow-Christians,—men whose influence in society was likely to be formidable on account of their sincerity and character. Against such a class and their mischief Davis would, in those days, employ the calm views and quiet sense of Paley. But the want of high spirituality, and a certain spirit of compromise in all his writings, prevented Paley from being a favourite with one so endowed with ardent feelings.

"In those days he had a very strong sense of the evils of religious fanaticism. I can speak with tolerable accuracy as to what was the complexion of his religious opinions. He was a Church of England man of the older and more liberal school. He was a frequent reader of the divines of the seventeenth century; the writings of Jeremy Taylor were heartily appreciated by him. He had at times a bold manner of putting his thoughts, which might mislead an ignorant person; but no man was more averse than he from licentious philosophy, or from profane discourse. I never recollect him speaking with levity on serious subjects. His frame of mind was naturally reverent, and the authors whom he habitually read were not of the mocking school. But when little men of little minds sought to strengthen their weak powers by allying themselves with fanaticism, he would expose their follies in a trenchant style, against which the refuted fanatic or convicted *Tartuffe* would defend himself by crying out with dissembled fright, 'Irreligious!' The exposure of hypocrisy is always a disagreeable, and often a dangerous proceeding. Political and religious affectation is oftentimes a vice with so many votaries, that from selfishness men are more tolerant of it than they ought. Probably Davis, on more than one occasion, experienced the dangers I have indicated.

"The value of moral philosophy he estimated very highly. He rejoiced very much that the late excellent Dr. Lloyd had given it so prominent a place in the college course. As long as I remember him, it was a favourite opinion of his, that the education of the higher classes of Irishmen was not of a kind that made them thoughtful. He wished that Ireland should produce more statesmen of action than mere orators, more philosophers and historians than novelists and sparkling *littérateurs*. He thought that the changes made by Dr. Lloyd would have a serious effect in awakening many a mind, and emancipating it from the routine of mere mechanical training. From his earlier days, that a high moral spirit should be raised amongst the upper classes was his eager aspiration.

"That he read for college honours was in some respects characteristic. At that time many men of parts, and of pretensions still greater than their parts, derided the system of college honours. They showered their wit upon premium men, and intimated that they would not condescend to such puerile objects of ambition. Alas! not a few of them paid a heavy penalty for their folly. When embarked in professions the preparation for which involves disagreeable drudgery, they regretted that at the fitting season they had not inured themselves to the habit of continuous exertion. The sole object of Davis was to discipline his mind.

"He was at that time as delightful a young man as it was possible to meet with in any country. All those virtues and peculiar charms which are to be looked for in a young man of energy and talent were assembled in his person. He was much more joyous than at the time he became immersed in practical politics. His good spirits did not seem, however, so much the consequence of youth and health as of his moral nature. His cheerfulness was not so much the result of temperament as of his sanguine philosophy, and of his wholesome, happy views of life. The sources of enjoyment were abundant to a man of his large faculties, highly cultured, possessing withal a body which supplied him with vigour and energy.

"In his politics he was at that time what would be called a hearty Liberal. It would be wrong, however, to call him a Radical, if that term is to be understood solely as indicating the English Radicals of the Hume and Warburton school. He had no superstitious veneration for ancient things, but neither had he any of that sour antipathy to them which marked the narrow-minded Radicals, who were utterly incapable of appreciating immemorial usages and time-honoured customs. A public measure was good or bad in his eyes, solely by its tendency to make men nobler, greater, more virtuous, or otherwise. The standing topics of party politics, even in these days, he despised. The rout and agitation about ballot—extension of suffrage, and short Parliaments, had little attraction for him. Not so, however, with corporations, with all questions of education, with all measures of social reform. From the first he saw how little genuine and permanent popular improvement could result from mere political changes of the kind aimed at by the English Radicals.

"At that time his mind was not particularly devoted to Irish affairs. There was then a close junction between the Irish and English politicians. The Irish Conservatives were perfectly satisfied with the professions of Sir Robert Peel; between the Melbourne Ministry and the Parliamentary Repealers led by Mr. O'Connell there was at least an affected sympathy, and a very decided purpose on both sides to be as useful to each other as circumstances would permit. They were the times when politics turned on the so-called Lichfield House compact. Wearied with the scenes of squabbling, and undignified altercations which had taken place between the retainers of the Castle and the supporters of the Corn Exchange, the Liberal party of Ireland (with some marked exceptions) appeared glad of a truce between the belligerents on any terms. Like most others of his contemporaries, Davis for the time chimed in indifferently well with the Liberal party of the time. It was not until about three years subsequently that he began to take very different views.

"Thus for a season, in his earlier days, he might have been said to be an Imperialist in his views—not, however, in preference to Nationalism, because at the time of which I speak (1838) the option was not fairly presented to him.

"On comparing him with his associates in the College Historical Society, and with the other collegians of his own standing whom I remember, two things especially distinguished him. First, the plainness of his character, and the perfect simplicity of his manners. There was, indeed, a vast quantity of ill-trained and ill-directed talent in the Historical. Men of bright parts and high hopes abounded in it. Some of these had been nine years in it. I remember one gentleman saying, in 1838, one night during what was called 'private business,' 'I was present myself, Mr. Chairman, at the time. The circumstances occurred *before the Revolution.*' I found that the Revolution alluded to was the French one of 1830, so that the speaker admitted that he was for nine years a member and frequenter of this talking club! Nor did the gentleman I allude to stand alone. An air of pretension, an assumption of precocious political importance very much disfigured the character of the young talkers. There was a theatrical manner about many of them, which was painful, and no drawing-room in Dublin ever witnessed so much absurd personal vanity as might have been met with in the Historical Society. The tendency of all such institutions in giving confidence and self-possession is to inflame self-esteem.

"I speak the plain truth when I declare that, from what I could see of Davis at the time, he was altogether free from affectation of every kind, and from all petty personal vanity. He had nothing of the showy air and varnished pretensions of others. No man could be less of a coxcomb. Vanities of appearance he utterly despised. He really was what he seemed to be. There is a passage in a sermon of Archbishop Tillotson, which every 'schoolboy who has been exercised in 'The Speaker' knows by heart— 'Truth and sincerity have all the advantages of appearance, and many more. If the show of anything be good for anything, I am sure the reality is better. For why should any man dissemble, etc.' Of this passage Davis was a living example.

"The second point in which he differed from his contemporaries was in the vastly extended course of his reading.

"He was a constant reader of history—of modern travels—of the biography of authors—and of the text writers in politics, such as Bolingbroke and Burke. Add to this that he had not, like others, neglected his college business. He had, besides, read some of the chief works in legal science. He was then a perfect *heluo librorum,* and he would really have become a mere 'book in breeches' but for the ethical discipline which he had given his mind. Much of what he read he cast from his memory, but what he deemed useful he rapidly assimilated with his previous acquirements.

"No one in the Historical Society at all came near him for extent of reading. Wallis was too lazy to be a strenuous reader. McCullagh probably read for effect, and despised many of the

works which Davis eagerly studied. In saying this I must not
be understood as disparaging Mr. McCullagh, with whom I was
at one period intimate, and who is decidedly superior to very many
of his rhetorical competitors. MacNevin and Keogh read only as
much as supplied fuel for their speeches. Ball read with ardour
at that time a good deal of English poetry, especially Wordsworth,
of whom he used to produce some very pretty imitations, when
his muse was kind. He read also ethics, and affected raptures
with Bishop Butler ; of his admiration of Butler I was sceptical,
because he was himself an extravagant Calvinist. Lefanu's reading I could form no opinion of. I saw him only once in the society,
and all he did that night was to scowl most magnificently at John
Thomas Ball, and utter something short, vehement, and fierce—
so much so that, though I have forgotten the word, I shall never
forget the appearance of 'pluck' and power Lefanu showed.
O'Hea was not a zealous reader, but I saw very little of him in
the society ; Butt was never there, during my time. Pollock was
no reader, but a most pleasing speaker, with a striking delivery,
and admirable manner. The men with whom Davis was to be
associated in reading were those who were studying for fellowship
—Tillett and the two Robertses. But Davis read from pure thirst
for knowledge, with a spirit of moral enthusiasm akin to the ardour
of a brave mariner, like Cook, voyaging to seek new countries.
He plunged into an ocean of reading, trusting to his mental elas-
ticity and thought for floating buoyantly under a deeply laden
memory.

    " If I am not mistaken, he was a member of the Law Debating
Society. I saw him there one night, but it might have been as a
visitor. I do not think he ever studied his profession with anything like attention. What Lord Bacon had written upon the
English law, he told me once, he had read through, and believed
that it was most useful reading for a lawyer. His idea upon studying the English law was that it should be read historically by the
student; he read Reeves's 'History of the Law,' and said it was
much more useful than Blackstone to a man wanting to make up
his knowledge as fast as possible. In 1838 I recollect that his
legal acquirements were spoken of very slightingly by one who
was a very competent judge. Yet he must have read a good deal
of jurisprudence, for he had a faculty of promptly referring to all
those parts of such works as treated of the philosophy of laws.

    " On the morning when he first came to see me, I well remem-
ber his taking up a Byron, and commenting on it. Of course he
was a great admirer of ' The Childe.' ' But, after all,' said he,

'there are some things that are better and grander in Wordsworth.' He was evidently charmed with the moral spirit of Wordsworth. It is not often one meets with a man who *heartily* appreciates such very opposite natures.

"He was fond of what was brilliant, rousing, and exciting. I remember his giving me graphic sketches of what he saw in the House of Commons during his visits to it while in London. He relished Sheil's pungent and exciting orations. I recollect his telling me one day, in the College grounds, of the stroke given by Sheil to Sir James Graham, in 1836. Discussing the Irish Church question, Graham made one of his elaborate, plausible, highly wrought speeches. His conclusion was the well-known passage from Lord Bolingbroke, in which that author states his conviction that, if the Church of England were destroyed, the Constitution itself must be buried in its ruins. The beautiful sentences of Bolingbroke were delivered by Graham with an imposing solemnity of manner; and the effect was very good, his own party cheering him heartily. While the plaudits were dying away up sprang Sheil, and while the fact of the quotation from Bolingbroke was in the memory of the House, he shouted forth, 'The right honourable baronet concluded his speech by quoting a deist and a traitor in defence of the *Church* and the *Constitution!* ' This happy epigram and pointed antithesis seemed to splinter the oration of Graham into fragments. Davis dwelt with great unction on the effect of this repartee.

"I do not remember any of his companions at that time. The only one I can positively speak of was his faithful loving friend Mr. P. R. Webb. I remember seeing Davis with him, and thinking that they were brothers.

"In his division at college were Mr. MacDowell (now F.T.C.D.), and Mr. J. Shaw Willes, now of the English Bar, where he is reaping at a very early period the fruits of vast talents and energy which knows no rest. These were two crack men of the division, both being mathematicians of the highest order.*

"At that time (1838) I did not discern much element of Irishry in Davis. In fact he was more like a young Englishman than an Irishman. He was always at work; he was no idler, or lazy coxcomb. There was a total absence of glare, of triviality, of theatrical manner, of affectation. He was thoroughly real. Simple, strong, unaffected; with proper pride, without any vanity, and with self-respect, he certainly showed more resemblance to the qualities of English nature than those commonly met with amongst Irishmen.

* Both now dead.

He had that broad, massive, and robust character which is, after all, the true genius of the Englishman, who in the brighter and more brilliant qualities of mind is surpassed by the Frenchman or the Irishman. He was more like a pupil of Charles James Fox than of Henry Grattan, judging him by his mental peculiarities.

"But he showed great ardour—I ought to say enthusiasm—of so vehement and at the same time tender kind, that its fervour would show him to have been an Irishman. 'Perfervidum ingenium Scotorum.'

"I was never 'introduced' to Davis. The auditor of the Historical Society always named the secretary. He walked across the room one night and asked me to become secretary. I did so at once. Hence our acquaintance. He had heard me make a Whig speech. This circumstance I mention because it may give some weight to the testimony I offer of Davis in 1838. It was only natural that I should regard him with some particular attention at that time.

"I left Dublin in July, 1838, and, with the exception of a letter relating to the College Historical Society which passed between us in that year, we were not again acquainted until the spring of 1841.

"I may add that at that time he seemed to me desirous of 'fame,' after the fashion of all high-spirited young souls. He told me, however, in 1841, that he had lost all his personal ambition—suggesting that he had once possessed it.

"In 1838 I had a book called 'Conversations at Cambridge.' It contained some literary *juvenilia*—bits of Macaulay's speeches at the Union Society, and some verses of Praed, the rival of Macaulay. With the 'Invocation to Madeline,' by Praed, Davis was excessively delighted. It is a sweetly tender poem, and pleased Davis vastly. He keep the book, and did not give it back, on account of this poem. Poor Praed's fine and subtle genius was never paid a higher compliment." *

* This is a quotation from one of Maddyn's notes to Davis in London : "I will be here for the winter, and am chumming with Willes [afterwards Mr. Justice Willes], who is engaged in piling a Pelion of Equity on an Ossa of Common Law. Keogh [afterwards Judge Keogh] is here also, and hard at work conveyancing. I saw him to-day, and heard him on Saturday last electrify Cogers Hall with one of the most able and powerful speeches I ever heard. Dec. 1839."

Another of Davis's friends, Denny Lane, had a high admiration for William Keogh's abilities. He was persuaded that if Keogh had had Davis's sincerity and integrity of nature, he would have become the most notable man of his generation, and, perhaps, have left even Davis behind in the race of public usefulness. Students may ponder with advantage on the career, the fate, and the reputation of these two men as an incitement to pursue the nobler path.

With these reminiscences of his college career the life of the student may close; that of the man of profound thought and decisive action was about to begin.

We can see through Maddyn's eyes the young auditor of the Historical Society among his associates, but he has not lifted the curtain from a more touching and impressive figure, the young student in his college cell. Secluded, unrecognized, and knowing himself only by casual flashes of insight, he was probably supremely happy because he was possessed by the passion which, to the boy of genius, is more engrossing than love of power or the love of women to manhood—the love of knowledge. He had access to a boundless library, the noble gateway to all the treasures of time, and he knew how to employ and enjoy that possession. The studies by which he gradually digested his mass of reading into principles and convictions exhibit astonishing industry and versatility. They are of all classes, from a chance thought scrawled on the fragment of a letter, to the exhaustive estimate of a standard book or a debated era. The patient analysis and protracted reflection from which conviction is born are mirrored in manuscripts many times revised. Systems of government, theories of philosophy, the habits and language of the people, the ballads and sayings popular among them, all pass in review in this process of self-education. The future poet was unconsciously nourishing his imagination, the future statesman collecting his data and framing his policy. Speaking of another youth of genius, he recalls his own debt to the college library:—

" Yes, books were his best, his unflinching friends ; they stood

by him in his greatest need; they solaced him; they comforted
him; they could not bestow wealth, but they supplied him with
all else he required; they were satisfactory, honest friends, who
told him the truth, a thing he was in search of, and much more
besides."

The stages by which Davis came to love all he had
been taught to deride or detest can only be a subject
of conjecture, but from the earliest record of his
opinions by his own hand, they are those of a confirmed Nationalist. He had silently grown into a
patriot. This result was not so unexampled as the
process by which it was attained. Some of the most
conspicuous figures in Irish history, between the fall
of Limerick and the emancipation of the Catholics,
are men who broke away from the party of Protestant ascendancy, and almost the first English
writer who recognized the essentially sordid character of Irish Toryism was John Sterling, the grandson of an Irish parson, and the son of a captain
of yeomanry. But to most of them their new opinions
came from contact with stronger minds; Davis
evolved them in the solitude of his college cell.

To complete Maddyn's survey of this early period
two or three facts must be mentioned. In 1836,
Davis took his degree of B.A., and in the following
year was called to the Bar.* Between these events,
after he had graduated but before his call, he was
president of a Dublin Historical Society, a group of

---

* Davis never sought college honours; the Davis who is sometimes cited
as a moderator in ethics and logic in 1835, was John Davis, no relation of
Thomas. The entry in the college books specifies that he "entered 4 July,
1831, as a pensioner; by religion, Protestant; father's name, James; profession, a doctor. The boy's age, 16; born in County Cork. Educated by
Mr. Mongan. Entered under Mr. Luby as college tutor." Mr. Luby, who
afterwards was a Fellow, was uncle of Thomas Clarke Luby, a Nationalist
of the generation succeeding Davis's, reared on the writings of the Young
Ireland party.

law students, of which the only memorial that remains
is an address which he delivered on the study of Irish
history, still unpublished; and at the same era he
made one of those premature and false starts in life
which ardent young spirits rarely escape, and which
have produced a crop of books the writers would
willingly let die, and of speeches which the mature
orator shudders to recall. This was the pamphlet
to which Maddyn alludes. He had close personal
friends among the Dublin Whigs, a party whose
policy was leavened at the moment by the generous
aims of Hudson, Deasy, O'Hagan, and others, who
were afterwards Federalists or Nationalists, and
rendered practical by the sympathy of officials of
a new type, like his remote kinsmen, Lord Morpeth
and Thomas Drummond, then Chief and Under
Secretary in Ireland. The House of Lords was at
that time making itself odious to reasonable men, by
resisting the reform of the Irish Church and Irish
Corporations—two of the most indefensible of human
institutions; and he made his first plunge into politics
before he was quite three and twenty by a plan for
the reform of the intractable chamber. This brochure furnishes a test of his intellectual discipline at
that stage. He had gathered political knowledge
abundantly and learned to think, but he did not yet
know how to use his materials. It is the only work
of his hands of which it may be said that the style
is tame, and the tone tepid and unpersuasive. It is
the argument of a young philosophical Radical for
an elected Upper House in the interest of the empire,
and it did not differ essentially from the more generous Whig opinions of the time. But it is notable
that, even in the storm of political passion which

then prevailed, he did not desire to abridge the authority of a second chamber. The absolute power of rejecting bills, he insisted, " should on no account be touched." It was an indispensable check on rash proposals, but it ought to be transferred from irresponsible to responsible hands.*

This pamphlet is the last incident in the era of silent meditation ; after his call to the Bar he had a higher call to the true work of his life.

* "The Reform of the Lords," by a Graduate of the Dublin University, Dublin : published for the author by Messrs. Goodwin & Co., Printers, 29, Denmark Street, 1837. (He still knew so little of the commerce of literature as to adopt a method of publication which rendered a successful sale impossible.)
The Dublin Historical Society, of which Davis was President, must not be confounded with the College Historical Society. The former consisted of a few law students, and met at the Dorset Institution, Upper Sackville Street. The society is so completely forgotten, that I have never met one man who was a member of it. It is worthy of note, that this address on the "Study of Irish History" was delivered in the middle of 1838, a period when Maddyn, like Wallis, erroneously supposes that he had not yet turned his attention to Irish affairs.

CHAPTER II.

THE THINKER.   1839, 1840.

IT was not to such a Society as Maddyn describes—
gay and sceptical, somewhat sensual and worldly,
devoured with ambition for immediate applause,
and scarcely more Irish in spirit than if it met by the
Isis or the Cam instead of the Liffey—that Davis,
in the summer of 1840, delivered his first public
address.   New men had joined in considerable
numbers since the reorganization of 1839, and the
Society had become more serious and sincere.

The address was a profound surprise to his few
intimate friends, almost as much as to the bulk of the
students.   Where they expected familiar platitudes
on a subject exhausted by use, they heard the voice
of an original man, who echoed no one, but uttered
unconventional opinions with the fervour of complete conviction.   The dumb man spoke, and spoke
like a mature teacher.   " Thoughts, prisoned long
for lack of speech, outpoured."   It was like the fruit
of the fig-tree, rich and succulent, but of which no
preliminary blossoms give warning.   Wallis, who was
present, and who was among those who expected
little, bears witness of its immediate effect.

" It excited the surprise and admiration even of those who

knew him best, and won the respect of numbers who, from political or personal prejudices, had been originally most unwilling to admit his worth. So signal a victory over long-continued neglect and obstinate prejudice, as he had at length obtained, has never come under my observation, and I believe it to be unexampled. There is no assurance of greatness so unmistakable as this. No power is so overwhelming, no energy so untiring, no enthusiasm so indomitable as that which slumbers for years, unconscious and unsuspected, until the character is completely formed, and then bursts at once into light and life, when the time for action is come."

The annual address had commonly consisted of an *éloge* on the art of oratory, with individual criticism on the great masters, and suggestions for the training by which an orator, whom the familiar axiom described as a manufactured article, might be made. He rejected this formulary and spoke to the sons of the gentry and professional classes, of the duties which would presently await them when they passed from the college to practical life, and bade them consider not how to harangue successfully at the Bar or in the pulpit, but how they might best become serviceable citizens and good Irishmen.

A *précis* or extracts will give an inadequate impression of this address, but it marks a starting-point in his life, and some fragments of it are essential to this narrative. If the reader thinks he has heard the same key-note struck in the English Universities in latter times, let him remember that Davis spoke more than fifty years ago.

In joining a society founded for the study of history, he reminded the students that they practically acknowledged how defective was the system of teaching in the University. There they passed the precious time between boyhood and manhood in studying two dead languages imperfectly, and left college loaded with cautions like Swift, or with

honours like many a blockhead whom they knew :
but ignorant of the events which had happened, the
truths which had been discovered, and all that
imagination had produced for seventeen hundred
years ; ignorant of all history, including that of their
own country, and for modern literature left to the
chances of a circulating library or a taste beyond
that of their instructors. When one compared the
gifted nature of the Irish race with the contemporary
literature of the country, it was impossible to doubt
there was some gross error in the education of the
only class which hitherto had received any education
in Ireland.

"Men," he said, "cannot master *all* knowledge. A knowledge
of his own nature and duties, of the circumstances, growth, and
prospects of that society in which he dwells, and of the pursuits
and tastes of those around him, is what every man should first
learn. If he does learn this he has learned enough for life and
goodness; and if he finds this not enough, he is prepared in the
only feasible way to profit by studying the works and thoughts of
ancient Italy, or Greece, or modern France, or Germany. The
masterpieces of classic literature ought to be read, not as school-
books or tasks, but as a noble recreation,—they were a mighty
mass of the picked thoughts of two renowned nations, the richest
mine of thought which time had deposited;—and history, as an
inspiration. If the student take more interest in the history, and
feel more admiration for the literature of these moderns than of
those ancients, let us not condemn his taste or doubt his wisdom.
The varieties of feeling, interest, and opportunity make these
differences, and a preference for the study of the modern continental nations is fostered and vindicated by the greater analogy
of the people of these islands to them than to the men of old
Greece or old Italy."

Many of the defects of the college system might,
he insisted, be remedied by a wise use of the Historical Society. It could teach the things which
a student ought to know—primarily the history of

his own country,—and lay broad and deep the foundations of political knowledge. Three out of four
of the orators of the last eighty years (the oratorical
period in these kingdoms) were trained, like all the
great orators of Greece and Rome, in such societies.

"'Tis a glorious world, historic memory. From the grave the
sage warns; from the mound the hero, from the temple the orator-
patriot inspire; and the poet sings in his shroud. On the field of
fame, the forum of power, the death-bed or scaffold of the patriots,
'who died in righteousness'—you look—you pause—you 'swear
like them to live, like them to die.' Men—I speak, having known
its working—learn history in this society with a rapidity and an
ease, a profundity in research, and sagacity in application, not
approached by any other mode of study. Suppose a man to prepare a defence of what most histories condemn, or to censure some
favourite act, or man, or institution, or policy, in his eagerness to
persuade he becomes more sensitive of the times of which he speaks
than could the solitary student, and we half follow him to the
scene over which his spirit stalks.

"With rare exceptions, national history does dramatic justice
to the transactions with which it deals; alien history is the inspiration of a traitor. The histories of a country, by hostile strangers,
should be refuted and then forgotten. Such are most histories of
Ireland; and yet Irishmen neglect the original documents, and
compilations like Carey's 'Vindiciæ;' and they sin not by omission
only—too many of them receive and propagate on Irish affairs
'quicquid Anglia mendax in historia audet.'

"I shall not now reprove your neglect of Irish history. I
shall say nothing of it but this, that I never heard of any famous
nation which did not honour the names of its departed great, study
the fasti, and the misfortunes—the annals of the land, and cherish
the associations of its history and theirs. The national mind
should be filled to overflowing with such thoughts. They are
more enriching than mines of gold, or fields of corn, or the cattle
of a thousand hills; more ennobling than palaced cities stored
with the triumphs of war or art; more supporting in danger's
hour than colonies, or fleets, or armies. The history of a nation is
the birthright of her sons—who strips them of that, 'takes that
which not enriches him but makes them poor indeed.'"

Not national records alone, but all history taught

great lessons. Who could discuss the revolutions
which reformed England, convulsed France, and
liberated America, without becoming a wiser man;
who could speculate on their career and not warm
with hope ?

It was the destiny of most of his audience to
enter public life, and he reminded them of its duties
and temptations to young Irishmen.

"In your public career you will be solicited by a thousand
temptations to sully your souls with the gold and place of a foreign
court, or the transient breath of a dishonest popularity; dishonest,
when adverse to the good, though flattering to the prejudice, of
the people. You will be solicited to become the misleaders of a
faction, or the gazehounds of a minister. Be jealous of your
virtue; yield not. Bid back the tempter. Do not grasp remorse.
Nay, if it be not a vain thought, in such hours of mortal doubt,
when the tempted spirit rocks to and fro, pause, and recall one of
your youthful evenings, and remember the warning voice of your
old companion, who felt as a friend, and used a friend's liberty.
Let the voice of his warning rise upon your ear; think he stands
before you as he does now, telling you in such moments, when
pride, or luxury, or wrath make you waver, to return to commun-
ings with nature's priests, the Burns, the Wordsworths, the Shake-
speares, but, above all, to Nature's self. She waits with a mother's
longings for the wanderer; fling yourselves into her arms, and as
your heart beats upon her bosom, your native nobility will return,
and thoughts divine as the divinest you ever felt will bear you
unscathed through the furnace. Pardon the presumption, pardon
the hope ('tis one of my dearest now), 'forsan et *hæc* olim me-
minisse juvabit.'

"What, though many a glorious expectation has failed ? What,
though even you have learned that toil and danger guard the
avenue to success ? What, though disappointment and suffering
have somewhat touched you, and made you less sanguine; yet, has
not time rewarded your sorrows?—has it not refined—has it not
purified—has it not strengthened, even when it humbled you ?

"I do not fear that any of you will be found among Ireland's
foes. To her every energy should be consecrated. Were she
prosperous, she would have many to serve her, though their hearts
were cold in her cause. But it is because her people lie down in

misery and rise to suffer, it is therefore you should be more deeply devoted. Your country will, I fear, need all your devotion. She has no foreign friend. Beyond the limits of green Erin there is none to aid her. She may gain by the feuds of the stranger; she cannot hope for his peaceful help, be he distant, be he near; her trust is in her sons. You are Irishmen. She relies on your devotion; she solicits it by her present distraction and misery. No! her past distraction—her present woe. We have no more war-bills; we have a mendicant bill for Ireland. The poor- and the pest-house are full, yet the valleys of her country, and the streets of her metropolis swarm with the starving. Her poet has described her—

> "'More dear in her sorrow, her gloom and her showers,
> Than the rest of the world in its sunniest hours.'

And if she be miserable, if 'homely age hath the alluring beauty took from her poor cheek, then who hath wasted it?' The stranger from without, by means of the traitor within. Perchance 'tis a fanciful thing, yet in the misfortunes of Ireland, in her laurelled martyrs, in those who died 'persecuted men for a persecuted country,' in the necessity she was under of bearing the palms to deck her best to the scaffold-foot and the lost battle-field, she has seemed to be chastened for some great future. I have thought I saw her spirit from her dwelling, her sorrowing place among the tombs, rising, not without melancholy, yet with a purity and brightness beyond other nations, and I thought that God had made her purpose firm and her heart just; and I knew that if he had, small though she were, His angels would have charge over her, 'lest at any time she should dash her foot against a stone.' And I have prayed that I might live to see the day when, amid the reverence of those, once her foes, her sons would—

> "'Like the leaves of the shamrock unite,
> A partition of sects from one foot-stalk of right:
> Give each his full share of the earth and the sky,
> Nor fatten the slave where the serpent would die.'

"But not only by her sufferings does Ireland call upon you: her past history furnishes something to awake proud recollections. I speak not of that remote and mysterious time when the men of Tyre traded to her well-known shores, and every art of peace found a home on her soil; and her armies, not unused to conquest, traversed Britain and Gaul. Nor yet of that time when her colleges offered a hospitable asylum to the learned and the learning of every land, and her missions bore knowledge and piety through savage Europe; nor yet of her gallant and romantic struggles against Dane, and Saxon, and Norman; still less of her hardy wars, in which her interest was sacrificed to a too-devoted loyalty in many a successful, in many a disastrous battle. Not of these. I speak of sixty years ago. The memory is fresh, the example pure, the success inspiring. I speak of ' The Lifetime of Ireland.'

"Look on our class in Ireland; are they worthy of their nature or their country? Are they like the young men of Germany: as students, laborious; as thinkers, profound and acute? Like the young men of France: independent, fearless, patriotic? Like the young men of England, Scotland, America: energetic, patient, successful? (I speak of the virtues of those foreigners.) And if not, if the young men of Ireland are careless, prejudiced, unhonoured—if their pupilage never ends—if no manhood of mind, no mastery in action comes from most of them—if preparation, thought, action, wisdom, the order of development in successful men, is not for them; if so, are their misleaders, the duped or duping apostles of present systems, alone to blame? No; you, young Irishmen, must blame yourselves. The power of self-education, self-conduct is yours; ' think wrongly if you will, but think for yourselves.'

"The college in which you and your fathers were educated, from whose offices seven-eighths of the Irish people are excluded by religion, from whose porch many, not disqualified by religion, are repelled by the comparative dearness, the reputed bigotry, and pervading dulness of the consecrated spot—that institution seems no longer to monopolize the education of Ireland. Trinity College seems to have lost the office for which it was so long and so well paid, of preventing the education of the Irish. The people think it better not to devote all their spare cash to a university so many of whose favourite *alumni* are distinguished by their adroit and malignant calumnies on the character, and inveterate hostility to the good, of that people with whose land and money they are endowed."

To each age God gave a career of possible improvement. In their time his young audience could foresee the speedy rise of democracy, and they had it in their power to accelerate and regulate its march.

" A great man has said, if you would qualify the democracy for power you must 'purify their morals, and warm their faith, if that be possible.' * How awful a doubt! But it is not the morality of laws, nor the religion of sects, that will do this. It is the habit of rejoicing in high aspirations and holy emotions; it is charity in thought, word, and act; it is generous faith, and the practice of self-sacrificing virtue. To educate the heart and strengthen the intellect of man are the means of ennobling him. To strain every nerve to this end, is the duty from which no one aware of it can shrink.

" I speak not of private life—in it our people are tender, generous, and true-hearted. *But, gentlemen, you have a country.* The people among whom we were born, with whom we live, for whom, if our minds are in health, we have most sympathy, are those over whom we have power—power to make them wise, great, good. Reason points out our native land as the field for our exertion, and tells us that without patriotism a profession of benevolence is the cloak of the selfish man. And does not sentiment confirm the decree of reason. The country of our birth, our education, of our recollections, ancestral, personal, national; the country of our loves, our friendships, our hopes; *our* country ——: the cosmopolite is unnatural, base—I would fain say, impossible. To act on a world is for those above it, not of it. Patriotism is human philanthropy."

Davis did not altogether omit the aids and suggestions for self-education of which the annual address had ordinarily consisted, and his counsel was of the most precise and practical character, and gives incidentally an insight into the studies by which he made himself a master of English prose.†

---

* De Tocqueville, preface to " La Démocratie en Amerique."

† For example : " There are so few English works on the philosophy of words, that I may enumerate them. Tooke's 'Diversions of Purley' is the most valuable for acquiring a critical habit in etymology and grammatical analysis; for the common use of words, Webster's Dictionary is the best; Todd's Johnson, as an authority and illustration for the modern variations; but Richardson is the handbook for him who would cultivate a pure English style. Horne Tooke, to be sure, was of opinion that each word had but one and an unalterable meaning in a language. Richardson has pressed this error still further, and has thereby enfeebled the otherwise admirable essay prefixed to his larger dictionary, but his errors (if so they be) only give a sterner purity and force to the language he teaches. When you have

But he passed speedily from the mere instrumental parts of knowledge to the higher methods by which it is acquired and used.

"Every prudent man will study subjects, not authors. Thus alone can you go through the wilderness of writers, and it is only by requiring ourselves to master subjects that we render this society what it is—a means of sound general education. Learning, as such, is the baggage of the orator: without it, he may suffer exhaustion or defeat from an inferior foe; with it, his speed and agility are diminished. Those are best off who have it in maga-

examined these books—and they are well worth reading—you must trust to the effect of your other literary studies, to the eager and full mind, to *supply* you with words and varieties of style, and to your metaphysical studies, to a patient taste, and habits of revision to *correct* them.

"I may mention that Spenser was the favourite leisure-book of that word-wielder, William Pitt, and of his great father, Chatham. Erskine and Fox are said to have known Milton and Shakespeare almost by heart. Curran's inspiration, next to the popular legends of Ireland, was the English translation of the Bible. Coleridge, indeed, says that a man familiar with it can never write in a vulgar style; but this, like many of Coleridge's show-sayings, is an exaggeration. For ordinary use, Bolingbroke, Swift, Hume, and even Cobbett, with all his coarseness, and the common letters and narratives of the last century, are safe though not splendid models. Amongst the orators—whom you will, and, perhaps, ought to follow more than other writers—you can study the speeches of Pitt for a splendid plausibility; Fox, for an easy diction and fluent logic; Sheridan, for wit; Curran, for pathos and humour; Burke and Grattan, for grandeur and sublimity of thought, language, and illustration. In wealth of imagination and in expressive power, Grattan is next to Shakespeare: his speeches are full of the most valuable information on Irish politics, and are the fit handbook for an Irishman. But his style is not for imitation; let no subject assume the purple. Erskine possesses most of these qualities, but with a chaster, and, methinks, less racy manner; but perhaps surpassing all, by combining the best qualities of all, are the speeches, so valuable and so little known, of Lord Plunket. His precise vigour marks him the Demosthenes of the English language. I shall hazard but one piece of advice: keep to the plainer styles. However you may dislike their opinions, or question their depth of judgment, the style of Southey, Smith, and some few more of the older reviewers is excellent. Coleridge, Carlyle, and the rest of the Germanic set are damaging English nearly as much as the Latinists did; their writings are eloquent, lively, and vigorous, to those who understand them; curry and mullagatawny to the literary world, but 'caviare to the multitude.' Carlyle is a more honest, but less learned thinker than Coleridge. Their opinions are unsafe, but their works are of the greatest use, in tempting men by their enthusiasm, or forcing them by their paradoxes, to think. Just as the dish possesses a high-cooked and epicurean flavour, is it unfit for the people or the men of the people. The literary style most in fashion is corrupt, and corrupting; the patois of the coteries, it is full of meaning and sensibility to them. But shun that jargon. The orator should avoid using it, for the people own not its power—it belongs not to the nations."

zines, to be drawn on occasion. Learning is necessary to orator,
and poet, and statesman. Book-learning, when well digested, and
vivified by meditation, may suffice, as in Burke and Coleridge;
but otherwise it is apt to produce confusion and inconsistency of
mind, as it sometimes did in both these men. Far better is the
learning of previous observation, the learning of past emotions
and ideas, the learning caught by conversation, invented or dug
up by meditation in the closet or the field; impressions of scenery
whether natural or artificial, in the human, animal, or material
world. Such learning is used by every great poet, philosopher,
and orator; perhaps it requires propitious training or nascent
genius to be able to acquire it, but ability to acquire insures
ability to use.

"When Grattan paced his garden, or Burns trod his hillside,
were they less students than the print-dizzy denizens of a library?
No: that pale form of the Irish regenerator is trembling with the
rush of ideas; and the murmuring stream, and the gently rich
landscape, and the fresh wind converse with him through keen
interpreting senses, and tell mysteries to his expectant soul, and
he is as one inspired; arguments in original profusion, illustrations competing for his favour, memories of years long past, in
which he had read philosophy, history, poetry, awake at his call.
That man entered the senate-house, no written words in his hand,
and poured out the seemingly spontaneous, but really learned and
prepared lullaby over Ireland's cradle, or keen over Ireland's
corse.

"Read, too, Burns's own account of the birth and growth of
some of his greatest lyrics. Read, and learn to labour, if you would
be great. There is no more common error than that great works
are usually the results of extemporaneous power. You have all
read an article on Sheridan by Lord Brougham, full of depreciating
criticism, founded on the evidences, the chisel-marks of composition, which Sheridan left, and so many others (Brougham among
the number) concealed. Henry Brougham is a *metaphysician*; he
made no mistake in this; but Lord Brougham is an *egotist*, and he
misrepresented.

"I entreat of you to abandon the notion that you will speak
well merely from speaking often. Of a surety, all your faculties
grow with use, but this very quality of mind behoves you to be
judicious as well as earnest in the exercise of your powers. A bad
style grows worse by repetition, as much as a good style improves;
or, more generally, bad habits grow as rapidly as good ones. Give
up the idea of being great orators *without preparation*, till you are

so *with it.* When you are, with your utmost labour, able to make one really great speech, you will be above me, my criticism, and my advice, but will, perchance, agree with my opinion."

These fragments, more than anything which he has left behind, enable us to divine the process by which the young Conservative became a Nationalist. It is plain that he had slowly thought out his opinions, and was sailing by no conventional chart, but by fixed stars. He resolutely determined to be just and fear no consequences. He desired to give these young men a country which it was a duty to serve and a disgrace to neglect, a country which they would love, as a tender son loves his mother, obedient to her voice, and ready to die rather than that she should endure any remediable wrong.

When the lecture was printed, the sympathetic student naturally sent it to the two or three contemporary thinkers who were the most familiar companions of his solitude. One was Savage Landor, in whose " Imaginary Conversations " he found a storehouse of noble thoughts, though his unbridled temper and rash spirit had left him shorn of the influence his genius might have commanded. Landor's reply was found among Davis's correspondence :—

"Bath, Sunday evening, December 15, 1840.
    " SIR,
        "I return you many thanks for the honour you have done me, in sending me the Address read before the Historical Society of Dublin.
    " I hope it may conduce to the cultivation of the national mind. Ireland, I foresee, will improve more in the next fifty years than any other country in Europe, between steam and Father Mathew.
    "That man has done greater good than all the founders of all the religions in the world within an equal space of time. I would

rather see your countrymen flock round such leaders than expose
their heads to the dangerous flourishes of declamatory demagogues.
               " I am, sir,
        " Your very obliged and obedient servant,
                            " W. S. LANDOR."

In John Forster's "Life of Landor" we find
Davis's rejoinder, and get a glimpse of the political
opinions which were consolidating into convictions.
He had no personal relations with O'Connell as yet,
but he recognized him as the legitimate successor
of the historical Irishmen whose lives were his
favourite study.

"I am glad to find you have hopes for Ireland. You have
always had a good word and, I am sure, good wishes for her. If
you knew Mr. Mathew you would relish his simple and down-
right manners. He is joyous, friendly, and quite unassuming.
To have taken away a degrading and impoverishing vice from the
hearts and habits of three millions of people in a couple of years
seems to justify any praise to Mr. Mathew, and also to justify
much hope for the people. And suffer me to say that if you knew
the difficulties under which the Irish struggle, and the danger
from England and from the Irish oligarchy, you would not regret
the power of the political leaders, or rather Leader, here; you
would forgive the exciting speeches, and perchance sympathize
with the exertions of men who think that a domestic Government
can alone unite and animate all our people. Surely the desire
of nationality is not ungenerous, nor is it strange in the Irish
(looking to their history); nor, considering the population of
Ireland, and the nature and situation of their home, is the expectation of it very wild."

He wrote also to Wordsworth, and received a
friendly answer; but this correspondence has been lost.*
The powers of the secluded student were now
confessed, and when he found wings it was as

---

* Davis told a friend that Wordsworth praised the address as a composition and as regards many of the sentiments, but said that it contained
" too much insular patriotism." The pamphlet was dedicated to the memory
of Francis Kearney, one of his early associates, who was now dead.

natural for Davis to use them as for a young bird to
fly. The *Citizen* was under the management of his
closest friends, and the studies which had occupied
his long leisure in college were poured without stint
into that barren soil. A youth of constant study, a
manhood in which he pondered over principles and
systems, prepared him to speak with authority on
many questions. It is a strangely touching experiment to turn over these papers to-day, and mark the
care he bestowed upon subjects of the profoundest
national importance, but to which scarcely any one
else gave a thought. "Udalism and Feudalism" is
a contrast of Norway and Ireland—the one solidly
prosperous with a peasant proprietary, the other
starving and desperate with a tenantry at will. He
put the moral of the case afterwards in the *Nation*
in one significant sentence, of which time has not
dulled the edge.

"Remember that many nations are as well off as the men of
cold, rocky Norway. Remember that no people on God's earth
are so miserably poor as the peasantry of soft and fertile Ireland.
Read and remember this; and then ask yourselves—and ask your
neighbours—why it is so? Ask them indoor and out—ask them
ere you do your business in the market, and after you have said
your prayers on the Sunday—ask till you are answered, ' Why are
the Irish so poor, when their country is so rich?'—' Why are so
many foreigners well off on worse land and in a hard climate?'—
' Is there no way of bettering us?' "

In the same spirit he investigated the constitutional difficulties which arose in the time of Grattan;
and in a paper on the natural relation of Irishmen to
the Afghans (then defending their liberties), opened
up views of a foreign policy suitable to a people
in the position of the Irish, which were afterwards
reiterated in the *Nation*, and which a thousand later

echoes have rendered commonplace, and sometimes *outré* and extravagant. But the most solid and valuable of these studies was a later inquiry into the work done by the maligned Irish Parliament of James II. A patriot has rarely undertaken a more necessary or generous labour than to justify that legislature, which was national in an unprecedented degree and patriotic in the best sense. These essays would have helped to train a generation in the knowledge that makes good citizens; but the public mind was still cold and indifferent. In truth, the Celtic temperament is averse to abstract studies, and will only bend to them under strict discipline, or when they have become the fuel of a great passion.

The friends with whom Davis was in the most affectionate and confidential relation at this time, outside the *Citizen* circle, were John Blake Dillon, William Eliot Hudson, and Robert Patrick Webb. Dillon was a fellow-student of his own age and character, whom he had encountered at the Historical Society—

"A simple, loyal nature, pure as snow."

Webb was a school-fellow at Mr. Mongan's seminary, and a constant associate from early days; a young man of leisure, culture, and liberal tastes, and, though of Conservative training and associations, disposed to follow his friend into new fields. Hudson was by several years the senior of Davis; a man of sweet, serene disposition, and singularly unselfish patriotism. He held the office of Taxing Master in the Four Courts, and had been associated with O'Loghlen Perrin and the leading Whig lawyers in reforming the administration of justice in Ireland. But his leisure and income were devoted to projects of public usefulness, in which ambition had no share, for his name was never heard outside of his own circle. National airs were collected and published at his cost, and various studies in Celtic literature promoted, and he bore the burthen of the *Citizen*, which was published at a constant loss, and contributed from time to time valuable papers in the region of political science. The maxim which declares that "a man may be known by his friends" was very applicable to Davis's case; it is only round such a man that such friends cluster.

CHAPTER III.

IT was in the spring of 1841, early in his twenty-fifth year, that Davis passed from speculation to action, and for the first time took a personal part in promoting the broad national policy which he had advocated in the *Citizen*. In the previous autumn the Whigs had committed a wanton outrage on the feelings of Irish gentlemen. To provide a conspicuous office for a few weeks for a political gladiator of their following, who had grown discontented, they compelled the greatest orator whom Ireland had sent to their aid since Edmund Burke to retire from the Irish Chancellorship, and placed a Scotch lawyer of hard and vulgar nature at the head of the Irish bar. Davis attended a bar-meeting of remonstrance, chiefly Whigs of national opinions who resented the appointment, not as a question of professional etiquette, but because it tended to humiliate Ireland. But the remonstrance caused scarcely a ripple of opinion. The middle class had tasted patronage and fallen asleep at the feet of the Whigs, and as O'Connell, who detested Plunket, was silent, the mass of the people did not know that there was anything amiss.*

* O'Connell is said to have approved of the transaction. It is manifest from his private correspondence that he did not share the professional or

It was in company with Conservatives resisting another Whig offence that Davis entered on the stage to do something which attracted universal attention, because it was something no other Liberal in Ireland of that day would have attempted.

The Royal Dublin Society was an institution created by the Irish Parliament for promoting the useful arts and sciences, and developing the natural resources of the country. After the Union, Leinster House, the palace of the Geraldines, was purchased for its use, and it received an annual grant of £5500 to defray the cost of its museum, schools of design, botanic garden, annual exhibition of cattle and agricultural produce, and occasional exhibitions of native manufactures. The lethargy which fell upon Irish enterprise after the provincialization of Dublin, was peculiarly felt in literary and scientific institutions, and the Dublin Society became, it was alleged, less and less a school of practical science and more and more a party club. It maintained a news-room and lending library for its members, with a subscription so high as to be nearly prohibitory to all but the landed gentry. When the era of reform came with the Whigs, its shortcomings fell under the review of Parliament, and in 1836 a select committee reported that, to answer the purpose for which it was endowed, it must be effectually reorganized.

Something was done to carry out the orders of Parliament, but not much. The high subscription was maintained, and it continued so exclusively a party club that the council was taken in a large

political heat on the subject. "Blessed be God, the danger is over! [defeat of the Government]. I believe Lord Plunket is about to resign. Campbell will be his successor" (O'Connell to P. V. Fitzpatrick, London, April 29, 1839, "Private Correspondence of O'Connell," edited by W. J. Fitzpatrick).

degree from the party of Protestant ascendancy. Two or three years after Catholic Emancipation a minority, who thought it not too soon to recognize the fact that religious equality among all classes of Irishmen was established by law, proposed Dr. Murray, the Archbishop of Dublin, a member of its council. He was a man who, from the sweetness of his disposition and the moderation of his opinions, had made no personal enemies; but he was a Catholic and a priest, and the society rejected him by a large majority. There was wide and profound indignation, which the Irish Government, of whom Dr. Murray was an ally, shared, and the transaction naturally brought the general shortcomings of the society into view. At the close of 1840, when the estimates for the coming year were in preparation, Lord Morpeth, then Irish Secretary, reminded the society that the House of Commons had recommended certain essential reforms which were not yet effected, and he desired to be informed of the intentions of the Council respecting them before the estimates of the new year were drafted. He intimated that they must abandon the political news-room, reduce the annual fee, and abolish the lending library on which funds granted for the promotion of science were expended, and carry out more effectually the instructions of Parliament, or the endowment could not be continued. The council, in reply, contended that they had carried out the instructions of Parliament as far as was reasonably practicable; that the news-room was supported, not out of the endowment, but out of the personal subscriptions of the members; and they insisted that the arbitrary command issued to them was not justified by any solid grounds, and was derogatory to the character of the society as an independent body. A general meeting of the society approved of this answer by a majority of 129 to 57. The Government organ, the *Dublin Evening Post*, immediately announced that the parliamentary grant would be withdrawn.*

In the state of public opinion in Ireland at that time, nine-tenths of those who called themselves Reformers, whether Protestants or Catholics, applauded this *coup* of the Government. It was an effectual method of punishing a bigoted coterie, who neglected the duties for which they were responsible and insulted a man of the blameless character of Dr. Murray. But to Davis the question was not one between Catholic and Protestant, or Liberal and Conservative, but between Ireland and the Imperial Government. He was offended by the arbitrary treatment of Irish gentlemen, and probably hoped that they would understand that they were insulted because they were only Irishmen. He wrote an article, marked by lofty national sentiment and an open contempt for party feeling on such a subject; and Dillon, who had some acquaintance with the editor of the *Morning Register*, took it to that journal. The readers of the Whig Catholic paper, famous for statistics and habitually respectful to the Castle, must have read next morning with lively surprise an appeal to sentiments of Protestant nationality

---

* An official letter from the Under Secretary confirmed the news. The society was informed that His Excellency could not recommend to Parliament any further continuance of the annual grant. He was, however, ready to receive from the council an account of any liabilities incurred previous to the receipt of Lord Morpeth's letter of the 17th of December, which were "essential to the promotion of the objects of the institution," that he might consider what sum should be introduced into the estimate of the present year for their liquidation.

long forgotten in Irish controversy.* He treated
lightly the charge that the Dublin Society had
refused to reform itself. All the recommendations of
Parliament except two had been adopted. One of
the two was promised further consideration, and only
one refused; and this one was rightly refused because
it was accompanied by an offensive threat.

"Was this the tone to adopt to a great national body?—'You
are our pensioners, do just as we bid you, without regard to your
own opinions or your own convenience, or we dismiss you.' . . .
Was this the treatment due to an institution which had grown
old in serving the interests of Ireland? Grant that the society
was wrong, yet surely it deserved respect and patience. It deserved
more: its opinions should not have been disregarded; its wishes
should in some degree have been yielded to. The society delibe-
rates; it sees that it has conceded much; it might have conceded
to civility what was refused to threats and rudeness. . . . We ask,
Would the French Government treat a public institution thus?
Would the English treat an English society of old standing, great
numbers, and respectability, thus? No, they dare not. Verily,
we are provincials. This society has existed over one hundred
years; it contains eight hundred members; it maintains a body of
professors of arts and sciences; it has schools, theoretical and
practical, for teaching; the agriculture, the manufactures, the
science, the literature of Ireland have been served by it; and now
it is to be flung aside at the caprice of an English Government.
It is not the child of that Government. It was founded by Irishmen; it was fostered by an Irish Government; an Irish Parliament,
while one existed, gave it, out of its scanty resources, £10,000 a
year—gave it generously and wisely. That Parliament perished,
and the grant was reduced to £7000 by the English Government;
it was afterwards reduced to £5000 by the English Government;
it is now taken away entirely by the English Government. Verily,
we repeat, we are provincials. But we ask the public, will they
allow the gardens to be sold, the model-room to be shut, the professors diminished, the shows of cattle and manufactures to be
given up, because the English Government quarrels with an Irish
institution? We laugh at the charge of faction in the late vote.
Many of the most determined Liberals, we know, voted in the

* Dublin *Morning Register*, Feb. 2, 1841.

E

majority. We remember well that the society did, on one remarkable occasion, richly deserve the charge of having acted factiously.
A venerated prelate, who united all that endears the man with all
that ennobles the public character, was rejected from political, or
worse, from sectarian feeling. We were not behind in censuring
them : but we deny that there is any connection between that step
and this ; neither the same men nor the same motives have influenced the society now. We will not visit the sins of the factious
voters of past years on the heads of the independent party, composed alike of Liberals and Conservatives, of the present. Nor
even, if we thought the society ever so blamable in that one
respect, would we look on quietly and see such a body insulted,
threatened, and trampled on ?

"In fine, we ask the public not to look on quietly and see this
old, useful, *Irish* institution sacrificed to the rashness or caprice of
an English minister ; and we ask the members of the society to
prove themselves mindful that it was the work of native legislature, that its assailant has been an Imperial Government ; and
that its only safe reliance can be on the national sympathy of the
Irish people."

The Castle press was bewildered by sentiments so
unprecedented. A Liberal journal, complaisant to
the Castle, and perhaps under obligations to official
persons, resisting the will of the Government ! It
was unheard of ; a base motive was the only one
intelligible to the official journalist, and he affirmed
that the proprietor of the *Register* must have been
betrayed in his absence by some untrustworthy
representative. His criticism is a characteristic
specimen of the journalism of that day.

"While writing, the *Morning Register* of this day was put into
our hands. On casting our eyes over a column of wordy and
furious stuff, our impression for the moment was that we were
reading an Orange journal. Certainly, we have not seen anything
so nauseous and so scandalous in the *Mail* of late ; nothing so personally offensive to ourselves since the *ruffianing* days. Our next
impression is more correct—of that we are certain,—that Mr.
Staunton has been most infamously used in his absence, by making
his journal the vehicle of a treacherous attempt to wound the
principles he has supported, and the party he has espoused, as well

as to assail the Government of the country because of its honest efforts to reform the abuses of a great public institution."

In a second article, Mr. Conway—this was the name of the Castle journalist—continued to lament that some "puny whipster" should place Mr. Staunton in a position dangerous, "not only to his character as a politician, but to the interests of his paper. Such conduct," he considered, "thoroughly infamous." * The Whig journalist naturally scoffed at the idea of Tory nationality; but Davis knew that Irish patriotism had been constantly recruited from the ranks of its hereditary enemies. Its greatest spokesmen in the century were sons of Government officials, while in every generation the sons of historical and tribunitial houses had passed over to the enemy, or silently relinquished the opinions which made their ancestors illustrious. He was persuaded that it only needed a Swift or a Grattan to revive the Protestant nationality of old.

* In a note to Webb, who was a member of the Royal Dublin Society, Davis asks for facts which would enable him to contrast the liberality displayed towards the British Museum with the parsimony with which the corresponding institution in Ireland was threatened; and he makes plain that his motive in taking up the question was to bring Irishmen of both extremes into friendly relations.

"I have received your letter and the *Post.* I had seen Conway's display on Friday (in the *Post* which came here to Mr. Hancock), and I immediately scribbled a reply, very much too civil, to Conway (for, *at the time,* I did not feel sure of Staunton), but repeating my former statements, and asking for a refutation, if it were to be had. I have since heard from Dillon; I find that he has replied to Conway—right well, I have no doubt. I have got the *Packet,* and have heard of the *Mail.* I am inclined to think something may be done, by following this up, to produce a better understanding between all Tories and Radicals who have any claim to be called Irishmen. Staunton, too, is to be entirely relied on; in fact, Dillon describes him as zealous; so pray have the facts about the British Museum, etc., written out, cyphers and all, to give them to me on Wednesday evening, when I shall be in Dublin. I am very glad you think well of the article. You did right to beat Pigot; it will make him more modest, and, as he really has the stuff in him, more devoted to the royal game. Remember me to Bessie and the son.

"Ever yours,
"THOMAS DAVIS."[1]

---

[1] Oldcastle, Sunday, Feb. 28, 1841.

Davis had gone to the country on private business, but Dillon next day restated the grounds on which the society was defended, denied that any wrong had been done to the proprietor of the *Register,* and challenged the official journal to point out any part of the original article which could possibly be described as personally offensive to any one. And he stated in two or three emphatic sentences the keynote of the new opinions.

" There is a section of Irish Conservatives," said Dillon, " who, with all their enmity towards the *religion* of the people of Ireland, combine a sincere regard for the honour of their country; who, through the struggles of party, have still clung to their nationality ; and who, if we can judge from their sentiments and their conduct on some occasions, do still entertain the hope that, sooner or later, the day will come when all our differences will cease, and our humiliation shall be no more. . . . We engaged in this dispute, not from any desire to quarrel with the Government, but from our firm resolve that whatever party be in office—Whig, Tory, or Radical—if we see it acting arbitrarily or using unjustly its Imperial strength against an *Irish* institution, we shall oppose it independently and decisively. Will any man be so base as to say that we ought to do less? . . .

" The writer [in the *Post*] affects not to understand what we mean by an Irish Government. We will be plain with him. We mean a Government under the control of an Irish Parliament. We think, and have always thought, that no honesty on the part of an Imperial Government can compensate for the want of this control, and have some hope that the time is not far distant when every honest man in Ireland will think the same."

The persistence of the *Register* was a marvel to the public. But Dillon was able to report to his friend that Mr. Staunton, who was a timid but dogged man, stood firm in the controversy, and had even admitted other articles from his new contributors, suggesting that Ireland had a foreign policy not necessarily an echo of the opinions prevalent at Westminster.*

The society was saved, and the sympathetic reader may mark that this transaction presents a key-note to Davis's entire career.

The friends felt that they had got an opening to the mind of the country which ought not to be lightly relinquished, and they resolved to propose a more permanent arrangement to Mr. Staunton. Dillon opened the subject, and in a few days was able to report the successful progress of the negotiations. Dr. Gray, who was brother-in-law to Torrens McCullagh, had recently bought the *Freeman's Journal*, in company with a few friends, and, since the articles on the Dublin Society had attracted attention, he proposed to Dillon that he and his friend should occasionally write for it. But they aimed to direct a journal, so that its teaching might be uniform and coherent, and that they might not be liable to be repudiated.

"I have just been talking to Staunton about our project," Dillon wrote on the 27th of February. "He seems to like it much

---

* Dillon's letter was addressed to Oldcastle, co. Meath, and is dated Feb. 17, 1841.

"DEAR DAVIS,

"You may perceive from the paper which I send you that the article on the Dublin Society has kicked up a row. Conway has come out with dreadful ferocity. I suppose Synan has sent you the *Post*, as I gave it to him on his promising he would do so. The *Mail* copied your article in full, together with my reply to the *Post*. I will send you the paper if I can get it. I understand that Conway meditates a general attack on the *Register* for its conduct of late. The foreign articles, particularly those relating to McLeod, have created a sensation at the Castle. I imagine I see you here putting your hand to your neck. Staunton is staunch. He wishes me to fight it out about the Dublin Society. He is, he says, for Irish institutions, whether they be Orange or Green. This is capital. You may suppose that I am impatient for your return. Let me hear what you think about all this. I will send you a copy of the *Post* to-night.
                                    "Ever yours,
                                        "JOHN DILLON."

better than I expected. In fact, from the tenour of his observations, I am inclined to think that we shall be able to accomplish an arrangement on the terms which we desired, as soon as you return. The offer of the *Freeman* made an impression on him, and he seemed rather obliged to me for making the disclosure to him."

The result was that the two young men were placed in control of the *Register*, for a limited period, and strictly as an experiment. Since a national press existed in Ireland it was never so low in character and ability as at that time. The popular journals echoed the speeches of O'Connell, but rarely supplemented them by any individual thought or investigation. One nowhere encountered the convictions and purpose of an independent man. There had been genuine fire in the Catholic struggle and the first Repeal movement, but it had expired, and the journalists at this time worked for the most part with the lethargy of men who believed little and hoped nothing. Thomas Moore summed up the case : " Look," he said, " at the Irish papers. The country in convulsion—people's lives, fortunes, and religion at stake, and not a gleam of talent from one year's end to the other." But though the press was feeble it was often malicious. Like a torpid viper, it awoke at times to inflict a sting.

National literature in a higher sense than journalism, like all our native institutions, had emigrated to England. The poet who, in the eyes of Europe, typified the Irish race vegetated in Devonshire. The novelist who aimed to win for the annals of Scotia Major the interest with which Scott had invested the annals of Scotia Minor was fagging for London booksellers. The young man of genius who had produced the most original drama of the

generation, and a novel which more than one of his
rivals has pronounced to be the best Irish story ever
written, was starving in a London garret because
he could not get even the employment of a hack.
Lady Morgan, after attempting for a time to sustain
a national *salon* in Dublin, followed the tide and
established herself in Mayfair. Maxwell was still
labouring, nearly as unsuccessfully as Maturin had
laboured before him, to attract an audience to pure
literature flavoured with a dash of Irish eccentricity;
and Maginn and Mahony, both intensely Irish in
nature and gifts, exhibited their nationality chiefly
in bitter gibes at O'Connell and the Repealers. The
Irish Penny Magazine, in which Petrie and O'Donovan
had revived for a time the study of Irish antiquities,
was dead. A *Dublin Penny Journal*, owned by a
Scotch firm, followed, but scarcely succeeded it. The
Citizen was little read, and, except for occasional
historical papers, was not worth reading. The *Dublin
University Magazine* alone maintained the reputation
of Irish genius, but it was more habitually libellous
of the Irish people than the *Times*. The stories of
Carleton and Lefanu, the poetry and criticism of
Mangan and Anster, the graphic sketches of Cæsar
Otway, and the sympathetic essays of Samuel Ferguson were smothered in masses of furious bigotry, manufactured chiefly by Samuel O'Sullivan, a parson who
had once been a papist, and brought to his new
connexion the zeal of a convertite. His brother,
Mortimer O'Sullivan, a man of notable ability, was
also a contributor, but rarely fell into the monotony
of hysterics which distinguished his junior. The
voice of Irish Ireland was heard nowhere but in the
speeches of O'Connell, and his position and ante-

cedents made him less the national than the Catholic
champion.

The young men wrote constantly in the *Register*
on foreign politics, and national organization ; and,
for the first time since the corpse of Robert Emmet
was flung into the mud of Bullysacre, a perfectly
genuine appeal was made to Protestant nationality.
The fervent exhortations on conciliation and bro-
therly love—which meant what they said,—the large
doctrines of national policy at home and abroad, the
wise speculations on the destinies of the country
(ripened and informed with familiar knowledge and
science), were new and strange. Was it deep philosophy or nascent madness? The first fate of new
truths is to be ridiculed, and the country was then
in no humour to be schooled in the sterner virtues.
Corrupted by the Whigs, who had kindled the lust
of place in a million of hearts—from the popular
member who wanted a sinecure, to the young peasant
who wanted to be a policeman,—the new principles
made slow way. The ordinary clientele did not
understand them ; and to gather new readers around
a long-established paper, with a fixed reputation
for respectable mediocrity, was a disheartening and
nearly impossible task. The prejudice to be assailed
was very intractable. Irish Protestants might well
be ashamed of the wrongs they permitted and
battened upon, but most of them only saw their
country through a haze of traditional prejudice. A
pane of coloured glass alters the eternal facts of
nature, her grass is no longer green or her skies
blue, and their prejudice was a coloured glass through
which all nature seemed orange and purple. The
experiment was to last for three months certain, and

then be reconsidered. Mr. Staunton, who was hard and parsimonious, but strictly honest in business transactions, reported, when the time came, that it had not succeeded. Measured by the financial thermometer it had failed indeed, for the circulation of the journal had not increased but diminished. In July he wrote to Davis.

" MY DEAR SIR,
"Our agreement was made on the 5th of March, and, according to my reckoning, you were engaged sixteen weeks subsequently to that date. You are therefore entitled to £32, for which I enclose a draft. There is, I am sorry to say, no dividend to be computed, our condition having been the opposite of one in advance.
" Yours very truly,
" MICH. STAUNTON.*

" Thomas Davis, Esq."

The two friends immediately retired from the *Register*, and employed themselves in other public work. They had found work by this time, destined to engross the remainder of their lives. While writing in the *Register*, it became plain that their position as national journalists, standing outside of the national organization which O'Connell had recently re-established at the Corn Exchange, was weak and anomalous. The philosophical nationality of the University was a feeble fire at best, kindled among rocks and mounds of solid earth, where there were few materials for combustion, and it was certain that it would only spread slowly and probably not very far. On the other hand, the popular agitation naturally repelled a young man like Davis, bred among a class to whom it was hateful and contemptible. For its methods were of necessity coarse, its instru-

* 80, Marlborough Street, July 24th.

ments rude, and the one conspicuous man of genius
who gave it its sole authority was the living embodi-
ment of political and religious passions inherited from
former contests. But however imperfectly it fulfilled
its office, it was the only guardian of the national
cause, and that cause was the cause of justice. The
result of reflection was that, to accomplish his purpose,
he must do what Tone had done before him—he
must associate himself with the people and their
trusted leaders whatever natural repugnance had to
be overcome. The most courageous incident in
Davis's career, which would not have been surpassed
in daring if he had mounted a breach in promotion
of his opinions, was to enter the Corn Exchange and
announce himself a follower of O'Connell.

It is difficult at the close of the nineteenth century, after fifty years of agitation for national ends
in which Protestants have been leaders or conspicuous spokesmen, to understand what such a
decision meant in 1842. The son of a Roman cen-
turion who left the retinue of Cæsar to associate
with the obscure Hebrews gathered round Saul of
Tarsus scarcely made a more surprising or significant
choice. A dozen years had barely elapsed since the
Celtic population were released from a code expressly framed for their extinction, so that "one
Papist should not remain in Ireland." The bulk of
the nation were simple, generous, and pious, but
ignorant and little accustomed to think for themselves. The middle-class Catholics scarcely dreamed
of any higher aim than to obtain some social recognition from the dominant race, or some crumb of
patronage from a friendly administration.

We have glanced at the Ireland into which Davis

was born in 1814. The generation which had since
elapsed saw political changes accomplished of great
scope and promise—Catholics were emancipated and
Parliament was reformed,—but the system on which
Ireland was governed by England had undergone no
effectual change. Every institution and agency per-
taining to authority was still strictly Protestant. The
towns were only a few months liberated from exclusive
corporations who had vindicated their right to govern
by plundering in every instance the endowments
provided by the State for their support. The counties
were still controlled by Protestant grand juries, in
whose selection the ratepayers whose money they
disposed of had no part. The judiciary, executive,
and local magistracy were Protestant in the proportion of more than a hundred to one, and they commonly regarded the people with distrust and aversion ;
for though time had mitigated, it had not extinguished
the sentiment which in official circles classified the
bulk of the nation as the " Irish enemy." Half the
rural population were steeped in habitual misery.
The peasantry in the genial climate of southern
Europe were better clad and fenced against the
elements than the tenant farmers who toiled under
the moist and chilly sky of winter in Ireland ; and in
the least productive countries in Europe, in the
barrenest canton in Switzerland, or the most sterile
commune in the Alps, they were better fed than
amongst the plentiful harvests of Munster. The
great estates were held by English absentees, who
ruled the country from Westminster, mainly for their
own profit and security. The resident gentry were
for the most part their dependents or adherents, and
had never wholly lost the secret apprehension that

estates obtained by confiscation might in the end
be forfeited by the same process. But they were
entrenched behind a standing army whose function
in Dublin was no more in doubt than that of the
Croat in Milan or the Cossack in Warsaw. The
country sent a few national and a few Catholic representatives to the Imperial Parliament, but the franchise was so skilfully adjusted to exclude the majority
that in some cases a freeholder with the required
qualification had to pay as many as ten separate
rates and taxes before he became entitled to vote.
One powerful tribune, indeed, constantly demanded
in Parliament and on the popular platform the rights
withheld from the people ; but his enemies scornfully declared that he did not represent the nation,
but only its frieze coats and soutanes. He had
against him, for the most part, the Irishmen whose
books were read or whose lives were notable, the
journalists capable of controlling public opinion, and,
universally, the great social power called good
society. His agitation was pronounced to be ple-
beian ; and, in truth, it was not free from faults of
exaggeration, offensive to veracity and good taste.
For nearly two years O'Connell, at this time, had
been making weekly appeals to public opinion in
favour of a native parliament, but he had not drawn
to him one man of station, weight of character, or
conspicuous ability. The sincerity of his policy was
doubted even among the patriot party, because he
impaired the simple force of the national claim by
coupling with it a radical reform of the House of
Commons, revision of the land code, and the abolition of tithe,—questions to be dealt with by the
Imperial Parliament, and each " good for a Trojan
war of agitation."

Between the agitator and the Government there was a section of the Protestant middle class, of humane culture and liberal opinions, who sympathized with neither, unless when the administration was in the hands of Whigs. They had been Emancipators, and wished to see gross wrongs redressed, but they were content that reforms should come as soon, and extend as far, as English opinion might approve—unhappily never very soon or very far. They were, in fact, merely the provincial allies of a political party in London.

The Tories, who were in a great majority among the gentry and the professions, looked on the popular movement with disdain. But the indolence and satiety which come of long possession leavened their scorn largely with contempt. Between these parties Davis, if he took any part in public affairs, felt he had no choice. He recognized in O'Connell the natural successor of Hugh O'Neil, Art MacMurragh, Owen Roe, and the other Celtic chiefs who had stood in the front of the nation in peril and calamity. No one saw more clearly that the leader was not free from faults—it is only in poetry and romance that one encounters blameless heroes; but his cause was the same as theirs, the deliverance of the Irish race from greedy and truculent oppression. Among the class Davis burned to enlist in the national movement, O'Connell had never stood so low as at this time. He had laid himself open to a suspicion hostile to his influence among men of public spirit. Little more than half a dozen years earlier he had pulled down the banner of nationality, in order to grasp the patronage of the Irish Government, and they feared that if the Whigs came back to power he would be liable to yield again to the same temptation. He could doubtless plead in defence that he had brought into power the Irish administration of Mulgrave and Drummond, and raised O'Loghlen and Woulfe to the bench. The true story of his relation with the Whigs was rarely recounted in his own day, and is still imperfectly understood. Immediately after the splendid success of the Catholic agitation, the first Reform Act was carried by the English party who had been Emancipators, with the effectual assistance of O'Connell. Political power was their immediate reward. In England Brougham, representing opinions which were then considered extreme, became Lord Chancellor; in Scotland, Jeffrey, long the standard-bearer of reform in that country, became Lord Advocate; but, instead of raising their great Irish ally to a similar authority, they disdainfully refused office to the foremost Irishman of his century, and maintained in power an executive and judiciary nurtured at the dugs of Protestant Ascendancy. There has rarely been a more shameless concession to English prejudice than this transaction. It was a blunder as well as an insult. O'Connell wished to become Attorney-General, that great wrongs in the administration of justice might be redressed by his hand, and that the Catholic nation might recognize by such a conspicuous fact that they were emancipated. The most capable statesmen in the Cabinet approved of the project, but Earl Grey, a man of cold and haughty disposition, met it with a contemptuous negative. O'Connell felt a just resentment, and, on his own part and the part of his race, he went into opposition to the Grey Government. He proposed to the people who had

won emancipation to organize anew for the Repeal
of the Union with England. It was a design which
he had meditated from early manhood, a just and
necessary design, but the period selected was undoubtedly influenced by his personal resentment.
The nation gave him prompt support, and, at a
general election which ensued, forty Repealers were
elected. The national demand was formally launched,
and could never be withdrawn without grave loss
and discredit. But when Lord Grey retired from
office his successor made peace with O'Connell, and
the Irish leader consented to make another experiment to obtain the redress of Irish wrongs from the
Imperial Parliament. He stopped the Repeal agitation in mid career, and became a parliamentary
supporter of the Whigs. The change was made more
offensive to Irish feeling by his permitting members
of his own family and many of his political friends,
who had been elected to Parliament at great popular
sacrifice, to become placemen and give up for ever
the cause to which they were pledged in the face of
the nation. When the Whigs fell from power in
1840, he took up the national question anew, but he
was impeded at every step by inevitable suspicions ;
the majority of the nation answered languidly to his
appeal, and the minority did not answer at all. This
was a country in which a public career offered no
prizes to ambition, but nowhere on the earth was a
noble, unselfish patriotism more imperiously solicited
to struggle and die rather than endure wrongs so
shameless.

The patriotism of the two young men was not
solicited in vain ; on the 19th of April, 1841, Davis
and Dillon became members of the Repeal Associa-

tion. They were cordially welcomed by O'Connell, and immediately placed on the general committee, which was the popular privy council, and on sub-committees charged with special duties. How they demeaned themselves there I shall describe more conveniently a little later, when I became their associate. But I may note how early Davis began to organize his work. Before he was a month a member of the association, O'Connell wrote to his son John :—

"Tell him [Davis] the want of funds is a decisive reason for not urging the Repeal as we otherwise would. This is really the secret of our weakness. I will press the appointment of Repeal wardens until every parish is provided with the machinery." *

They were assiduous in their attendance on committees, but they did not limit their labours for the national cause to one field. Davis continued his contributions to the *Citizen*—now become the *Dublin Monthly Magazine;* and Dillon, who had succeeded to the auditorship of the Historical Society, prepared the closing address for the year 1841.

Dillon's address followed the general line of his friend's in teaching public duties, rather than rules of art; but it was calmer and statelier in tone. Nearly devoid of ornament, it was eloquent with strong convictions and lucid principles. It was an appeal to the judgment and conscience rather than to the generous emotions. But it was persuasive in a singular degree. One of the most eminent judges in Ireland told me a fact which enables us to estimate its value better than much criticism. "The night before I read Dillon's address," he said, "I was a

* O'Connell to his son, London, May 29, 1841, "Private Correspondence of O'Connell."

Whig; next morning and ever after I was a Nationalist." Dillon was so closely associated with Davis, so intimate a confederate and counsellor throughout his career, that I must pause for a moment on the Catholic Nationalist's first confession of faith as an essential part of the new opinions which they brought into Irish affairs.

If the Historical Society were solely a school of eloquence (he told them) the greatest lesson it could teach was that the way to be eloquent was, not to study the tricks of rhetoric, but to cultivate the passions of which eloquence is the natural language. It was usual on occasions like that to praise the care and perseverance of Demosthenes in mastering the art, but it would be more to the purpose to recall " the great passions by which he was inspired; the ardent love he bore his country; his fear for her safety; his undying hatred of her foe; and his fierce indignation against the traitors to her cause." His speeches were not loaded with ornament, there was slight care bestowed upon the structure of sentences or the selection of words; but " one spirit pervades them; throughout they breathe one great desire—to awaken his fellow-citizens to a sense of their dignity and their danger. This was the secret of his eloquence. His heart was in the cause in which he spoke."

And history everywhere repeated the same lesson.

"Look," he said, " to the records of any nation, and inquire what is that period of its history when eloquence shone forth in the greatest splendour? You will find it to be, when great events were being enacted, and great interests in conflict, and great and stormy passions roused in the breasts of men. Compare France in the Revolution with France ten years before, and ask the cause of the change which that short period brought about in the

F

genius of its people? You will find that it was not because they were more accomplished rhetoricians, that the men of the Revolution were greater orators than those who went before them, but because of the bursting forth of new passions, and the diffusion from breast to breast of high and fierce desires. It was this that roused the sensual nature of Mirabeau, and touched his tongue with fire. It was this that redeemed from that oblivion, into which it otherwise had sunk, many a name that is now immortal. And when Henry, the Demosthenes of America, issued from the recesses of the forest, and summoned his countrymen to arms, with an eloquence as deep, and as strong, and as rapid, as the rivers of his native wild, whence did *he* draw his inspiration? Was it from the pages of Longinus, or Quinctilian, or Blair? or was it not rather from the tumultuous emotions that heaved within him? He loved his country; he saw it in danger; and passion touched his heart, and its fountains opened, and the sacred stream gushed forth unsolicited and free."

He spoke of the example which their own history furnished :—

"We are apt, when we contemplate such a rare collection of great men as the Irish Parliament at that time exhibited, to attribute to *them* the greatness of those events which occurred in their time; and to suppose that the splendour in which that period appears clothed, was borrowed from the brilliancy of the genius in which it abounded. I would be inclined to reverse this arrangement, and to place the greatness of the time the first, and the greatness of the men the second, in the order of causation. . . . The age, I think, was not so much indebted to fortune for having blessed it with so many great men, as the men were indebted to it for having thrown them on so great an age. And I am confirmed in this opinion by a conviction which I have always entertained, that the intellectual powers of those men are generally overrated. Great orators they were, no doubt—amongst the greatest the world ever saw; but I do not think they deserve to be classed amongst the greatest men. As men, their greatness should be judged, not from what they *said*, but what they *did;* and, judged by this test, they are found wanting. Their language abounds in great conceptions and brilliant thoughts; but in their actions we seek in vain for that lofty determination which marks the conduct of the truly great—the Hampdens, the Washingtons, and many a countryman of our own, whose name is now forgotten, or preserved by lying history as an object of ridicule and scorn. At a time when they had the enemy completely at their mercy, and might have dictated whatever terms they pleased, they should have insisted on something more than permission to meet and amuse one another with elaborate orations, and to make laws which they had no power to enforce. They should have known that, no matter what forms of liberty it may possess, a nation is not free which has not the means of defending itself from aggression; that a constitution is but a mockery which has no security for its existence but the faith and the forbearance of strangers; that a Parliament is nothing more than a debating club, if it be not sustained by the sympathy, and, if need be, by the arms of the people."

He warned them against the modern cosmopolitanism which taught that nationality was a prejudice; that one spot of earth, because we chanced to be born there, was not on that account to be preferred to another, and that we had no duties to perform to our mother country. The man who knew how much more the happiness of a people depended on the spirit and disposition prevailing among them, than on the quality of the food which they ate or the clothes which they wore, viewed with more alarm the progress of such opinions than a pestilence or a famine, or the presence of a hostile army on our shores. For the effects of these things were speedily effaced; the ravages of pestilence and famine were soon repaired, and fields laid waste soon grew green again : but when cold and grovelling selfishness took possession of the minds of a people and drew them away from virtue and honour, there was then a wound inflicted which festered at the heart, and which centuries might not heal.

What was to prevent the objection taken against patriotism being brought to bear on family distinctions and the affections growing out of them ?

"Shall we not presently hear (or rather, do we not hear even now, from those pestiferous missionaries of vice that swarm throughout England) attempts to reason or to ridicule men out of their affections for their brothers and their parents? Might not a very virtuous lamentation be composed on the calamities that spring from those affections? upon the ruinous lawsuits that arise from the father's anxiety to preserve the property of his children, and the sanguinary duels that are occasioned by the sensitiveness of the brother to a stain upon a sister's honour? . . . National patriotism is as much a part of our nature as filial or fraternal love; I ground the assertion on the universality of its existence. And if we would pity or abhor the man who should advise us to transfer our filial affection from its proper object to such other object as interest might point out, why do we listen with patience to the men who tell us that we should transfer our patriotism from our own to other countries, when self-interest prompts us to do so? The latter of these affections is just as independent of our will and of self-love as the former; and it is so for the same reasons. It is a passion which springs out of the past, and the past we cannot alter. It is formed at a period when we are altogether incapable of reflecting on its uses; it grows, like summer flowers, in calm and cloudless times—those sunny days of childhood, when the heart is fresh and prone to love. Chilled it may be by selfishness or crushed by sophistry, but it cannot be transplanted. Uproot it from its native soil and it blooms no more, but the place in which it grew will remain empty and desolate for ever."

He spoke of the blessings patriotism conferred and the sacrifices it entailed, and it lends a noble charm to the sentiment of the young man to remember that in later times when called upon to put the sentiment into action he did not fail.

"The patriot revels in a thousand pure delights, which the cold cosmopolite can never taste. It is sweet to look back upon those times when our country was great and free. It is sweet to muse amidst moss-grown ruins, the memorials of her pride. It is sweet to read of the valour of her sons in their unequal struggles with the invader; to contrast their high-souled gallantry with the little arts and the ruffian fraud by which their ruin was effected It is sweet to gaze upon the flag that waved above their heads in

battle; it is sweet to hope that it shall wave again. The very
sorrows of the patriot are, like our own soft-breathing music,
sweetly sad. The tears of the exile are not all tears of grief, when
he sits down pensive in a distant land and thinks of home—the
remembered scenes, and the loved companions of early pleasures,
and the green churchyard where he would wish to sleep. Even
death itself lays down its grisly terrors, and smiles on him who
meets it in his country's cause. Deep generous raptures thrill
through the hero's breast, and his heart bounds lightly, and his
pulse beats high, when duty summons him to the post of danger.
And though fortune frown upon his arms, and his banner sink,
and he be doomed to press the plain; although, as he lies upon
his 'gory bed,' sad images of weeping friends and blighted love
afflict his spirit, and the cheers of successful tyranny send to his
grieved and death-sick heart the sad forebodings of wrongs and of
dishonour that await his native land; yet when his pangs have
passed away, and he is laid where the insults of the stranger or
the groans of his country cannot reach him, oh! who would give
his glory and that chainless grave for a few short years of slavery
and shame?

Students familiar with the ante-revolution literature of France and America will note that Davis's
address belonged to the first, Dillon's to the second
school. The one suggests the passion of Vergniaud,
the other the stately strength of Patrick Henry or
Alexander Hamilton. Davis's address was like a
vivid stream rippling musically over impediments,
and leaping into cascades, sometimes sparkling in
the sun, sometimes diving into subterranean places,
and reappearing coloured with the veined soil through
which it forced its way. Dillon's was like a calm,
strong level river, whose force may be measured by
the unbroken rapidity of its course.

He illustrated by examples the decisive and salutary results patriotism had produced in the world,
and by principles drawn from moral science the
depths of our nature from which it is derived. In

Ireland even what were called "the prejudices of patriotism" were symptoms of a nature undebased.

"The national character of Ireland, with its passions and its prejudices, its religious affections (called 'superstitions' by the cold of heart), ay, and its aversions and just resentments—this character has not been produced in a day, or in a year, or in a hundred years. Long centuries of trial and affliction have made it what it is. Its roots strike deep into antiquity, and its branches have been watered, from time to time, by the blood of the unforgotten brave. And is it not vexatious to hear little assimilating politicians talk about bending and fashioning this ancient tree, as if it were a twig?"

The end for which he aimed was brought back to view at the close of the address :—

"If the observations I have made have the effect of raising a doubt concerning the wisdom of those politicians who make light of nationality, who think that they serve their country by depreciating her power and resources in the estimation of her own people and of the world, and by representing her as unfit to enjoy, and unable to defend, her freedom; if anything I have said should cause you to think that national patriotism and common sense are by no means inconsistent with one another, as they are very commonly supposed to be, then my object is accomplished, my trouble more than rewarded, and your time, I think, not altogether thrown away."

These generous thoughts fell upon fit soil. In the short interval since the delivery of Davis's address, the Historical Society had undergone a notable change. It would seem, indeed, as if he had inspired it with his own soul. The old notabilities had all disappeared, and their successors were for the most part serious students fit to profit by lessons of public duty. Among the new members who afterwards won honourable reputation in the professions or the university were included John K. Ingram,* John O'Hagan, John and David Pigot, and Nelson Hancock.

* Now Senior Fellow of Trinity College, and a man of high distinction as a scholar and writer.

The adhesion of Davis and Dillon to the popular movement is a memorable event to Irishmen. There are men who make epochs in our history. Lawrence O'Toole, who combined the Celtic tribes against the invader; Art McMurrough, who effaced the crimes of his ancestor by heroic services; Hugh O'Neill, who baffled the enemy by culture and policy he learned from themselves; Roger O'Moore, who evoked hope among a moribund people; Sarsfield, who restored to their imagination the figure of a national soldier; Grattan, who used the institutions of the conquerors to conquer them in turn; Wolfe Tone, who combined the Presbyterian Republicans of the north with the Catholic serfs of Munster; O'Connell, who taught the trampled multitude their strength; and Davis, who once again aimed to unite the whole force of the nation in honourable union, are such men. He was the first Protestant since Tone, of recent times, who not only sympathized with the wrongs of the Celts, but accepted and embraced the whole volume of their hopes and sympathies. He was not a patron of the old race, but its spokesman and brother.

It was at this time, in the autumn of 1841, that I made Davis's acquaintance at the Repeal Association, and Dillon's at the *Register* office, where I had preceded him in an apprenticeship to journalism. I was in town only for a few days, to keep terms at the King's Inns, and had no opportunity of cultivating their acquaintance before returning to Belfast, where I then edited a bi-weekly newspaper. But they were so unlike all I had previously seen of Irish journalists that I was eager to know more of them. On returning to Dublin in the spring of 1842, I met them in the hall of the Four Courts, and they put off their gowns and walked out with me to the Phœnix Park, to have a frank talk about Irish affairs. We soon found that our purpose was the same—to raise up Ireland morally, socially, and politically, and put the sceptre of self-government into her hands. I knew their connection with the *Register* had ceased, and that the *Dublin Monthly* had no audience in the country, and I proposed that we should establish and conduct a weekly paper as organ of the opinions we held in common. Sitting under a noble elm in the park, facing Kilmainham, we debated the project, and agreed on the general plan. I was to find the funds and undertake the editorship, and we were to recruit contributors among our friends. Davis could count upon John Cornelius O'Callaghan, whose " Green Book " * was attracting attention at that time; Dillon named two young men in college, who afterwards did valuable work—John O'Hagan and John Pigot; and I could promise for Clarence Mangan and T. M. Hughes,† who contributed to the journal I was then editing, and O'Neill Daunt (formerly O'Connell's private secretary), whom I had sounded on the subject. We separated on an agreement to meet again in summer, and launch the journal in autumn.

Davis's correspondence during his early connection with the Repeal Association exhibits him constantly engrossed in work. One of his school-fellows ‡

---

* In 1841 appeared "The Green Book; or, Gleanings from the Writing Desk of a Literary Agitator:" a miscellany of poetry; the notes, valuable historical studies; the verses, rather slipshod, being more than ten years older than the establishment of the *Nation*, and belonging to quite a different school.

† Afterwards author of " Revelations of Spain," the " Ocean Flower," etc., and editor of the *London Charivari*, a periodical which preceded *Punch*, and was illustrated by Leech.

‡ Cadwallader Waddy, county Wexford.

asked his advice on an effective style in journalism, and got prompt counsel.

"I received this morning your letter, and the *Wexford Independent.* With something of jest or flattery, I fear, you ask my poor opinion on the 'matter and style' of your article? To punish you I shall give it. I can assure you sincerely that anything written by an old friend and school-fellow would be welcome to me. I think you have written a sensible and, I may add, eloquent article on the most important of national manufactures, mind-making; appropriate too, for the public must learn much, and that quickly, on the subject, if they would prosper. There is no subject which interests me so much as education. I shall give you next month a pamphlet of mine on it, and shall pray your candid opinion. [The allusion is to his Address, which was printed in October, 1841—ten days after the date of this note.] I know you will pardon my pointing out a defect or two in your forcible style; the sentences are rather long and complicated, the parts of each sentence might be more *accurately distributed*, and, lastly, let me beg of you not to employ newspaper phrases so much. These are faults which you need only bear in mind to amend. You have 'metaphysical consciousness' enough to watch and correct yourself. Do so, and you will soon acquire a more consistent and precise style. You possess sufficient force and invention, as I can see, and I have no doubt your information is extensive. You see I am no flatterer; you asked my opinion, and I fancied it might be of service to you. I should never have intruded it unasked. You will, I know, pardon its freedom. You mention Lord Ebrington's Declaration [Lord Ebrington, then Lord Lieutenant, declared that no Repealer would receive any share of the patronage of the State]: I think O'Connell has made a right use of that part which recognizes the constitutional right to agitate for repeal, as it will impede the next Whig Coercion Bill, which nothing but a French war will prevent the introduction of. The passage which threatens to withhold all favour and patronage from Repealers I think worthy of Lord Castlereagh, and one of the most insolent speeches I have ever read. But Thiers will soon make the Whigs sing another tune. You promised to give me a call on your return—do not forget it. We shall then talk more of these things.

"I remain, your sincere friend,

"THOMAS DAVIS."

His friend Webb complains that he is neglecting him for politics, and receives an adequate excuse.

"MY DEAR ROBERT,

"I am a brute for not having written to you before. After that admission you must forgive me. I envy you your leisure, and the country, and your thoughts. I am up to the tips of my hair in business. I am secretary to the Franchise Committee, ditto to the Municipal Election Committee, and, on account of Clement's illness, I am obliged to give some of my time to the Dublin Registry, which is now going on. There is no hope of my getting out of this 'decayed metropolis' for the summer, or autumn either.

"Do you walk four Irish miles an hour for two hours consecutively? [As Davis had doubtless instructed him to do.] If so you are in speed at least quite my match; but I get dogged, and would endure any amount of fatigue or disgust with the object of my toil and not give up—in walking at least.

"When you are at Capel Curig go and see a lake between it and Trefriew; there is no road, you must cross the hill.

"Are you getting more passionately patriotic? You are away from poor Ireland. Poor, poor Ireland! Well, who knows? 'Old Erin *shall* be free' says the 'Shan Van Vocht.' I wrote 'will;' I have changed it to '*shall*.' How is Bessie? and how go on the babes? My love to you all, with a heart and a half. Next summer maybe we shall be together in Connaught. I shall be all alone here by this day week. Have you made as much way in De Beaumont as in walking? [Davis gave him De Beaumont's 'Irelande Sociale, Politique, et Religieuse' to study.] Talking of histories, 'as you do in your note,' there's a 'History of Conway.' Get it, and Price's (I think that's the name) 'History of Wales,' and be happy. Pray write to me soon, and I may be in a more scribbling mood. Good-bye, my boy.

"Always yours,
"T. D.*

"To P. R. Webb, vagabond in Wales."

And again :—

"Write, for I like to hear from you, for thus only am I reminded by anything outside myself that we are to spend, as we have spent, many an hour pleasantly, and not without purpose, together. And tell me how Bessie is, or tell her to write to me. Talk to me all you have been thinking among the 'chiefless castles.' I am already

* 61, Bagot Street, August 4, 1841.

getting sick of 'citizens and burgesses.' I never *will* be a Lucas; you, little impudence, will add I could not, but—— [Lucas was the popular Protestant leader in Dublin between Swift and Grattan.] . . . Lest I should forget to tell you when we meet, remember to read a book called 'The Rationale of Religious Enquiry,' by James Martineau. It has two or three important thoughts on religion that were new to me; perhaps they will be so to you, at any rate you will like the book." *

As the season approaches its close he is still busy at public work :—

"I learn from your mother that you have been very ill. Attribute this to your lazy, sedentary, pedantic, fire-loving, chimney-worshipping, mopish habits. Amend your ways, use your limbs, breathe God's air, and see His world, or, by the holy St. Patrick (I swear by your patron in compliment to you), you'll evaporate and cease to be. O'Connell refers me to son John (as himself has not the authority for the story of Sarsfield at Landen), and the said son John is at Darrynane; but I'll remember your quest and get it answered. [The authority, probably, for the story of his dying words, 'Would that this were for Ireland.'] Will you oblige me by sending me at once a note to the librarian R.D.S. Library, to admit the Rev. John McHugh, Catholic Curate of Kinsealy. This, my client for your favour, is somewhat read in Irish history, and occasionally comes to town. O'Callaghan is in London, staggering with Parisian lore. His book is beginning to sell, and will be noticed in the *Dublin Review* next month. Do you know Mackintosh's letters to R. Hall about his madness? Do you know Mackintosh's life? or anything? I only just read it myself, but I can swagger judiciously." †

And to the same friend, still touring in Wales, he sends practical suggestions for turning his excursion to the best account :—

"Why don't you write to me? To be sure I owe you a letter but then I have nothing to tell; you have much to say to me, as you are the traveller, the seer of new sights, the feeler of new thoughts, while I am jogging on in the old way, intending much

* Saturday, August 28, 1841.
† 61, Bagot Street, September 28, 1841.

and doing nothing, or worse. I am alone, and grow lonely; the weather is miserable, O'Connell in low spirits; so write to me and rehumanize me. If affairs here do not come to a crisis in a year I shall turn Unitarian preacher. You will be glad to hear that O'Connell will (he says) have a book on Irish History from 1172 to 1612 (when the Irish were made not-outlaws) published in October. It will consist of some thirty pages of text, and seven or eight hundred of notes and illustrations, including most of Carey's book to that date. [Carey's ' Vindicæ Hibernicæ,' a defence of the Irish rising in 1641.] O'Connell's name will get all these collections read, and the memory of Ireland will be enlarged. We may all take advantage of this beginning, and put thoughts into the mind of the country. By heavens, 'tis maddening to see the land without arts or arms, literature or wealth! I am for the sharp remedies. Oh for another Clontarf! the crowded hour, and the worthy grave. But you have other thoughts, calm, unfevered, for though nestling in the battlements of Caernarvon or striding through the pass of Llanberris, you hear the clash of arms, see waving banners and charging knights and struggling mountaineers. Yet 'tis all a pleasant vision; not personal, nothing of duty, or faith, or anxiety, in it; fanciful, passionless, and oh, the dark tarn rippling where it rippled, or lay still, in the time of Glendower or Caractacus, in the times of minstrel and bard, when no damned slate quarries and earth-stabbing mines, and cold, fitful, imbecile races were there. I hate England and Anglicism, isolated, yet not original. I wish the Chartists would seize the lands, and burn all the machines in England. Is the human race progressive, or oscillating? The progress of the last six hundred years—printing, gunpowder! Christianity says the race has a destiny as well as the individuals; yet surely (may God forbid it!) we are not to settle down into utilitarianism—making the most use of the world, and cramming it with as many wealthy, gymnasticated, schooled people as it will hold, in social parallelograms or cottages and gardens, and it does not matter much which. . . . Is it not possible to have moral and intellectual progress in religion, and happiness, without a simultaneous growth of mechanics and material pursuits and condensed population, which leaves no mountain untilled, no sea unfathomed, no valley lonely? Do you feel any necessity for a creed to satisfy your feelings? Unless one has something of the sort he is apt to grow inactive and uncomfortable. A strong mind must preach or govern or love, a mission or occupation or a paradise. I must choose between the two first, but I waver and grow sensual and misty (for mine is not a strong mind), so shall probably end in doing neither." *

After our general design for the new journal was settled, Davis proposed modifications to which his colleagues could not cordially assent. He feared that a weekly paper spoke too seldom to be an effective teacher. The *Evening Freeman*, an unprosperous offshoot of the morning paper which appeared twice a week, was understood to be in the market, and he suggested that we should farm it for a fixed period, and be heard twice a week instead of once. I was unwilling to make this experiment. A weekly journal was my ideal. One of my first purchases with money of my own earning had been a set of the *Examiner* in the time of Hazlitt and the Hunts. When a schoolboy, I had fallen in with the early volumes of *Blackwood's Magazine*, and its base vituperation of Hazlitt and the Cockney school excited a longing to read Hazlitt, and, after him, Charles Lamb, De Quincy, and Leigh Hunt. A paper like the *Examiner* in its best days,—different in form as well as in spirit from the existing weeklies,

* 61, Bagot Street, Sunday, August 15, 1841.
There are so few of Davis's letters playful, that this one is worth preserving as an example. His mother instructed him to issue certain invitations, to Webb and some of his relatives, but, being busy or lazy, he transferred the duty to his friend in the jargon of the profession to which they both belonged :—

"Therefore it behoves you to intimate the contents of these presents unto them, the aforesaid. Provided always that if the said Robert Webb, Bessie Webb, or Isabella Woodroffe, shall fail in any of the things deeds or acts herein and hereby intimated and expressed or intended so to be, it shall and may be lawful to and for the hereinafter named Thomas Davis, or his assigns, to break the heads of them the said Robert, Bessie, and Isabella, in such manner as to him or them shall seem pleasing, to wit on the day and year last mentioned, at Dublin, aforesaid.

"The writing on the appended quarter sheet of paper, and on both sides thereof, was written by me on this 20th day of December, 2nd Vict., A.D. 1838.

"THOMAS DAVIS.

original instead of a reprint, and literary as well
as political—seemed to me the fit medium for criticism and speculation. After much debate it was
suggested, probably by Dillon, that we might try
both projects simultaneously. Happily the division
of forces which the double task would have imposed
was avoided by the refusal of the *Freeman* proprietary
to accept the arrangement. They shortly afterwards
purchased the *Morning Register*, in which Davis and
Dillon had recently written, amalgamated it with
their daily paper, and the unprofitable *Evening Freeman* slipped quietly out of existence.

But Davis had not yet reconciled himself to the
limitations of a weekly paper. He had studies in
hand too extensive for the columns of any newspaper.
He was about to reprint the statutes of the Irish
Parliament of James II., with suitable comments,
and nothing short of a monthly periodical could find
space for them. And his college friends, Wallis
especially, were angrily opposed to any political
journal, which, they insisted, must fall under the
dictatorship of O'Connell, and lose all initiative and
independence. The *Dublin Monthly Magazine*, if it
were only strengthened by the men and money about
to be wasted on a weekly paper, would, they contended, do the work designed more effectually—the
work being, to create a sounder and more generous
opinion on all branches of the Irish question, and
cultivate the sympathy of Protestants. On the other
hand, if its best men were diverted to other projects,
the only organ of high nationality in the country
must perish. A weekly paper was a mistake; there
were several weekly papers already in existence, but
they were never seen in the hands of the educated

classes. Objections to a periodical, because it only
appeared once a month, were. futile. Was there not
a periodical in Edinburgh, which appeared only once
a quarter, which had saved the fortunes of the Whig
party, and won the mind of England to Reform?
And the political and literary services of the rival
quarterly in London to the Tory party had been
scarcely less signal. London, no doubt, had excep-
tional opportunities; but if such things could be
done in Edinburgh, why not in Dublin? These were
the arguments pressed upon Davis, especially by
Wallis, whom he was accustomed to hear with
deference. Though the magazine had been a complete failure, only kept in existence at the cost of
Hudson, Davis had still a strange hankering for
putting his new wine into this damaged vehicle.
Wallis, who was as inventive, as persuasive, and as
unpractical as Coleridge, was ready with a plan to
supersede the new journal, the very name of which
was an offence to him. *Nation*, forsooth, when it
could not escape its fate of becoming the washhand-
basin of O'Connell! This was the plan. Let the
magazine become the property of its contributors;
let a fund be raised to carry it on for three years
certain; let the new proprietors form a social club
meeting weekly, to consider the public questions
which they were about to treat; and there would be
a focus of opinion and practical work such as had
wrought wonders in America, France, and Germany.
Davis promised to sound his friends on the subject.
He did not propose to abandon the *Nation*, but to
leave me to consider whether the limited assistance
he could give under the circumstances would be
worth retaining. When the new project was com-

municated to Dillon, then in the country, his vigorous good sense rejected it peremptorily.

"DEAR DAVIS (he wrote),

"Although I received your letter two days since, it was quite impossible for me to answer it sooner. I have been unable to do anything, or even to think of anything since I came to the country, from the state of perpetual motion in which I have been kept. In compliance with your request for a categorical answer to your proposal, I say 'No.' I need hardly tell you that nothing would give me greater pleasure than to make one of those of whom your club will consist, if you succeed in establishing it; but with my present opinions regarding its principal object, it would argue a great want of common prudence in me to join it.

"You must not understand me to mean that it is not desirable that the *Citizen* should flourish. I have not, as you are aware, so high an opinion of the utility of a monthly periodical for this country as you and others have; but, at the same time, I think it would be by no means without use if it could succeed. But is your project likely to insure its success? I see no reason to think so. It is now two or three years in existence, and it is still a losing speculation; and what chance is there that it will not be the same at the end of the next three years? What advantage will it have that it has not had? I cannot see any, and I think it a pity that the energies of the best men in the country should be wasted in an occupation neither profitable to themselves nor to any one else; for you know a magazine which does not pay is not read. Under these circumstances, if you engage in the undertaking, I must be content with wishing you success.

"As to the prospectus [of the *Nation*], it was my intention (and unfortunately, like most of my intentions, it still remains unfulfilled) to write one, and to send it together with yours to Duffy. This is the reason why I have kept yours so long. I do not altogether approve of the one you wrote. It contains many good passages; but, as a whole, I think it would not answer the purpose for which it was intended. I have taken a copy for Duffy, which I will send him immediately. The original I send back to yourself, as you might wish to improve it. It would be highly desirable to have a good prospectus, and you have done first-rate things in that way.

"Have you seen Duffy's letter in the *Vindicator?* It struck me as a first-rate production. A weekly paper conducted by that fellow would be an invaluable acquisition. I should like to hear when you intend to leave town, and how you are succeeding in the club affair.

> " Ever yours,
> " JOHN DILLON." *

After Dillon's letter, Davis began to speak to his friends of the new journal. He still helped the *Dublin Monthly* with important papers, and urged old contributors to help it, but the project of re-organizing it was silently abandoned. On the 6th of July, he wrote to Waddy—

"I am going to resume my connection with the Irish press in the autumn, but in a way which will enable me to effect more with less demand on my time than last year. And, as I am talking of myself, you will see some very treasonable papers of mine in the *Dublin Monthly* for the two last and the ensuing months, on the Afghan war. What say you to Blackburn? He has produced an angry feeling amongst moderate Liberals and even Tories here ; and as to Pennefather, he has damned himself past recovery.† Norbury never uttered so atrocious a charge as he did. To keep the ball up they are this day prosecuting a Drogheda printer for publishing the *Shan Van Vocht!* Only think of such madness! Is it possible Peel sanctions this? But thank God, for with a persecuting Government we need only be true to ourselves, and Ireland will be ready whenever an opportunity offers to emancipate herself. I leave for the north on Tuesday, so if you write to me to Belfast, care of C. G. Duffy, Esq., *Vindicator* Office, next week or the week after, I shall get your letter. Burn this.

> " Ever yours,
> " THOMAS DAVIS."

Next day he wrote more fully to Maddyn :—

"You won't write to me, so I write to you, perhaps it's the

---

* Dillon's letter has no date; but the letter in the *Vindicator*, to which he alludes as recent, is dated June 23, 1842.

† The allusion is to the prosecution of Mr. Gavan Duffy, editor and pro-prietor of the *Belfast Vindicator*, for an alleged libel charging Attorney-General Blackburn with a partial administration of justice by trying a Catholic prisoner, in what was called " a party case," by an exclusively Protestant jury, while a directly opposite practice was employed in the case of Protestant prisoners. The case was tried before Chief Justice Pennefather, and some account of the circumstances out of which it arose, and the speech for the defence, will be found in Lord O'Hagan's "Selected Speeches," p. 75.

same in the end. Well, I'll philosophize by-and-by, but must scold now. When you withdrew your animal self from us Irishers, did you mean to subtract the spirit? If I'd known your design I'd have *nobbled your soul* as the Kilkenny boys did the Carlow electors. In good sooth, won't you write to me and tell me what you are doing, or dreaming, or hoping? Do you take any interest in the twig you so richly nourished—the *Citizen?* We have had all manner of doubts and discussions, and have at last resolved to continue it, blow high, blow low, for some time longer. For charity and for memory's sake, send us something—we die, we faint, we fail! Well, well, I meant to write you a grave letter, and here I am scribbling nonsense. Now don't say 'of course,' for I'm in savage health, and won't bear a gibe. Webb and I leave for the north on Tuesday next. After seeing the County Down, Belfast, and Benburb, we mean to loiter round Antrim cliffs to Derry, and maybe to Donegal; and from either I shall return by the Fermanagh Lakes to Dublin, leaving him to close the autumn in the north with his wife and his little ones—God bless them! Webb is always asking for you, and what can I say? I am going to take another dash at the press here, but under better auspices than last time. If you write to me any time before the 25th, care of C. G. Duffy, Esq., *Vindicator* Office, I'll get the letter."

Maddyn, in reply to his appeal for a contribution to the *Dublin Monthly,* promised a sketch of Stephen Woulfe—a lawyer who had distinguished himself in the Catholic agitation, and, after emancipation and reform, became Chief Baron in Ireland. On his northern journey Davis answered him, and opened his heart to his friend on his policy and hopes.

"I picked up your letter yesterday, on my way here. Webb and I have been over the battle-ground of the Boyne, through Dundalk, Rostrevor, the Mourne Mountains, and mean, after seeing Benburb and Belfast (the home of heroes and conventicle of swine), to go round the Antrim coast to Derry. Your sketch of Woulfe will be invaluable. Are you aware that he wrote a pamphlet on the Catholic question? I have it in Dublin. Would you wish for it? I agree with most, and differ from some, of what you say; but I am so sun-stricken and plethoric that I hardly am able to tell you which is which."

He concluded in language which enables us to

understand how mature and well-considered were the opinions which the young recruit brought to national counsels :—

"The machinery at present working for repeal could never, under circumstances like the present, achieve it; but circumstances must change. Within ten or fifteen years England must be in peril. Assuming this much, I argue thus. Modern Anglicism — *i.e.* Utilitarianism, the creed of Russell and Peel, as well as of the Radicals—this thing, call it Yankeeism or Englishism, which measures prosperity by exchangeable value, measures duty by gain, and limits desire to clothes, food, and respectability,—this damned thing has come into Ireland under the Whigs, and is equally the favourite of the 'Peel' Tories. It is believed in the political assemblies in our cities, preached from our pulpits (always Utilitarian or persecuting); it is the very Apostles' Creed of the professions, and threatens to corrupt the lower classes, who are still faithful and romantic. To use every literary and political engine against this seems to me the first duty of an Irish patriot who can foresee consequences. Believe me, this is a greater though not so obvious a danger as Papal supremacy. So much worse do I think it, that, sooner than suffer the iron gates of that filthy dungeon to close on us, I would submit to the certainty of a Papal supremacy, knowing that the latter should end in some twenty years—leaving the people mad, it might be, but not sensual and mean. Much more willingly would I take the chance of a Papal supremacy, which even a few of us laymen could check, shake, and prepare (if not effect) the ruin of. Still more willingly would I (if Anglicanism, *i.e.* Sensualism, were the alternative) take the hazard of open war, sure that if we succeeded the military leaders would compel the bigots down, establish a thoroughly national Government, and one whose policy, somewhat arbitrary, would be anti-Anglican and anti-sensual; and if we failed it would be in our own power before dying to throw up huge barriers against English vices, and, dying, to leave example and a religion to the next age. I have for some time had two sets of articles in contemplation for the *Citizen*—one 'Illustrations of Nationality,' being some account of the peculiarly national things of Hungary and Norway at present, and of Switzerland in the past, and perhaps the free cities of the Middle Ages. The second series to be passages of Irish History, such as the lives of the O'Neills, the settlement of Munster and Ulster, etc. What do you think of these projects? Did I tell you that I am going to resume writing for the press in a couple of months? Don't mention it to any one. It is necessary for me to get involved in projects, otherwise my mind would fall into the old melancholy or the older love which wasted most of my life. Write to me soon again, and believe me

" Ever yours,

" Thomas Davis." *

In July, Davis visited me at Belfast, and all the preliminaries were settled for the issue of our prospectus. Davis's draft was adopted with a single amendment, and an addition which I considered of importance; the names of the intending contributors were published as a guarantee of good faith and personal responsibility. Davis suggested the significant title of the *Nation* for the new paper, and a sentence from the prospectus will indicate our specific aim :—

"Nationality is their first great object—a Nationality which will not only raise our people from their poverty, by securing to them the blessings of a Domestic Legislature, but inflame and purify them with a lofty and heroic love of country—a Nationality of the spirit as well as the letter—a Nationality which may come to be stamped upon our manners, and literature, and our deeds—a nationality which may embrace Protestant, Catholic, and Dissenter—Milesian and Cromwellian,—the Irishman of a hundred generations and the stranger who is within our gates;—not a Nationality which would prelude civil war, but which would establish internal union and external independence;—a Nationality which would be recognized by the world, and sanctified by wisdom, virtue, and prudence."

The Belfast of the United Irishmen and the Volunteers, which still claimed to be the chief seat of liberality and letters in the island, had a strong fascination for Davis, but I warned him that he would find the "Athens of Ireland" as ugly and sordid as Manchester; its temples hideous little

* July 24, 1842.

Bethels, where Pentilic marble was replaced by unwholesome bricks from the mud of the Lagan, its orators noisy fanatics, and the old historic spirit soured into a bigotry worthy of Rochelle, the Belfast of France, where Protestants, newly escaped from chains, maintained what they called religious liberty by refusing a Catholic permission to worship God or exercise the smallest authority within their dominion. To my northern friends Davis was a new and puzzling phenomenon. The Belfast Whigs were Protestant Liberals, in general sympathy with the English Whigs, but a genuine Nationalist was nearly unknown among them. The Catholic Bishop and clergy to whom I presented him saw for the first time an Irish Protestant who recognized the old race as the natural spokesmen of public opinion, who sympathized passionately with the historic memories of which they were proud, but never forgot or permitted others to forget that the Protestant minority were equally Irishmen, however party politics might have separated them from their brethren.

Though his apprenticeship ended and his public life began when he entered the Repeal Association, it was only in the new journal he was free to utter his whole mind and able to make himself heard by the nation. His public life lasted barely five years, and seldom in the history of a people have five years been more fruitful of beneficent changes in opinion and action. The story I have to tell is not so much the career of a gifted man as the development of a new era. It is nearly half a century since he entered the Corn Exchange; it is over five and forty years since he was buried at Mount Jerome; and during all this interval the opinions which he

taught have been widening their scope, and his name
growing dearer to his countrymen.   He influenced
profoundly the mind of his own generation, and it is
not too soon to affirm that he has made a permanent
change in the opinions of the nation which he served.
It needed patience and forbearance of a kind not
too plentiful among Irishmen to harmonize his aims
with the juggles and devices of traditional agitation.
But there was still " one great aim, like a guiding
star above."   The rights of a nation were again
demanded for his country without stint or limitation,
by its accredited leader.   The cause was as good as
any recorded in history, and he was persuaded and
resolved that the contest should become as noble
and spiritual as the great enterprises which had
moved his sympathy in the annals of struggling
nations.   The sentiments already in his heart afterwards blossomed into song :—

> " May Ireland's voice be ever heard
>   Amid the world's applause !
> And never be her flag-staff stirred,
>   But in an honest cause !
> May freedom be her very breath,
>   Be Justice ever dear ;
> And never an ennobled death
>   May son of Ireland fear !
> So the Lord God will ever smile,
> With guardian grace, upon our isle."

From this date all the incidents of his career are
familiar to a hundred witnesses, and pass before us
like a panorama.

CHAPTER IV.

THE new journal was announced to appear on the 8th of October, 1842. Davis had only undertaken to contribute one article a week, and he arrived in town from his northern excursion on the eve of publication.* But he speedily came to see that he had found the true business of his life, and he entered on it with all the decision and energy of his nature. The public were on the alert for the appearance of the *Nation*. The prospectus and the disclosure of the writer's names had awakened a certain curiosity, and there was already at the publishing office a considerable list of subscribers, and large orders for the first number from country agents. The two earliest subscribers were symbolical—men who took slight interest in current journalism, but much in native literature—the eminent antiquaries, Eugene Curry and John O'Donovan. But the existing journalists, as I encountered them from time to time, warned me, in spite of these omens, to expect a collapse. We are apt to think of an eminent man as having

---

* I found this note among his papers: "I have been expecting you in town for some days. Our first number must make its appearance to-morrow fortnight, and there are many questions to be considered, which will require time and you. Pray come home" (Duffy to Davis, Sept. 23, 1842).

been to his contemporaries all he has become to
posterity, but this rarely happens ; and it will be an
encouragement to modest men to know that it was
far from happening to Davis. It is not strange that
he was for a time imperfectly recognized at college ;
but when he began to act in public, he was the
subject of contemptuous banter to the veteran
agitators around O'Connell. He spoke a language
which they did not understand, and pursued aims
which they believed to be quixotic. The jolly unprincipled editor of the *Pilot*, understood to be much
in the confidence of O'Connell, assured me that
Davis was a simpleton who nearly ruined Alderman
Staunton by eccentric proposals in the *Register*, and
might be counted on to frighten men of sense from
any enterprise in which he was concerned. And the
proprietor of the *Monitor*, who had no *malus animus*,
told me that he had seen Davis representing the
Repeal Association in the Dublin Revision Court,
and that he was unskilful and unready, ignorant of
practice which had become traditional, and incapable of holding his own with the Conservative
agent.

When expectation and the conflict of opinion
were at their height, a mischance in the printing-
office rendered it necessary to postpone the appearance of the journal for a week, and I was consoled
on various sides with the assurance that such a delay
was fatal; the public expectation was disappointed,
and could never be revived.

On the 15th of October the long-expected first
number was issued. Maddyn had suggested a happy
motto from a speech of Stephen Woulfe, " To create
and foster public opinion, and make it racy of the

soil." [The form and appearance of the journal were
new in Ireland ; political verses were printed among
the leading articles as claiming equal attention, and
there was a distinct department for literature.   The
first leader declared, as the chief article of our creed,
that, political nicknames—Whig, Tory, and so forth
—notwithstanding, we would recognize only two
parties in Ireland—those who suffered by her degrada-
tion, and those who profited by it.] Clarence Mangan
proclaimed our second purpose to be the emancipation
of the trampled tenantry.

> " We announce a New Era—be this our first news—
> When the serf-grinding landlords shall shake in their shoes,
> While the ark of a bloodless yet mighty Reform
> Shall emerge from the flood of the popular storm !
> Well we know how the lickspittle panders to pow'r
> Feel and fear the approach of that death-dealing hour;
> But we toss these aside—such vile, vagabond lumber
> Are but just worth a groan from ' THE NATION'S ' FIRST NUMBER."

By a curious coincidence the arrangements were
completed on Davis's twenty-eighth birthday, and
next morning the journal was flying through the
city.   In his correspondence with Maddyn we have
the story of its success.

> "The *Nation* sold its whole impression of No. 1 before twelve
> o'clock this morning, and could have sold twice as many more if
> they had been printed, as they ought to have been; but the fault
> is on the right side.   The office window was actually broken by
> the newsmen in their impatience to get more.   The article called
> ' The Nation' is by Duffy; ' Aristocratic Institutions,' by Dillon;
> ' Our First Number,' by Mangan ; ' Ancient Irish Literature,' ' The
> Epigram on Stanley,' and the capital ' Exterminators' Song,' are
> by O'Callaghan.   The article on ' The English Army in Afghan-
> istan, etc.,' the mock proclamation to the Irish soldiers, and the
> reviews of the two Dublin magazines, are by myself. . . . The
> articles you propose will do admirably in your hands.   Duffy is
> the very greatest admirer of the sketches of Brougham and Peel

that I ever met. [Sketches by Maddyn in the *Dublin Monthly Magazine.*] Perhaps in a newspaper the points should be more salient and the writing more rough and uncompromising than in a magazine. Duffy seems to think that if number three, your lightest, dare-devilish *poteen* article, were to come first, it would most readily fall in with the rest of the arrangements."

Wallis, who was nothing if not critical, administered a bitter to correct any excess of sweets.

"MY DEAR DAVIS,

    "Where's the article—'The Beauties of the Boyne Water,' or whatever it was to be—that you promised positively for next month's magazine? Did you not, or will you not, strike the iron while it is hot? Or have you been so much occupied with your *accouchement,* with your parturient and obstetrical responsibilities, that other things have been naught to you? Certainly the antenatal baptism having been (*me saltem judice*) so lamentably botched, it was the more important to provide that cradle, caudle, cake, and all other ceremonials should be unexceptionable. I have not yet seen the 'new birth to unrighteousness,' the unclean thing, with the holy name embroidered on its frontlets and phylacteries. [He objected vehemently to the title of the journal.] Not a copy procurable by me, and sundry other speculative individuals, even at a premium. One thing you may be sure of: the newsmen are open-mouthed against you. I have listened with pastoral patience to several of their diatribes. They say you might have sold in Dublin *ten times* what you printed for the city circulation ; and that they warned you early in the week, and offered to lift you and your compeers to the Seventh Heaven on a pyramid of two hundred quires, and you had not the spunk to venture." *

Maddyn, who had made difficulties at the outset in helping a journal with whose main aim he was not in sympathy, soon became a regular contributor of critical and biographical papers ; and Davis treated him with a frank confidence and affectionate deference which soothed the sensitive literary spirit. He sent him suggestions for articles from time to time, and kept him acquainted with the secret history of the enterprise.

* October 17th.

" The paper is selling finely. The authorships this week run thus—' War with Everybody,' by J. F. Murray; ' Reduction of Rents,' and the ' Faugh a Ballagh,' by Duffy; ' Time no Title,' ' The Sketch of Moore,' and ' The Grave,' by myself. . . . The *Mail* says we are at work to establish a French party! They'll say by-and-by we have Hoche's ghost or the National Guard in the back office ; but devil may care—

' Foes of Freedom *Faugh a Ballagh.*' "

And again :—

" Duffy and I are delighted at your undertaking the notice of Father Mathew. In your hands, and with your feeling, the article will be worthy of the man. The portrait of him will not be out of Landell's hands for a little time. The Shiel or the Avonmore and O'Loghlen would probably come best next. Four thousand copies to-day, equal to the *Freeman*, and double any other weekly paper. The country people are delighted with us if their letters speak true. We have several ballads, ay, and not bad ones, ready ; ' Noctes' squibs, etc., in preparation. In the present number, ' The Reduction of Rents,' and the ' Continental Literature,' with the translation from La Mennais (who has, I see, turned missionary), are by Dillon. ' The O'Connell Tribute' is by Daunt (aided by Duffy's revision and my quotation from Burke). ' The Revolution in Canada' and ' An Irish Vampire' are mine."

Davis asked his friend for specific information on the Paris press, where he hoped to find light on foreign politics, to correct the British or parochial opinions which prevailed in Ireland. In judging the application and the answer, it must be remembered that they were written nearly fifty years ago, when Paris journals were as unknown in Ireland as Berlin journals are at present, and the *Revue des Deux Mondes* was still in its adventurous youth.

" Will you allow me," he wrote, " to put you to some trouble ? We want to subscribe to some French papers. Would you, either from your own knowledge, or from accurate inquiry, let me know as soon as possible the relative ability and position of five or six of the leading political newspapers in Paris ; also for what papers Victor Hugo, Janin, Georges Sand, etc., write fiction; also what, and how dear, is the *Revue des Deux Mondes;* or is there any other thing of the kind that would be more useful? Do you know enough of Griffin to put down such a page on him as sparkles before each of the portraits in Frazer? [A portrait of Griffin was in preparation for the *Nation*.] Poor Maginn—but that's the end of it in this rotten artificial world we're living in."

Maddyn replied immediately.

"I write at once to say that if you will look to *Chambers' Journal* for the year 1840, you will find two very full articles on the French press. Perhaps it is in 1839, or later. In 1840, in the *Quarterly Review*, is a very *minute* article from original sources on everything about the French press—I think by Thackeray. This also deserves your perusal.

"Your choice lies between the *Journal des Débats* and the *Constitutionnel*. My brother-in-law for a long time took the *Courier Français*, which had a great deal of literature in it.

"Bohain's *Courier de l'Europe*, published in London every Saturday, giving the cream of the articles for the week, would be worth your getting. All the French in London take it.

"The *Revue des Deux Mondes* is not worth getting. Occasionally there is a good article, but it would be enough to purchase odd numbers.

"I would spend a part of your spare money on American periodicals: for example, the *Democratic Review*—monthly, New York—a 'Jacksonite' in its faction, and a 'whole hog' in its theories—would be worth taking.

"I know nothing of Griffin, except what everybody knows. Sergeant Talfourd some time since, before several literary men, spoke of Griffin's genius with enthusiasm: he admired its 'stern reality;' such were his words. On the 'Collegians' his fame depends. I think it is, as a mere work of genius, the most dramatic fiction I ever read. In Catholic power of sympathetic appreciation he is unrivalled.

"After what Wallis wrote on Griffin, nobody could touch the subject. The notice in the *Citizen* announcing his death could not be surpassed.

"Give my address to no one. I will put your letter before a proper quarter for exact and *late* information about the Paris Press, and send you an answer as soon as I get one. Meantime read what I told you. *Vive et vale*, O'Sullivan Davis." *

* Maddyn addresses him in bantering allusion to his Celtic descent, "Thomas O'Sullivan Davis." In youth he wrote his name Thomas *Osborne* Davis, but abandoned the practice in manhood.

Ballads and songs, founded on incidents of Irish history, had been a speciality in the Belfast journal which I edited, and I consulted Davis and Dillon on continuing them in the *Nation.* Neither of them had ever published a line of verse, but they were willing to make the experiment. In the third number some verses of Davis's were published, but Dillon was discontented with his own production, and never could be got to renew the attempt. It was in the sixth number that Davis suddenly put forth his strength. The night before publication he brought me the "Lament of Owen Roe O'Neill," a ballad of singular originality and power. The dramatic opening arrested attention like a sudden strain of martial music :—

"'Did they dare, did they dare, to slay Owen Roe O'Neill?'
'Yes, they slew with poison him they feared to meet with steel.'
'May God wither up their hearts! May their blood cease to flow!
May they walk in living death who poisoned Owen Roe!'"

The enthusiastic reception of this ballad by friends whose judgment he trusted was like a revelation to him. He came to understand that he possessed a faculty till then unsuspected. He could express his passionate convictions on the past, and his rapturous reveries on the future, in the only shape in which they would not appear extravagant or fantastic. He assumed the signature of "the Celt" to signify his descent from the Welsh and Irish Gael, and it was soon widely recognized that the soul of an old bardic race throbbed again in his song. He recalled with pride that the greatest modern lyrists—Béranger, Moore, and perhaps Burns —were Celts, and, as he insisted, brethren of the same family :

" One in name and in fame
Are the world-divided Gaels." *

But Burns was an utter Lowlander.

Strength comes to the strong and wealth to the rich. After a little time, verses often as good as Davis's or Mangan's flowed in from new contributors. It was suggested in a provincial paper in the north that the poetry of the *Nation* must be written by Moore and the prose by Sheil and Carleton. And the fourth number contained a paper which, when its author made himself known (as he did in a little time), rendered these wild stories probable. O'Connell, who had not written anonymously in a newspaper for nearly a generation, was so impressed by the astonishing success of the journal, that he sent us a long and vigorous paper entitled " A Repeal Catechism ; " and John O'Connell returned to the fold which he had recently deserted, with a leading article and a number of verses.† Davis announced O'Connell's contribution to Maddyn, and seemed to regard it as an attempt to take possession of the paper in a sense that could not be permitted.

" Your sketch of Roebuck is admirable, and you have contrived *safely* to give some useful hints against what you most condemn here. The ' Repeal Catechism ' is by Daniel O'Connell. I like it greatly, though I came to it prejudiced against it. The time he sent it was ten o'clock on Friday night, which sent some of our leaders spinning out. But we will manage things better in future, and the name of his being a contributor will give the paper new circulation. I am resolved to be practical, and there-

* T. D. McGee.
† " Mr. Daunt brought in John O'Connell, who, as the favourite son of the national leader, was counted an important accession—for the prospectus at any rate ; but on the remonstrance of some of the existing journalists, who considered themselves injured by the publication of his name in that character, he separated from us before the issue of the first number, and only returned when to be a writer in the *Nation* had become a distinction worth coveting " (" Young Ireland," chap. iii.).

fore sacrifice some of my projects, otherwise his alliance with its natural results would have driven me from the journal. Meantime we are getting power, in circulation already exceeding any weekly papers here, and in character. Moreover the soldiers are beginning to read and write to us." *

The success was vigorously pushed. The principal contributors met once a week at a frugal supper to exchange opinions and project the work of the coming week. These informal conferences proved a valuable training-school, less, perhaps, for what the young men taught each other than for what each taught himself. It is the silent process of rumination, doubtless, which determines the main lines of thought, but some men never know thoroughly their own opinions on a subject till the train of slumbering reflection has been awakened by controversy, and the obscure points lighted by the sparks struck out in conflict. An illustrated gallery of distinguished Irishmen was commenced, to set up anew on their pedestals our forgotten or neglected patriots; feuilletons, original and translated from the French, appeared in every number for a time; and a system of "Answers to Correspondents," real and imaginary, was opened, in which new projects were broached, books and men briefly criticized, and seeds of fresh thought sown widely in the popular mind. The ballads and songs were our most unequivocal success, and Davis, who doubted at the outset the feasibility of the experiment, not only made the most brilliant contributions to it, but interpreted its purpose most sympathetically.

"National poetry," he afterwards wrote, "presents the most dramatic events, the largest characters, the most impressive scenes, and the deepest passions in the language most familiar to us. It

* November 6, 1842.

magnifies and ennobles our hearts, our intellects, our country, and our countrymen; binds us to the land by its condensed and gem-like history—to the future by example and by aspiration. It solaces us in travel, fires us in action, prompts our invention, sheds a grace beyond the power of luxury round our homes, is the recognized envoy of our minds among all mankind and to all time."

We had soon to repress a rage for versifying, often merely mimetic, sometimes as mechanical as the music of a barrel organ, which the success of the *Nation's* poets begot. [Correspondents were told that the student who could rescue an Irish air or an Irish manuscript, or preserve an Irish ruin from destruction; who could make a practical suggestion for bettering the social condition of the people, gather a fading tradition, throw light on an obscure era of our history, or help to instruct the people among whom he lived, would do a substantial and honourable service to his country, which need leave him no regret for wanting the gift of song. There was no mercy for nonsense, and the judgment on new verses or projects which the people applauded was often considered harsh and peremptory, the reader little suspecting that the merciless critic was often the author himself in masquerade.] One of the earliest biographical sketches was one of Thomas Moore, by Davis, which he had the satisfaction of learning proved very agreeable to the poet.*

The reception of the paper in the provinces was a perplexity to veteran journalists. From the first number it was received with an enthusiasm compounded of passionate sympathy and personal affection. It went on increasing in circulation till its

---

* In January, 1843, one of his friends (the editor of the *Globe*) wrote to me: "The sketch of Tom Moore I was successful in obtaining through a friend in Dublin, and sent to Moore, whose note in reply, if not a private one, would raise a blush on your editorial face.—E. A. MORAN."

purchasers in every provincial town exceeded those of the local paper, and its readers were multiplied indefinitely by the practice of regarding it not as a vehicle of news but of opinion. It never grew obsolete, but passed from hand to hand till it was worn to fragments. The delight which young souls thirsting for nutriment found in it has been compared to the refreshment afforded by the sudden sight of a Munster valley in May after a long winter; but the unexpected is a large source of enjoyment, and it resembled rather the sight of a garden cooled by breezes and rivulets from the Nile, in the midst of a long stretch of sandbanks without a shrub or a blade of grass.

The doctrines which the new men taught have a permanent interest, for they were the seed of many harvests to come. Though they were daring to rashness, and to timorous ears sounded like the tocsin of revolution, they were restrained by habitual submission to the eternal laws of morality and justice. Nothing was taught which was not, in their belief, intrinsically just and right, or which did not appeal to the noblest motives a generous but untaught people could be made to comprehend. Much of this teaching was the direct work of Davis, and much his indirect work—sparks kindled at the fount of fire which burned in his bosom; but all his colleagues were busy completing the cosmos of Irish nationality, and a skilful critic will discern a variance of style, corresponding with variations of character of which natural style is a sure reflex.

Davis was well equipped for his task. He had framed his code of opinions, as we have seen, by long meditation and systematic industry, and they were

H

ready for use. The methods by which success in the national struggle might be won, seemed to him neither few nor doubtful. He knew the history of the country as familiarly as he knew the succession of the seasons. He knew that of the scanty concessions which had been won at long intervals, there was not one that was not yielded to fear of consequences. A little loosening of the Catholic bonds when Irish soldiers were fighting in the army of George Washington, a little more when the French Republic beat back the confederated kings of Europe, a great national deliverance when the officers of an army of Irish citizens deliberated at Dungannon, and Catholic emancipation when it was the alternative of civil war. The expected deliverance might come like the others by diplomacy, or by arms, but it was certain to him that, for either end, the essential preliminary was to inflame the people with that passionate determination to be free at any cost, which tyranny in all ages has found its most formidable difficulty. Our resources were not trivial. There were seven millions of one mind on the question, and fewer Batavian burghers and peasants held their own against the most powerful sovereign in Europe between Charlemagne and Napoleon. The annals of little states, less populous than Irish provinces, which in successive centuries had served the world so well in arts, arms, civil government, and the discovery of new fields for human enterprise, gave the measure of what a resolute nation might accomplish; and why not our nation, if only the distracted people could be gathered into one company.

The policy of Wolfe Tone, half a century earlier, had been to induce the oppressed Catholics to forget their prejudices and join hands with the enlightened reformers among the Protestant minority. The present problem was a harder one—to induce the wealthy well-placed haughty minority, in possession of whatever the State or the law could bestow, to forego their monopoly, and unite with the trampled multitude in demanding a change which most of them considered revolutionary, and many feared would endanger their Church and their possessions.

The shepherd boy who went forth with sling and scrip against the Pagan giant scarcely fought at greater odds. But the fear of failure is the palsy of faith and action. The same sentiment has since been sung in language which vibrates with courage and devotion—

> " Had fear of failing swayed against redress
> Of public wrong, man never had been free ;
> The thrones of tyrants had been fixed as fate,
> And slavery sealed the universal doom."

The opinions of the new men might well constitute a primer of generous nationality.

" The restoration of Irish Independence," it was said, " has been advocated too exclusively by narrow appeals to economy, and sought by means which neither conciliated nor frightened its opponents. We shall try, and God willing we shall succeed in arraying the memories of our land, the deep, strong, passions of men's hearts, in favour of our cause. And while we shall shrink from repeating any factious or offensive cry, we shall counsel and explain those means of liberation which heroic freemen from Pelopidas to Washington have sanctioned.

" The restoration of land to the people had for a century no reason to support it save the musket of the ejected heir, desperate from suffering, and no witness save the peasant when the scaffold saw him martyred. We shall strive not merely to explain the workings of landlord misrule in Ireland, but to show how similar wrongs have been remedied in other countries ; seek to satisfy quiet intelligent men that the people cannot and ought not to be

patient under the lash, and to urge such men to prevent the
unguided vengeance of that people by leading them to redress.
We shall confront those who yell out murder and assassination
when any one attacks the landlords, but have neither eyes to see,
ears to hear, tongues to speak, nor hearts to understand the
miseries and plights of the peasants.

"The people of Ireland are few enough for the size and capabilities of their country, but they are too many for their present
state.   They have no manufactures, there are no home-spent rents
to give agricultural wages, there remains only the land; from
that they are being ejected by the wicked and stupid scheme of
consolidation, or, if left, it is under rack-rents, in wet wigwams,
with rags not enough on their backs, and potatoes not enough for
their food.   The landed gentry mistake their position, and are
ignorant of their times.   In every country in the world democracy
is moving on.   Its march may be slow and discriminating; if
violently opposed, it will be overbearing and rude.   Let the Irish
aristocracy aid the people in getting manufactures, in improving
their means of home and foreign trade; let them spend their
incomes at home, and be mild and just in their dealings; and
they will make the transition slow and gentle.   But if they persevere in exacting rack-rents, in clearing and consolidating; if
absenteeism, want of employment and want of manufactures leave
the people nothing between starvation in freedom or half starvation in bondage in a workhouse,—if this come to pass, other
things, not dreamed of just now, will follow.

"The popular organization is too exclusively political.   It
ought to be used for the creation and diffusion of national literature, vivid with the memories and hopes of a thoughtful and
impassioned people.   It may guide and encourage our countrymen, not only in all which concerns their libraries and lectures,
but what is of greater importance, their music, their paintings,
their public sports, those old schools of faith and valour.   It
may and ought to apply to some practical and creative end, the
present intellectual and moral activity, before it passes away, like
so many things in which we trusted, leaving despair behind.
Ireland, a large and fertile island, owned by eight millions of
a virtuous, brave, and intelligent race, has the natural capabilities
of a rich and strong nation.   But however great her resources, it
will require the application of all her wealth, all her industry, all
her intellect, to her own exclusive service, to make her prosperous
and great; and this, an Irish Parliament, devoted to Irish interests, and wielding the whole strength of Ireland, without let,

stay, or hindrance from any other legislative power, can alone accomplish.

"Men still spoke of compromises, and material compensation for our lost nationality. But though Englishmen were to give us the best tenures on earth, though they were to equalize Presbyterian, Catholic, and Episcopalian, though they were to give us the completest representation in their Parliament, restore our absentees, disencumber us of their debt, and redress every one of our fiscal wrongs in the names of liberty and country, we would still tell them, in the name of enthusiastic hearts, thoughtful souls, and fearless spirits, that we spurned the gifts if the condition were that Ireland should remain a province. The island, instead of being a prosperous nation, was an impoverished dependency, because its people spent ages in religious and political quarrels, instead of using their powers to educate, enrich, and ennoble themselves. It was inhabited by men of many different races and creeds. The lot of all was cast together, their interests were the same, and their only chance of prosperity was in union. For many ages they fought because some were of Danish, some of Milesian, and some of Saxon descent. There was, perhaps, no country on earth where there are not many races mixed into one nation. Why should the races in Ireland hate and ruin each other because their fathers came here at different times from different countries, and hated and ruined each other in ages long past? Nor was religious difference any better ground for disunion among Irishmen. Religion rests between each man and his God. No man has a right to dictate his own creed to others, or punish them for rejecting it.

"Work was the necessary price of success in the undertaking to raise up Ireland anew. The people ought to perfect their organization, perform faithfully the tasks assigned to them by their leaders, and win over opponents by courtesy and fairness. The Repeal Association sought to array the Irish people in a peaceful league to demand and obtain their rights. It determined to have Repeal fully represented in the corporation, in the poorlaw boards, and in Parliament. It tried to educate Repealers, and to persuade those who were not so, by its publications and meetings. Publications, meetings, the registries, and the Repeal organization, involve great expenses; and to meet these expenses the Repeal rent should be large, certain, and uniform, so that it might serve the purposes for which it was subscribed."

Let it be remembered that O'Connell's doctrine

was that the Irish race were endowed with all good gifts, physical and moral without stint, and were poor and obscure only through the sins of their oppressors. The *Nation* taught that to the evils inflicted on them by misgovernment were added other evils created or fostered by faults of their own. They wanted, not only education and discipline, but the priceless habit of perseverance. They had committed painful follies and crimes, but they still possessed native virtue which would infallibly redeem them at the cost of the necessary labour and sacrifice.

"To make our liberty an inheritance for our children and a charter of prosperity, the people must study as well as strive, and learn as well as feel. Of all the agencies of freedom, education was the most important. It was in the mind of a people the seeds of future greatness and prosperity were stored. The destruction of her industry only made Ireland poor—the waste of her mind left her a slave. Education, from being a crime punishable with heavy penalties, became, under the gradual change of weapons which tyranny was compelled to adopt, a wicked and deliberate scheme of proselytism. There was still no system of national education adequate to the wants, and adapted to the genius of our people. A little time ago there was none that was not an insult and a curse. But with all its drawbacks, when the system at work for the last nine or ten years had lasted as many more, the whole of the Irish young men would have got more education than any similar class in the world out of Germany and America. The books they used were Anglican and utilitarian, but it was the duty of the political teachers of the people to spiritualize and nationalize them with higher and nobler aims. In schools the youth should learn the best knowledge of science, art, and literary elements. And at home they should see and hear as much of national pictures, music, poetry, and military science as possible.

"A people not familiar with the past would never understand the present or realize the future. One of the tasks the *Nation* humbly desired to perform was to make the dead past familiar to the memory and imagination of the Irish people as the greatest and surest incentive to reclaim the control of their country; and not merely the past of their own country, but of the old and new worlds. The people did not recognize this imperative want. They were accustomed to consider themselves abreast or ahead of the rest of the world. The melancholy fact was that in all education—scholastic, social, and professional—our adults were behind most civilized nations. Energy, endurance, tenderness, piety, and faith—the natural elements of the highest moral and intellectual character—they still possessed as fresh as they existed in France or England centuries ago, in the ages of Faith and Action. But their best powers were unorganized and undeveloped, from want of that severe discipline so essential to bind in its harness the impetuous irregular vigour of our Celtic nature. Of all races the Celts most demand discipline, and profit most by it. This education must reach to the peasant in his cot and the artisan in his workshop. They· paid the penalty of ignorance in unprosperous lives at home and abroad. A people with natural gifts which, under favourable circumstances, would produce not only artisans of the finest touch, but painters, musicians, and inventors, sweated under the heaviest toil in the world—felled the forests of Australia and drained the swamps of Canada.

"Discipline was necessary, not only to develop good qualities, but to correct bad ones. The most fatal want of the Celt was want of will, instability ; the tendency, not to bend and turn, but to waver and gyrate, had been the curse and reproach of our race. There was a real tenacity in the national character, but it was so intermittent in its action that it lost half its use. What were the means by which leaders of the people had produced revolution? They laboured at the outset to create the educated opinion from which alone springs a national purpose. They gave a direction and aim to the vague aspirations of patriotism. For on educated opinion, as the political philosophers taught, even the most despotic authority ultimately rests.

" We Irish were *incuriosi suorum.* For ten who read Mac-Geoghegan a hundred read Leland, and for one who looked into the *Rerum Hibernicarum Scriptores* a thousand studied Hume. Thus we judge our fathers by the calumnies of their foes. If Ireland were in national health, her history would be familiar by books, pictures, statuary, and music, to every cabin and workshop in the land ; her resources, as an agricultural, manufacturing, and trading people, would be equally known ; and every young man would be trained, and every grown man able to defend her coast, her plains, her towns, and her hills—not with his right arm merely, but by his disciplined habits and military accomplishments. These were the pillars of independence.

" Some of us were base enough to do cheerfully the work of the enemy. It was a mistake to imagine that the only Irish hodmen in London were those poor fellows who were always ascending and descending ladders with bricks and mortar. There were hodmen in Parliament, who fetched and carried all sorts of rubbish for their masters—newspaper hodmen, ready to knock their country down with a brickbat—pamphleteering hodmen, who get a despicable living by mixing dirty facts and false figures together, and flinging them at Ireland, wherever they see a chance of getting their mortar to stick. Thus we abandoned self-respect, and we were treated with contempt ; and nothing could be more natural, nothing more just. It is self-respect which makes a people respected by others, as order makes them strong, virtue formidable, patience victorious.

" Irishmen must learn what other nations were doing and thinking. The exaggeration of England's strength and glory, in which English rulers and writers indulged, the deprecation of the force and morals of England's foes (Ireland being in the front), was never very hurtful to an Englishman ; but when Irishmen accepted these falsehoods, a secret distrust of themselves unfitted them to resist oppression or maintain their rights. But they would speedily come to know better. An accurate, unexaggerated knowledge of their own strength and weakness multiplied many times the power of a people. God had given the Irish people all the gifts of nature in abundance ; if they wanted the blessing of liberty it was their own fault.

" To preserve, fortify, and increase the good qualities for which the people were noted was the highest work of patriotism.

" The man who was drunken, quarrelsome, idle, or selfish might shout for Repeal, but he brought disgrace on the cause, and was not worthy to be a free citizen of an Irish nation. The murderer, the intimidator, and the ribbonman were foes to Ireland. It should be the boast of every Repealer that, having his mind fixed on the holy and glorious object of his country's regeneration, he had conformed himself to a virtuous and manly life, as a proof that he was fit for freedom : a vicious province could never become a nation.

" Let Repealers, then, lift up their own souls, and try by teaching and example to lift up the souls of their family and neighbours to that pitch of industry, courage, information, and wisdom necessary to enable an enslaved, darkened, and starving people to become free, enlightened, and prosperous. And let them never forget what gifts and what zeal were needed to perform that work effectually—what mildness to win, what knowledge to inform, what reasoning to convince, what vigour to rouse, what skill to combine and wield. They had been sometimes driven to employ the 'coward's arms, trick, and chicane;' but they must renounce these vices. Extreme courses might be necessary in the struggle on which the country had entered, but dishonourable means never."

These were the teachings by which the new men announced themselves. They might be dangerous to misgovernment, but they were surely in harmony with integrity and good sense. These were seeds and saplings from which many harvests have grown.

The journal broke frankly with the past, declining to be responsible for its errors or its quarrels, and was original from cover to cover; but nothing amazed and charmed the country like Davis's articles. His political writings were commonly exhortations or remonstrances to the people on faults to be amended or virtues to be cultivated, couched in language which, to borrow his own words, was "fresh, vehement, and true." His literary papers corrected some popular error, vindicated a slandered leader, or lighted up an obscure era. "His style," says a competent critic, "was as original and individual as Grattan's or Goldsmith's, and far more Irish than either." * Some one said of his articles that they were like unspoken speeches of Grattan. But though they were sometimes as rhetorical in form, and generally as intensely real in purpose, they were more natural and unstudied in expression. They suggested a man who was not proffering ingenious criticism, but uttering his long-weighed convictions on questions of immediate interest. The political papers were often quite colloquial, and when

* Martin McDermott.

they rose into passion and poetry they had still a
practical aim, and rarely parted company with solid
good sense. This intensely individual style was
often imitated · by correspondents, whose feeble
mimicry suggested the original as the faint murmur
in a sea-shell recalls the music of the ocean. His
plans and projects, stamped with force and reality by
a powerful imagination, in the same way became
fantastic and incredible in other hands. There was
as wide an interval, MacNevin used to say, between
his theories and theirs as between the visions of
Dante and the visions of Joe Smith. His master-
gift was the power of persuasion. He moved and
charmed his readers, but, still more, he sowed in their
minds seed of opinion which ripened into action.

But the work of the journal was necessarily subordinate to that of the national organization, and to
this it is now necessary to turn. O'Connell had rashly
promised that 1843 should be "the Repeal Year"—
the year when his great object would be accomplished, and he brought all the prodigious force of
his will and intellect to redeem this promise. Nature
gave him a physical vigour which labour could
scarcely exhaust, an imperturbable good temper, a
courtesy before adversaries, and a diplomacy which
was dexterous and versatile. Under these lay a
subterranean rage against injustice or opposition,
which burst out at times like a volcano. His passionate oratory in the Catholic struggle raised the
heart of the people as military music refreshes and
stimulates the weary soldier, and this fire was not
exhausted. Though he was tormented by the public
and domestic troubles which a man so placed rarely
escapes—for cares gather round the high-placed as

clouds round the mountain summits—he worked with unwavering perseverance. In February he published a little volume in which the wrongs inflicted on Ireland since the invasion were collected from annals and records, and presented in one huge indictment. In March he raised the national question by a motion before the Dublin Corporation, in a speech of remarkable power and provident moderation. He was answered by Isaac Butt on behalf of the Conservative party; and the controversy was conducted with so much capacity and mutual forbearance, that it kindled desire and hope in many minds which long were apathetic.

Davis reported his impression of these events to Maddyn :—

"I 'know' that much good has already followed from the explanations, the good temper, arguments, and concessions which came out during the discussion. O'Connell's two speeches were greatly superior in style and argument to those in St. Stephen's in 1834. I sat out the whole affair. Staunton's was the next in real worth. His statistics were mature and unanswerable. Butt was very clever, very fluent, and very ignorant. I feared the debate would do mischief from the strength and contagion of the opposition. I fear it not now. O'Connell's book ('Memoirs of Ireland, Native and Saxon') is miserable in style, but popular in plan and highly useful. Irish history 'must' be read henceforth." *

Davis and the principal writers of the *Nation* were active members of the general committee of the Association. The ordinary business of a committee-man was to second, or, if he could not second, at least to echo the proposals of O'Connell. But the new men, as we have seen, had a policy and ideas of their own—a policy not designed to thwart, but to complete and consummate the purpose O'Connell

* March 3, 1843.

aimed to accomplish. Davis hoped to enlist the middle class in the movement, and to inflame young men of both races with a national spirit. Dillon desired that the condition of the peasantry should receive immediate attention, and the question of land tenure and poor-laws to be promptly taken into consideration. Others had plans of systematic popular education and a legion of projects more or less practical for advancing the cause. They commenced to develop opinion, and to act on principles which have since become the common property of all enlightened Irishmen. There was naturally surprise and jealousy at the outset, but the new recruits were not men to whom it was possible to attribute sinister motives. Dillon was always sweet, placid, and open; and the transparent sincerity which looked out of Davis's large candid eyes, and from his open earnest face, dissipated suspicion; while an energy that prompted him to engage in all the labour of the largest designs and all the drudgery of the minutest details disarmed jealousy. The result was a transformation scene which only those who have witnessed it with their eyes will fully understand. In the midst of the old traditional agitation, grown decrepit and somewhat debauched, a new power claimed recognition. The servile and illiterate agitators who acknowledged no law but the will of their leader, saw among them men of original ideas and commanding intellect, who pressed their opinions on their audience with becoming modesty indeed, but without the smallest fear or hesitation.

Davis avoided wounding dangerous susceptibilities less from policy than from the generosity and modesty of his nature; and, at this time, O'Connell certainly felt that he had got colleagues whose ability and zeal would do effective service, though they did not always run in the traditional grooves. Looking back through the rarified atmosphere of experience, I cannot insist that all our designs were discreet or practical. We were defeated by a narrow majority on the proposal to maintain an agent in Paris, as the centre of political activity in Europe, which, had it been accepted, would certainly have been savagely misrepresented by the enemies of the national cause. O'Connell's sons were at times defeated in the committee on questions arising between them and the new men, and once or twice O'Connell himself had to accept proposals which he did not entirely relish. The practical man of the world bore a slight reverse with a good humour which disarmed opposition; for he knew the proposals were always designed to feed the flame of nationality.

Much was done to enlarge and vitalize the old traditional system. An historical and political library of reference was collected, peculiarly rich in the rare Anti-Union and Emancipation pamphlets. The cards of membership were made an agency for teaching the people national history and statistics, and familiarizing them with the effigies of their great men. A band was trained to play national airs in public for the first time since the Union, for Davis knew that the Celts were peculiarly subject to the spell of music.

"Music," he wrote, "is the first faculty of the Irish; and scarcely anything has such power for good over them. The use of this faculty and this power, publicly and constantly to keep up their spirits, refine their tastes, warm their courage, increase their union, and renew their zeal—is the duty of every patriot."

The Repeal wardens were exhorted to watch over historic ruins in their district, and to encourage the people to found news-rooms and local societies. Some one proposed, in pursuance of the same policy, to clothe the messengers and attendants of the Association in green livery, but Davis opposed this scheme. "I will not," he said, "be a party to putting on hired servants the uniform last worn by Robert Emmet."

We are apt to regard as somewhat trite and commonplace the transactions of our own day. Drape these young men like Rienzi in the forum or the Swiss foresters who led the Alpine spears at Morgartan, and they become picturesque and heroic. Rightly understood, the work they had undertaken was of the same scope and magnitude, though it was not projected in the gloom of forests or the shade of august ruins, but under the glare of sunshine in committee rooms and newspaper offices, by men clothed in paletots and chimney-pot hats.

After the serious business of life began, Davis had no longer leisure for elaborate correspondence. He wrote constantly to a chosen few, but only notes as brief as bulletins. His mind produced abundantly the fresh fancies, the just reflections, and the graceful badinage which make the charm of perfect letters, but all went to swell the stream of public work, on which his heart was set. His correspondence is valuable chiefly because it tells us what he was doing, and thinking of, and makes plain the unbroken purpose of his life.

He still found time to help the magazine, and Wallis received his contributions somewhat with the air of a pedagogue acknowledging the theme of a favourite schoolboy.

" ' Colonel Napier,' " he wrote, " is very much to the purpose;
but I fear such very lengthened quotations swamp and weaken
the force of the arguments in the text. The more a man quotes,
the less hath he an air of speaking with authority—the great
essential to all effective persuasion."

To Maddyn he wrote most habitually. He desired
to engage him in a project for a high-class periodical
on Federalistic principles—Federalism being then
much spoken of among National Whigs as a possible
compromise.

"Enclosed are some suggestions for *Nation* papers, by Duffy,
which of course you'll accept, change, or reject, as you like. Munster Society would give you fine subjects—sketches of classes of
characters. Now to your letter. I never asked you to join the
party I am immediately connected with, for I supposed you alien
from its opinions. What strength and pleasure I should receive
from working by your side I need not tell you.

"The party who would sustain the *Review* are Federalists—
men thoroughly national in feeling, Catholic in taste, and moderate
in politics. Things have come to that pass that we must be disgraced and defeated, or we must separate by force, or we must
have a Federal Government. Mere repeal is raw and popular.
The Federalists include all who were Whigs in Belfast, the best
of your Cork men, Wyse, Caulfield, and several excellent men
through the country. Hudson and Torrens McCullagh, Deasy,
Wallis, and all that set, are Federalists. I will not ask you to
come until matters are fixed and safe and clear; all I wished now
was to know might you come? You would make a great, a perfect
editor. I'm glad you've given up the Bar, you're too good for
a woolsack. Don't think of writing on religion for three or four
years. We must parochialize the people by property and institutions, and idealize and soften them by music, history, ballads, art,
and games. That is if we succeed, and are not hanged instead;
but I *know* my principles will succeed."

After the Corporation debate the Repeal Association received important recruits and a great accession
of friends, and it was determined to summon a muster
of the whole population in each of the counties in
succession. These assemblies were so gigantic that

the *Times* described them as "monster meetings "—
a title which they retained.   During the summer the
monster meetings increased in number and enthusiasm, and the Irish Tories called upon the Government to check them by some sharp stroke of authority.
Sir Edward Sugden, an English lawyer, at that
time Lord Chancellor of Ireland, answered their
appeal by removing Lord Ffrench and four and twenty
other magistrates from the Commission of the Peace,
for the new offence of attending public meetings
in favour of the Repeal of the Union.   Mr. Smith
O'Brien, till then known as an Irish Whig of popular
sympathies, inquired in Parliament if the same discipline was to be extended to English magistrates ;
and not getting a satisfactory reply, he resigned his
commission, which could no longer, he conceived, be
held by an Irish gentleman without humiliation.
Lord Cloncurry, Henry Grattan, and a number of
other country gentlemen followed his example.   The
Bar struck a more effectual stroke.   Twenty barristers
joined the Association in one day as a protest against
the unconstitutional character of an executive who
degraded magistrates for taking one side of a debat-
able public question, while they applauded other
magistrates for taking the opposite side.   Among
these recruits were Thomas O'Hagan, afterwards
Lord Chancellor ; Sir Colman O'Loghlen, afterwards Judge Advocate-General ; and Thomas Mac-
Nevin, and M. J. Barry—the two latter of whom from
that time became constant associates of the young
men of the *Nation.**

Twenty barristers were a great gain ; but, instead

* Barry soon began to write squibs and political verses in the *Nation.*
His contributions were sometimes signed Brutus, for the whimsical reason
that Marcus Junius Brutus had the same initials as Michael Joseph Barry.

of twenty, there ought to have been two hundred. Their excuse for selfish neutrality was turned effectually inside out by Maddyn.

"The Dublin lawyers, forsooth, have no time to attend to anything but their profession. Lord Kames was a philosopher and author, as well as a learned lawyer; Jeffrey edited the *Edinburgh Review* while engaged in heavy legal business. The English barristers find time to attend the House of Commons, and take an active part in its proceedings. Sir Samuel Romilly had a larger practice than any one amongst them, and he found time to rouse the public mind and reform the criminal laws. Brougham was in heavy practice while leader of the opposition. Sergeant Copley was famous in parliamentary debates while he pursued his profession. Sir William Jones and Sir James Mackintosh obtained legal eminence without relinquishing philosophic pursuits. The Dublin barristers, forsooth, have no leisure! Yet Daniel O'Connell, in the height of his professional practice, when he was making at least five thousand a year, found time to organize a great association, carry on its political affairs, address the people of Ireland in speeches and letters, and make his name heard of through the world."

In answer to some remonstrance on the rashness of his policy :—

"You seem to me," he wrote to Maddyn, "to underrate our resources. The Catholic population are more united, bold, and orderly than ever they were. Here are materials for defence or attack, civil or military. The hearty junction of the Catholic bishops is of the greatest value. The Protestants of the lower order are neutral; the land question and repeated disappointments from England have alienated them from their old views. Most of the educated Protestants now profess an ardent nationality, and say that, if some pledge against a Catholic ascendancy could be given them, they too would be Repealers. You will see by the accompanying paper that fourteen barristers, most of them men of good business, joined yesterday. Before a month we are likely to have as many lawyers as ever joined any decided agitation here. The Americans are constantly offering us men, money, and arms. . . . Crowds of soldiers and police are enrolled Repealers. These are some of our resources. The present agitation will not fail for want of statesmanship, though it may for want of energy. Even O'Connell has looked very far ahead this time, and knows he cannot

I

retreat. I think we can beat Peel. If we can quietly get a Federal
Government I shall for one agree to it and support it. If not,
then anything but what we are.

"I fear it is impossible to get the Sheil's 'Life of Mathew'
[Life, by Dr. Sheil of Ballyshannon], but I shall make another
trial before I send this. I am told that it is wretched trash,
without facts or taste."

And again:—

"Your 'Sheil' was perfectly successful. Every one praised it.
Even O'Connell called it admirable, and only objected to 'one or
two mistakes' in fact. That is, he was crotchety about justice
having been done to Sheil *quoad* the Catholic Association. Upon
the whole, however, he liked it greatly. There is, however, I
believe, one error in it—attributing the articles on Ireland in
L'Étoile to Sheil exclusively. I have heard from the second best
authority that they were principally written by the editor of it,
who refused a large sum for doing the work, which he did gratis."

Davis's character is exhibited, not only in what he
did and wrote, but in the echoes of it which came
back to him from friends, even when they took the
character of objections or remonstrances. Denny
Lane wrote at this time:—

"Short, narrative, and *not* descriptive, ballads are greatly
wanted in Irish literature. By all means stick to poetry, but
pray do not abandon professional success—you are fully equal to
two strong pursuits. If you should meet political disappointment,
your literary talents and poetical longings will always keep existence fresh."

Maddyn applauded an attempt by one of Davis's
colleagues to expose the ignorance and dishonesty of
the school of pseudo-Irish romances then becoming
popular in England.

"I have read with delight an article in the *Nation* on Lever's
works. It is most admirably done; whoever the writer is, he has
certainly displayed no ordinary literary abilities; and never did
any Irish writer deserve more richly the treatment he has met
with at the hands of honest Irish criticism. I cannot conceive the
spurious liberality which affects to patronize the anti-national ten-

dencies of all this man's writings, on account of the rollicking devil-may-care sort of factious fun and ferocious drollery of his slipshod, flimsy, fashionable, novelish style of writing." *

Shortly after the Corporation debate, an incident occurred which promised for a moment to become memorable. Coach-building was a prosperous industry in Ireland, and the mail-coaches for the service of the post-office were built and run by Mr. Peter Purcell, a Catholic country gentleman, who had quarrelled with O'Connell and become a *protégé* of his opponents. The Postmaster General, who never advertised English or Scotch contracts in Ireland, advertised in Scotland the contract for the . Irish mails, and Mr. Croal, of Edinburgh, became the successful tenderer. An active sympathy with Mr. Purcell sprang up, in which the Duke of Leinster, the Provost of Trinity College, the Lord Mayor, and other eminent Unionists took part; and O'Connell, forgetting old feuds, aided and encouraged them. Even Thackeray, who had recently visited Ireland, wrote a squib or two against the Scotch intruders, illustrated with his own pencil. Here is a specimen from the *Nation :—*

" For daddy and children, for daddy and mammy,
No work and no hope, O, the prospect is fine !

---

* June 10, 1843.

To me he wrote, at this time, of a poem which I had lent him with an exhortation to read it as a storehouse of original thought :—

" I read some forty pages of this 'Festus,' and return it to avoid reading more. It is a marvellous anatomy of soul with a sunbeam for a lancet, but I don't want theories; I have had too much of them, and of grief—the latter chiefly at my own shortcomings. But there are dishonoured truths (such as that scorn of repentance) in the book, and when I have a longer leisure I'll ask you for it again.

" Would you have the *Nation* of the 1st of July found out and committed to safe keeping for me ? It has eloped from my file. Was this a good omen, to lose the *Nation* July the 1st ? " [the date on which the Irish cause was lost at the Boyne].

But I fancy I'm hearing your lordship cry—' Damme,
  Suppose they *do* starve, it's no business of mine.'

" Well, it's 'justice,' no doubt, that your lordship's observing,
  And that must our feelings of hunger console ;
We're five hundred families, wretched and starving,
  But what matters that so there's ' Justice for Croal ! ' "

The Government journals scoffed at a national
tumult about such a contemptible trifle, but Davis
reminded them that a greater trifle, Wood's half-
pence, united the whole nation against foreign
government.

The *Nation*, while it urged on the monster meetings and the entire O'Connell programme, never
neglected its individual policy. It was a puzzle to
the people to find Irishmen of genius honoured
and applauded without any regard to their political
opinions. Up to that time the popular test was
simply their relation to the great tribune. If a man
hurrahed for O'Connell with sufficient vehemence,
much was forgiven him in conduct and opinion; if
he criticized the darling of the nation, scarcely any
service was an adequate set-off. Even Moore fell
into disfavour for singing, in one of his later melodies,
the decay of public spirit in Ireland.

This independent criticism, which began to attract
the attention of Conservative and Liberal Nationalists to the journal, was not well received at head
quarters. The *Pilot*, whose *rôle* was to do for
O'Connell what he would scorn to do for himself,
began to growl. The editor published a letter from
his American correspondent, who was well known in
Dublin, suggesting that the writers of the *Nation*,
who were not sufficiently deferential to O'Connell's
opinions, were probably identical with certain writers

in the *Dublin Review* who assailed him openly, and
Ireland was warned to be aware of these conspirators.*
Unfortunately for the *Pilot*, the device of using the
American correspondence to assail the *Nation* had
been employed before, and the correspondent had
written to me from New York repudiating the
language attributed to him, and authorizing me, in
case the practice was continued, to publish the repu-
diation. The forgery was quietly exposed in the
Nation, which was equivalent to binding over the
offending journal to good behaviour for a time. But
O'Connell himself, from the tribune of the Corn
Exchange, took us to task for praising bitter Tories
like Maxwell and Maginn, and neglecting an excellent Liberal like Samuel Lover. It was my duty to
reply, that our loyalty to the national leader did not
include any renunciation of our individual opinions
on questions of taste or feeling, and that for our part
we regarded Lover's caricatures of the Irish peasantry
as more offensive than the banter of open opponents
like Maxwell and Maginn. Davis afterwards placed
the question on a nobler footing. He insisted that
gifted men were a treasure and a strength to their
country, irrespective of their opinions.

"It behoves every people to 'love, cherish, and honour' its
men of ability, its men of service—the men who can adorn it with
their pencil, make it wise by their teaching, famous by their pens,
rich by their ingenuity, strong by their statesmanship, triumphant
by their valour. Doing thus, Athens became the pole-star round
which the lights of the earth turn; doing thus, Italy gave laws,
literature, and arts to half Europe. This might be lesson enough
for Ireland; yet she has another motive. If, in addition to the

* The New York correspondent of the *Pilot* was Thomas Mooney, a man
of surprising energy, very notable afterwards in Melbourne and San Francisco,
and known in later times as a dynamitard in the New York *Irish World*,
under the signature of "Transatlantic." He is now dead.

rewards, the society, the station, which England offers to emigrant
ability, there be added neglect, poverty, and want of recognition
at home, the motives for the serviceable men of Ireland to enlist
with England become, what they actually are, too great to be
withstood by most men. . . . The first and greatest duty of an
Irish patriot, then, was to aid in retaining its superior spirits.
Men make a state. Great men make a great nation. Without
them opportunities for liberation will come and go unnoticed or
unused. Without them liberation will come without honour, and
resources exist without strength—corruption and slavery, if they
do not keep watch, will resume their sway without alleviation or
resistance." *

This uniform courtesy and firmness towards
opponents, though it was new in Irish controversy,
did not offend popular feeling, because it was accompanied by an unsparing exposure of the system they
maintained. Though it was a main aim of the young
men to reconcile the gentry and the Protestant
minority with the whole nation, it was an aim never
pursued by ignoring the intolerable injustice of the
Established Church and the existing land system.
"Be just, and you shall be the acknowledged leaders of
a devoted people ; but justice must be done, for they
are withering under your exactions." This was the
language held. The gentry were told that they had
never done their duty, and that their neglect of it
lay at the root of Irish misery. The land system
which they had framed in the Irish Parliament
seemed an instrument of torture needlessly stringent
for a people so broken and dependent, but, like a

---

* It is proper to note that on one occasion Davis wrote in direct reference
to O'Connell's habit of jeering at the Duke of Wellington as the " stunted
corporal "—
    " We dislike the whole system of false disparagement. The Irish people
will never be led to act the manly part which liberty requires of them, by
being told ' the Duke,' that gallant soldier and most able general, is a scream-
ing coward and doting corporal."
    On another occasion Southey was defended from the hackneyed Whig
libel of being a mercenary turncoat.

great bridge over a small stream, it gave the measure
of the slumbering force which it was intended to
restrain. The awakening of this force was the object
of their constant apprehension, and it was now
appealed to weekly with ideas that struck it like
electric shocks. The *Nation* taught as axioms that
the land was not the landlord's own to do as he
would with, but could only be held in proprietorship
subject to the prior claim of the inhabitants to get
food and clothing out of it. No length of time and
no solemnity of sanction could annul the claim of the
husbandman to eat the fruit of his toil, or transfer it
to a select circle of landed proprietors. The minute
one human being died from the denial of this fundamental right, an injustice would be committed as
positive in its nature as if the landlord class con-
spired to throw the soil of the country out of cultivation, and left the whole population to starve. Why
should landlords be the only class of traders above the
law? There was no more inherent sanctity in selling
land, or hiring it out, than in selling shoes; and the
trader in acres ought to be as amenable to the law,
and as easily punished for extortion, as his humbler
brother. The existing system had lasted long indeed, but fraud and folly were not consecrated by
time, they only grew grosser fraud and more intolerable folly. The landlord was entitled to a fair rent
for the usufruct of his land; all claims beyond this,
over the tenant's time, conscience, or opinions, were
extortion or usurpation.

It would be unjust and unskilful criticism to
judge the verses Davis wrote in intervals of this
busy and stormy life by the canons we apply to a
poet in his solitude. They altogether mistake his

character, indeed, who regard him as distinctively
a poet or a writer. His aims were far away from
literary success. All his labours tended only to discipline and stimulate the people. He looked to share
in guiding the counsels of a nation he had prompted
into action and marshalled to victory. The place
he would have loved to fill was not beside Moore and
Goldsmith, but beside O'Neill, Tone, and Grattan.

A song or ballad was struck off at a heat, when
a flash of inspiration came,—scrawled with a pencil,
in a large hand, on a sheet of post-paper, with unfinished lines, perhaps, and blanks for epithets which
did not come at once of the right measure or colour;
but the chain of sentiment or incident was generally
complete. If there was time it was revised later and
copied once more in pen and ink, and last touches
added before it was despatched to the printer; but
if occasion demanded, it went at once. For his
verses were written to make Irishmen understand
and love Ireland better, as the poet understood and
loved her, and sometimes a quite transient circumstance furnished an opportunity. It does not detract
from the merits of Freiligrath and Béranger that their
songs had commonly some public ends in view, for
they sprang from a passion which was burning in the
poet's breast; and Davis's verses were always either
the expression of feelings uppermost in his mind at
the moment, or which belonged to it habitually,—
never mere flights of fancy or literary experiments.
What Robert Burns wrote of his own purpose and
inspiration as a poet, Davis might have written of
himself, changing only the nationality.

"Scottish scenes and Scottish story are the themes I wish to
sing. I have no dearer aim than to make leisurely pilgrimages

through Caledonia, to sit on the fields of her battles, to wander on the romantic banks of her rivers, and to muse by the stately towers or venerable ruins once the honoured abodes of her heroes." *

And in one sense he was more of a national poet than any of the illustrious writers whom I have named. He embraced the whole nation in his sympathy. Béranger scorned and detested a party which formed a substantial minority of his country-men; Moore scarcely recognized the existence of a peasantry in his national melodies; even Burns, a Lowland poet, had imperfect sympathy with the natives of the mountains among whom Walter Scott was to find his heroes. But Davis loved and sang the whole Irish people.

" Here came the brown Phœnician, the man of trade and toil—
Here came the proud Milesian, a-hungering for spoil;
And the Firbolg and the Cymry, and the hard, enduring Dane,
And the iron Lords of Normandy, with the Saxons in their train.

" And oh ! it were a gallant deed to show before mankind,
How every race and every creed might be by love combined —
Might be combined, yet not forget the fountains whence they rose,
As, filled by many a rivulet, the stately Shannon flows."

But the native rulers who held their own for centuries against the invader touched him most. Here are a few verses from a vigorous and pictur-esque balled entitled, " A True Irish King "—

" The Cæsar of Rome has a wider domain,
And the *Ard Righ* of France has more clans in his train ;
The sceptre of Spain is more heavy with gems,
And our crowns cannot vie with the Greek diadems ;
But kinglier far, before heaven and man,
Are the Emerald fields, and the fiery-eyed clan,
The sceptre, and state, and the poets who sing,
And the swords that encircle A True Irish King !

* Robert Burns's letter to Mrs. Dunlop.

" For he must have come from a conquering race—
The heir of their valour, their glory, their grace :
His frame must be stately, his step must be fleet,
His hand must be trained to each warrior feat,
His face, as the harvest moon, steadfast and clear,
A head to enlighten, a spirit to cheer ;
While the foremost to rush where the battle-brands ring,
And the last to retreat, is A TRUE IRISH KING !

" God aid him !—God save him !—and smile on his reign—
The terror of England—the ally of Spain.
May his sword be triumphant o'er Sacsanach arts !
Be his throne ever girt by strong hands and true hearts !
May the course of his conquest run on till he see
The flag of Plantagenet sink in the sea !
May minstrels for ever his victories sing,
And saints make the bed of THE TRUE IRISH KING ! "

He loved the Norman, too, when the Norman
became an Irishman.

" The Geraldines ! the Geraldines ;—'tis true, in Strongbow's van,
By lawless force, as conquerors, their Irish reign began !
And, oh ! through many a dark campaign they proved their
    prowess stern,
In Leinster's plains, and Munster's vales, on king, and chief, and
    kerne ;
But noble was the cheer within the halls so rudely won,
And generous was the steel-gloved hand that had such slaughter
    done ;
How gay their laugh, how proud their mien, you'd ask no herald's
    sign—
Among a thousand you had known the princely Geraldine."

It is curious how soon and how thoroughly this
town-bred bookish man caught the characteristics of
social life in an Irish village. Griffin or Carleton
could scarcely surround a modest Irish girl about to
become a bride with more characteristic incidents
than these :—

" We meet in the market and fair—
    We meet in the morning and night—

He sits on the half of my chair,
  And my people are wild with delight.
Yet I long through the winter to skim,
  Though Eoghan longs more, I can see,
When I will be married to him,
  And he will be married to me.
        Then, oh! the marriage, the marriage,
          With love and *mo buachaill* for me!
        The ladies that ride in a carriage,
          Might envy my marriage to me.

" His kinsmen are honest and kind,
  The neighbours think much of his skill,
And Eoghan's the lad to my mind,
  Though he owns neither castle nor mill.
But he has a tilloch of land,
  A horse, and a stocking of coin,
A foot for a dance, and a hand
  In the cause of his country to join.
        Then, oh! the marriage, etc."

This stanza, from another song, is in the same vein :—

" Come in the evening, or come in the morning,
  Come when you're looked for, or come without warning,
Kisses and welcome you'll find here before you,
  And the oftener you come here the more I'll adore you.
    Light is my heart since the day we were plighted,
    Red is my cheek that they told me was blighted :
    The green of the trees looks far greener than ever,
    And the linnets are singing, ' True lovers ! don't sever.' "

There is not, I think, in the lyrics of Burns a more spontaneous gush of natural feeling in unstudied words than this other song of a peasant girl :—

" His kiss is sweet, his word is kind,
    His love is rich to me ;
  I could not in a palace find
    A truer heart than he.
  The eagle shelters not his nest
    From hurricane and hail
  More bravely than he guards my breast—
    The Boatman of Kinsale.

" The wind that round the Fastnet sweeps
　　Is not a whit more pure—
The goat that down Cnoc Sheehy leaps
　　Has not a foot more sure.
No firmer hand nor freer eye
　　E'er faced an autumn gale—
De Courcy's heart is not so high—
　　The Boatman of Kinsale.

" The brawling squires may heed him not,
　　The dainty stranger sneer—
But who will dare to hurt our cot,
　　When Myles O'Hea is here ?
The scarlet soldiers pass along ;
　　They'd like, but fear to rail ;
His blood is hot, his blow is strong—
　　The Boatman of Kinsale.

" His hooker's in the Scilly van,
　　When seines are in the foam ;
But money never made the man,
　　Nor wealth a happy home.
So, blest with love and liberty,
　　While he can trim a sail,
He'll trust in God, and cling to me—
　　The Boatman of Kinsale."

In these ballads he is never guilty of the bad taste of undervaluing the enemy with whom his people struggle. How fine is this picture of the English column at Fontenoy !—

" Six thousand English veterans in stately column tread,
Their cannon blaze in front and flank, Lord Hay is at their head
Steady they step a-down the slope—steady they climb the hill;
Steady they load—steady they fire, moving right onward still,
Betwixt the wood and Fontenoy, as through a furnace blast,
Through rampart, trench, and palisade, and bullets showering fast ;
And on the open plain above they rose, and kept their course,
With ready fire and grim resolve, that mocked at hostile force :
Past Fontenoy, past Fontenoy, while thinner grow their ranks—
They break, as broke the Zuyder Zee through Holland's ocean
　　banks.

" More idly than the summer flies, French tirailleurs rush round ;
As stubble to the lava tide, French squadrons strew the ground ;
Bomb-shell, and grape, and round-shot tore, still on they marched
    and fired—
Fast, from each volley, grenadier and voltigeur retired.
' Push on, my household cavalry !' King Louis madly cried :
To death they rush, but rude their shock—not unavenged they
    died.
On through the camp the column trod—King Louis turns his
    rein :
' Not yet, my liege,' Saxe interposed, ' the Irish troops remain ; '
And Fontenoy, famed Fontenoy, had been a Waterloo,
Were not these exiles ready then, fresh, vehement, and true."

He was at times a moralist, and he touches the deepest chords of a generous heart when he sings, as he often does, our duty to our native land. In one of his finest historical melodies, after picturing the men who fought and ruled of old, he exclaims—

" We are heirs of their fame, if we're not of their race—
And deadly and deep our disgrace,
If we live o'er their sepulchres, abject and base :—
    As truagh gan oidhir 'n-a bh-farradh ! *
Oh ! shame—for unchanged is the face of our isle ;
    As truagh gan oidhir 'n-a bh-farradh !
That taught them to battle, to sing, and to smile ;
    As truagh gan oidhir 'n-a bh-farradh !
We are heirs of their rivers, their sea, and their land,
Our sky and our mountains as grand—
We are heirs—oh, we're not—of their heart and their hand,
    As truagh gan oidhir 'n-a bh-farradh ! "

The number of poems produced in three years supply evidence of his promptness and fertility. Moore, we know from his diary, spent day after day over one of his "Irish Melodies." Béranger with the same frankness describes the prolonged labour a song cost him. Half a dozen a year were as many as he could finish to his satisfaction. Davis in the midst

* " What a pity there are none of their company ! "

of engrossing political labours, produced three times as many—nearly fifty in three years; and his friends might place the " Battle of Fontenoy," or the "Sack of Baltimore," beside " Remember the glories of Brian the Brave," or "Le Chant du Cosaque," as confidently as Turner hung one of his landscapes side by side with a Claude.

Davis's associates, who had yet no political designation or nickname to distinguish them, and no common platform except the journal, were drawn more and more together by personal sympathy. The connection grew as political connections are apt to grow; they had a common stock of opinions, a journal to formulate them, much social intercourse, leaders whom they trusted, and opposition enough to discipline and consolidate their union.

The weekly supper became an institution, and was held at each other's houses in succession, to preserve the sentiment of equality and fraternity. It was a council table in effect, where every one brought his intellectual offering of frank criticism, practical suggestion, story or song, and might be sure of unstinted recognition; for this friendly gathering of men running the same race was as free from envy or rivalry as any assembly of men ever was on the earth. Every one was busy in a common cause, and a brotherhood of design is the essence and poetry of what in ordinary circumstances is mere *esprit de corps.* . Davis was a peer among his peers, never aiming at any lead that was not spontaneously accorded him, and scarcely accepting that much without demur. He loved to be loved, but he was totally indifferent to popularity, and is distinguished from all Irish tribunes who preceded him or have followed him by a perfectly genuine desire to remain unknown, and reap neither recognition nor reward from his work. As I re-read this last sentence, I recognize how imperfectly it conveys to the reader the nearly unexampled phenomenon of a man whose whole force was spent on public affairs, who served the country with the zeal with which a good son serves his mother, who helped the men most in the public eye with authorities, illustrations, and trains of thought, but never exhibited himself, and never desired to be mentioned in connection with his work. In a long lifetime I have encountered no other man of whom this could be said without qualification or drawback.

Thinkers who habitually debate the serious interests of life are apt to oppress their audience by the gravity of their speech. But Davis's conversation was cheerful and natural, and his demeanour familiar and winning. At this time he was under thirty years of age, a strongly built, middle-sized man, with beaming face, a healthy glow, and deep blue eyes, set in a brow of solid strength. There was a manly carelessness in his bearing, as of one who, though well-dressed, never thought of dress or appearance. When he accidentally met a friend, he had the habit of throwing back his head to express a pleased surprise,* which was very winning; a voice not so much sonorous as sympathetic, a cordial laugh and cheerful eyes completed the charm. And this strong self-controlled man, if the generous emotions were suddenly awakened, would blush like a girl.

* "I see that start of glad surprise,
  The lip comprest, the moistened eyes;
  I hear his deep impressive tone,
  And feel his clasp, a brother's own " (O'Hagan).

Considering the matter and purpose of his talk, its most surprising characteristic was its simplicity. He was never a colloquial athlete, making happy hits and adroit fences; he spoke chiefly of the interests of the hour with plainness and sincerity, but his opinions were apt to come out in sentences which would be remembered for their justice or solidity. He was best in committees and conferences, where his rapid allusions and pregnant suggestions were better understood than in a popular assembly. When moved, which was rarely, he spoke with a proud, earnest sententiousness, which was very impressive. There were men among his associates, and men of notable ability, who announced a new opinion like a challenge to controversy, but Davis ordinarily dropped it out like a platitude, on which it was needless to pause. He loved to condense a new truth into a familiar winning phrase, as much as some men love to fabricate a novelty out of a maxim of Epictetus, or an epigram of Rochefoucauld. To circulate truth was his object, never to appropriate it and stamp his own name on it. He naturally spoke much, as he wrote much, for he had a fulness of life which broke out at all the intellectual pores; and his talk had a flavour of wide reading and exact thought, like the olives and subtle salt which give its piquancy to a French *plat*. But he never spoke as a leader or pedagogue, but always as a comrade. As a natural result he was loved as much as he was trusted. To be original, to be deeply in earnest, and at the same time to be loved, supposes rare qualities, not only in him but in his consociates, for few men can endure to be taught. They sought his counsel in difficulties, and always found more than they

sought. In political conferences it was impossible
not to remark a certain abrupt, but not uncourteous
dogmatism, but in a *tête-à-tête* not a trace of it
remained :—

> " He spoke and words more soft than rain,
> Brought back the age of gold again." *

If ever there was a gleam of anger in his eyes you
might be sure it was just wrath against some intolerable wrong, like the pious rage of Dante. One of his
friends insisted that his talk possessed the stimulating properties which Southey attributes to Humphry
Davy's wonderful gas, it excited all manner of mental
and muscular energy and a pervading courage and
confidence.

His temper was perfect. I have seen him tried
by unreasonable pretensions, by petulant complaints,
by contemptuous dissent from what he held most
certain and sacred, but he maintained a sweet com-
posure and was master of himself. In these trials
nature had need to be repressed by a disciplined will,
for beads of perspiration on his broad brow often disclosed the contest within. But angry word or
gesture none of his comrades ever saw. Among
them he was always serene. Starting from the perfectly just assumption that they loved and trusted
him, he made light of dissent. Controversy he knew
was one of the processes by which opinion is created
or regulated, and a man often modifies his opinions
in the very act of defending them. Even his enthusiasm, which was singularly contagious, was regulated
and restrained, never clamorous or aggressive. Celtic
Irishmen have a tendency to take offence easily and

* Emerson.

K

to stand upon their dignity quite gratuitously; his
example tended to correct this weakness, and if it
exhibited itself he encountered it with a grave
sweet courtesy which made the offender ashamed of
himself.

Like Charles James Fox he was a " very pains-
taking man," and this quality never exhibited itself
so assiduously as in the service of his companions.
When he promised anything, however trivial, or made
a casual rendezvous, one could count on a definite
fulfilment—not a common characteristic of gifted
young Celts. He loved to make his knowledge their
common property. When he met in his readings a
new book which enlarged his horizon of political
knowledge, or suggested some new device for serving
the cause, he exhibited such generous rapture that he
roused congenial feelings among his associates, and
inspired even the sceptical with somewhat of his own
ardour of study and hopeful views of life.

He did nearly as much work as all his friends
united, and had leisure not only to " carol his native
wood-notes wild," but to be the soul of their social
gatherings. One of them who had been a traveller
saw a porpoise in the Indian Ocean run a race with
a steamer of four-thousand-horse power, and not only
beat the gigantic machine, but express its enjoyment
of the contest by exulting somersaults in the air,
and he declared that the spectacle reminded him of
nothing so much as Thomas Davis among his associates. The force of his faculties was multiplied by
a purpose which never slackened. Even his rare
gifts and a character in perfect equilibrium might
have been wasted in an enterprise so tremendous as
the one he had undertaken, but a powerful will

devoted to a noble purpose is a force before which impediments disappear.

> "Such earnest natures are the fiery pith,
>   The compact nucleus, round which systems grow :
> Mass after mass becomes inspired therewith,
>   And whirls impregnate with the central glow." *

Mangan never came to the weekly suppers, and I had to invent opportunities of making him known to a few of our colleagues one by one. He had the shyness of a man who lives habitually apart, and the soreness of one whose sensitive nerves have suffered in contact with the rude world. Like Balzac, Scribe, and Disraeli, he commenced life in an attorney's office, and was tortured by the practical jokes and exuberant spirits of his companions.

William Carleton,† whom I had known for many years, called at the *Nation* office from time to time to criticize or applaud what we were doing, and in the end to help us. He was cordially received by the young men, invited to excursions we made occasionally to historical places, fêted and encouraged to become frankly a Nationalist ; but it is a significant fact that to the weekly suppers, which were our Cabinet council, he never found his way. He liked the men cordially, found their talk agreeable and their historical excursions pleasant picnics, at any rate, but their purpose was something which, with all his splendid equipment of brains, he was incapable of comprehending.

MacCarthy was our Sydney Smith. His humour was as spontaneous as sunshine, and often flashed out as unexpectedly in grave debate as a gleam of sun-

* Lowell.
† Author of " Traits and Stories of the Irish Peasants," etc.

shine from behind a mask of clouds. Some practical
man proposed that there should be a close season for
jokes, but they did not impede business, but rather
seasoned it and made it palatable. MacNevin and
Barry were wits, and sayers of good things ; Mac-
Carthy was a genuine humourist. MacNevin's mer-
riment was explosive, and sometimes went off without
notice, like steam from a safety-valve. Barry uttered
his good things with a gravity which set off their dry
humour, and was accused of preparing the *mise en scène*.
Denny Lane, on some such occasion, told a story of
one of his fellow-citizens who used to produce a pun
once a year, and gave a dinner party to let it off,
sometimes getting up appropriate scenery, machinery,
and decorations for the new birth which turned his
annual into a little melodrama.

Davis was never a *faiseur de phrases*, but sayings
of force or significance sometimes fell from him as
spontaneously as pearls from the lips of the princess
in the fairy tale. Some one quoted Plunket's saying
that to certain men history was no better than an
old almanac. " Yes," he replied, "and under certain
other conditions an old almanac becomes an historical
romance." I brought to breakfast with him one
morning a young Irish-American recruit, burning to
know personally the men who had probably drawn
him across the Atlantic, and possessing himself many
of the gifts he loved in them. I asked Davis next
day how he liked Darcy McGee. " With time I
might like him," he said, " but he seemed too much
bent on *transacting* an acquaintance with me." A
certain new recruit brought a pocketful of projects,
good, bad, and indifferent, some of them indeed
excellent, but he exhibited them as if they were

the Sibyl's books.   Speaking of him next day, some one said to Davis that his talk was like champagne. "No," said Davis, "not like champagne, like a seidlitz-powder; it is effervescent and wholesome, but one never gets rid of the idea that it is physic." But though he had a keen enjoyment of pleasantry and loved banter and badinage, he did not possess the faculty of humour.   When he occasionally made experiments in this region he became satirical or savage.   Like Schiller, he looked habitually at the graver aspect of human affairs, and was too much in earnest for the disengaged mind and easy play of faculties necessary to be sportive.   But if we judged Burns by his epigrams, how low he would be rated !

The youngest of the associates were John O'Hagan * and John Pigot.   O'Hagan was a law student, labouring to acquire the mastery of principles which alone makes the law a liberal and philosophical profession.   He was modest and reticent, speaking rarely and never of himself or his works.   MacCarthy, in his poem of the "Lay Missionary," has painted his social life.   In literature he made himself gradually known to his colleagues by sound criticism in the sweetest of wholesome English, and by poems which constantly extended the range of his powers into new regions.   John Pigot was a bright handsome boy, son of an eminent Whig lawyer afterwards Chief Baron of the Exchequer, and Davis held him in great affection.   He was a diligent and zealous student, and a perpetual missionary of national opinions in good society.   He contributed sometimes, but very rarely, to the *Nation*, for he was not as yet a writer of the requisite vigour or skill for that office.

* Mr. Justice O'Hagan, lately head of the Land Commission in Ireland.

O'Callaghan was older than his colleagues, and of another school. He had gone through the first Repeal agitation, and had never quite recovered from its disillusions. He was a tall, dark, strong man, who spoke a dialect compounded apparently in equal parts from Johnson and Cobbett, in a voice too loud for social intercourse. "I love," he would cry, "not the entremets of literature, but the strong meat and drink of sedition," or, "I make a daily meal on the smoked carcase of Irish history." Some one affirmed that he heard him instructing his partner in a dance on the exact limits of the Irish pentarchy and the malign slanders of Giraldus Cambrensis. O'Callaghan was a thoroughly honest man, but he brought into Irish politics in his train a younger brother, whose sly furtive character none of the young men could tolerate. He was never admitted to the weekly suppers, never permitted to write a line in the *Nation*. He betook himself to other associates and other journals, and, in the end, ripened into a Government spy.

Davis was my senior in age, and greatly more my senior in knowledge and experience. Educated in a city, disciplined in a university, living habitually in society where he had friends and competitors of his own age and condition, he got the training which developed the natural forces in the healthiest manner. I had lived in a small country town, where I had not the good fortune to encounter one associate of similar tastes and studies, except Henry McManus, the artist, and T. B. McManus, who has left an honourable name in Irish annals ; and I had paid the penalty of being a Catholic in Ireland by being withheld from a university which still maintained the agencies of proselytism and the insolence of ascendancy. I took my new friend into my heart of hearts, where he has maintained the first place from that day forth.

Davis's abnegation contrasted strangely with the practice of some of his contemporaries. One occasional contributor, who wrote about a dozen articles in three years, contrived to introduce his own name into half of them, and O'Callaghan frankly declared that he could not afford to waste a grain of his reputation by hyper-modesty. Whatever he wrote was published under his name, or a recognized *nom de plume*, and was generally some extension of the field of historic research opened in the "Green Book." A note of this period will illustrate his ingenuous individuality.

" *Tuesday*, July 1st (Anniversary of the Battle of the Boyne, both as to day of the *week* and day of the *month*).

" DEAR DUFFY OR DAVIS, OR DAVIS AND DUFFY,

" I'm much obliged for your insertion of my little note to the Editor of *Limerick Chronicle;* and as it strikes me that you'll have a good opportunity for an article this week, I may as well mention it.

" There's the festival the Orangemen are to hold, I believe, this evening, anent the so-called glorious victory of the Boyne; and really you ought not to let slip such an occasion as will present itself for putting an end to that humbug in Saturday's *Nation*. You may have seen what a capital hand the *Mail* lately made of O'Connell's tumble in the mud with regard to Galileo's business, which never cost us here anything equal to the bad consequences resulting from the false notions, so long, and even still, sought to be kept up, on the subject of the Boyne affair. The exact number of British, Northern Irish, Huguenot, Dutch, and Danish infantry and cavalry regiments are stated in full from official data in my second edition; from which all the real merit of the English and their Ulster allies on that day can be deduced for the public, in the way you'll be so well able to do in the *Nation*. And as what you'll say will be believed, even by men of anti-Catholic notions in politics, when other papers would not be minded, it's in your power to do much good by at least contributing to put a stop to such 'revivals' as those Orange ones connected with the affair of the 1st of July and 12th. They have been the foundation of a great deal of evil to Ireland, so do what you can to coffin them. Until the Koran is destroyed there will be Mahometans.

"As ever, sincerely yours,

"In the singular and dual number,

"J. C. C."

The young men had as yet no visible following, and might be described in the contemptuous language which Jefferson flung at the friends of Alexander Hamilton, "as a party all head and no body." But the future Young Irelanders were estimated as unskilfully as the future Federalists; for, like them, they grew into a decisive power. Even now there was a surrounding of youngsters who neither wrote nor harangued, but constituted a sympathetic chorus almost as essential to the success of the drama as the actors themselves. They sang their songs, repeated their *mots*, carried their opinions into society, and sometimes quite honestly mistook them for their own.

Whenever men are combined for a large purpose, good or evil, posterity is apt to select one of them to inherit all the honour. In the Reformation we think only of Luther, but without Calvin and Knox the Reformation might have remained a German schism. Of the Jesuits the world remembers chiefly St. Ignatius, but he was far from being the first in genius, or even in governing power, of that astonishing company. Among the forerunners of the French Revolution opinion settles upon Rousseau and Voltaire, but Denis Diderot sapped the buttresses of authority and stubbed the roots of faith with a more steadfast and malign industry. Wilberforce is hailed

emancipator of the negroés, but without Clarkson and
Zachary Macaulay he would have gone to his grave
without seeing them emancipated. The hour and the
man is always rather the hour and the men. Original
men come in groups, and so it was now. Davis was
the truest type of his generation, not because he was
most gifted, but because his whole faculties were
devoted to his work; and because he was not one-
sided, but a complete and consummate man. But
the era produced a crowd of notable persons. Mangan
was a truer poet, but altogether wanted the stringent
will which made Davis's work so fruitful. MacNevin,
and still more in later times Meagher, uttered appeals
as eloquent and touching, but each of them kindled
his torch at the living fire of Davis. Dillon had,
perhaps, a safer judgment, and certainly a surer appreciation of difficulties; but his labours were intermittent. Most of their separate qualities united in
Davis, and every faculty was applied with unwavering purpose to a single end, which ruled his life "like
a guiding star above."

Irish history had been shamefully neglected in
school and college, and the young men took up the
teaching of it in the *Nation;* not as a cold scientific
analysis, but as a passionate search for light which
might help them to understand their own race and
country. When this attempt began, Irish history
was rather less known than Chinese. A mandarin
implied a definite idea; but what was a Tanist?
Confucius was a wise man among the Celestials; but
who was Moran? One man out of ten thousand
could not tell whether Owen Roe followed or preceded
Brien Boroihime; in which hemisphere the victory of
Benburb was achieved; or whether the O'Neill who

held Ireland for eight years in the Puritan wars, was
a naked savage armed with a stake, or an accomplished soldier bred in the most adventurous and
punctilious service in Europe.   They soon lighted up
this obscure past with a sympathy which gilded it
like sunshine, till the study of our annals became a
passion with young Irishmen.   On this teaching
Davis constantly strove to impress a precise aim and
purpose.   He ransacked the past, not to find weapons
of assault against England, still less to feed the
lazy reveries of seannachies and poets upon legends
of a golden age hid in the mists of antiquity, but to
rear a generation whose lives would be strengthened
and ennobled by the knowledge that there had been
great men of their race, and great actions done on
the soil they trod ; whose resolution and fidelity would
be fortified by knowing that their ancestors had left
their mark for ever on some of the most memorable
eras of European history; that they were heirs in
name and fame to a litany of soldiers, scholars, and
ecclesiastics, no more fabulous or questionable than
the marshals of Napoleon or the poets of Weimar;
and to warn them by the light of the past of the
perilous vices and weaknesses which had so often
betrayed our people.

"This country of ours," Davis wrote, "is no sand-bank, thrown
up by some recent caprice of earth.   It is an ancient land,
honoured in the archives of civilization, traceable into antiquity
by its piety, its valour, and its sufferings.   Every great European
race has sent its stream to the river of Irish mind.   Long wars,
vast organizations, subtle codes, beacon crimes, leading virtues,
and self-mighty men were here.   If we live influenced by wind,
and sun, and tree, and not by the passions and deeds of the past,
we are a thriftless and hopeless people."

When students were exhorted to make themselves familiar with native history, we were met on the threshold with the difficulty that there were no books available. An Irish library was as costly as an Irish freehold; and, when you got it, there was no skeleton map forthcoming of the territory to be traversed. It was a "mighty maze, and all without a plan." Nobody but a few antiquaries studied our annals. To the masses it was a story of disaster and defeat, from which they shrank. The cloud of 1798, and the Union, lay heavy upon it.

The intellectual stagnation of the time will be best understood by examples. In early numbers of the *Nation*, a long list of James Duffy's publications is advertised—James Duffy, who was afterwards the national publisher,—but, without a single exception, they are works of Catholic piety. Denis O'Brien, a popular retail bookseller, occupies two columns of the journal with his wares; * and among fifty-three periodicals and serials, forty-eight are English or Scotch; and among fourteen works of fiction or travel, only two are Irish; out of eleven miscellaneous books, only one is Irish; out of thirteen volumes of poetry, there was not one native in subject or authorship; and of a hundred and seven works of popular instruction, the entire were English or Scotch. To teach the people that they had a history as harmonious as an epic poem, illustrated with great names and great transactions, was like awakening a new sense, and created a tumult of enthusiasm. They loved and pitied their country; but that they might honour and worship it, was a revelation.

"This teaching," said one of the next generation of patriots, no longer living, "made impressionable

---

* *Nation*, Dec. 24, 1842.

people, like myself, feel as if our dear Ireland was a living thing, whom we must love, honour, and serve." Its aim cannot be better described than in language of Davis's :—

"To create a race of men full of a more intensely Irish character and knowledge, and to that race to give Ireland. It would give them the seas of Ireland to sweep with their nets and launch on with their navy; the harbours of Ireland, to receive a greater commerce than any island in the world; the soil of Ireland to live on, by more millions than starve here now; the fame of Ireland, to enhance by their genius and valour; the independence of Ireland, to guard by laws and arms."

We were warned by the *Times*, and a chorus of smaller critics, that these historical reminiscences fostered national animosities. Perhaps they did; but is there any method of exposing great wrongs which does not beget indignation against the wronger? We were of opinion that writers who habitually employed the epithet Swiss to signify a mercenary, Greek a cheat, Jew a miser, Turk a brute, and Yankey a pedlar, who symbolize a French-man as a fop, and a Frenchwoman as a hag (beldam ⸗ belle dame), and who called whatsoever was stupid or foolish Irish—an Irish argument being an argu-ment that proved nothing, and an Irish method a method which was bound to fail—were scarcely entitled to take us to task for truths which, how-ever disagreeable, were at least authentic.

The journal alone was not a sufficient agent for this purpose, and books to fill some of the greater voids in our history began to appear. The work which Davis and his friends did in this way was of wider scope and greater permanence than anything they could accomplish in the Association. They were slowly, half unconsciously, laying the foundations of a national literature. Their first experiment was a little sixpenny brochure, printed at the *Nation* office, and sold by the *Nation* agents—a collection of the songs and ballads, published during three months, entitled " The Spirit of the Nation." Its success was a marvel. The Conservatives set the example of applauding its ability, while they condemned its aim and spirit. Frederick Shaw, then leader of the Irish Tories, read specimens to the House of Commons as a warning of a new danger. Isaac Butt, his rival in Ireland, made the little book the main subject of his speech at a Conservative meeting in Dublin, and declared the writer—supposing the book to be the production of one man instead of a dozen— " deserved the name, and had the inspiration of a poet." And Mr. Lefanu, the most gifted journalist of the party, taking the prose and poetry together, pronounced the *Nation* to be the most ominous and formidable phenomenon of strange and terrible times.

" The *Nation*," he added, " is written with a masculine vigour, and with an impetuous singleness of purpose which makes every number tell home. It represents the opinions and feelings of some millions of men, reflected with vivid precision in its successive pages, and, taken for all in all, it is a genuine and gigantic representative of its vast party."

This interest, curiously compounded of anger and sympathy, spread to England. John Wilson Croker, in the *Quarterly Review*, praised without stint " the beauty of language and imagery," but declared, in his habitual slashing style, that " they exhibited the deadliest rancour, the most audacious falsehoods, and the most incendiary provocations to war." The *Times* affirmed that O'Connell's mischievous exhor-

tations were as nothing compared with the fervour
of rebellion which breathed in every page of these
verses. The echo of those strong opinions ran
through the chief critical and political journals, and
the *Naval and Military Gazette* added a dash of
vitriol to the flame when it announced that the
songs made their way into the barracks, and were
sung at the public houses frequented by Irish soldiers.
It had now reached the point when the literary Paul
Prys became interested, and, as a matter of course,
Monckton Milnes got an Irish member to procure him
secretly half a dozen copies, which he was afraid to
send for in his own name; and his secret was kept,
as is usual in such cases, by his confidant transmitting his letter to the *Nation* office. A little later
Macaulay set his *cachet* on their merits, by frankly
recognizing the energy and beauty which many
of the poems displayed, and deploring that such
genius should be employed in inflaming national
animosity. A second part was speedily published,
and the little volume, swollen into a large one, was
reprinted in endless editions in Ireland and America,
and has been the companion of two generations of
Irishmen, wherever an emigrant, missionary, or
soldier has carried the Irish name. The newspaper
office could not produce the book fast enough for the
demand, and at an early period it was transferred to
Mr. James Duffy, a publisher then in a small way of
business in a by-street, to whom it was the beginning of great prosperity. Remembering the pre-
cedent of Robert Burns, who refused to make money
by the songs of his country, the copyright was bestowed on the publisher.

The second experiment was a collection of the

orators of Ireland. It was designed to bring into
one series the greatest speeches of the men who
fought the battle of parliamentary independence in
the eighteenth century; next, the great Irishmen
who had served the Empire with conspicuous ability—
Burke, Canning, and Wellesley; and, finally, of the
two tribunes of the Catholic agitation, O'Connell and
Shiel. To say that the renowned orators who graced
the era of independence were not read in Ireland,
is to give an imperfect conception of the case. The
speeches of Grattan, Flood, Curran, or Plunket were
nearly as little read as the "Annals of the Four
Masters," and almost as inaccessible. Some of them
were never collected, and the costly editions of
others, which had been published, had long gone out
of print, and it was only in a public library, of which
there were not half a dozen in the island, or in Whig
manor-houses, or occasionally in the book-case of an
aged priest, that a stray volume might be found. To
create an appetite for these treasures of passion and
knowledge, and to gratify it abundantly, was a fruitful work. Davis gathered the materials for the
volume on Curran, with which it was proposed to
begin; and when the most laborious part of the work
was completed, he invited Wallis to write a memoir,
and edit the collection. Wallis failing, he pressed it
on Maddyn :—

"I asked Wallis to write the 'Curran,' and he refused. He is
getting nervous and distrustful. I don't mean in heart, for he is,
with all his oddities, affectionate; but in his judgment and temper.
He'll do nothing till others have done everything important, and
then maybe he'll chronicle, and insult or glorify us, or lament us
if we fail. As the notice of Curran has been delayed so long,
perhaps you might now be able to write it. If you can, it will be
a great gratification to me to see you do it."

And again :—

"I am most anxious that you should write the memoir. You will really do justice to Curran, the honest valorous patriot, the wit never excelled, the most poetical of all secular orators, the unrivalled advocate, the thorough Irishman."

Maddyn made difficulties, though the proposal was very grateful to him.

" To Irishmen," he wrote, " Curran is what Burns is to Scotch-men, the genuine poetic product of the soil. It provokes me that I cannot avail myself of ' coming out' upon such a subject, and conciliating some sympathy from my countrymen. I think I know how it ought to be done, which vexes me more. . . . Byron said he heard more poetry from Curran than he had read in all his life."

Let a reader, to whom Davis is new or unknown, consider how few men he has encountered in life who, having himself done the hard preliminary work of a literary project, would labour in secret to transfer the credit and honour to another, and he will begin to understand the man I am endeavouring to de-scribe. When the speeches were in type he renewed his appeal to Maddyn :—

" Enclosed is one page of a proof copy of Curran's speeches, of which Mr. James Duffy is about to issue a thousand copies, with Reynolds's portrait also enclosed. His proof reached me here much pressed for time, and therefore I wrote to him, if he were so inclined, I would ask a friend to write the sketch, but of course he should be paid. I enclose you his answer. Will you write this? . . . It is settled that James Duffy is to pay fifty pounds to the writer of the Memoir and selector and editor of each volume of speeches. No one can do the three volumes of the series, ' Bushe,' ' Burke,' and ' Grattan,' so well as yourself. . . . It was O'Hea, an old College Historical Society friend, who joined the association, not the goose O'H——. O'Hea, as you know, is a man of vast powers, and is succeeding at his profession. O'Loghlin is an abler and firmer man than his letters would show ; I thought it a very poor letter. Lane is all you describe him, a fine fellow. O'Hagan has the best business of any Outer Bar man on his circuit. He is a good man and of great energy, and a trained speaker. McCullagh is Federalist, and has done nothing till the last three days. He is now sobered, and working for Federalism."

Maddyn finally pleaded that he had too many engagements already, but promised a little help to whomsoever undertook the task.

"Curran," he wrote, "was a glorious enthusiast, without deluding day-dreams or romantic misbelief. I will jot down some odd remarks upon him on a sheet of paper and send them to you next week; they may be of use to whoever will do it, and they shall be at your service." *

In the end Davis did the work himself. The volume was published without his name, and not as one of a series, but practically to determine the prudence of the general design. He accompanied the collection of speeches with a fresh, vigorous, and sparkling memoir. The book has since run through twenty editions, and is in the hands of every student of Irish history. It had to encounter the conceited dogmatism which a work of original genius seldom escapes, but we can read this rash disparagement with something of the sensation which Brougham's estimate of Byron, or Jeffrey's of Wordsworth, or John Wilson's of Tennyson is apt to create in a reader of to-day. It used to be said with some justice that if you put an Irishman to roast, another Irishman would turn the spit. The turnspit on this occasion was Mr. Marmion Savage, a gentleman who commenced his career at the Corn Exchange declaiming against tithe, and ended as clerk of the Privy Council. He pronounced judgment on Davis's volume in the *Athenæum*, and the opening paragraph is worth preserving as one of the curiosities of criticism.

* Maddyn to Davis, September 8th.

"A greener book than this has not yet issued from the Green Isle. The cover is greener than the shamrock; the contents greener again; and the style and execution are green in the superlative degree. In short, it is 'one entire and perfect *emerald*,' saving the value of that precious stone. It must needs be an emanation from some very green and unripe genius, who sees every object through a pair of green spectacles; nay, we have a suspicion that the author is no other than the actual Green Man. It ought to be called 'The Green Book;' but we fear, from the extravagant verdure of the language and crudity of the composition, that the Barrister will hardly succeed in 'making the green one—*read*.' *Vert* like this is not easily convertible into *Venison*. We never thought the epithet '*green*' very complimentary to Ireland, any more than the appellation '*old*.' There is *indeed* such a thing as a 'green old age.' But Ireland must be either in her *infancy* or her *dotage*, if she is not more displeased than charmed with the work before us."

After describing the style as one which "combined all the absurdities of Carlyle with all the vulgarity of Ainsworth," the writer was good enough from his sublime altitude to drop a crumb of encouragement to his victim. If he would abandon everything that was characteristic in his style and essential to his purpose, he might in time become not altogether intolerable.

"He produces upon us, when he is lively, somewhat the effect of an hour in Donnybrook Fair; and when the mood changes to pathos, we fancy we have been assisting at the funeral of an O'Rourke, and listening to the mercenary howlers of a provincial wake. We have not been slow to commend the productions of Young Ireland, where they seemed worthy of praise; we saw evidences of poetry in the 'Spirit of the Nation,' and it gave us pleasure to record our opinion to that effect, although we were not, of course, amongst those who approved of the *animus* of those effusions. But the present is a work to be rebuked; and if our rebuke be more sharp than usual, it is because we believe that, with all its sins, it proceeds from one who has faculties for something better, would he but mix a little grey discretion with his green politics, and correct his green composition by a few years of brown study."

MacNevin followed Davis with a collection of the State Trials in Ireland from 1794 to 1803—the era of Castlereagh and Carhampton. It was carefully edited, and the period lighted up with a vivid introduction.

A popular edition of MacGeoghegan's "History of Ireland" followed—a valuable book published in Paris by an emigrant priest,—and Barrington's "Rise and Fall of the Irish Nation," and Foreman's famous "Defence of the Courage, Honour, and Loyalty of the Irish,"—the last edited by Davis.

Every week the journal contained counsel to young Irishmen on education, discipline, the use they might make of their lives, and the services they could perform for their country, and the same spirit animated their work in the Association.

A disease fatal to local organization is want of work. O'Connell thought that to collect and remit the Repeal rent was employment enough, but the new men were constantly suggesting tasks which touched the imagination and warmed the hearts of their disciples.

" Watch over our historical places," they said; "they are in the care of the people, and they are ill-cared. All classes, creeds, and politics are to blame in this. The peasant lugs down a pillar for his sty, the farmer for his gate, the priest for his chapel, the minister for his glebe. A mill-stream ran through Lord Moore's Castle, and the commissioners of Galway have shaken, and threatened to remove, the Warden's House, that fine stone chronicle of Galway heroism. [A warden of Galway was the Brutus of Ireland, and sacrificed his son to his country.] But those ruins were rich possessions. The state of civilization among our Scotic, or Milesian, or Norman, or Danish sires, was better seen from a few raths, keeps, and old coast towns, with the help of the Museum of the Irish Academy, than from all the prints and historical novels we have. An old castle in Kilkenny, a house in Galway give us a peep at the arts, the intercourse, the creed, the indoor, and some of the outdoor ways of the gentry of the one, and of the merchants of the other, clearer than Scott could, were he to write, or Cattermole, were he to paint for forty years. Yet year after year more and more of our crosses are broken, of our tombs effaced, of our abbeys shattered, of our castles torn down, of our cairns sacrilegiously pierced, of our urns broken up, and of our coins melted down."

All this work had to be done with a constant watchfulness against giving offence to the national leader, who had small sympathy with the philosophy or poetry of politics, and a general disrelish of unauthorized experiments. Maddyn proposed to republish Woulfe's famous pamphlet on the Catholic claims, entitling it, "An Essay on Irish Government by the late Chief Baron;" but the proposal was not adopted, probably because the brochure would revive forgotten controversies with O'Connell. He also suggested that Dr. Doyle's essays, omitting what was temporary, would furnish a useful handbook of Irish thought; but the same objection existed in this case. Even the managers of the *Dublin Monthly*, whose obscurity protected it from any active censorship, were alarmed at Maddyn's O'Connellphobia. He wrote a paper for the magazine on Richard Ronayne, popularly known as " Radical Ronayne," a Munster Catholic who, in controversies between O'Connell and Cobbett, on poor-laws and national policy, commonly sided with the English Radical; but it was necessary to dock it considerably, and smuggle it into the *Monthly* under the form of a contribution from an American sympathizer.

"Hudson and I agree," Davis wrote to his friend, "in asking you to change the name of the article to 'Richard Ronayne'— Radical R. is a nickname; also to change the introduction. There is no good in imitating Moore's lament [over the decay of public spirit in Ireland]; and lastly, because I have written the opposite at length, in an article on O'Connell in the same number."

The monster meetings went on with unflagging spirit and still increasing numbers. Many millions of Irishmen had now been paraded and battalioned as Nationalists determined at all costs to raise up their country anew. The influence of a resolute organized people was tremendous. It made itself felt in every fibre of the nation, among the most hostile section as well as the most sympathetic. Here are two or three significant illustrations. In the absence of the National members from Parliament, the Government proposed an Arms Bill of unexampled stringency; but the public spirit was alert, and it was resisted by Irish Whigs, led on this occasion by Lord Clements, Sharman Crawford, and Smith O'Brien with stubborn persistence. Half of the session was wasted before it was forced through the Commons. A reply from Mr. R. R. Moore, one of the organizers of the Anti-Corn Law League, to a note on the question, will sufficiently indicate that Davis was busy promoting the resistance.

"I have shown your note with all due discretion to some good friends of freedom—Villiers, Gibson, Bowring, Cobden, and Ricardo have promised to oppose that Devil's instigation, the Arms Bill; I intend to speak to all the members I know on the subject. . . . The truth is, they will not be persuaded that O'Connell is not playing the game of Repeal agitation merely to get the Whigs in again, and they never will forgive him his indiscriminate support of that miserable faction when they were last in power." *

The Bill proposed to issue arms only to a limited class who had received a licence from a bench of magistrates, and even these weapons were to be stamped with an official brand. The branding was

* National Anti-Corn Law League, 448, Strand, London, June 7, 1843.

very offensive to Irish gentlemen; it would degrade
the historical weapons of the Volunteers which they
still possessed, and disfigure their *armes de luxe.*
The authorities were reminded that, if the people
became exasperated, these precautions would prove
worthless—

> "For rage finds weapons everywhere
> For nature's two unbranded arms."

When these Irish Liberals had failed in Parliament
they addressed themselves directly to the English
people, inviting them to consider the condition to
which the fatal policy which they supported had
reduced Ireland. The people were poor, estranged,
and exasperated by a long course of vicious legislation. The labouring population lived habitually on
the verge of destitution. Irish commerce, manufactures, fisheries, mines, and agriculture attested
by their languishing and neglected condition the
baneful effects of misgovernment. Was there any
remedy? It was in vain that the representatives of
the nation claimed redress, their complaints and
remonstrances were unheeded. But they appealed
now to the higher tribunal of public opinion, and
demanded perfect equality with England as the only
secure and legitimate foundation upon which the
Union could permanently rest.[*]

Half a year later a number of Irish Peers, led as
of old by the Duke of Leinster and Lord Charlemont,
followed the example of the Commoners, and peti-

---

[*] The names appended to this address, which appeared on August, 1843,
were Thomas Wyse, Waterford City; D. R. Ross, Belfast; Thomas Esmonde,
Wexford Town; William Villiers Stuart, Waterford County; R. S. Carew,
Waterford County; D. Jephson Norreys, Mallow; M. E. Corbally, Meath
County; John O'Brien, Limerick City; M. J. O'Connell, Kerry County;
Robert Archbold, Kildare County; Robert Gore, New Ross; Hugh M. Tuite,
Westmeath County; James Power, Wexford County; Wm. S. O'Brien,
Limerick County.

tioned Parliament to take the condition of Ireland
into immediate consideration. They enumerated the
wrongs which the people endured, and denounced
the policy of the Government as erroneous and futile.
The army was increased, barracks were fortified,
armed vessels were stationed off the coast, and upon
the navigable rivers of the country. But the use of
force, though it might be effective for the suppression
of disorder, could not remove discontent.

Even the English Whigs did not escape the prevailing influence. A party manifesto was published
in the *Edinburgh Review*, revised by Lord John
Russell,* offering among other concessions an annual
visit of the Queen, and a residence in Ireland long
enough to make the presence of the Sovereign no
unusual element in national life, the holding of
parliamentary sessions in Dublin, a provision for
middle-class education by erecting Maynooth into
a university, reform of land tenure, the disestablish-
ment of the Protestant Church, and a permanent
provision for the Catholic clergy, and for the maintenance of their churches. A sum yielding an annual
income of three hundred thousand pounds must be
granted for the purpose of carrying out these reforms.

A more curious and significant evidence of progress was an Irish Club started in London. A dozen
peers, more than twenty members of Parliament, as
many baronets, knights, or privy councillors, and a
considerable muster of artists and literary men united
in the Irish Society. It was to be independent of
religious and political distinctions, and the names of
men so widely divided as Frederick Shaw, Emerson

---

* See "Select Correspondence of Macvey Napier," then editor of the
Edinburgh Review.

Tennent, and Colonel Taylor on one side, and
Anthony Blake, D. R. Pigot, and Thomas Redington
on the other; with an intermediate section, of whom
Colonel Caulfield, D. R. Ross, and Morgan John
O'Connell were representatives, promised that it
would be national in a high sense. Irish artists like
Maclise, MacDowell, John Doyle, and men of letters
like Father Prout and Dr. Croly, gave it an attraction more piquant than rank can furnish, and it
opened with satisfactory prospects.*

The land question was more and more debated in
the *Nation* as the most urgent of Irish grievances,
and one for which redress might perhaps be obtained

* The progress of national opinions may perhaps be best gauged by their
influence on the Conservative press. Here is an extract from the *Evening
Mail*, the most authoritative organ of the Tory party in Ireland, which
exhibits it in the "Precursor stage," one day's march from Repeal :—

"Ireland is deprived of her fair proportion of influence and power in the
administration of public affairs. Irishmen are treated with neglect and scorn.

"The Queen's cabinet contains not a single Irishman.

"The subordinate offices of the Government, with the exception of the
petty place assigned to Mr. Emerson Tennent, and two or three more of
'such small deer,' are exclusively held by English and Scotch.

"From all the public departments in Great Britain, Irishmen are
excluded, whilst English and Scotch officials shoulder them out of the
direction of affairs in their own country.

"Towards the liberal professions the same partial course is pursued; and
never was it pursued with a more unvarying monopoly than within the last
four years.

"Next comes the Church, towards which the rule is rigidly enforced—
namely, that Englishmen are worthy to be set in the highest offices in
Ireland, but no Irish clergyman entitled to aspire to the meanest preferment
being in the gift of Government. Did any one ever hear of an Irish clergyman being made an English bishop, or an English dean?

"The difficulty experienced by Irish gentlemen in procuring the promotion of their sons in the *Royal Navy* is almost as great as if the *gun-room*
were a cathedral, and every midshipman a holden prebendary.

"Even the *Army*, which is indebted in a great degree for its high renown
and pre-eminence to the valour and conduct of Irish gentlemen, is now
assuming the character of an exclusively British institution. Numerous
complaints have reached us from quarters of the highest rank and respectability, of the influence of national partiality at the Horse Guards. Irish
gentlemen in vain solicit permission to purchase commissions for their sons.
The answer they receive is invariably the same—full of smooth hope and
delusive promise, ending in nothing.

"These things tend to make the Repeal movement the formidable engine
of anarchy it is" (*Evening Mail*).

from the Imperial Parliament. Maddyn asked Davis for the plan of settlement contemplated in Ireland, and, being then engaged on a book which he afterwards published, "Ireland and its Rulers," inquired for authorities on the period which it covered.

"Carlyle and his numerous crew of imitators," he wrote, "turn up their noses at the word '*plan*,' and think them all formalists who demand one. They preach about the folly of Sieyes, forgetting that Sieyes really had no plan at all. A man with twenty schemes has no scheme. With all that is said and written on the subject in Ireland, it is strange if no measures have been indicated that might bear even their *proposition* to Parliament. Could you also from your multifarious resources indicate to me any books wherein I might read up in a summary manner the chief political events of the years 1829, 1830, 1831, and 1832 in Ireland? In short, I want the history of the first Repeal agitation, its accidental impulses, and its aggravating causes. Is there any work published where there is an Irish retrospect of these years? . . . Don't tell me any secrets, or to any one else who is not in your political confidence. Recollect that most honourable men might injure you by thoughtlessness or imprudence." *

When the monster meetings had arrayed the bulk of the nation on his side, and the time for mere demonstration was over, O'Connell promised that he would summon a Council of Three Hundred to consider the question of international securities, and form the nucleus of an Irish Parliament. The Convention Act forbade the election of delegates in Ireland, but he proposed to escape its penalties by accepting as members of the Council such gentlemen as their neighbours designated by entrusting them with £100 each for the Repeal Fund. The project was daring and even revolutionary, for such an assembly would be entitled to present an ultimatum to England, and support it by the force of the whole nation. The young men took it up warmly, but not

* July, 1843.

without a secret apprehension that O'Connell meant
it to create alarm in England rather than to perform
the noble work for which it seemed fit.

The meetings still swelled in numbers, passion,
and purpose. O'Connell's oratory kept measure with
the quick march of the nation. At Davis's birthplace he used language afterwards known as the
" Mallow Defiance." Speaking of a rumour which
attributed to the Government the intention of suppressing the movement by force, he said—

"Do you know, I never felt such a loathing for speechifying
as I do at present. The time is coming when we must be doing.
Gentlemen, you may learn the alternative to live as slaves or die
as freemen. No! you will not be freemen if you be not perfectly
in the right and your enemies in the wrong. I think I perceive
a fixed disposition on the part of our Saxon traducers to put us to
the test. The efforts already made by them have been most
abortive and ridiculous. In the midst of peace and tranquillity
they are covering our land with troops. Yes, I speak with the
awful determination with which I commenced my address, in consequence of news received this day. There was no House of
Commons on Thursday, for the Cabinet was considering what they
should do, not for Ireland, but against her. But, gentlemen, as
long as they leave us a rag of the Constitution we will stand on
it. We will violate no law, we will assail no enemy; but you are
much mistaken if you think others will not assail you. (A voice—
We are ready to meet them.) To be sure you are. Do you think
I suppose you to be cowards or fools?"

He put the case that the Union was destructive
to England instead of Ireland, and demanded whether
Englishmen under such circumstances would not
insist on its repeal.

"What are Irishmen," he asked, "that they should be denied
an equal privilege? Have we not the ordinary courage of Englishmen? Are we to be called slaves? Are we to be trampled
under foot? Oh! they shall never trample me, at least (no, no).
I say they may trample me, but it will be my dead body they will
trample on, not the living man."

The Repeal Association, to stamp this sentiment on marble, voted a statue of O'Connell as he spoke at Mallow, with the final sentence of his declaration carved on the pedestal, in eternal memory of a great wrong adequately encountered.

These transactions excited profound interest throughout the civilized world. The United States sent back an answer to them in immense meetings held in the great cities, at which eminent senators, judges, and statesmen took part. England was warned that if she coerced Ireland, she would do so at the risk of losing Canada by American arms. Seward, afterwards Secretary of State, and John Tyler, then President of the United States, declared that the Union ought to be repealed.* One of the great meetings sent an address to France, inviting her to help a nation which had helped her on a hundred battlefields. France answered by a memorable meeting in Paris, at which deputies and journalists took part who before four years had themselves become the Provisional Government of a new republic. They offered arms and trained officers to a country resisting manifest injustice. In these transactions it became plain that France and America recognized as a spokesman of the Irish race, not only O'Connell, but the *Nation.* The writings of the paper were spoken of in their correspondence, and quoted in a hundred newspapers from New York to New Orleans, and were universally translated by the press of Paris. The attendance at the monster meetings continued to grow, till it was alleged that at Tara little short

---

* "The proceedings of the Convention at Philadelphia are most, or rather would be most glorious, if we were in a position to avail ourselves of such help. But—but—but—— No matter, the time is coming in spite of the Devil" (T. McC., to Davis).

of a million of men met to claim self-government for their country.

To his friend Maddyn, Davis wrote the most secret hopes of his heart at this time. It is characteristic that he desired to see the Federalists become a strong party; if his own aims were baffled he was ready to promote theirs.

"You in England quite overrate the likelihood of war here. We have the people as docile and exact in their obedience to us as possible. They see that discipline is the greatest element of success. Unless the Government begin the contest, either with their own troops or with an Orange mob, there will be no fight for the present. We are making more way with the upper classes than you fancy. They will not yet, at least, join the association, but many of them will join a Federalist party which is about being founded. If that Federalist party be managed by bold clear-headed men it will impose its own terms on England in two years. We Repealers hold peace and war in our hands. O'Connell could in three months have possession of Ireland, but he is adverse, wisely, humanely adverse, to fighting, save in the last extremity. He prevailed in '29 by the power of fighting, not the practice of it; may he not do so again? You will say, 'No, for England is dead against us.' What's the proof of her being so? I see little; on the contrary, I believe a portion of the intelligence and half the populace of England will aid us, if things go on peaceably, as they are going. Do you see the provincial press of England and Scotland? It is generally favourable; the Whigs, undesignedly perhaps, are serving us, and the Ministry and their Press are acting and writing so irresolutely and rashly that we can hardly fail to overcome them if we do not copy their blunders. Should sterner counsels prevail, they will come to the contest greatly weakened by what has passed, and we, some of us at least, know our duty and see our course. It may be very sad, but 'tis not very unpromising, as, were you here, I could satisfy you."

Maddyn pressed his objections on Davis with affectionate persistency, for he wrote less as a partisan of authority than a man eager that his friend might not make a mistake.

"Differences of speculation never vex me, but I feel half annoyed when any one whose powers of mind are entitled to high respect obviously miscalculates. Talking of O'Connell and his power of getting Ireland in three months, you say 'He prevailed in 1829 by the threat of fighting and not the practice of it; may he not do so again?' Answer: Never, because the questions *then* and *now* are vastly different in their intrinsic value, and, besides, are very differently regarded by the British public. Because, firstly, the Catholic question was one that had been earnestly advocated by the whole of the Whig-Radical and Dissenting parties of England; because the British public was in its favour; because, in the eye of a statesman of any calibre, from Chatham to Castlereagh, its concession could not possibly injure the Empire, but rather strengthen the authority of England; because, three or four times in 1802, 1808, 1812, 1822, and 1825, it had been almost conceded by Parliament. A civil war under such circumstances would have been criminal on the part of an English Minister. England never would have supported Wellington in 1829, when she herself was divided upon the question; but what is the case now? The British Empire is struck at; the authority of England is endangered. Repeal of the Union, if carried, will destroy the glory of England and her power along with it, and will ruin her character throughout the globe for sagacity, ability, and capacity for ruling. Give Ireland a Parliament, and England will at once cease to be a substantive power.

"You attribute much value to the press. You appeal to it as if it were in your favour. Tell me any *influential* paper that has written a line in your favour. The Metropolitan press, of all parties, is against you, and so is all the Conservative and Whig press in the rural districts. At either side of the argument the press is nothing to appeal to. It has been sinking in this country year after year in social influence; one or two of the London morning papers are barely able to carry on.

"Were the Government unprepared for a struggle? Were they not ready to repel force by force? Were they caught napping?

"Both parties know all that the Repealers have been trying to do in Ireland; and in America Lord Palmerston knew every movement of the Irish sympathizers. I rather think he had scouts there, from what I have been told. Besides, the American Democracy is nothing to count upon—a beggarly, bankrupt set of boasting vapourers that cannot pay their common trade debts, let alone the expenses of a war. Why didn't the braggarts seize

Canada if they had any ability for fighting? *That* was their time to show fight, but they *didn't*.

"The Opposition has been thrashed in France, and it never can gain power unless it abandon its unprincipled and rascally politics. Thiers is the vilest politician alive. He is a man who has no moral power whatever; and Lamartine is a mere declaiming waverer. It is not the interest of the French throne in this age, whether it be occupied by the elder or the younger branch of the Bourbons, to incur a war with England.

"As a Minister for Ireland, Peel has been a miserable failure, and the fact is confessed by all parties. *Laissez faire*, in his position, was disgraceful; he might have done wonders, but he lacks all the qualities of *high* statesmanship.

"T. B. C. Smith has been a total and, I'm afraid, hopeless failure [in Parliament]. I was anxious that he might have maintained the credit of the Irish Bar, but it is confessed that Jackson was an orator compared to him. He was coughed down on one occasion. He is miserably nervous, and is actually pitied by his opponents. On one occasion F. French was cheering and encouraging him ! P—— was Lord Chatham in comparison.

"I implore you not to entangle yourself in what is *now* a hopeless and vain endeavour. This country will fight to the last against you, and the present and late Governments have wary sentinels that watch your movements. Lord John would go on to the last in a war for the integrity of the Empire. Therefore keep out of mischief."

But to all his persuasions, Davis replied : "I shall go into the Three Hundred. Would that you were with us there ! It will be a post of danger, and of power for good or ill."

The grounds of hope, which he omitted to state to Maddyn, may be found in public correspondence which I shall presently quote.

Tait's Magazine had been for years an authentic organ of British Radicalism, and Davis sought to enlist it more actively in the Irish cause. But the Radicals were alarmed at the tone of menace which O'Connell's speeches at the monster meetings and the writings in the *Nation* had given to the Irish movement; and Mr. Tait answered, I fancy, the apprehension in his own mind rather than any suggestion made by his correspondent.

"Sir,

"My answer must be short. I write in bed, recovering from a severe illness. War would be perfect madness. Ireland would be crushed in an instant, and the justice or injustice of her cause be utterly disregarded, until the bloody doings were over. While nothing but ruin be looked for from armed resistance to Britain, everything is to be hoped for from peaceful agitation.

"Why not imitate the Anti-Corn Law League, and send missionaries to explain the grievances of Ireland and plead her cause through every part of England and Scotland? Scotland is likely to be the first to understand and feel for Irish wrongs. But any attempt at violence would be looked upon in the same light in Scotland as in England. Except as to religion, music, and to some degree, literature, Scotland has no separate nationality. The union with England is complete.

"I am, sir, your very obedient servant,

"W. Tait.*

"Thomas Davis, Esq."

* Edinburgh, May 30, 1843.

CHAPTER V.

THE RECREATIONS OF A PATRIOT. 1843.

A MAN's character is often best read in his amusements. He may pose on the platform, or in the
salon, but in holiday undress he needs must follow
the bent of his nature.

Davis's labours at the *Nation* office were free
from the slavery which journalism sometimes im-
poses. The obligation to be at a particular place at
a fixed hour daily is an excellent discipline, but it is
not compatible with such a task as he had imposed
upon himself. He worked for the newspaper with
prodigious energy, but at times and places which
suited him, reserving leisure always for other claims
of duty. He employed himself largely in friendly
conferences with men of his own generation. It
might seem that he was already busy preparing for
the task that awaited him in the near future, for he
was forming alliances, making friends, choosing
colleagues and selecting agents. At the very climax
of popular agitation in the autumn of 1843, a meeting
of the British Association was fixed to be held at
Cork, and Davis, as a native of the county, promised
to attend. He proposed at the same time to take
a holiday from work, and employ it in an extensive

tour in Munster and Connaught, which would enable him to communicate with important political allies, and probably to make new friends for the cause. He needed not merely leisure, but solitude. To be wholly alone at times, disengaged from the closest friendships and the tenderest domestic ties, is a necessity to the strong and fruitful thinker.

His correspondence during this excursion, with some help from memoranda which he made at the moment, enables us to follow him closely. During the greatest stress of work or travel he was an incessant student, and in his leisure the practice clung to him. The " Paradise Lost " and the " Transfiguration of Raphael," says Emerson, are results of a note-book ; and Davis has left behind him a bundle of note-books during his excursions or studies. Unhappily they are often quite undecipherable ; or, if legible, phrases which to him were doubtless symbols of vivid impressions yield small results to any one else. They were sometimes written in pencil, and, after nearly half a century, have faded into shadows. Where pen and ink were employed, he trusted so largely to his memory that the notes constitute a sort of *memoria technica*. He probably felt the truth of the poet Gray's memorable saying—that half a word set down at the moment is worth a cart-load of recollections. But, such as they are, they enable us to watch the student hiving with loving care the materials which gave local colour and dramatic character to national ballads, or furnished the statesman with data on which opinion was founded. He gathered traditions of historic events where they happened, studied the aspect and topography of memorable places—there are such studies of Limerick, Galway, Derry, and Drogheda, for example, with rude maps and drawings of the battle-fields. Scraps of local songs and vocabularies of Irish phrases are interrupted to set down the names of men who might be useful to the national cause or who were familiar with the local antiquities, notes on the administration of justice in the provinces, drawings of old coins, or memoranda of articles to be written by himself or others.

Speaking of another young enthusiast, Samuel Forde, the artist, Davis used language very applicable to his own case :—

"His acquisitions are numerous, and rapidly, though unconsciously, made ; unknown even to the man of genius himself, they are obscurely recorded, nor are they seen until knowledge and power so signally display themselves in his works. Then the hints and almost forgotten suggestions and impelling impulse in which they may have originated, rise remembered, and the magnificent design may be traced to the most frivolous circumstances that have undergone some beautiful expanding process in his mind."

He travelled by Kilkenny, Waterford, and Cashel, and reported in a letter to his friend Webb the official business transacted at Cork :—

"The association meeting was successful for its science both to natives and to strangers ; but because the Repealers and the educated shopkeepers of Cork sustained it, the county Conservatives declined to join it, so the number was only six hundred instead of fifteen hundred, as had been usual. However, we had a thousand at the ball.

"Old Bishop Murphy is a glorious hearty Johnsonian bookworm. He'd hardly let me out of his house. But he's a courtier ; and with all his 100,000 volumes, his book-lined mansion, and his help to Hogan, I am not yet quite sure of him.

"I have to see some things and men at Cork, and shall not leave it for four or five days. Write to me there."

In his diary we find more at large his impressions

of Dr. Murphy, the Catholic Bishop, who had collected a great library which he proposed to bequeath
to some public purpose.   His method of purchase
was duly noted, and some of his recollections of
Rome chronicled : —

"Dr. Murphy : met me, drove [with him to his] house ; some
middling pictures and prints. 100,000 vols. (catalogue in Feast-
book). 6000 this year, great in classics and illustrated books.
Buys second-hand ; gives 5 per cent. to dealers ; does not go to
auctions nor order them ; buys much in Belgium ; says that the
convents supplied the great libraries of France and Belgium. The
Bishop said—

"'I was dining with Cardinal Gonsalvi when Canova arrived
with the rescued pictures and statues from Paris. All rose. Gonsalvi embraced him and saluted him Marquis, with a pension of
5000 crowns a year. He refused. "Oh, his Holiness must not
be refused." "Well, I accept it on condition of its being given
to poor artists in Rome."' "

He heard from the Bishop and others stories of
an eminent sculptor, at that time in Dublin, having
recently returned from Rome.   John Hogan was
originally a carpenter, and by force of native genius
raised himself to be one of the greatest artists of his
generation in Europe.

"Hogan ; 2 [of his] chalk drawings at Macroom's ; they are in
a carpenter's [named Hogan] ; H. worked in Mrs. Deane's [as
a carpenter], Sir T. D——'s [Sir Thomas Deane, a local architect]
mother. After nine month's vain entreaty, Sir. T. got him for
Dr. Murphy, for Mrs. D. Murphy was then about to fit up the
chapel, had the plaster done, and the bracket and canopies and the
niches ready ; he got pictures of the apostles, etc., cut the likeness
and drapery, all boldly but loosely. He has 27 wood figures in
that sanctuary, a half-relief altar—Leonardo's 'Last Supper,' free,
clear, and noble. Carey saw the altar-piece, etc., and asked
for the carver. 'He is a carpenter.' 'Bring him hither.'
Carey took a hand and a Socrates' head to Dublin Society. They
could not, as he was not a pupil, but they gave him 25 guineas
for the head and hand, and offered £100 [to start him in an artistic
career] if Cork gave another (see their books). Hogan got £300,

gave £150 to his family, and started for Rome, with many letters
from Dr. M.; delivered none of them, but bought a block, hired
lodgings, shut himself up for six months. [A shepherd boy,
playing on his pipe, was his first success;] and then an Italian
bag-piper was there to play for Rome for ever. He was commissioned to make Dead Christ for Dr. M. He did so, and was
allowed by Dr. M. to exhibit and then sell it in Dublin. Clarendon
Street Chapel has it, but he did another in Italy. When 'twas
opened, after it came from Leghorn, the head was found unfinished.
' Why ?'   ' I wished to prevent jealous people saying I got Italian
help.   I shall do this here under their eyes.' (This fine work is
now under the high altar in the Carmelite Church, Clarendon
Street, Dublin.)   Mr. J. Murphy has bust of Dr. M. and himself
by H.   Dead Christ, large noble man in full health; drapery
round, fine, and true, but at side too heavy stone-lying; head on
right shoulder, right foot over left, elbows on ground, hands on
sides, wedged-up head, neck, flesh. A cemetery angel by him,
deep, gentle, reflective, wing exquisite." *

When he left the city for the county Cork he
picked up traditions which, when they were carefully
sifted, might furnish materials for history.   Nearly
every great estate in Munster is the result of some
great crime, and he found a notable instance :—

* One of his friends a little later sent to Davis estimates of some of the
leading politicians he had met in Cork, for his private guidance, and time has
made them as harmless as the " Annals of the Four Masters."

"Joseph Hayes, Alderman—singularly clever, equally intemperate,
thoroughly impracticable, hating everybody in general, and the Murphy
family in particular; cannot, I presume, do the entire work of this city
himself, and will not, I am convinced, work with anybody else. . . . Richard
Dowden—clever, business-like, practical, much in favour with the democratic
section, with which he has always steadily worked. Of his honesty I know
nothing, but I have no reason to doubt it. . . . George Mason—I believe
(and it is the general belief) this man to be an honest enthusiast. He is an
ultra-democrat, a universal-peace and cold-water man, considers honesty and
poverty synonymous terms, and so forth. He has a kind of ability, but
can, I think, be easily made a tool of more designing men. . . . There are
the Murphy and Lyons parties, having their origin in trading rivalry. The
influence of each is extensive; but from their great number, wealth, perfect
union amongst themselves, and the various branches of trade, in which they
have nearly a monopoly, the Murphy family has a much more extended
influence than the Lyonses. The former, too, are backed by the great body
of the clergy, from their connection with the Bishop, and have all the
doubtful and dishonest professors of liberal politics on their side, while the
only wealthy man who has steadily connected himself with Repeal is Tom
Lyons " (M. J. Barry, Blackrock, Cork, August 2nd).

" Beecher's great grandfather came here possessing nothing. Young O'Driscoll got him to take care of his house while he was abroad with his sister.   When he came back Beecher prosecuted him under the Penal Laws (as a Papist) and got his property."

" O'Leary shot for outlawry for refusing horse for £5 at Mallow, and Matthew of Thⁿ. on being asked for his 2 fiery chariot horses drove to the Archbishop's and read his recantation."

He looked at the landscape with the eye of a soldier and a poet :—

" All these Southern heads have castles and as many are peninsulas ; these castles are on the necks—thus securing some 20, or 30, or 50 acres for tillage, cattle, plunder, and stores.   There the galleys were beached, doubtless, in winter, [when they were not] plundering in more gentle seas.   All these O'Heas, O'Donovans, O'Sullivans, Burkes, O'Malleys, O'Loghlens, O'Driscolls, O'Mahoney's, etc., were doubtless pirates or sea-kings (see in Waterford Hist.).   O'Dᵐˢ alliances and invasions, Burke the marine, Grace O'Malley's galleys in 1172, privateers in 1645.   Thorpe's pamphlets and coast traditions."   [Thorpe's pamphlets are a valuable collection in the Royal Irish Academy.]

" In Tipperary and Kilkenny, grey eyes, black lashes, rich brown hair, middle or small size, oval-faced arch girls ; now dark hair, flashing black eyes, brunette, sunny cheeks, bearing graceful. Tela girl lovely horsewoman."

To Pigot he sent further details of his excursion, and a glance at Mount Melleray, the famous Trappist convent in the Waterford mountains.

" Fermoy, Aug. 26, 1843.

" I was at Cape Clear yesterday in a hooker.   I have seen much to admire, and some places worthy to live in in Cork, but the Cape is neither sublime nor beautiful beyond the common necessities of an Atlantic island.   It is crawling with people, and is not savage nor sweet enough for me.   In fact I have met nothing of the merely stern kind in Cork equal to Donegal.

" Introduce me descriptively to Hogan.   I heard much of him from Dr. Murphy, the Bishop of Cork, and I've taken a strong liking to him.

" I wish you were here to take down word and music from every second person I meet.   I'm going to dine with a very fine fellow, Father Tom Barry, and have no more time to write.

Remember me to Wallis. Is his heart so hard, or are his joints so rusty, as to look idly on now?

" I doubt if I should ever have had the energy to overcome my dislike to letter-writing but that I am waiting in a dismal book-less inn for a truant acquaintance. Since I left you I have tracked the Nore and Suir, roused the echoes of Comushenam, drunk potheen through Tipperary, and stomached science in Cork. I came here from the last place in company with a retreating squadron of the British Association under the special care of the oddest, brazenest-faced dog on earth, Cooke Taylor (Whateley's friend). We were humbugged into a meeting at Youghal, dinnered by Sir Richard Musgrave, and taken by him this morning in his steamer to Cappoquin. From thence Signor Mayer, a Florentine; Dr. Olave, the Vicar-General of Bengal; the Roman Catholic Bishop elect, of Clogher; and I drove to Mount Melleray, three of us to visit it—the Bishop 'to make his retreat.' By the way, I find that O'Connell made a retreat here some three or four years ago, and the prior assured me that so severe a retreat was unknown even in the abbey, and was considered a hard and noble example by the monks. The institution consists of a *mitred* abbot, the only one in Ireland, one prior, nine other priests, besides religious and lay brothers—in all about seventy. The priests, besides their religious duties, are as teachers in the schools, superintendents of work, etc., and they alone speak—the rest are eternally silent day and night, in and out. They are engaged in tilling their land, and in the trades necessary to their indepen-dence. They have five hundred and sixty acres on the mountain, of which over two hundred are under cultivation. They have a fine garden highly tilled, and a hot-house with vines, flowers, etc. I send you a geranium blossom of theirs. Until lately they were dependent for many things; now they raise their food (vegetables and milk and butter), grind their corn (wheat and rye), make and mend their own clothes, tools, harness, build their houses, paint and carve pictures and statues for their chapel, and are grooms, carpenters, smiths, foresters, masons, schoolmasters, and wheel-wrights. Their school is new but not bad. Fancy this abbey with its tall white spire and thriving ascetic unnatural community staring in heaven's face from the side of the great free lordly wild mountain, and you have Mount Melleray. They all wear brown gowns and hoods and brogues, save the priests, who wear white. St. Bernard was their founder, and they have a fine manuscript of the Psalms with music in his writing. I have got a most pressing invitation to go there for some time, and whenever I like. I have written you all this, knowing you would prefer it to geology."

In Tipperary, on his downward journey, he found traditions of scornful and wicked oppression which have borne bitter fruit in latter times.

" Father F—— says, ' I remember Sir John Fitz-Gerald bidding all the people in Cashel fair kneel, and they knelt, and he waved his sword over them, walking through them.'

" Pierce Meagher's ancestor was at the wake of Lloyd of Meldrun, who was his kindest friend.   Jacob of Mewbarn came to young Lloyd, afterwards, with list of Catholic conspirators.   One of them was Meagher, and the great meeting-night was the night of Lloyd's wake.   ' He was at my father's wake that night, and your informer lies,' says Lloyd.   ' Well, we'll leave *him* out and hang the rest.'   ' If you offer to touch one of them I'll denounce you all.' "

He found among the peasantry a new version of the old Gaelic ballad " Shule Aroon,'' which he sent to Pigot and afterwards gave me for the " Ballad Poetry of Ireland ; " and another song, which seems to have been new to him though it was still habitually sung in the northern counties.   Like the French chansons under the First Empire, it is the whine of contented slavery.

" From morning dawn I'd never grieve,
    To toil a hedger, ditcher,
    If that when I came home at eve,
    I might enjoy my friend and pitcher.
    Though Fortune ever shuns my door
    (I know not what 'tis can bewitch her)
    With all my heart can I be poor,
    With my sweet girl, my friend, and pitcher.''

The grandeur of the scenes he saw fed the loftiest convictions of his life :—

" That chainless wave and lovely land
    Freedom and Nationhood demand—
    Be sure, the great God never planned,
    For slumbering slaves, a home so grand,

> And, long, a brave and haughty race
> Honoured and sentinelled the place—
> Sing oh ! not even their sons' disgrace
> Can quite destroy their glory's trace."

Among the letters which followed him to the
country was one from John Pigot, offering very
sound advice, that the Repeal Association should
be prorogued during O'Connell's annual holiday at
Darrynane, instead of being subjected to the mis-
guidance of Mr. John O'Connell. But it was,
unfortunately, advice which would inevitably be
rejected at head-quarters.

"I need not say I was not at Tara ; but John O'Hagan tells
me it was a transcendent sight. I hear that if ever a million of
people assembled it was there ; at least, if measurement of the
ground could support a good guess. Oh that they knew how to
meet also in earnest ! O'Connell's reception was royal. John
O'Hagan says they literally made a road for his carriage to pass
through the crowd, dividing on each side, he, sitting on the box,
seemingly as much astonished as elated at the sight of the people.
Surely it is impossible for a man to fill such a position, even for an
hour, without an ambition beyond the petty trammels of 'constitutional' hypocrisy. It appears he goes to Darrynane before the
close of the fine season. It is very well, but why do not some of
you propose an adjournment—prorogation—of the association also ?
The rent must fluctuate and must decrease : there is nothing new
to be said ; nothing new to be done in Dublin. The Congress of
Three Hundred does not meet till November, and the association is
next to useless, at least meeting every week, and a committee
could do the business as well. . . . Another thing—I wish you
were in town to interfere about the statue of O'Connell. You are
aware Hogan is to have it, and that he is in town. I greatly fear
the Repeal Committee will embarrass him. There must be no
tampering dictation, as the Drummond Committee attempted.
Hogan must be left to himself, and, as it is to be undertaken, it
must be done at his own price. Surely this, of all, must be our
national statue of O'Connell. Let it be worthy of the country for
ever. Let it be fit as the statue of the President, some years
hence, as well as the leader of now. I spent most of Saturday
with Hogan. He is delighted at the idea. He seems quite to rise

with it. He wishes a figure at least ten feet high, and thinks it
should express all the power and grandeur of concentrated Ireland.
He desires a figure for Ireland, no more of weeping and weakness,
but of pride and command. It will be a glorious one in his hands.
No terms have yet been proposed, nor was he speaking of them;
but a friend of his told me that he was so disgusted with the
English Committee he had last to deal with (Drummond's), that
he will not now undertake anything unless all be left to himself.
Could you not write to the men of the Repeal Committee about it?
Reilly, you know, was proposer: but just imagine Tom Steele
asking to be allowed to design a pedestal! If you or some one
of sense and taste does not interfere, I predict there will be some
infernal blunder." *

Smith O'Brien's recent proceedings in Parliament
made him a man worth cultivating for public ends;
and Davis asked Webb to send him an introduction,
Webb being a near kinsman of Mrs. O'Brien.
To Webb, Davis wrote:—

"Bantry, Sept. 8, 1843.
"My DEAR ROBERT,
"Will you have the goodness to give, or get me, an
introduction to Smith O'Brien? I shall be in Limerick in a week,
or less. I want, not his hospitality, but to know his character.

"I have just arrived here after a trip by Kinsale, Bandon,
Cloughnakilty, Baltimore, Cape Clear, Skull, etc. Kinsale, I
know, is dear to your genealogical soul. Every second house in it
is in ruins. I could make nothing of its antiquities in the short
time I was there. The Cistercian abbey, built, as its own inscription tells, 1594, has no beauty left. The gaol, once a Desmond
castle, has a handsome door with well-cut vines and grapes in
stone between the upright pillars and the spring of the arch.
Ringrone Castle (De Courcy's) is on the opposite side from the
town; it is a poor ruin, and was a poor tower. Charles Fort, below
the town, is on the site of Rincooran Castle (see the *Hiberna
Pacata*). There was a pamphlet about Kinsale printed there in
1795. I had not time to look at it, but the Rev. Mr. MacNamara,
the parish priest, a most accomplished gentleman, has a copy of it.
" The Old Head is the best bit of coast in this country. I felt
a pirate as I stood on its green top, cut off by a castled ravine from

* Pigot to Davis, August 23rd.

the rest of the promontory, so 'handy' for supporting a garrison and guarding plunder. The Old Head is far better than Cape Clear. I was much pleased with Baltimore and its neighbourhood [his last and, in some respects, his best ballad was 'The Sack of Baltimore'], but the glory of the coast I have hitherto passed is Lough Hyne; it is a lagoon surrounded by the craggiest hills. On its longest bank is a pretty, small cottage and demesne; on the west corner, close to the shore, is a smaller cottage guarded and caressed by trees. In the centre is a straggling rocky isle with a ruined tower; on the north is a ravine overhung by one of the steepest mountains I know. The mountain is a heap of chequered terraces of rocks and trees, with a white cabin strung on it, like a baby at the breast. The lagoon joins the sea through a narrow, twisted, rocky gap, through which the stream actually leaps. Place yourself on the east side of this gap, with the demesne on your right, the small cottage at the opposite side of the lake, the mountain and ravine mouth north of it, the crag stretching south, and the isle before you. Write to me. Give my love to Bessie and the rest of my friends about you."

A little later he wrote to the same friend:—

" I went through the whole course of the Blackwater before finally leaving Cork city, and since then I have been through Kinsale, Bandon, Cloughnakilty, Baltimore. I went yesterday in a hooker from Baltimore to Cape Clear, and thence to Skull, and so to this town. I shall be in Tralee in four or five days. Write to me there. I am now listening to Lane taking down an English and an Irish version of a glorious song on the fight of Ceim agan Feigh, a Whiteboy battle in 1822."

He went to Kerry chiefly to confer with Maurice O'Connell, whom he believed more disposed to resolute policy than the other members of his family; and, doubtless, he was, before domestic troubles drained his life of all purpose. He loved and honoured Davis and longed to share his noble aims, but his will was a bow unbent for ever. From Tralee he wrote to Pigot:—

" Arrived here to-night. I got your notes. I am content if the things be done. I am vain enough to suppose that they will tire executing sooner than I shall in designing—thus we can all work in our own ways. I spent the night before last at Darrynane." *

Here are memoranda, probably of the same date, containing hints for work and study :—

"I feel more and more that a good novel is the greatest of works, the natural combination of all objects and natures, whereas other things are selections from feelings or subjects, and admit of a magnifying with consistency, as in Shakespeare ; but it, perhaps, would be impossible to write consistent a superhuman novel from the multitude of objects . . .

"Colonel Shaw's 'Portugal' contains valuable hints on working drill, military economy, outpost duty, and the rationale of discipline, etc. *The Soldier's Friend*—once a month, price sixpence, eighteen quarto pages, of three columns each ; eight columns to the state of the army, English and foreign, the advocacy of soldiers' promotion, anti-flogging; and the remainder to a military treatise.

"The late owner of Castle R——, to preserve it, contracted with a mason to build a wall round it. He did so with the stones of the castle itself !

"Mr. Hunter states that, in the schools on his own and Mr. Maxwell's property, the Irish blood is first in the class, as all his female connections inform him."

At Limerick he met the gifted brother of Gerald Griffin, author of "The Collegians," a novel which has since rivalled the circulation of "Guy Mannering" and "Tom Jones," and he gathered some facts about that unhappy man of genius :—

"Griffin was sensitive, not strong. Tall and fair, and kindly as a girl. He entered London plump and fresh, in six weeks was starved and sallow. Avoided help. J. B. [John Banim] loved and tried to help him [but he would not be helped]. J. B. sent Mrs. Banim to see him. Griffin, in coming downstairs, had to hold his coat or dressing-gown behind, for 'twas in rags. No love disappointment. His passions deadened from grief."

Davis sketched the Treaty Stone—on which the surrender of Limerick was signed, on conditions which were infamously violated.

* Davis to Pigot, Sept. 17th.

The Treaty-stone was a pillion-stone that stood out at a public-house on the Dublin road, near Ginkle's quarters. [A pillion-stone is a stone which enables women to mount on the pillion behind a horseman.]

It was in memory of this visit, doubtless, that his friend Denny Lane, at a later period, bantered him on the impression he had left on the beautiful city:—

"How I laughed this week at the opinion the people of Cork formed of you! 'Oh, this Mr. Davis, what a modest young man he must be! He writes prose and poetry so well, and he draws up reports admirably, and yet he is too retiring to speak even about his own report at the association.' Oh, Thomas! Thomas! I felt the cordial influence of a glorious laugh cheering and warming me inwardly, for I was obliged to wait until I got to secret places to guffaw, at the credulity of the people of Cork who thought Thomas Davis a modest man,—the man who sels to at every art and science with a perfect certainty of beating any one—who makes bold attempts to surpass Grattan, Courier, and Carlyle in their respective styles,—who's as ready to deliver his opinion on a theory of refraction or the metaphysics of Fichte, as on a sonata, a painting, or a lobster salad,—and who utters all his judgment with an *ex cathedra* air that tempts his best friends to throw him out of the window! Talk of Tom MacNevin, why he is no more able to hold a candle to Tom Davis, than Davis himself is to—draw a declaration on a bill of exchange!" *

* Before he started on the southern journey, Maddyn, who knew that he had a student's carelessness of appearance, wrote to him:—

"As you may be meditating what clothes to carry with you, recollect that Cork is a very dressy place, and that *Sartor Resartus* ought to be much meditated by them. Therefore carry your, etc. . . . Never take off your gloves while in Cork, and affect for the time a pretty strut, and you will be sure to fascinate."

Davis replied: "Lane will, I know, do all he can to show me what's to be seen. He and I get very intimate. He is a fine fellow, but hardly selfish enough for great success, unless as an apostle.

"As to Cork being 'dressy,' *hæret in cortice*, but let it do as it likes. I'll do as I like and dress as I like, and let it like me or not as it likes, and be damned to it. I fear no one, and I hope I shall court no one for vanity, applause, or anything but a great end. You need not fear a rebellion. The rents will be refused, and the consumption of excisable articles stopped if necessary. So the people think, and, I fear, intend. My projects begin where they end."

His correspondence with me during this journey was naturally on the political business transacted in Dublin.

The young men saw great possibilities in the project of a Council of Three Hundred, and immediately looked out for constituencies. Davis asked me to find him one, preferably in the North.

"I am slow to write directly on the Three Hundred," he said. "If the people were more educated I would rather postpone it for a year; but they would grow lawless and sceptical, so I fear this cannot be done. If O'Connell would pre-arrange, or allow others to pre-arrange, a 'decided' policy, I would look confidently to the Three Hundred as bringing matters to an issue in the best way. As it is, we must try and hit on some medium. We must not postpone it till Parliament meets, for the Three Hundred will not be a sufficiently free and brilliant thing to shine down St. Stephen's and defy its coercion. Yet we must not push it too quickly, as the country, so far as I can see, is not braced up to any emergency. Ours is a tremendous responsibility, politically and personally, and we must see where we are going."

On the 29th of August, he wrote a characteristic note from Cork :—

"Enclosed is an article against hanging. I was present at a capital trial in Kilkenny, and was horrified by the witness system. The government of this country is damnable. Pray do not at any inconvenience omit the article from the next *Nation*. I am seriously anxious on the subject. If you see Haughton [James Haughton, a notable philanthropist] tell him not to neglect the memorial I sent him. . . . I came here this evening, and shall not go to Killarney for a few days. Perhaps I may send you something else, as I feel scribbleways. Here the people are British Associationized and cold, but Lane and many others have begun to work. A meeting was held here last night. Lane and Barry's speeches were, I am told, good. I send you two verses of Barry's. Perhaps if he goes on you ought to do with him as with O——. I do not know where he lives, but any letter enclosed to Denny Lane, 4, Sydney Place, will reach him. Query, Should you get him to write something humorous? I am not neglecting the Three Hundred [the proposed Council of Three Hundred]. 'Grattan's

Memoirs' by his son, Hardy's 'Life of Charlemont,' *Walker's Magazine* (of which there is a copy in the Association Library) contain materials on Dungannon. Notice the Catholic Committee of 1792, Wyse, Tone, Grattan, etc. Tone says 'twas one of the noblest assemblies he ever saw. Copy the passage. You ought to print the Census sheet I left you, at once, correcting it by the large volume of the Census which you should buy and notice, or send to me to notice, and by Captain Larcom's paper read here. By the way, the Repealers had the whole association here. Who wrote the 'Ways and Means?' * 'Twas excellent. Write to me soon. . . . You seem to have a turn for genealogy. I wish you knew my eldest brother, who has the most extraordinary gifts in that way I ever met. There is no family in Munster but he knows the pedigree of; but, alas, he is an English-minded man."

He wrote again from Tralee on the 17th September :—

"On my arrival here to-night I found a note from [John] Reilly, saying that I would have no difficulty in getting chosen either for the city or county of Dublin, and that O'Connell would do anything for me. Will you speak to John O'Connell on the subject, and write to me immediately after?

"You can fancy reasons why it would be desirable to have me, and, perhaps, two or three more, including Maurice O'Connell (whom I saw ere yesterday), out of the Assembly and out of the power of our foes, under certain circumstances. Still, I think it possible to secure both advantages (if my efforts in either way can be of use). The *Nation* of yesterday is very good and varied. I did not see that of the 9th."

I replied :—

"I have secured your return (and your £100) for county Down. Mr. Doran [Rev. John Doran, P.P., Loughbrickland] undertakes to manage it all without further flapping. I did not consult John O'Connell, for reasons that I will tell you when you return; but if you prefer Dublin, and can secure it, you are not bound to Down—it only waits your convenience. I am glad you intend to do an anniversary article. Do not forget the influence of our songs, and popular projects, or the foreign notice the national question obtained through the *Nation*, or the universal adoption of its tone by the provincial press. I meditate a song upon the same happy occasion.

* See "Voice of the Nation," p. 35.

" Your report was confirmed—the way the crow killed the hare—by chance. John O'Connell read it to the Committee, or rather *in* the Committee, for not a soul seemed to be listening, as the great man was telling a story about Watty Cox. When the story and the report were finished, I said that I would be happy to move the adoption of the latter, if I could hope that anybody knew what it was about ; whereupon O'Connell, who has the most extraordinary faculty of knowing what is going on without apparently attending to it, said he quite agreed with me in approving of it, and would second the motion. The work was then, of course, done, and I announced the general fact, assuming that you would go into detail thereafter." *

This was Davis's rejoinder :—

" I have thought much of the place for which I should go into the Convention, and think, after all, that Down would be a proper place for me to represent. I cannot reconcile the two things—a Protestant constituency and a large available population. Tell them that as I am one not likely to shrink should the duty imposed on me be dangerous, so I should look for real confidence and manly backing whatever turn affairs take. I shall not work for praise or popularity. I want our cause to succeed, and shall in pursuit of success shrink from nothing but dishonour. I am not, nor shall I try to be, an orator. I would, if possible to my limited powers, be a politician. If your friends think such a man fit for their purposes, I shall do their work as cautiously, firmly, and honestly as I can. I want them to understand me. In such a struggle as ours mistakes in character are terrible things. We can succeed if we earn success."

He had now reached the west, and wrote from Galway on September 30th :—

" Many thanks for your kindness about Down ; but I am unwilling to be tied to any place till I see how things run, which I cannot satisfactorily do till I get to Dublin, which I fear will not be till the 14th, as I have been stopped here by wet weather.

" I send you an anniversary article, written very calmly. I was desirous really to say what we had done, and wanted to do so without bragging. From this and its length (which I thought unavoidable in a useful article on such a subject) you will probably

* September 27, 1843.

dislike it. If so, to the fire with it, without ceremony. If I think of anything else I shall scribble it. Good night." *

About the same time, he wrote :—

"MacN——'s article [in the *Nation*] on the Whigs has given great offence in many quarters. I think, to say truth, it said too much, and looked like a cruel attack, when the Irish Whigs at least were doing nobly in the House. Take some opportunity to distinguish that you did not mean them (S. O'Brien and the like) in attacking the Whigs, and do not notice anything in the London Press on it. I speak advisedly. We have need of tolerants as well as allies for a while."

Before turning to the west, he wrote to Maddyn :—

"What do the Britishers mean to do with our Three Hundred? What do the longheads think of it? What do *you* think of it? I am offered various places in it. Ought I to go in? I think 'yes,' from policy and conscience. Pray write to me at length, and very soon."

Maddyn strongly dissuaded him from entering the Council.

"The Government," he wrote, "will never permit it to assemble. They will put it down, and challenge the country to resist, and all reasonable men of the Whigs, Conservatives, and Moderates will approve of the Government resolution. By the 1st of March, 1844, it will be seen that no man will have lost more reputation than O'Connell, and no man gained more than Peel. I would strongly advise you not to fetter yourself more than you are at present. Do not shackle yourself by assuming responsibilities, while you will not be allowed to retain your own right of decision. . . . As to policy, what influence or permanent power would you acquire by becoming a leading member in a council which will never dare to do anything great? What more could you do for your ideal Ireland than you can now achieve? It is pretty plain that you must have either a pen or a pike in your hand, and is the council the place for you to work with such

---

* He wrote to John O'Connell to make sure that he was not outrunning the wishes of the leader, and had a satisfactory reply. "As to your sitting in the Three Hundred, my father said he would not wish to have it without you. I should think we would easily get you a seat for a northern district, where men will be wanting, but not money. To have a non-Catholic would also be a good thing there."

implements?* . . . . All parties here are ready unsparingly to employ force, if you will persist in your resolution to plunge into a bloody civil war. The Irish think Peel is cowed because he holds back and does not obey the counsels of the ultra Tories. 'Twas so with Pitt in 1790, and subsequently. He did not go to war until he saw that it was absolutely necessary; and the moment he gave the word he regained his popularity with the governing public of England. Depend upon it that O'Connell will be defeated in this business. The moment that blood begins to be shed O'Connell's prestige vanishes. 'Ethereal Revolution' and moral agitation will vanish. Like the Revolution of 1688, O'Connell's reputation is lauded as 'glorious' because it is largely historical and completely bloodless, but his renown will be destroyed when he forgets his caution, and confounds the enthusiasm of applauding multitudes with the steadiness of an army, or a swaggering orator with a Napoleon or Cromwell."

During this autumn Sir Charles Trevelyan, a Treasury official, who had seen service in India, and, as brother-in-law of Macaulay, had the ear of the Government, visited Ireland to report on the state of public feeling. He disbelieved in O'Connell's sincerity, but he found the bulk of the people determined Nationalists, eager to fight when called upon by their leader, and the Catholic clergy he believed were in complete sympathy with them. But he added :—

"There is another estate in the Repeal organization, of the existence of which the people of England are imperfectly instructed—the young men of the capital. As far as the difference in the circumstances of the two countries admitted, they answered to the 'jeunes gens de Paris.' They were public-spirited enthusiastic men, possessed, as it seemed to him, of that crude information on political subjects which induced several of the Whig and Conservative leaders to be Radicals in their youth. They supplied all the good writing, the history, the poetry, and the political philosophy, such as it was, of the party."

His judgment of O'Connell seemed at the time shamefully unjust. But the private correspondence of O'Connell has since been published, and we find

* London, September 27th.

that, after the muster of the nation at Tara, when
the soul of the people was on fire for self-government,
he addressed a letter to Lord Campbell, the party
gladiator who held for a few weeks the office from
which Lord Plunket had been driven, recommending
measures for conciliating Ireland by concessions, and
restoring the Whigs to office.

" Why does not Lord John [Russell] treat us to a magniloquent
[? magnificent] epistle declaratory of his determination to abate
the Church nuisance in Ireland, to augment our popular franchise,
to vivify our new Corporations, to mitigate the statute law as
between landlord and tenant, to strike off a few more rotten
boroughs in England, and to give the representatives to our great
counties? In short, why does he not prove himself a high-minded,
high-gifted statesman, capable of leading his friends into all the
advantages to be derived from conciliating the Irish nation, and
strengthening the British Empire? " *

A better insight into the purpose and hopes of the
young men than Sir Charles Trevelyan had attained,
will be found in a letter which Davis addressed to
the Duke of Wellington, under the signature of a
Federalist, debating the pros and cons of coercion
and concession :—

" This is not the place to examine whether a country with two
thousand miles of coast can be blockaded—whether a territory of
thirty-two thousand square miles can be occupied by a man a mile
—whether the science of cities would not furnish important supplies to the strong hands of the peasants—whether a country so
uneven in surface, so cut up by clay ditches, and cabins, and
villages, and little ravines, and inhabited by so many field-
workers, could be traversed by squadron or field battery,—for
these questions I must refer others to Keatinge, Cockburne, Roche
Fermoy, the maps, and to the fore-mentioned lists of books. I beg
your Grace's pardon—I refer them to a higher authority on the
military resources of Ireland and on the doctrines of war than
any one living or dead—to the Duke of Wellington."

* Letter to Lord Campbell, Sept. 9, 1843.

He goes on to tell the Duke the state of opinion among the educated classes, the great factor in all political changes; but paints, it must be confessed, rather his hopes than his experience.

"I heard hints of a diplomacy embracing rich and angry spirits, and extending to more than one state. I heard of a system of retaliation, severe, just, and systematic enough to insure for Irish insurgents what it won for Washington and the American rebels —all the rights of war. The sober organization and the manageable fury of the people were dwelt upon. I heard of field works, and plans for subdividing a mob in a few hours. I heard of an ingenious and formidable commissariat, of American steamers, of Colonial and Chartist insurrections, of friendly foes and leading genius. Most of the Conservatives, and many of the Whigs said that an insurrection would occur, and would be suppressed, unless France interfered, either by going to war at once, or by winking at private expeditions, such as went to Greece and Spain. But the rich men among them seem to dread a defeated as much as a successful insurrection. The break-up of trade, the terrible shock to English reputation, and the enormous expenditure which an insurrection would occasion, were not the only grounds of their fear.

" Your lordship will readily understand the connection between the land tenures here, and insurgent hopes. The landlords believe that the first act of an insurgent general would be to proclaim the abolition of rents, and to bid the people 'take the land, and fight hard to keep it.' Such an appeal they speak of with terror. They believe that the thoughtful and adventurous yeomen of Leinster would adhere to a cause so advocated. They think that the Presbyterians, discontented at the tenancies-at-will, to which, in spite of the rules of the Ulster settlement, and of common creed and common right, their tenures are limited, would rise to a man. They fear that the trampled serfs of Connaught would learn hope by vengeance, and courage by example; and they know that the chivalrous peasantry of the South would sweep all before them till some great army was brought on their front, if even that would check their course.

" Nor did the Leinster and Munster gentlemen seem sure that the Irish soldiers or police could be got to shoot or sabre their countrymen. 'Times are changed,' said a Whig friend to me, with a sigh—' Times are changed—the people will never provoke the soldiery when under the influence of drink; they are a sober

and a dangerous race, sir.' And then he added a story about
Sir Parker Carroll. You knew him, and so did I, my lord. He
was a fearless man, and one familiar with Ireland. Happening to
be in a club-room in London when some young lord declared that,
for his part, if he had the management of Tipperary, he'd march
an army in at one end of it, and hang every man till he came out
at the other, ' My lord,' said Carroll, ' that plan was tried in
a Spanish province by the French, and before they were half
through the province the people were hanging them. The same
thing would happen in Tipperary to your lordship's executioners.
The rising of an entire people,' he added, ' rarely takes place, and
rarely fails.' This last was the opinion of another of your countrymen, who seems much respected here. In 1803 Robert Emmet
asked John Keogh, ' Ought I to go on if ten counties rise ?' ' Ay,'
said Keogh, ' if five counties rose, and you would succeed.' . . .

" One thing I am sure your Grace will admit, that the power
of coercion depends as much on the sort of men who suffer as on
those who inflict it. If the sword of the despot strike a coward, he
falls or flies. But beware, my lord—beware of striking some hard
and devoted man with your battle-axe over such a combustible as
Ireland. You remember your brother's saying, ' Ireland is quiet
—quiet as gunpowder.' "

In another letter, signed " A Protestant," he specified the resources of the country for a contest more
deliberately :—

"Ireland is strong enough for absolute independence. It has a
wider and deeper fortification (the sea) round it than any other
European State, and a larger population and revenue than any of
the twenty-one independent States on the Continent. These are
the raw materials of independence.

" Prussia, with about one-third more population and revenue
than we have, surrounded by the hungry eagles of Austria and
Russia, and scattered like a fallen angel hither and thither in
Europe, holds her ground. She finds it possible to maintain
122,000 troops of the line and 408,000 militia men.

" Starting under Frederic with 2,500,000 people she has grown
to be the fifth power in Europe. She became so by avoiding no
contest—she, and her chief, never grew pale at the din of war nor
shrunk from the responsibility of independence. She used her
opportunities, nursed her strength, never sacrificed her allies to
passion or pedantry, struck in the right time, and struck home.

"She is independent and powerful; Austria dreads, and Russia courts her.

"Would we want 122,000 men if Prussia needs but that number? Would not 60,000 be more effective in this entrenched and hill-ramparted isle than 150,000 on the unditched flats of Prussia? Cavalry is a joke in Ireland, and artillery could not act here for a month in winter time. And why could we not maintain a militia of 300,000 trained men when Prussia has 408,000? If England so blunders her army that it would exhaust us to imitate her, why could we not imitate Prussia, which, as M'Culloch says, had to organize an army ' so that it might embrace the maximum of force with the minimum of expense,' and 'solved the problem.' We require less force in proportion to our resources. Why could not we 'solve the problem' too? Are we dolts and dastards, and are these Prussians demigods?

"What I say of the army applies to all the other departments. Prussia is able to maintain a most efficient civil government, to attend to her complicated affairs from the Rhine to the Vistula, to keep ambassadors at every court, and to educate every child of her fourteen millions of people, and all with her eight and a half millions a year.

"Nor is the analogy limited to Prussia.

"Twenty-one states, inferior to Ireland in population, revenue, and military position, pay their military and civil expenses, and the interest upon their debts.

"Why could not Ireland do as well in proportion as Prussia does, with her army and her church, and schools, and poor? Why could not Ireland do better than any of these twenty-one inferior states? Why could it not maintain as large an army as Naples? Why not support double the expenses and possess double the power, as it has more than double the revenue and men of Bavaria or Portugal? Why not have more ships than Holland, the swampy den of three millions? Where has God written down our inferiority?

"'Tis an idle and imbecile thing to allege the cost of independence, or the difficulty of it, as reasons against separation, or Repeal, or Federalism, or any other phase of nationality."

During Davis's tour in Munster the political work of the Association, and the educational work of his colleagues went on vigorously. At Mullaghmast the Nationalists of Leinster assembled in immense numbers. The trades and citizens of Dublin met at Donnybrook, fed on memories of what great cities —Athens and Rome, Bruges and Ghent, had done for liberty; and the population of the Metropolitan County was summoned to assemble at Clontarf, a memorable battle-field. But a trivial incident arrested the tide of success. The vast troops of horsemen who attended the monster meetings were named Repeal Cavalry in some provincial newspapers; and an indiscreet secretary of the Clontarf meeting, in issuing the programme of proceedings, assigned a place to the "Repeal Cavalry." This political blunder was promptly corrected by order of O'Connell; but the Government, who understood perfectly well that it was the folly of a subordinate,* seized on the incident as a pretence for suppressing the meeting. A proclamation was issued forbidding it to assemble, and warning all loyal and peaceful persons from attending.

It is useless to debate in this place what O'Connell ought to have done to maintain the right of public meeting, or what he might have been expected to do after the specific language of the Mallow defiance. What he did was to protest against the illegality of the proclamation, and submit actively and passively to its orders. He was the leader, alone

---

* " When we were assembled in the drawing-room before dinner, the Duke [of Wellington] entered, with the proclamation issued at Dublin Castle, to repress the Repeal meeting at Clontarf on the 18th inst., which he had just received from town by express. . . . I could see that he was much pleased with this exercise of authority, and that he thought the Government had been dilatory in not adopting these strong measures at an earlier period. He said—' We must now show them we were really in earnest; they give us now a fair pretext to put them down, as their late placard invites the mob to assemble in military order, and their horsemen to form in troops. This order probably was not written by O'Connell himself, but by some eager zealot of his party, who has thus brought the affair to a crisis. Our proclamation is well drawn up, and avails itself of the unguarded opening which O'Connell has given us to set him at defiance ' " (" Raikes's Diary ").

commissioned to act with decisive authority, and he
warned the people from appearing at the appointed
place. By assiduous exertions of the local clergy
and Repeal wardens they were kept away, and a col-
lision with the troops avoided. But such a termination of a movement so menacing and defiant was a
decisive victory for the Government; they promptly
improved the occasion by announcing in the *Evening
Mail* their intention to arrest O'Connell and a batch
of his associates on a charge of conspiring to " excite
ill will among her Majesty's subjects, to weaken
their confidence in the administration of justice, and
to obtain by unlawful methods a change in the constitution and government of the country, and for that
purpose to excite disaffection among her Majesty's
troops."

Next day, Saturday, the 14th of October, O'Connell, his son John, T. M. Ray, Secretary of the Association; three journalists of the national party, John
Gray, Charles Gavan Duffy, and Richard Barrett;
and two country priests, Fathers Tyrell and Tierney,
were arrested, but admitted to bail to take their trial
for the imputed offence.

In the same number of the *Nation* which announced
the Clontarf proclamation, there was a poem from
Davis exhorting the sculptor to make the intended
statue of O'Connell a likeness in which the history
of his country and the epic spirit of resistance, never
quelled in the Irish race, might be read as in a book.

> " On his broad brow let there be
> A type of Ireland's history;
> Pious, generous, deep, and warm,
> Strong and changeful as a storm ;
> Let whole centuries of wrong
> Upon his recollection throng—

Strongbow's force, and Henry's wile,
Tudor's wrath, and Stuart's guile,
And iron Strafford's tiger jaws,
And brutal Brunswick's penal laws;
Not forgetting Saxon faith,
Not forgetting Norman scath,
Not forgetting William's word,
Not forgetting Cromwell's sword.
Let the Union's fetter vile—
The shame and ruin of our isle—
Let the blood of 'Ninety-Eight
And our present blighting fate—
Let the poor mechanic's lot,
And the peasant's ruined cot,
Plundered wealth and glory flown,
Ancient honours overthrown—
Let trampled altar, rifled urn,
Knit his look to purpose stern."

But the likeness of the chief must recall Ireland's victories as well as her reverses.

" Let the memory of old days
Shine through the statesman's anxious face—
Dathi's power, and Brian's fame,
And headlong Sarsfield's sword of flame;

" And the spirit of Red Hugh,
And the pride of 'Eighty-Two,
And the victories he won,
And the hope that leads him on!

" Let whole armies seem to fly
From his threatening hand and eye;
Be the strength of all the land
Like a falchion in his hand,
And be his gesture sternly grand."

Above all, it must picture the Mallow defiance, when he was " content to die but never yield."

" Fancy such a soul as his,
In a moment such as this,
Like cataract, or foaming tide,
Or army charging in its pride.

> Thus he spoke, and thus he stood,
> Proffering in our cause his blood,
> Thus his country loves him best—
> To image this is your behest.
> Chisel thus, and thus alone,
> If to man you'd change the stone."

When the news of the proclamation reached him at Galway, he saw that the supreme crisis of the cause had arrived. He knew that O'Connell was pledged to resist any violation of the right of public meeting till the aggressor passed over his dead body, and he was persuaded that the people at the slightest sign would fly to his assistance. He started straightway for Castlebar to consult John Dillon on ulterior measures, and, as he had papers at Bagot Street which might compromise others, he sent instructions to his mother to burn them. But, when the arrests provoked no resistance, he hurried back to Dublin. When he met his friends we found him painfully discomposed by the retreat before the proclamation. The gathering confidence of the people in their own strength, their reliance on the promises of their leader, as well as the new desire which Davis had done so much to plant, that their acts might adequately correspond with their words, were all dissipated. After such an anti-climax it was impossible to believe that a conflict with England, in which the whole nation would be arrayed under the green banner, would take place during the lifetime of O'Connell.

It is needless to detail how disastrously our dreams were scattered,—

> " How toppled down the piles of hope we reared."

It was a time of despondency and misery, of rage, and almost of despair. Davis's first emotion was expressed in mingled wrath and scorn :—

" We must not fail, we must not fail, however fraud or force assail ;
   By honour, pride, and policy, by Heaven itself!—we must be
     free.

" We called the ends of earth to view the gallant deeds we swore
     to do ;
   They knew us wronged, they knew us brave, and, all we asked,
     they freely gave.

" We promised loud, and boasted high, ' to break our country's
     chains, or die ; '
   And, should we quail, that country's name will be the syno-
     nym of shame.

" Earth is not deep enough to hide the coward slave who shrinks
     aside ;
   Hell is not hot enough to scathe the ruffian wretch who breaks
     his faith.

" But—calm, my soul !—we promised true her destined work our
     land shall do ;
   Thought, courage, patience will prevail ! we shall not fail—we
     shall not fail ! "

Up to this time Davis's policy might be expressed
in the simplest formula.   He desired that the passion
and purpose of the people should be raised to the
scale of 1782, when England would again yield to the
will of a united nation, or, if she would not yield,
that the Repealers should do what the Volunteers
would assuredly have done, fight for the liberty denied
to them.   When these hopes disappeared, his first
thought was to quit the Repeal Association for ever,
and serve Ireland in some other field.   A great
purpose is like a great river, dammed at one point it
forces its way by some other towards its unchanging
goal.   It was only a question of where he might
most usefully and honourably devote his life.

After repeated conferences, we resolved to accept
the situation, and turn it to account in preparing for

the future. Nothing could be done now, everything
might and must be done hereafter. From that time
the energy of the young men was employed in projects of education and discipline. Between the arrest
of O'Connell and the era of the famine and the French
Revolution, the *Nation* swarmed with projects fostering a lofty but not impracticable nationality. The
fruition of our hopes was admitted to be distant,
but it might be made more sure and more precious
by a wise use of the interval.*

The O'Connell trial can only be glanced at in a
memoir of Thomas Davis. It proved a signal con-
summation of the system of misgovernment on which
he made war, and rendered its hidden iniquity intelligible to Europe and America. The Catholic
chief of a Catholic nation was tried in a Catholic
city before four judges and twelve special jurors
among whom there was not a single Catholic. But
among the four Irish judges there was an Englishman, and among the twelve Irish jurors there was
another of the same race and opinions.

The trial lasted five and twenty days, and at
every stage was marked by the infringement of the
settled law or established practice governing trials
of this nature. At the close the Chief Justice charged
for a conviction with what proved to be illegal violence; and a jury of partisans, as carefully selected
as the juries which tried the State prisoners of the
Stuarts, found a prompt verdict against all the traversers of whom one had only attended a single

---

* One of the poets of the era illustrated in a striking image the change
that in good time would be sure to come.

"Our hope, like some revolving light, but turns its darker side,
And soon will shine our beacon light as quenchless o'er the tide"
(De Jean Frazer).

meeting of the Association and been a member barely
five days.

The prosecution brought a great accession of
funds and a large body of recruits to the Repeal
party. The most notable recruit was William Smith
O'Brien. He was younger son of a house famous
in Irish annals, since more than a century before the
English invasion. He was a man of good estate,
long discipline in Parliament and public life, of active
intellect, but, above all, of universally acknowledged
probity and disinterestedness. He was received with
enthusiasm, and immediately became by common
consent the second man in the movement.

Between the verdict and the sentence, O'Connell
was urged by Whig friends to visit England, and
promised a significant ovation. He might help
them to overturn Peel, and if this could be done
promptly, he would never be called up for judgment.
At worst his reception in England would remind
Peel what sort of prisoner he had to deal with.
But the most serious of the national party greatly
dreaded the experiment. O'Connell, as they knew,
stood between two dangers. He was strongly
possessed with the apprehension that Peel would
improve his victory by a Coercion Act, enabling
him to suppress the Association and forbid public
meetings. And he was surrounded by Whigs of
the official class, wooing him back to the bosom
of that party. Immediately after the verdict he
went the length of proposing in committee to dissolve the Repeal Association; and this disaster was
only averted by the young men declaring that they
could not follow him into a new association if the
existing one was sacrificed to a panic. O'Connell

was made to realize, almost for the first time, that a
new class had grown up about him, who were his
faithful and zealous allies, but would never be his
servitors or henchmen.

Davis wrote to Smith O'Brien, who was in the
country, warning him of the danger, but suggesting
that a visit to England by O'Connell was a smaller
peril than a series of meetings at home, which was
the necessary alternative.

"If O'Connell were firmer," he said, "I would say he ought
not to go to England; but fancy his speeches at ten meetings here
with the State trial terror on him! I fear we must keep him out
of that danger by an English trip till Parliament meets, and then
all will be well."

O'Connell went to England, and was rapturously
welcomed to Parliament by the Whig opposition;
went to an Anti-Corn Law League meeting at Covent
Garden Theatre, and was the hero of the occasion;
was invited to public meetings in various large towns
in the north, and to a public dinner in London.
But what his English sympathizers claimed on his
behalf was such justice to Ireland as would supersede
Repeal. The official organ of the Whig party
invited him to abandon an unattainable end, and
trust to Lord John Russell to do to Ireland the complete justice which he meditated. O'Connell's
language before his English audience was not
reassuring; and he alone of all men could sacrifice
the national cause. He could no longer induce the
people to retreat openly as in 1834, but he might
render success impossible during his lifetime. Davis
was deeply pained and alarmed. He wrote a letter
to John O'Connell, intended as usual for his father's
eyes, and his grief and fear pierce through its
courteous and moderated phrases.

"61, Bagot Street, March 8, 1841.

"MY DEAR O'CONNELL,

"I meant to have called on you, but, being unable to do so, I must write instead. I for one recommended your father to go to London on Sheil's and Pigot's repeated assurances, that he was not to be asked to recede, but, on the contrary, would be urged to take a peculiarly bold and Irish course, and to return immediately after the Debate. The reverse of all this has happened. His speech on the Debate was able and dignified, though surely not very strong. No Repealer, however, could complain of it. But I am certain that his present course is not politic. He roused Ireland by staying at home—is he not letting her spirit sink by going abroad? While he was holding monster meetings, he breathed the most fiery and jealous nationality. He now prizes the cheers, the rights, and the feelings of the British, as much or more than the Irish. Repeal and Federalism all go on the doctrine of leaving England to settle her internal affairs, and Ireland her own internal affairs exclusively. And he expressly avowed, and publicly and repeatedly preached, that we would neither depend on the aid nor meddle with the business of England. He is now interfering with it in all important matters, he calls Ireland and her representatives to interfere, he attends Anti-Corn Law meetings, he has brought in a Bill in the Commons, and *seems* to rely on English sympathy for redress. Now, I do not complain of this (though if Mr. Sheil or Mr. Pigot [D. R. Pigot, afterwards Chief Baron] are parties to the course I would have reason to complain of them), but I question the policy of it. I see that he has not got one sympathizer more than he had a year ago. These men are powerless to achieve their own end. The [Anti-Corn Law] League may use your father's name and oratory, and seek in exchange to keep him from prison, but it will not help Repeal. I know this. Mr. Sturge is very amiable, but he has little ability and less influence.

"The late and coming meetings and speeches are contradictory to the whole policy of the past Repeal agitation, and equally opposed to what that agitation must be if vigorously resumed. They therefore shake the Irish people now, and will embarrass them hereafter; for, believe me, John O'Connell, every single inconsistency injures the character and weakens the power of a statesman. If all this be true, the only effect of this English movement will be to check and embarrass Repeal. I do not, and cannot suppose that your father ever dreamt of abandoning Repeal to escape a prison, yet that is implied in all the Whig articles. If he had such a purpose, this partial conciliation of Leaguers and demi-Chartists would not accomplish it. Peel, not Sturge, wields the judgment. Nothing but a dissolution of the association would, we are directly told, prevent the sentence. To dissolve the association would be to abdicate his power, and ruin his country. He is incapable of it; you of whose fidelity to Ireland no one feels a shadow of doubt, you, would be no party to it; 'tis not thought of, and so I gladly pass from this insulting suggestion of the Whigs.

"Then, why should your father embarrass his future Repeal policy by a sojourn in England, and still more by identifying us with the English as if he were (still) a Precursor and sought to cement the Union, not dissolve it? Why for a momentary and delusive gain, why for the 'hurrays' and 'Never, never' of London or Birmingham which are powerless to prevent his imprisonment, why cloud the future? In six months or twelve he will be obliged to throw all this overboard with much loss of time, labour, and strength. Ireland is not what she was a month ago. If this continues we shall have neither a Repeal agitation nor a Liberal Government, whereas a vigorous pursuit of Repeal now would retain the one and give the only chance of the other.

"I am anxious to avoid this subject in public; I entirely rely on your personal kindliness and your devotion to our country; I want to see if we cannot pull more surely together; and I am

"Most truly yours,
"Thomas Davis."

The private correspondence of Davis was rarely more extensive and varied than at this period. He wrote to Maddyn in the interest of a poet whom we all cherished.

"I think you were a reader of the *University Magazine*. If so, you must have noticed the 'Anthologia Germanica,' 'Leaflets from the German Oak,' 'Oriental Nights,' and other translations, and apparent translations of Clarence Mangan. He has some small salary in the College Library, and has to support himself and his brother. His health is wretched. Charles Duffy is most anxious to have the papers I have described printed in London, for which they are better suited than for Dublin. Now, you will greatly oblige me by asking Newby if he will publish them, giving Mangan £50 for the edition. If he refuse, you can say that Charles Duffy will repay him half the £50 should the work be a failure. Should he still declare against it, pray let me know soon

what would be the best way of getting some payment and publication for Mangan's papers. Many of the ballads are Mangan's own,
and are first-rate. Were they on Irish subjects he would be paid
for them here. They ought to succeed in London nigh as well as
the 'Prout Papers.'"

Maddyn doubtless did his best, but he did not
succeed, and the greatest poet of his generation lived
and died unknown to London publishers. After a
little, Davis renewed the subject :—

"The care you took about Mangan was very kind. He, poor
fellow, is so nervous, that it is hard to get him to do anything
business-like; but he is too good and too able to be allowed to go
wrong. But I want to inflict another labour on you. Chapman
and Hall tell James Duffy that their arrangement with him does
not include political poems, so they refuse the agency of the
'Spirit of the Nation.' Now I am, for half a dozen reasons, more
anxious about this than any other book of his, and I venture to
ask you, therefore, to show it to Moxon; tell him that it will be
completed in eight numbers, and in London bound in a volume in
green silk with double titles, English and Irish indexes, etc., on
the 1st or 2nd of January, price 10s. 6d. Show him some of the
notices; ask him, as the poem publisher, to act as London
publisher and agent.

"How are your spirits and strength? O'Connell and the
Tablet have created some bigotry here, but with God's blessing
we'll crush that too."

In the same letter he finds time, amid the hurricane of excitement in Ireland, to watch over the
interest of the magazine.

"Your article [for the *Dublin Monthly*] will be most welcome,
and the sooner it comes the better. Let me know whether I shall
send you proofs, and whether I may mention the authorship to
William Hudson. The management of the magazine and the
expense of it are on his shoulders. He is full of hope, and
delighted with the quiet sure progress nationality in knowledge,
art, and feeling is making here. The new number will not be out
till to-morrow or Monday, or else you would have received it, and
the two preceding ones at the Garrick Club. The change of
publisher disturbed all our details, but we'll go on better for

the future. I have a long paper this month, on the men of the Parliament of 1690. By next month, when we shall close the subject for the present I think, at least as much will have been done for the civil history of that epoch as for any other in our history."

Maddyn replied :—

"London, July 3rd.
"I am much obliged by the trouble you have taken about the magazines, which I received safely. Hudson's article disappointed me on the land question very much. It is wild and rambling, unlike the calm head of a contriver. The State papers [on James II.'s Parliament] are most interesting and valuable. Your brief summary of the events that caused 1688 is very *fair*, hardly could be more so. Wallace, McCullagh, the Westminster Reviewers, etc., are wasting breath in debating the meannesses and peccadilloes and duplicity of the Whig leaders. Is the Protestant religion to be held responsible for Henry the Eighth and Co.? or the Catholic for the many guilty popes, besides the shameless cardinals Dubois *et hoc genus?* No more than the moral lustre of 'the Repeal' is to be dimmed by that prominent agitator, who is now a violent Repealer, though he abused Pigot in the columns of the Dublin papers, because he (Pigot) gave him (agitator) no place; or by Alderman Hayes's consistent career (he worked hard for the Brunswicker, Gerard Callaghan), or Dan Callaghan's ditto. What Burke said of 1688 is the best theory of it : 'In truth, it was rather *a revolution prevented* than a revolution *effected.'* It secured the parliamentary government of England, and that was a great deal. I don't see that McCullagh has taken either a profound or novel view of it, and his ostentatious parade of notes with references to authorities in every one's hands is ridiculous. His quoting Wallace is ridiculous. *He* is not the slightest authority. You are aware of his superb fluke of Barnett."

In the end, Maddyn suggested that a literary pension should be asked for Mangan out of the taxes to which we all contributed.

"I entreat that there may be no democratic or high republican squeamishness shown in this matter," he wrote. "So long as we are living under a monarchy, let us at least have the advantages of it. And the Repealers do not profess to be anti-monarchical— neither are they, I am sure. Therefore let Mr. Mangan's friends

o

not scruple to do for him what Leigh Hunt's friends did three or four years since, when they sought to interest Queen Victoria for the Radical poet. In short, this point is really of consequence, and if Mangan could be well launched, his future voyages would be easier and more agreeable. . . .

"Whoever told you that Mr. Mahony [Father Prout] is not addressed as 'Revd.' said what is not the fact. He is invariably styled 'Revd.' in society, and he stands by his order manfully. O'Connell or his informants probably confound him with Maxwell, who was a 'Revd.,' but who has dropped the title and added 'esquire' to his name. By the special terms of Mahony's ordination he need only perform ecclesiastical functions, he is not compelled to do so; he is ordained *titule patrimonii*, and not *titule missionis*."

The magazine on which he had spent so much care and pains was staggering towards a final fall. In January he wrote to Maddyn:—

"Wallis has finally given up the *Dublin Magazine*, for that is its last baptism, and Hudson and every one else of us looks a little after it. What will come of the new experiment of gossip-editing remains to be seen. I have written a couple of little introductions to the statutes of 1689. Banim, by the way, has not done justice to that time."

The experiment answered as might have been expected; three months later he wrote to the same friend:—

"61, Bagot Street, April 13, 1843.

"Our poor magazine is really dead at last. The expense had kept increasing, and the sale diminishing, and it was necessary to stop. The amphibious politics of the magazine, the high price and unequal ability were enough to sink anything. The publishers were careless and without influence, and the perpetual change of size and price most absurd."

Other educational projects were pushed on vigorously. Davis negotiated successfully between James Duffy, the recognized publisher of the party, and the author's brother, for a uniform edition of the national novels of Gerald Griffin, and with Dr. R. R.

Madden for a new edition of his "United Irishmen."
One of his colleagues induced the publisher to accept
a manuscript novel from William Carleton, up to
that time a name odious to Catholic booksellers; and
"Valentine McClutchy" marked a new departure in
the career of a man of genius. O'Connell's "Memoir
of Ireland, Native and Saxon," had been originally
published in America, and the European copyright
was presented by the author to O'Neill Daunt, on
whom the labour of collecting the materials had
chiefly fallen; and the same colleague induced James
Duffy to purchase it at three hundred pounds—a large
price for a volume to be published at a couple of
shillings. A "Pictorial History of Ireland," consisting of coloured lithographs by Henry MacManus,
with short biographical or historical illustrations by
O'Callaghan, proved unhappily a failure—the only
complete collapse among the projects of the party.

The signs of intellectual success, which were dis-
cernible on all sides, have been described elsewhere
in language which it will be convenient to borrow:—

"Books upon the history and condition of Ireland were now
published in France, Prussia, and Belgium, and portraits of the
conspirators were to be found in every town and village between
the Atlantic and the Pacific, and in almost every city on the
continent of Europe. More than a quarter of a century later,
when these transactions were nearly forgotten by a new generation in Ireland, I was startled to find for sale under one of the
piazzas of Turin a large lithograph designated 'Capi e Promotori
della Questione Irlandese'—being no other than the convicted
conspirators of 1844.

"The association, in pursuance of its new policy, offered a prize
for the best essay on a Constitution for Ireland, and exhorted
competitors to remember that 'the difficulties of the case must not
be evaded, but frankly stated, and the means specified by which
they might be best met.' The Celtic race, though obstinate in its
habits, is very susceptible of discipline; no peasant is so easily

transformed into a soldier; no peasant girl so speedily acquires ease and intelligence by living among the cultivated classes. The enthusiasm of the time which had enabled an entire nation to become water-drinkers would, it was hoped, enable them to submit to other discipline and other sacrifices. It was admirable to see how young men of all ranks entered into this idea. Townsmen took up the defence of farmers who were unable to assert them-selves before a landlord armed with a merciless code; the ancient seats in piety and learning were wantonly desecrated as granaries, cattle-sheds, and ball-courts, or as quarries for the neighbouring squire or parson; and young persons volunteered to become their guardians till the time arrived when a National Government would take them in charge. This progress was obvious; but there was progress more important which could not be measured. Davis possessed the rare faculty of exciting impatience of wrong without awakening the deadly hatred of those who profit by it; and it was only in after years men came to know how deeply the new ideas penetrated among cultivated Protestants. Joseph Le Fanu was the literary leader of the young Conservatives, and Isaac Butt their political leader; both were at this time engaged, privately and unknown to each other, in writing historical romances which would present the hereditary feuds of Catholics and Protestants in a juster light to their posterity. Their books were published anonymously, and not for some years after they were begun; but I can state on their authority respectively that they had constantly in view in pursuing their task to gratify the new sentiment which the *Nation* had awakened. Samuel Ferguson, more essentially a man of letters and more indisputably a man of genius than either, broke through the hostile silence of the Dublin *University Magazine*, by predicting with generous exaggeration that, if no untoward event interrupted their career, the time would come when the national writers in Dublin would be read with something of the same enthusiasm in Paris as men in Dublin were reading Béranger and Lamartine. Mr. Lever, who winced under contemptuous criticism in the *Nation* (for the young men rejected his drunken squires and riotous dragoons as types of the Irish character), could not altogether resist the same sentiment; his historical stories took a tone so national that his cautious Scotch publisher demanded if he was 'repealizing like the rest.' Even in Ulster, the home of prejudice in latter times, they had reason to know that their songs found favour, and, like Moore's, were heard in unwonted places. And in the stronghold of bigotry, in the office of the *Evening Mail*, at the feet of the astute parson who directed its politics, there was growing up a lad who in a few years broke away from hereditary prejudice to become the laureate of Irish treason.

"History and historical poetry, which elsewhere are the food of patriotism, were wholly excluded from public teaching in Ireland, and it was well entitled to be regarded as a notable event when professors of Trinity College and professors of Maynooth, Protestant and Catholic clergymen, Conservative and National barristers and journalists, were seen side by side in the Rotundo while Moore Stack recited ballads and speeches alternately from the classics of Irish literature and the recent writings in the *Nation*. A little later a similar combination took place on behalf of the widow of John Banim, a writer intensely national in his scope and spirit, and whose name at an earlier period would certainly have frightened away Conservatives. A committee, selected alternately of Repealers and Conservatives or Whigs, was organized to purchase her an annuity, but were relieved from the duty by the frank concession of a pension by Sir Robert Peel, impressed perhaps by the unprecedented phenomenon of such a combination. Society, which in Dublin was like a British camp, began to open its doors to the young orators and poets, and the songs of the *Nation* were heard in drawing-rooms where nationality had never penetrated since the Union, except in the disguise of Moore's 'Melodies.' Good old Tories shook their heads and predicted perilous consequences. There was a story of a dowager who, after one of the national songs, gathered her flock and carried them off in a pretended panic, crying, 'Come away, my dears, before we are piked out.'" *

Before this time Dillon had ceased to write in the *Nation*, except on an occasional spurt; MacNevin took his place, and gay banter and persiflage succeeded to philosophical speculation and humanized Benthamism. But he was not idle; he was a constant critic on his friends, and his lenient and sympathetic strictures sank deep. MacNevin declared that Dillon's scraps of advice were not like beads strung at random, but, when you came to think of it, each took its place as part of a complete whole, like links in a chain of demonstration.

* " Young Ireland," chap. iv., bk. ii.

Of the *Nation* of this period Davis has written, "Duffy and I wrote most of the paper;" but he wrote much more than I did, as the business of administration fell exclusively on me. A modern editor, sometimes, like the leader of an orchestra, never plays a bar, but is content to direct the movement and determine the time of his band. This was not my idea of the duties of the position. I wrote as much as an office permitted which involved a large correspondence and a constant supervision of whatever was published, that the character of the journal might be guarded as scrupulously as a gentleman guards his personal honour.

While the " Spirit of the Nation " continued to win praise from representative Englishmen for its originality and vigour, we could find no London booksellers to circulate it, other than the Catholic tradesmen in back streets who dealt in Irish newspapers and books of piety ; and the first batch of Mangan's poems, which will live as long as Tennyson's or Browning's, were not accepted by any London publisher, and only got published in Dublin by a bonus of £50 being paid by one of his friends to Curry and McGlashen, whose magazine they had enriched.

The verdict against the State prisoners was not followed, as we have seen, by immediate punishment, the sentence being postponed, according to practice, until the opening of next term. In the interval eminent lawyers at the English and Irish bar pronounced the proceedings to be illegal in essential particulars, and advised an appeal to the House of Lords by writ of error. O'Connell, when he returned from his English expedition, found the people exasperated by the idea of his imprisonment, and attempted to tranquilize opinion by a device which, like an accommodation bill, helped to swell his liabilities to an impossible total. "Give me," he said, "but six months of peace, and I will give you my head on a block if we have not a parliament in College Green."

Davis reported to his friend Pigot the state of affairs in Dublin at this period.

"The newspapers will tell you the news. Your Whig friends are wrong. There *is*, at last, a dogged spirit in this country which will tell in any way we have to use it. The only danger is that the sudden news of O'Connell's imprisonment, which was not expected, may cause some petty rows. But it is so late in the week that, though he will probably be sentenced to-morrow, he will not be in gaol before Saturday or Monday, and meantime we'll have warned them and make them sullen, not rash.

"O'Brien and I are in particularly good spirits. If Wyse and his Federalists would work as we're working, all might end quietly in our favour in two or three years; but the chances are in favour of a more remote and sterner ending. I hope the former.

"O'C[onnell] and Duffy are in good health and spirits, and they are the most important [of the Repeal convicts]."

Davis esteemed Wolfe Tone to be the most sagacious Irishman born in the eighteenth century. He projected a union of Catholics and Protestants in the distracted country, and accomplished his design in the United Irishmen. He landed in France without credentials or money, and negotiated successfully with Hoche and Carnot. He launched a French expedition against the British power in Ireland, which failed, like the Armada, only because it was scattered by a hurricane. His name was familiar to students, but, though he had a monument in the United States, there was no memorial of his services in the land for which he died. A few friends subscribed funds to place a tombstone on his grave in Bodenstown cemetery,* and Davis reported progress to Pigot, who took a lively interest in the project.

" (Private). Wednesday, April 17, 1844.

" DEAR JOHN,

" Inclosed is a sprig of ivy from over the grave at Bodenstown. Gray and I were there to-day, and the first Irish monument to him will be put on his tomb on Sunday next at half-past eleven.

" The monument, you know, is a plain black marble slab, very massive; on it are to be the words—

" ' THEOBALD WOLFE TONE,
Born 20th June, 1763;
Died 19th November, 1798,
FOR
IRELAND.'

I like the inscription, though 'tis mine. It says enough for this, and perchance enough for all time. The reason of its being put down now is that Mrs. Tone wrote to say she wished it. Her letter is plain and heroic; better than ever a woman of Sparta wrote. She says she had wished and had hoped to have done this last office, and to have laid her bones beside his, but the infirmities of seventy-six years prevent her."

" . . . I suppose you see J. O'Hagan often. Tell him that three several persons who worship his ' Dear Land ' are displeased with ' crimson red,' and that he ought to alter it. Also say that the concluding line of Ingram's first verse is bad English; it should run ' his glass ' not ' your glass ' [in the song ' Who fears to speak of 'Ninety-eight?']. But, then, ' your ' is a far better singing word; so let him write forthwith to Ingram to shift the line, so as to secure the English and smoothness. I think the two last lines, in

* The design originated with Dr. Gray, but was probably suggested by a stanza in a little poem of Davis's :—

" Once I lay on that sod—it lies over Wolfe Tone—
And thought how he perished in prison alone,
His friends unavenged, and his country unfreed—
' Oh, bitter,' I said, ' is the patriot's meed;

" ' For in him the heart of a woman combined
With a heroic life, and a governing mind—
A martyr for Ireland—his grave has no stone—
His name seldom named, and his virtues unknown.' "

verse one, would sing better and read better thus than as at present—

"'But you man, a true man,
Will fill your glass with us.'

"I have the first-proof sheet of first part of the new edition [of the 'Spirit of the Nation'] on my desk. The music is very well done, and the paper and letter-press are superb. Nothing like them have been attempted here before. Have you musicked 'Tipperary' yea or nay?

"O'Connell is in spunk and spirits, and very civil these times. Our parliamentary committee is working admirably. I have a hundred pages of their reports laid by already. In another week I'll have another hundred.

"When Parliament rises we are to publish the 'Statistics of Ireland,' with maps, etc.

"My poor sister continues dangerously ill. She is at Ennis-kerry.

"Your translation of Venedy * was corrected by Anster. I believe I shall go to London in the summer, but am not sure. I fear you and I would idle each other cruelly there.

"My latest project is a 'Ballad History of Ireland;' not a continued metrical chronicle, but a rosary of ballads by every one who could write one. I *calculate* that a fifth of such a work or more has been done. Would it not be the most potent and imperishable of books, if well done? Besides, it could be continually improved by the insertion of new, or the re-writing of old ballads.

"Why don't you write? Make, force, drive J. O'Hagan to write. It is cruel of him not to do so. I wish he'd write on Aughrim or Clontarf, or anything down to the rent [the Repeal Rent, a subject no one adopted willingly], if he'd but write. Ingram, too, is inexcusable. One poem now is worth twenty to be brought out in five years. Have you heard W. J. Fox, the negative Pantheist of Finsbury? You will see him *cleverly* sketched in the next *Nation*. He is well worth hearing."

On the subject of Tone's monument Davis again wrote to Pigot, that it was considered discreet to postpone the project till after the sentence on O'Connell and the other traversers.

* Herr Venedy, a German democrat who visited Ireland in this year, and wrote an account of his visit.

" I did not forget you or your rights. None of us have yet
paid our quotas. The tomb is *not* set up. It was taken to Bodenstown, and all the parties were to have gone down to have lent a
hand in placing it over the sod where he lies; but some of the
' Conspirators' ' counsel objected to its being done just then; so it
was postponed and will, I think, not be done till the end of June.
Do not speak of *any* of these facts.

" My poor little sister has not mended much. She says she
is better. God grant it : but I doubt, and so does her medical
attendant. The wind is very bad for her. If J. O'Hagan is
writing songs, make him do so to Irish airs, for which no good
words are extant.

" Smith O'Brien wants, as soon as the ' Spirit of the Nation' is
out, to reissue the songs and music of the ' Citizen.' After that
' Spirit of the Citizen' a re-issue of ' Bunting,' with new words,
would be sublime. I'm going to try an air or two, and be damned
to your objections against my metre ! "

" May 29, 1844.

" Parties here are just now looking for the healthiest gaols, for
they expect to be sentenced to-day. It will task our energies to
keep the people quiet. They did not believe O'Connell could be
imprisoned—he, the thirty years' king of their hearts.

" Make Prout balladize for us [Fr. Mahony, whom Pigot met
in London]."

On May 30, 1844, the traversers were brought up
for judgment. They claimed to stand out till the
writ of error was tried by the House of Lords; but
they were immediately sentenced to fine and imprisonment, and sent to Richmond Bridewell. The
metropolitan prisons were under the control of the
Dublin corporation, and by their connivance the
imprisonment amounted to mere detention in a
country-house with handsome and extensive gardens.
The governor and deputy-governor were authorized
to let their official residences to the prisoners. We
had separate suites of rooms, our own servants, a
common table, which was rendered luxurious by gifts
of venison, fish, game, and hot-house fruits, and the

unrestricted society of our friends. O'Connell proposed to write his memoirs in this retirement, and the journalists worked unrestrictedly at their profession. John O'Connell, who liked to play at journalism, set up a *Richmond Prison Gazette*, consisting chiefly of banter and pasquinades on the prisoners by each other ; and we gave audience to sympathizers on fixed days, and had a conference with Smith O'Brien on the business of the Association twice a week.*

During the weary progress of the State trial, Davis spoke to me for the first time of a long retirement from the *Nation*. He would travel, he would employ himself in historical or political studies, but he still doubted if there was any useful or honourable work for him at Conciliation Hall. These designs, as we shall see, were not altogether relinquished, but his fidelity to O'Brien and to his more intimate associates, and the necessity which a strong man feels to face the danger nearest at hand kept him at his post, and to do his best while he was on duty was the

---

* The imprisonment was borne cheerfully, but no doubt it was easily borne. Davis sung the spirit in which such an ordeal should be encountered if its perils were graver :—

> " 'Tis sweet to climb the mountain's crest,
> And run, like deer-hound, down its breast ;
> 'Tis sweet to snuff the taintless air,
> And sweep the sea with haughty stare :
> And sad it is when iron bars
> Keep watch between you and the stars ;
> And sad to find your footstep stayed
> By prison-wall and palisade ;
>   But 'twere better to be
>   A prisoner for ever,
>   With no destiny
>   To do, or to endeavour ;
>   Better life to spend
>   A martyr or confessor,
>   Than in silence bend
>   To alien and oppressor."

practice of his life. He made suggestions to the counsel of the traversers, especially to Whiteside, on the historical defence relied on, which proved of substantial value.

A design which Davis long cherished was to write a history of Ireland. It was a great want. There was no history which could be put into the hands of a student or an inquirer without shame, and no one was so fit as he for the task. But its chief attraction for him was the escape it would afford him from Conciliation Hall, and his friends, who knew that he would leave a fatal void in the national ranks, discouraged the design. He was engaged in work which was not indeed higher, for a Prescot or Thierry is one of the greatest gifts Providence could bestow upon Ireland, but was far more pressing. It would have been a bad economy of life to lay down his habitual task, and seclude himself from the interests of the hour, even for such a purpose; yet this is what he desired to do. Confident in the variety and accuracy of his studies, he spoke of a few weeks or months as sufficient leisure ; but not months but years were needed to produce such a book as he designed. In the middle of the State trials he pressed the project on me for the second or third time.

"My dear Duffy,

"I think it better for me to begin my history at once, and give the next five weeks exclusively to it, and I can work for the same time in summer for you, which will transfer the term of our arrangement to the beginning of July instead of the end of May. I can be much more useful to you then than now; and, at any rate, I know that, as it will convenience me, you will manage without me for a while. I have been thinking what you had best do, and here is my thought. To arrange the paper in the way I have indicated in the enclosed plan. To give the second literary

page to the trials, which will prevent breaks. To get our London
friend [Maddyn] to write critical letters or sketches of Irishmen
as literary leaders. His would be the most efficient, simply to
keep up the literary character of the paper. To keep the P.C.
[Poet's Corner] good, and the leading poetry brilliant. To get
MacNevin to write gay finished special articles, and not loose
generalities on subjects which he has not mastered. Doheny
would write too; or possibly an article from Dillon or Godkin
could be got as a good substitute.

" I think that, obliged as you are to be in court, it would be
most easy for you to write the State Trial articles, and that it
would prevent your getting idle or *ennuyé* at court. You ought to
rise and breakfast at seven, and take half an hour's run before you
go to the court, and, in fact, resolve to lead a most fresh vigorous
life to sustain you against *Qui Tam's* speeches [Qui Tam was a
nickname for the Attorney-General]. I'll see you at court to-
morrow."

He set to work making a ground plan of his proposed history, estimating the space each era would
require, putting previous studies in order, and seeking
new materials wherever they were to be found.*
Here is a note from John O'Connell in reply to an
application for papers relating to the service of Irish
troops on the continent :—

" MY DEAR DAVIS,

" It was but yesterday evening I got your note, referring
to the matter of my 'Irish Brigade' documents. Your patriotic
object, of course, has my very valueless approbation; but I had,
previous to hearing from you, deprived myself of control over the
documents you wish to see. They are in O'Callaghan's hands
since Monday, and have been out of mine and lying waiting for
him at the association during two previous days. I do not expect
to see him for some days—and you live near him—(I believe his
address is 37, Upper Merrion Street)—and I am sure he will not
hesitate to convenience you. I have made them entirely over to
him. I have been looking for an opportunity of telling you that,
knowing you were lending Ray 'Brown's' trade-pamphlets of
early last century, I looked over them in his possession, and made
some extracts, to appear in the species of ' Repealer's Manual ' that

* See Appendix.

I am compiling, and that if you had, or have, any objection to
their being made use of, I will destroy them at once. I have felt
I ought to have taken care to ask your permission ere taking my
extract from them.

"I have not seen my father since Monday, nor expect to see
him before to-morrow afternoon, so cannot yet answer your questions respecting Sarsfield's death-words and the T.C.D. MS. account
of Brian O'Neil's murder. Banim's novel, the name of which I
forget, upon the sieges of Derry and Limerick, has, I think, the
Sarsfield anecdote with its authority. O'Neill Daunt was the
collector of the more out-of-the-way matter in 'Ireland and the
Irish.' Wishing you success in your excellent undertakings,

"I remain, my dear Davis,
"Very faithfully yours,
"JOHN O'CONNELL." *

A month later Davis recurred to his project :—

"DEAR D.,
"Here are some scribbles, hard and tender mixed. I saw
O'C. yesterday; he is very Repeal, and vigorous and polite; says
he would not go to Cork were't not to be a Repeal dinner. I'll
give your printer a literary leader on the state of Wales and the
'Haverty,' and, in fact, I'll work at the *Nation* till April, if you
don't go to gaol or do. Is not that as rude and rapparee a way of
talking of your liberty as I could adopt?

"Yours,
"T. D."

The remonstrance of his friends and the intractable difficulties of the case induced him to modify
his plan into the project of a history in eras, each
era treated by a separate writer. Among his papers
I find a note of the latter design :—

"'History of the Pale,'—C. G. D.
"'The Civil Wars,' *i.e.* from end of Pale to Cromwell's, and the
Acts of his Parliament *quoad* Ireland,—T. D.
"'Patriot Parliament,' 1689 to 1792, and from 1792 to 1800,—
T. D.; 1800 to 1844,—D. O. M."

But three men can no more write history to the

* Carysfort Avenue, Blackrock, March 8, 1843.

accompaniment of a State trial than one man. In the end it was determined to begin modestly, and put off the larger design for calmer times. The Committee of the Repeal Association were induced to offer a prize for a school history of Ireland, and I find among his papers a letter discussing this project :—

"I wish you would consider these two suggestions about the proposed history while the notice is still unpublished.

"1. It ought to come down to the Union, and no later. If it come to the present time, you will have odious and lying exaggerations about O'Connell, and, what is worse, injustice to the other men engaged in the Catholic Agitation. Depend upon it there will be no avoiding this, but by stopping the history at the Union. Moreover, proceedings so recent will occupy such an undue share of the book as to crush out more material facts. Let the O'Connell Agitation be glorified in a book published for the special purpose, and written by Dr. Stephen Murphy!

"2. Eight months is obviously too short a period to write a history in. Take an average writer, and he would need three months to collect his materials, three months to arrange and digest them, and, if he wrote the book in three months more, it would be at the rate of a hunt. This would be nine months. But, as a writer is a man and not a steam-engine, you would need to throw in a couple of months for relaxation and his other employments. He may be a farmer (John Keogh's grandson), an attorney (Mitchel), a doctor (Cane), or some other man with his hands full of work, and it is surely more important to have a good book than to have one a few months before the seasonable time. I think you ought to allow a year for a book that you intend to be permanent and standard ; but if it be desirable to avoid so long a delay, fix the first of March instead of the first of January, 1846. This will only postpone the book two months—nothing to the Association, everything to the writer plunging hopelessly through his last chapters.

"I am anxious about this, not only on public grounds, but because one of our friends [MacNevin] proposes to try his chance ; therefore don't set down my letter entirely to the credit of public feeling. But I do fully believe that the delay will be as necessary for every possible competitor as for him. If you think with me

the changes can be easily made in committee, and will equally
affect Trojan and Tyrian.

" Thomas O'Hagan has seen a good deal of Grey Porter lately,
and he tells me that he has a pamphlet nearly ready for the press,
in which he takes a strong tone against the Association, and recom-
mends a reconsideration of the Act of Union simply with a view
to increase the number of Irish representatives. You ought to
see to this (without mentioning O'H.'s name), for a useful man
like Porter ought not to be let run into a foolery that will render
him ridiculous for evermore." *

Early in 1844 he renewed the proposal to retire
temporarily from the *Nation,* but was again dissuaded.

" Will you or MacNevin," he wrote to me, " deal with the
Debate? My mother's sister is dying in our house, and I cannot
bring myself to this work.

" And now I want to know could you postpone the second half
of my engagement with the *Nation* till autumn, or entirely? I
know this is a very unreasonable request. But I find that I must
either give up the notion of writing the history, or absolutely
stop writing for the *Nation* during the spring. Would not the.
sum you agreed to give me procure a sufficient variety of other
writing to compensate for the absence of my harum-scarum
articles? But do not decide hastily. I am in a very sobered
mood, and feel doubts, serious doubts, of my ability to write the
history at all. But I shall speak to you next week of this.

" I do not expect my poor aunt to live out the night, so I'm
not likely to see you for a few days."

While he still meditated writing the history immediately, he had correspondence with Maddyn and
John O'Donovan, the antiquary, which is of permanent interest, though perhaps the latter permits his
opinion to be a little too much tainted with jealousy
of a rival, and quite inferior, translator from the
Gaelic.

O'Donovan wrote to him :—

" Having heard that you are engaged on a history of the English Invasion of Ireland, I beg to say that I am anxious to show

* Duffy to Davis.

you some notes of mine on certain facts connected with this period of Irish history. I do not want to force any opinions upon you, but, having spent years in comparing the different English and Irish authorities, I wish you to see certain observations which I have written, and which may be of some use to you. The translation of the 'Annals of the Four Masters,' published by Mr. Geraghty, though put into readable English by Mangan, is full of errors, and you will find it very unsafe to trust it. Truth is one thing and national honour another; and, though it may be but prudence to suppress certain facts at certain periods, no historical work will live but that which has truth for its object. In translating the monuments of the history or superstitions of a people, we should suppress nothing, nor should we make the language of the translation better than the language of the original; that is, if a story be badly told in the original, it should not be well told in the translation; if an original author thought proper to introduce into his chronicle, as an historical fact, that a certain ancient crozier held a conversation with a certain priest, the translator of that chronicle should not write, in English or in any other language, that this crozier never spoke a word. Again, if an original chronicler has written that, at the siege of a certain town or castle, the besiegers put men, women, children, horses and fools to death, his translator should not omit the *women*, and *children* and *fools!* And, again, if an original writer in an original language has recorded that a certain Hugh de Lacy was killed while accompanied by three of his people, his translator is actually guilty of historical forgery if he changes *three of his people* to *one-third of his nation.* Small forgeries of this kind very much affect the phases of historical events, and the person who indulges in them deserves the opprobrious name of 'historical charlatan.' . . . I see that Mr. Duffy has made a slight allusion to the stiffness of my translations from the Gaelic, because I do not know English. I know English about six times better than I know Irish, but I have no notion of becoming a forger, like MacPherson. The translations from Irish by Mangan, mentioned by Mr. Duffy, are very good;[*] but how near are they to the literal translations furnished to Mangan by Mr. Curry? Are they the shadow of a shade? Mr. Duffy speaks as if Mangan had translated directly from the original! But the world is now too knowing for silly assertions of this kind. . . . It may be useful just now to talk of long-faded glories; but it is my opinion that we have but few national glories to boast of in our history, which only proves that, though we were vigorous and

[*] " Ballad Poetry of Ireland."

partially civilized, we never had any national wisdom. The day
is approaching, however, when we shall be wiser, and our past
history will then amuse, and perhaps also instruct us, by exhibiting
to our view many glorious examples of the sad results of disunion.
The great Dan knows this well, for, though he is but a bad his-
torian and worse antiquary, he has a big head. Let me conclude
by one remark, that it is my opinion that the *Nation* newspaper,
even though it is no child of the tribe of Dan, has done more to
liberalize the Irish and implant in the minds of the Anglo-Irish
and Iberno-English the seedlings of national union, than all the
histories of Ireland ever written, and that, if it continues to live
as long more as it has already lived, without flinching from the
noble principles it has hitherto maintained, its effects on the
national mind will not be easily removed. I wish I could boast
of our having had such literature in the days of Cormac Mac Art,
or even of Brian Boru."

As Maddyn had a book of three volumes in hand,*
he could not undertake any portion of the history,
but he was enthusiastic in his reception of the idea.

"Depend upon it you are quite right in supposing that all
that humanizes any portion of mankind, must be thoroughly useful
to the mass. The leaven spreads, and admiration of ideal excel-
lence has effects profoundly useful, even for the multitude. The
curse of our age in Ireland is, that only the coarse agencies
are employed upon Irish society. The British Power governs by
a coarse terrorism; the Irish Democracy seeks to vindicate itself
by a coarse O'Connell-born demagogism; Irish individual ambition has coarse and palpable objects — it courts broad notoriety
instead of permanent fame, and aims at table-talk celebrity instead
of the glory that springs from the acclaim of posterity. Irish
religion is coarse—bear witness the Calvinism of the miscalled
Church of England prevalent in Ireland, the utilitarianism of the
Unitarians, and the unpoetical as well as unphilosophical dogmatism of the Catholicism. The last is proportionably the best in
Ireland, and most true to its own ideas. Again, oratory, more than
poetry or philosophy, is worshipped by the coarse student-mind of
Ireland. We have a people amongst whom is widely spread a
capacity for the ideal and romantic, but we have no peasant minds
like Burns, Elliott, or the hosts of artisan intellects of England.
But *cui bono, cui bono?* all this? The remedy is not to wish that

* " Ireland and its Rulers."

things were otherwise in Ireland, but to will that we ourselves at least should be as much as possible above the faults of our time, while we at the same time remain vitally true to the instinct of country. Lavater says, 'Wishes run with loquacious impotence, but will presses forward with laconic energy.' Ireland has been eternally wishing, but never willing. Let some twenty or thirty Irish minds determine to be true to their individual psychology, while they will purpose to represent and illustrate the spirit of their country, they would create an age of which the effects would remain when the Corn Exchange was a thing of mere historical recollection. But enough of a futile topic." *

On a detached sheet of his diary, without date, I found a significant entry, which, as I conjecture, belongs to this period. He had never travelled, and he longed to obtain the practical acquaintance with races and institutions, and with art and political geography, which travel alone supplies. It was only at this period of his short public life that he could have withdrawn himself from his engagements for six months, and he still feared that there would be a long interval of timid and wavering counsels when he would be best employed in training himself for the future.

"Write for *Nation* till August, then Scotland and Norway for two months (£50), Hamburg, Prussia, Munich, Austria, Venice, Switzerland, Paris, Turin, Italy, Spain and home ; £250 or £300 in all. Or go in June to Scotland, Hamburg, Berlin, Munich, Vienna, Trieste, Venice, Switzerland ; in all, three months : then September and half October in France, half October, November, and half December in Italy, home to Christmas : in all, six months. Good ! Morning, finish letters to Dillon and Duffy."

But the imprisonment opened an era and an opportunity which put these dreams to flight.

* It was probably in relation to the projected history that he applied to the controller of the ordnance survey for certain information. Major Larcom, who was his personal friend, replied, " I do not know that any remains of the Strafford army exist, but I shall obtain more information on that point when I get to work on Sir W. Petty's account of the Down survey. It was once doubted whether there ever were maps with the Strafford survey, but I am already tolerably sure there were, and that they existed in Petty's time."

CHAPTER VI.

THE STATESMAN. 1844.

O'CONNELL and half a dozen selected agitators were locked up in prison, and now the critical question arose, Could the agitation live without the agitators ? It is a strange craze of English politicians to believe that discontent in Ireland depends upon the action of this man or that, instead of springing perpetually from the condition of the people. It is a power which may be regulated and disciplined, indeed, but it is no more created by human skill than one of the unintermittent forces of nature. It was now about to become more vigilant and formidable, more patient and determined after defeat, than it had been at the height of the monster meetings.

The new leader was a man of good capacity, careful training, and large experience in public affairs. His manners were a little rigid and formal, and his utterance too deliberate for Celtic taste, but his generous heart kept him young and fresh. He was ready to compete with his juniors in labour and to surpass them in sacrifice. As a scion of a great historic house descended from King Brian, the Alfred of Ireland, and a member of Parliament of unstained probity and recognized success, he occupied a unique position. He was not only the greatest recruit the cause had won, but he created the hope of a decisive movement among the class to which he belonged. O'Connell had proclaimed him his personal representative, and the mouthpiece of the national cause during the imprisonment; and O'Brien devoted every faculty of his being to the task imposed upon him. He loved to be surrounded by men of probity and capacity, and had no jealousy of their gifts. He had large belief and confidence in Davis, who speedily came to bear the same relation to him that Alexander Hamilton bore to Washington. He formulated the policy of the official chief, supplemented his projects with kindred proposals of his own, and clothed their common purpose in the persuasive language of genius. O'Brien visited O'Connell and the State prisoners almost daily, consulted them on his plans that nothing might be done which had not the assent of the imprisoned leader, but his own character, and that of Thomas Davis, were soon broadly stamped on the national movement.

Davis for the first time had a free field for his policy, and a direct control of public affairs, and we are able to judge of his gifts as a statesman. There was no more thought of travel or of retirement; no more despondency : like a vigorous young tribune called from the ranks of Opposition to be a Minister of State, he began to act and direct like one who had found his proper work, and his influence was soon felt in every province of public affairs. His policy was ready for the hour and for the generation. He had lived in solitude with the great thinkers and reformers, and was accustomed to note the currents and undercurrents which govern opinion and to foresee the forces which would be at work to-morrow.

The new administration of national affairs opened with a characteristic incident. The Government press circulated a rumour that it was intended to suppress the Association and shut up Conciliation Hall. O'Brien immediately declared, with an intrepidity which was universally felt to be spontaneous and unaffected, that if such an attempt were made he would request the committee to place him in the chair, that he might try in his own person the question whether the constitutional right of public meeting could be extinguished by official authority in Ireland.

A parliamentary committee, organized by O'Brien during the State trial, now completed a series of reports dealing with the main branches of the national question in an exact and practical manner, like men who might soon be called upon to exercise the unctions of a national Government. Davis believed that the chief men engaged in this work were more competent and resolute than the advisers who surrounded Grattan in 1782. "'The Parliamentary Committee,'" he said, "is a deal tougher than 'the Whig Club.'" Somewhat later, O'Brien discovered that these political studies had excited interest among a class unusually cold and sceptical, the gentlemen who sit on both sides of the Speaker's chair.

"I find," he wrote to Davis, "that our reports have produced in the minds of the English members an extraordinary effect, and that my notion of making the Repeal Association an introductory legislature has been completely realized. Every intelligent M.P. says that they are calm, able, and most useful."

Robert James Tennent, an indolent man of genius, who long led the Liberal party in Belfast, and might have done anything with them if his great faculties had been associated with a great purpose, applied to one of his friends in Dublin for a copy of these State papers.

" Do you know," he wrote, " if it would be possible to procure a complete set (*ab initio*) of the Repeal Association Reports? My friend, Thomas O'Hagan, has given himself trouble for me about this, but, I fear, unsuccessfully."

It was welcome news to Davis when the Congregational minister of his native town * echoed this criticism :—

" The members of the parliamentary committee," he wrote, " are doing wonders. I am astonished, amazed; I did not think there were such men, such thought, such true nationality combined with such indomitable perseverance, in the country. We have in this department of the association something like the best part of our Parliament; and of this there can be no doubt, that you fairly represent the country. And what is better, you are attaining more strength and life and vigour, and consequently more importance in the eye of the nation, every day. Go forward, and may God bless you ; and He will bless you, for you labour for the country which you love."

His friend Webb, whose connections by birth and marriage were intensely anti-national, sent him a report of good work in which he was engaged:—

" I employ myself at present a good deal in giving my womankind here some inkling of Irish history. They begin to take an interest in it, are becoming somewhat alive to the disgrace of ignorance respecting it, and seem much astonished at its revelations. I am thus a humble and far-off gleaner in the field, whose harvest your sickle has entered so deeply—*Parva sed apta mihi.* Even this, however, tends perhaps to save some of the coming generation from those thick and impenetrable prejudices, which have so long and so fatally been interposed between Ireland and the affections of her children."

* Rev. Mr. Gibson.

Davis's share of the work he projected was commonly to do half of it, and revise the other half. He wrote to O'Brien:—

"Either you or I, or some one, should compile a short account of the geography, history, and statistics of Ireland, to be printed in fifty or sixty pages of a report, accompanied by a map, and circulated extensively. We must do more to educate the people. This is the only moral force in which I have any faith. Mere agitation is either bullying or preparation for war. I condemn the former, others of the party condemn the latter. But we all agree in the policy of education. . . . The members of the Franchise Committee should apply themselves, under your guidance, to the Grand Juries. I suppose we shall be able to work up some account of the Customs, Excise, and Post Office from Stritch's and Reynolds's reports. We should get Mr. Mullen to make a report of the Poor Law Commission and its working. I shall make up the Education and Police as soon as the Estimates Report is out. Dillon and I have agreed to prepare facts, etc., on (land) tenures (Irish and foreign). Thus, I think, we are on the way of having proper materials for a statistical account of Ireland both internally and in relation to the British Empire."

As agencies for local action, Repeal Reading Rooms were multiplied. There were already three hundred: it was determined to increase them to three thousand; and they were directed to contest every elective office in the interest of Repeal, with candidates of the best character and capacity obtainable. Though the main agency relied upon was education, it was not merely the education of books, but still more the education of action and responsibility. To plant opinion and create habits, is to form men, but discipline in public duties alone can form citizens; and corporations, boards of guardians, public schools and colleges, if occupied by men of public spirit, might, he felt assured, help—

"To gather up the fragments of our State,
And in its cold, dismembered body breathe
The living soul of empire."

Davis rarely spoke in the Association, but his friends O'Brien, Dillon, MacNevin, Barry, and O'Gorman were often in the tribune, and gave a tone of confidence to debate, to which it had been a stranger of late. Nature gave him the passions and convictions which make an orator, but he thought the art of oratory greatly overrated. In conversation, as well as in his writings, he often repeated the truth—"A great orator is of no use, unless he is also a great man. Nay, the most eloquent orator can never become great if he wants moral power."

The Repeal members were summoned to attend the weekly meetings at Conciliation Hall, and the leading Repealers in the provinces came up in batches for the same purpose, carrying addresses to the State prisoners. Preparations were begun for a general election, and candidates of honour and capacity, fit to be the spokesmen of a nation, were sought for. What sort of representatives the new men wanted was not left in doubt. The existing members had been elected before the country was awakened on the national question, and were for the most part despicable in character and capacity. As missionaries of a subject nation to a dominant one, they were like Lascars sent to convert Brahmins. Davis, in lieu of speaking in Conciliation Hall, wrote on the subject in the *Nation* with admirable frankness:—

"If our members were a majority in the House," he said, "it might not be very moral, but at least it would have some show of excuse, if we sent in a flock of pledged delegates to vote Repeal, regardless of their powers or principles; though even then we might find it hard to get rid of the scoundrels after Repeal was carried, and when Ireland would need virtuous and unremitting

wisdom to make her prosper. . . . We want men who are not
spendthrifts, drunkards, swindlers,—we want honest men—men
whom we would trust with our private money or our family's
honour; and sooner than see faded aristocrats and brawling pro-
fligates shelter themselves from their honest debtors by a Repeal
membership, we would leave Tories and Whigs undisturbed in
their seats, and strive to carry Repeal by other measures." *

And again :—

" We want legislators; we do not want mere farmers, mere fops,
mere scamps, or mere fools.   We want, in London or Dublin,
men trained in the whole circle of knowledge—familiar with the
country's agriculture, and trade, and resources.   We want men
who have learned how to wield the present, by having studied the
past—men familiar with our history and the history of other nations.
An Irish Representative should not only know the statistics of this
country better than the names of his neighbours; he should be
familiar with the government, tenures, and condition of other
countries, especially of countries in a half-provincial state.   He
should have studied human nature and natural science.   He will
have to deal with men's motives, not only in policy, but legislation,
—not only in managing a party or a committee, but in making
civil and criminal laws, whether here or in London, for Ireland
or the empire.   He will have to deal with the physical resources
of the country, and the useful arts, and the bearing of laws on
production.   Let constituencies look about them, and say are they
represented thus?"

The tone of strict and haughty discipline, designed
to make the people fit to use and fit to enjoy liberty,
was illustrated in the method of dealing with a
public riot at this time.   One of O'Connell's jurors
had an establishment in Kilkenny, and a mob
avenged themselves on him, for his partisan verdict,
by wrecking his shop.   The transaction was promptly
censured in the Association, and in the *Nation* Davis
used this emphatic language :—

" We have heard with surprise and anger that a house in
Kilkenny, belonging to one of the jurors in the State trials, has
been wrecked.

* *Nation*, June 29, 1844.

"Such an outrage is an outrage against law, which we hope and believe the law will sharply punish.

"It is much worse—it is a direct violation of the principles of the agitation—it is a gross breach of Repeal discipline—it is a crime against Ireland.

"If a soldier, no matter from what motive, rushes from his rank in battle, he is, very properly, sabred or shot instantly. If we had the men who perpetrated this outrage before us, and a clear field, we should just as unhesitatingly cut them down.

"If we are to carry Repeal—if this is not to be another of these damnable failures that have disgraced our intellect and our character—there must not be one other popular crime. The Irish people deserve to rot in slavish poverty if they will not keep the discipline under which they enlisted."

And he taught the rationale of this rigid discipline in language of transparent plainness :—

"We are not men who bid the people to expect Repeal in the change from leaf to fruit in any year. We have never said it was certain. It is not certain; for if the people do not persevere with a dogged and daily labour for knowledge and independence they will be slaves for generations. It is not at hand, for the Protestants must be in our array, or foreign war must humble our foe; Ireland must be united, or our oppressor in danger, ere we can succeed by moral force ; but we ask those who require knowledge, discipline, and civic wisdom as guarantees for our fitness for nationality—Has not Ireland done something to solve their doubts and satisfy their demands ? "

He appealed to the minority in language they had never heard before—in language, indeed, never heard in Ireland since Grattan was laid under the flag-stones of Westminster Abbey.

"Poor deluded Irish Protestants!" he said,—"brave! fierce! impotent! You have denied the country for which a race of Protestant patriots—Daniel O'Neill, Molyneux, Swift, Lucas, Flood, Grattan, Tone, and Saurin—fought and spoke. You, who threw off the uniform of '82, and used its muskets against liberty— you, who would not listen to Stuart, became the clients of Castlereagh. You saw commerce extinguished, manufactures withered, your militia abolished, your parliament abolished—your gentry,

and your genius, and your revenue swept away,—and now the vile
pelf, and now the haughty lordship, for which you bore all this,
are wrenched from you without pity, without compromise. Are
you men and bear it? Are you fools and cowards? Or have your
hearts grown so base that interest, patriotism, and vengeance
plead alike in vain?—and are you content to accept the degrada-
tion of your country as reward enough for your subserviency
to England? "

And again :—

" Where else in Europe is the peasant ragged, fed on roots, in
a wigwam, without education? Where else are the towns ruined,
trade banished, the till and workshop and the stomach of the
artisan empty? Where else is there an exportation of over one-
third of the rents, and an absenteeism of the chief landlords?
What other country pays four and a half million taxes to a foreign
treasury, and has its offices removed or filled with foreigners?
Where else are the people told they are free and represented, yet
only one in two hundred of them have the franchise? Where
beside do the majority support the clergy of the minority? In
what other country are the majority excluded from high ranks in
the University? In what place, beside, do landlords and agents
extort such vast rents from an indigent race. Where else are
the tenants ever pulling, the owners ever driving, and both full of
anger? And what country so fruitful and populous, so strong, so
well-marked and guarded by the sea, and with such an ancient
name was reduced to provincialism by bribery and treacherous
force, and is denied all national government.

" And if the answer be as it must, 'Nowhere is the like seen,' then
we say that union amongst Irishmen would make this country
comparatively a paradise."

And, like Swift, he sought to arrest the ear of
the Protestant democracy by associating their party
tunes with generous and patriotic sentiments.

> " Fruitful our soil where honest men starve;
>   Empty the mart, and shipless the bay;
> Out of our want the Oligarchs carve;
>   Foreigners fatten on our decay!
>   Disunited,
>   Therefore blighted,

> Ruined and rent by the Englishman's sway ;
> Party and creed
> For once have agreed—
> Orange and Green will carry the day !
> Boyne's old water,
> Red with slaughter !
> Now is as pure as an infant at play ;
> So, in our souls,
> Its history rolls,
> And Orange and Green will carry the day ! "

He had somewhat earlier formulated the policy on which, and on which alone if arms were relinquished, O'Connell's great design might be realized. He strove to keep steady and uniform a policy which had a tendency to run sometimes into insincere violence, sometimes into offensive bigotry.

" Conciliation of all sects, classes, and parties who oppose us, or who still hesitate, is *essential* to moral force. For if, instead of leading a man to your opinion by substantial kindness, by zealous love, and by candid and wise teaching, you insult his tastes and his prejudices, and force him either to adopt your cause or to resist it,— if, instead of slow persuasion, your weapons are bullying and intolerance, then your profession of moral force is a lie, and a lie which deceives no one, and your attacks will be promptly resisted by every man of spirit."

And on another occasion :—

" If Irishmen were united, the Repeal of the Union would be instantly and quietly conceded. A Parliament at whose election mutual generosity would be in every heart and every act, would take the management of Ireland. For oh ! we ask our direst foe to say, from the bottom of his heart, would not the people of Ireland melt with joy and love to their Protestant brethren if they united and conquered? And surely from such a soil noble crops would grow. No southern plain heavy with corn, and shining with fruit-clad hamlets, ever looked so warm and happy as would the soul of Ireland, bursting out with all the generosity and beauty of a grateful people. . . . Fancy the aristocracy placed by just laws, or by wise concession, on terms of friendship with their tenants, securing to these tenants every farthing their industry entitled

them to, living among them, promoting agriculture and education
by example and instruction, sharing their joys, comforting their
sorrows, and ready to stand at their head whenever their country
called. Think well on it—suppose it to exist in your own country,
in your own barony and parish. Dwell on this sight. See the
life of such a landlord and of such farmers—so busy, so thoughtful,
so happy! How the villages would ring with pleasure and trade,
and the fields laugh with contented and cheered labour. Imagine
the poor supporting themselves on those waste lands which the
home expenditure of our rents and taxes would reclaim, and the
workhouse turned into a hospital or a district college. Education and art would prosper; every village, like Italy, with its
painter of repute. Then, indeed, the men of all creeds would be
competent by education to judge of doctrines; yet influenced by
that education, to see that God meant men to live, and love, and
ennoble their souls; to be just, and to worship Him, and not to
consume themselves in rites or theological contention, or, if they did
discuss, they would do so, not as enemies, but inquirers after truth.

" The clergy of different creeds would be placed on an equality,
and would hope to propagate their faith, not by hard names
or furious preaching, but by their dignity and wisdom, and by the
marked goodness of their flocks. Men might meet or part at
church or chapel door without sneer or suspicion. From the
christening of the child, till his neighbours, Catholic and Protestant,
followed his grey-haired corpse to the tomb, he might live enjoying much, honoured much, and fearing nothing but his own carelessness or vice."

In the midst of his serious labours, he burst constantly into verse, as into the region where he was
free to speak his mind without limitation. His
ballads were for the most part historical or legendary,
and were in effect Irish history in the costume of
verse; for whatever he wrote had still the same
aim, to raise up his people by making them better
men and better patriots.

It is not easy to evoke poetry out of morals or
metaphysics, but he knew that verse is the best
vehicle to pass current maxims for the people, and he
often employed it to teach them their higher duties:—

" Then, flung alone, or hand in hand,
    In mirthful hour, or spirit solemn ;
In lowly toil, or high command ;
    In social hall, or charging column :
In tempting wealth, and trying woe,
    In struggling with a mob's dictation ;
In bearing back a foreign foe,
    In training up a troubled nation :
Still hold to Truth, abound in Love,
    Refusing every base compliance—
Your Praise within, your Prize above,
    And live and die in SELF-RELIANCE ! "

It sometimes served even the purpose of controversy. O'Connell had elevated into an axiom the
preposterous paradox that no political amelioration in
any time or country was worth one drop of blood.
It would have been unwise to raise a controversy
with the leader where it could be honourably avoided,
and Davis contented himself with putting into
enduring verse the nobler and truer sentiment :—

" The tribune's tongue and poet's pen
    May sow the seed in prostrate men ;
But 'tis the soldier's sword alone
    Can reap the crop so bravely sown !
No more I'll sing nor idly pine,
    But train my soul to lead a line—
A soldier's life's the life for me—
    A soldier's death, so Ireland's free !

" The rifle brown and sabre bright
    Can freely speak and nobly write—
What prophets preached the truth so well
    As HOFER, BRIAN, BRUCE, and TELL ?
God guard the creed these heroes taught—
    That blood-bought Freedom's cheaply bought.
A soldier's life's the life for me—
    A soldier's death, so Ireland's free ! "

One of his disciples echoed this sentiment later,
in graver tones :—

" When on the field where freedom bled,
  I press the ashes of the brave,
  Marvelling that man should ever dread
  Thus to wipe out the name of slave ;
  No deep-drawn sigh escapes my breast—
  No woman's drops my eyes distain,
  I weep not gallant hearts at rest—
  I but deplore they died in vain."

If the conciliation preached on the platform and
in the press were to prove a real force in affairs, it
was manifest that it must be translated into action.
In selecting candidates for Parliament, an excellent
class would be men who had been honestly converted
to Nationality. There was a wide distinction between
Whigs who had been, and might again be, dangerous
enemies to Nationality, and Whigs who were Federalists or likely to become so. These Davis regarded
as our natural allies, and he framed resolutions in
this spirit to be proposed in the Association, and, as
they amounted to a new departure, sent them to
John O'Connell for his father's consideration.

" 1.—That we think it will be the imperative duty of the
Repeal constituencies in future to return no one to Parliament
who is not an avowed and certain advocate of Domestic Legislation
for Ireland, and a man eminent for patriotism, virtue, and ability.

" 2.—That whereas the majority of persons holding Federalist
opinions are worthy and patriotic men, and are advocates of
Domestic Legislation for Ireland (though they superadd thereto
Irish representation in an Imperial Parliament), we are of opinion
that pledged Federalists, if otherwise desirable, *may* be supported
by the Repeal constituencies wisely and consistently, and if members
of the association, *should* be ; and that we strongly deprecate contests between simple Repealers and Federalists.

" 3.—That it is desirable to postpone all attempts to pledge the
Irish members to the advocacy of Domestic Government, until the
certain approach of a general election, and then that such pledge
should be sought in the most conciliatory manner, and that its
refusal should not be resented in angry words, but repaired by the
substitution of a National candidate."

" My dear Davis" (John O'Connell replied),

" My father has considered your resolutions and made amendments which Crean [Acting Secretary of the Association] will communicate to you. He has written his reasons on them. We can talk the matter over here when you come. Dinner, you know, every day at five sharp, and a corner of a chair, at any rate, vacant for ' The Celt.' " *

One of the hardest tasks an Irish leader could attempt, was to teach his countrymen to respect the law in a country where the law was so often used as an instrument of torture, but Davis did not shrink from the attempt, for he knew that deference for authority is an essential basis of good citizenship, and that France had tossed in unrest for half a century because she remembered too exclusively the abuses of a power shamefully misused.

"It has been our fondest aim," he wrote at this time, "to shelter the administration of the law from suspicion. Coarse, and criminal, and crude as it is, we had rather see it observed in the sincerity of a delusive confidence in its integrity, than see wronged men loose themselves from its obligations, and take vengeance into their own hands, or weak men bowing to it with slavish fear."

To complete the records of public duties which Davis taught, it will be necessary to cite here language which he employed somewhat later to rebuke agrarian crime in the south, language in which the sternness of an indignant judge is miti- gated by the passionate tenderness of a father who sees his children misled to their ruin.

"The people of Munster are in want—will murder feed them ? Is there some prolific virtue in the blood of a landlord that the

* For those to whom the story is unfamiliar, I may state that after a time O'Connell adopted this policy of supporting only Nationalists at elec- tions, enforced it with great vehemence, and with threats and warnings to individual Whigs that they must become Repealers or retire from Parliament; but finally, in 1846, suddenly abandoned it, and broke with the Young Irelanders on the point of supporting Richard Sheil at Dungarvan, Sheil being at that time an official Whig who had renounced National opinions.

fields of the south will yield a richer crop where it has flowed?
Shame, shame, and horror! Oh, to think that these hands, hard
with innocent toil, should be reddened with assassination! Oh,
bitter, bitter grief, that the loving breasts of Munster should
pillow heads wherein are black plots, and visions of butchery, and
shadows of remorse! Oh, woe unutterable, if the men who
abandoned the sin of drunkenness should companion with the
devil of murder; and if the men who last year vowed patience,
order, and virtue, rashly and impiously revel in crime!

"But what do we say? Where are we led by our fears?
Surely Munster is against these atrocities—they are the sins of
a few—the people are pure and sound, and all will be well with
Ireland. 'Tis so, 'tis so; we pray God 'tis so; but yet the people
are not without blame!

"Won't they come and talk to us about these horrid deeds?
Won't they meet us (as brothers to consider disorders in the
family) and do something—do all to stop them! Don't they
confide in us? Oh, they know, well they know, that our hearts
love them better than life—well they know that to-morrow,
if 'twould serve, we would be ready to die by their side in battle;
but we are not ready to be their accomplices in crime—we would
not be unsteady on the scaffold, so we honestly died for them, but
we have no share with the murderer!"

The new policy did not long escape notice. Some
of the best informed of the English journals pronounced that the agitation had become far more
formidable and menacing than in its boisterous days,
for it was now sincere and practical, and the ex-
tremest of the Orange journals at home declared that
the moderation of the leaders was a cover for the
worst purposes.

Tait's Magazine was at that time the chief organ
of cultured Radicalism in Great Britain, and its
editor was among the first to recognize the change.
Two months after the imprisonment had commenced,
he published this remarkable estimate of the reorganized movement :—

"In Ireland, agitation goes on with a quiet, self-assured
strength, that seems remarkably independent of extraneous excite-

ment. It lived once in the breath of the Agitator—it has now a life of its own. The 'Rent of the Captivity' flows in—sometimes a little faster, sometimes a little slower—on the whole, in a full, deep tide, that betokens something more serious than 'enthusiasm' as its source. The chief thing we note in the more recent aspects of this agitation is, that, as the Repealers grow more powerful, they grow more conciliatory and more cautious. They treat their non-repealing countrymen with a respect and cheerful good temper, from which we Saxon agitators for Free Trade and Suffrage might, perhaps, take a lesson; are most tolerant of one another's diversities of opinion; dissuade over-zealous constituencies from pressing too hard on their present representatives; exhort their Orange brethren to leave off 'looking at Irish things from opposite sides of the Boyne;' and pay particular attention to the registration. As their power increases, so does their vigilance, their anxiety to make no mistakes. The old English notion—we suspect still the prevalent one—of Irish patriots and agitators, as being a herd of boastful and frothy rhetoricians, is now ludicrously false. They are most careful and earnest men of business. They rejoice in their strength, but it is with fear and trembling. With the exulting consciousness of power that men must feel who hold in their hands the allegiance, and sway the volition of a nation, they seem to live in perpetual dread of making a false move. In their own words, 'There is *the demon of repeated failure* casting his shadow by us as we move on;' and they are determined, once for all, to exorcise this same demon out of their country's history. The rumours of a Whig accession, to be followed by a gracious and merciful liberation of the Liberator, made them quite nervous; *that* would be a difficulty, indeed: yet they think they could get through it. Even the decision on the writ of error is anticipated, by these impracticable and hard-headed patriots, with much less of eager excitement than one would suppose. We repeat the expression of our conviction, that the state of Ireland is formidable and menacing, to a degree far beyond what public opinion in Great Britain has yet realized to itself. It is frivolous now to talk of Sir Robert Peel's 'chief difficulty.' Ireland is coming to be an Imperial difficulty — a perplexity and peril to Tory, Whig, and Radical alike. The difficulty is growing, at a rate at which it must very soon outgrow the best statesmanship of our most able and honest public men."

Frederick Lucas,[*] the Catholic publicist, who

[*] Editor of the *Tablet*, and afterwards M.P. for Meath.

was a steady supporter of O'Connell's policy, and a
better judge than most men of political forces, held
language more precise :—

"Never," he said, "were both the leaders and the led more
deeply in earnest or more assiduous in their labours. The contest has become less noisy, and this deceives the vulgar, but it has
in exactly the same proportion become more real, more true, (shall
we say it?) more honest and more respectable. It has now become
a recognized fact that the struggle for Repeal may be a long one;
and all parties are girding themselves up for that march through
the wilderness which is to prepare them for the possession of the
promised land. . . . And in the mean time the years of the
pilgrimage will not be wasted. They will be spent in earnest,
anxious, painful efforts to acquire knowledge and discipline, and
every spiritual, moral, and intellectual quality which can accomplish and adorn freedom. . . . Instead of the pike and drum
with which we were distracted last summer, this year shows us
the reading-room, maps, books, papers—the furniture of the mind,
not of the barracks. Instead of battlefields and assembled myriads,
we are to have a more peaceful discipline—combination against
the excise, against spirits, tobacco, tea, coffee, and against all
manufactures that are not of Irish production. When to this we
add a very possible revival of the Arbitration Courts, we have
described a system of agitation which, if properly and heroically
worked into practice, will succeed."

But though there was a new policy and new
leaders, it was a change of cabinet, not of dynasty,
which had taken place. Business was conducted in
the name and with the sanction of the imprisoned
chief, and his position in the confidence and affection
of his race was carefully maintained. Davis wrote
on this point with striking effect in a second letter
to the Duke of Wellington, in the character of a
Federalist :—

"You have got O'Connell at last into gaol. But does your
Grace really believe *that* will stop the agitation? Don't you know
that all the Roman Catholics, Repealers or not, look upon him as
their 'Liberator'? Indeed, my lord, I think they underrate the

service done by Grattan, Wolfe Tone, Plunket, and your Grace, in bringing about emancipation. But this, you see, is an error that makes his imprisonment more unpopular.

"Then, O'Connell is a great man—has stood in the foreground of Irish history for near thirty years. Much as we may sneer at it, he, in some sort, represents Ireland, and *every* Irishman feels this. The imprisonment of such a man is, after all, a national insult. I doubt its being forgiven for a long time. He is imprisoned against the will of the majority of the Irish people, to satisfy the policy of England. This, in some sort, lowers all Irishmen, even his opponents.

"Recollect, the populace idolize him. His person is more known than that of any man alive. There's hardly a man, woman, or child, from Newry to Tralee, but has looked on his manly figure and his winning manner, and heard his wonderful voice, and plausible and tender eloquence. They think more of him than of their farming, or religion. They prefer him to priest, or neighbour, or angel. He is their hero. They pray for him, endure for him, obey him, would die for him. If you had doubled the tithes, or restored the hearth and window-tax, or put an excise on potatoes, you could not have so deeply and lastingly irritated the people. I think better of the people for such devotion; but, whether better or worse, the *fact* is material, and you seem to have forgotten it. The repute of having carried Emancipation, reduced the tithes, obtained corporations, praised and defended the people, were his. His person was equally known and prized by them as his deeds; he only wanted the martyrdom or its appearance to make him a saint all out in the mind of a people who naturally connect suffering under the law with piety, valour, and patriotism. The hereditary love of the Irish for tragedy, even in their greatest affairs, is satisfied at last in him who seemed hitherto to have plucked danger from the patriot's path."

A note from O'Brien to Davis, before the first month of imprisonment had expired, will illustrate the care that was taken to avoid any difference with O'Connell :—

"I was much concerned to find that some parts of your report on Kane [Kane's 'Industrial Resources of Ireland'] did not altogether accord with the views of the prisoners. I think that we are bound to show much greater deference to their wishes, now that they cannot speak for themselves, than if they were free."

The imprisonment at Richmond was, as I have said, a detention on parole, in a pleasant country-house, where a good table, and troops of visitors on appointed days, and leisure for study or business on the other days made time pass without *ennui*. Davis described to Pigot what he found at the Bridewell :—

"The prisoners have two large gardens, a sitting-room and bed-room each, constant visitors, good health and good spirits. The last we all have. We have played our game well and out-manœuvred the Government, and, as far as I can judge, we are an overmatch for them. But 'tis 'a long cry to Loch Awe,' as the Scotch say, and I'm in no hurry. I need not say I am busy at everything but speech-making, which I resolutely avoid and so shall continue.

"My sister is better, but still very weak. Duffy says your song is high treason at least; but I'll read it with him to-morrow again.* D. is certainly better since the key turned on him, but he got a cold from dining in a big tent which they set up in one of the gardens. Just think of their audacity—they had a tricolour flag at the head of the tent, till the governor of the gaol struck it! .

"Matters are glorious in Ulster. The Belfast Whigs coming out at last. The '98 drop is in them yet, God bless them therefor! What is J. O'H. at? His is the pen for this time.

"Don't say how well off our friends are [the Repeal prisoners]. All anxiety for them is over, so we can move on with light hearts.

"Henry Grattan and Alexander McCarthy come to-morrow, and we shall have a great day. We are organizing the rent system, and methinks 'twill be sure and ample henceforth."

The *Nation*, which I continued to edit without interruption at Richmond, seconded the new policy *con amore*. The high prerogative law of the Queen's Bench was repudiated or ignored. On the week the

---

* Pigot fell into occasional extravagancies, which it was necessary to repress. Davis laughingly suggested that he had better set up a journal of his own for these ecstatics, and call it *Pigot's Penny Pike.*

imprisonment commenced the journal was printed with green ink, to express hope and confidence; the articles which had been pronounced seditious were republished in a little volume entitled " The Voice of the Nation," and the prosecuted verse in a new and costly edition of " The Spirit of the Nation."

" You have imprisoned three newspaper proprietors," Richard Sheil exclaimed in Parliament, " and the Irish Press is as bold and as exciting as it was before. Eleven thousand copies of the *Nation* newspaper circulate every week through the country, and administer the strongest provocation to the most enthusiastic spirit of nationality which the highest eloquence in writing can supply." *

Literary projects, designed to educate and fortify public opinion, were pushed on towards completion, and Davis's correspondence at this time is largely occupied with them. The success of the " Spirit of the Nation " induced the publisher to bring out a quarto edition, in monthly parts, with music, and Davis took endless pains to have the Irish phrases corrected and the songs adapted to national airs. To Pigot he wrote :—

" Will you take some trouble for me? 'Tis to write on one side of music paper the ' Corravath Jig,' the ' Siege of Belleisle,' your air to the ' Gilla Machree,' the ' Boyne Water,' and ' O'Connell's March;' and would you try and discover some woeful old air for the ' Lament of Owen Roe,' and fit ones for the ' Girl of Dunbuidhe,' and the ' Men of Tipperary'?'

Eugene Curry answered inquiries about Dathi, an Irish king who plundered Britain and Gaul before the Christian era.

" ' Dathi's body was brought to Cruachain, and was buried in Relg-na-Riogh at Cruachain, where the great part of the kings

* The *Nation* was then price sixpence, and eleven thousand of a circulation which will appear small in the age of penny papers, represented £550, which the people paid weekly for the pleasure of reading it,—sometimes more than the Repeal rent.

of the race of Heremon were buried, where unto this day remains the Cairrthe dearg (Red rock) as a flag over his grave in his Leacht (Carn) near the Rath of Cruachain, even to this time, 1666' (Duald MacFirbis).

"The name of Dathi's burial place is spelled, in modern times, Roilig-na-Riogh, 'Burial-place of the Kings.' The above curious notice is now printed as part of the essay or chapter on the ancient pagan cemeteries of Ireland in Mr. Petrie's 'Round Towers;' therefore you will not anticipate him in putting it in any shape before the public. You will see more on Dathi at page 21 of the forthcoming volume of the Irish Archæological Society's Transactions, which is now in the binder's hands. Could you look in at me for a moment?"

To me he wrote at the same time :—

"I send you the poetry that appeared from October 14th to December 30th, and was at all noticeable, except some of which I had no copies. Fortunately I think all these ought to be omitted. They are McCarthy's 'Intercepted Despatches,' 'The Siege of Waterford,' my lines to Nogan, all too long; also my lines 'We must not fail,' which are rhetoric, not poetry, and I hate them. I have altered some of the 'Girl of Dunbuidhe,' and rewritten my 'Christmas Carol.' I hope you will agree with my notions on these matters. I have turned them about in my mind, and am very deliberate in my liking for them."

"H. [Hudson] has written music for the 'Men of Tipperary,' and will do so for the entire series. B—— wants time only, so I suppose he will make the sketch. But don't mention his name to any one at all. I feel bound to secure him in this, as it is for me he is going to make the design. . . . In comparing the list [for the new edition] with the [old] 'Spirit of the Nation,' I recall that you were to have spoken to Walsh about his 'Voice of Tara,' and got Williams to unite three of his war songs into one—leaving his admirable Munster war song untouched, but giving it some other name, such as 'Hymn of Thurles.' Walsh's poem on quiet re-reading I think very well of, and there are several strong thoughts and racy lines in Williams's verses. I enclose both. . . . The oftener I see our names printed under the titles of our verses, the more immodest it seems. If you at all concur with me, a pen stroke to each poem will cure them. Some names being fictitious is another reason for the change. J. E. P. wishes to be signed Fermoy, not Roche Fermoy. He and John O'Hagan are writing songs. . . . What will you do with Maddyn's long story? Keep, publish it, or send it back? Have you reviewed the magazines? Mind, I'll not give the 'Black Cabinet' unless you have the magazines done in time. I am just going to write it, and shall not see you, as I dine out to-day; but shall to-morrow. I extirpated the historical error of the 'Stone of Fate' from Dathi [a ballad by Davis] and now defy your criticism there anent. Can you let me have the 'Invasion'? [a novel by Griffin.]"

"I leave with you a 'Hesiod' [Flaxman's "Illustrations"], and you can send me the volume you have. I think 'The Golden Age,' and 'The Carrying of Pandora by Mercury,' two of the most beauteous and true compositions I ever saw, and well worth ten 'Spirits of the Nation.' Glory to Flaxman, though he was Saxon."

Davis, who set slight value on what is called fame, used to say that, if he had his will, the songs of the *Nation* would be remembered in after times, and the authors quite forgotten, or survive only in a legend attributing them to some O'Neill or McCarthy, whose existence critics would naturally dispute. But the age of myths ended when the printing-press was set up.

In his own verses he made some corrections which were excellent, but one to which I strongly objected. The dramatic opening of "Owen Roe" is a striking beauty, but he proposed to efface this effect, by inserting a prefatory verse describing how the interlocutors in this dialogue came on the stage. He appealed to two of his friends in London on the point.

"I have rewritten the two first verses of 'Owen Roe,' or rather a line in verse one, and three lines in verse two. The dialogue before was complex and unnatural, and the rhythm nil. Now the second verse belongs entirely to the messenger, who states in some detail how Owen died, having before the ballad opens just told that Owen was dead, poisoned by the English. The whole first verse belongs to the lamenter. Tell me what you and John O'Hagan think of this change, and tell me at once."

Judgment went against him on the appeal, and he submitted like a man of sense. He wrote to me:—

"I find every one, including John O'Hagan, etc., are against me on the 'Owen Roe,' so I must surrender. Will you take the blame of restoration with James Duffy? [the cost of alterations fell on the publisher]. If so, put back verse one as in the present 'Spirit of the Nation,' but I plead to have verse two run thus—

'From Derry we were marching, false Cromwell to o'erthrow,
And who can doubt the tyrant's fate had he met Owen Roe?
But the weapon of the Saxon met him on his way,
And he died, etc.'

"You, I think, agree with this. Will you put my 'Aileen Aroon' into the first number, where the 'Corravath' comes now, and push that farther on? This will oblige me. Inclosed is the correct copy. I shall leave the music of the 'Corravath' to-morrow."

To O'Hagan he wrote :—

"The last number of the 'Spirit' will appear on the 24th of December next. I wish you had something of a ballad going into it. Write on the Volunteers. My 'Dungannon' is unanimously put aside, and you could not have a better subject. Your Munster begins number seven, and Duffy has your 'Expostulation' to suggest some changes. . . . I wish you would write words to some popular airs. Your 'Paddies evermore' shows you could do anything you tried in that way. Pray think of this; 'tis well worth doing."

To Maddyn he wrote :—

"One of your recent letters made me hope that you were coming to reside here for a time. Should you do so, I think we could, immediately after, reduce the project of a history of Ireland in the eighteenth century to certainty. Could you not, on Willis's return to London, come directly here? You would see how things are; we could project, and discuss our projects; you would come to know every one of every party worth knowing, and you would draw fresh life from resting awhile on your native earth. Do come within a month; the weather will then be 'settled fine;' our summer excursions to the Castles of the Pale and the sites of Finian glory will have begun; I shall show you Glennamole and Glenolam and Tara and the Boyne. I am anxious, too, that you should come before the meetings of the Royal Irish Academy close, as our evening meetings will give you endless opportunities of making agreeable acquaintances."

Among the sympathizers with O'Connell in prison, the Whig journals were conspicuous. If a change of Government took place, they insisted that the victims of a packed jury and a partizan judge should be immediately released. But what some of us feared most—not without reason as it proved in the end—was a renewal of confidential relations between O'Connell and a Liberal Government. It was not thirty months since he had been their submissive ally in Parliament, and the chief controller of their Irish patronage, and a renewal of these relations must be fatal to the national cause. And he still maintained, though we little knew it at the time, correspondence with some of them, unbecoming his position and professions in Ireland. The *Nation* aimed to avert the danger of a new Whig compact, by recalling the offences of the party against the country. But we were unexpectedly met by private assurance, that the worst of these offences had been prompted or approved by O'Connell himself. Thomas O'Hagan,* who had been my counsel in the State trials, and whom I had the happiness of including among the most valued of my private friends, was asked to remonstrate with me on the subject. In July he wrote to me at Richmond prison :—

"I am sorry that I shall be unable to get out to you to-day, but I have several cases to dispose of, and I am considerably pressed. I enclose a letter which I had from our friend Deasy. It will explain itself and the views which he wishes to press, better than any account I could give of it. I need not tell you my own notions,

* Afterwards Lord O'Hagan.

which you know, but we can talk of the matter when I see you, as I hope to do, to-morrow.

> " Affectionately yours,
> " THOMAS O'HAGAN."

The enclosed letter addressed to O'Hagan by Mr. Rickard Deasy is of historic interest. Mr. Deasy was at that time a young barrister in good practice, associated with the most liberal of the Whigs, the men who in the end became Federalists, as he did himself. Ten years later, however, when the national spirit had collapsed, he was a Law Officer of the Crown, and, in the end, became a Baron of the Exchequer.

" During the period I have mentioned," he wrote, " some of the worst acts of the Whig Government were those which the Repeal party most loudly applauded, and that Government prevented the commission of some errors which the very same party tried to force them into. You may remember how O'Connell himself proposed a Coercion Bill for Ireland, which I believe the Government refused to adopt, and which Sharman Crawford was ' blackguarded ' for opposing. You also remember how O'Connell supported the appointment of Lord Campbell [to the Irish Chancellorship], which but for that support I believe would not have taken place. I do not know whether you are aware that the Irish popular members, including O'Connell, pressed upon the Whig Government the adoption of Shaw and Peel's plan for *abolishing* corporations in Ireland, and that it is principally to the firmness of Lord John Russell that you are indebted for the existence of Repeal Mayors, etc., to sign municipal declarations for you. Of personal meanness on the part of some of your most high-flown patriots I shall not speak, as I believe you and I are of the same opinion respecting them.*

These disclosures, so far from being an answer to our fears, only increased and confirmed them.

The new policy of the Association was not too welcome at head-quarters. O'Connell, like both the

* June, 1844.

Bonapartes, was determined to found a dynasty at all costs; and his second son, his destined successor, was already known among his parasites as the Young Liberator. That he had none of the essential gifts of a tribune did not quench his ambition, and he dreaded the rise of men who would be unlikely to accept a lay figure as a national leader. To him the best-informed writers agree in attributing troubles which now began to appear. It was the practice of the Association that no resolution should be proposed which had not been previously submitted to the general committee, but Daniel, the cadet of the O'Connells, a young man whose share in public affairs consisted in the task of reading at Conciliation Hall a weekly bulletin from his father in prison, proposed, without previous consultation with the committee, a vote of thanks to the most discreditable and untrustworthy of the Irish members, for a speech in which he had assailed, in violent language, the most influential of the Irish Federalists. Davis was deeply moved, less by the dangerous breach of discipline than by a deliberate reversal of the policy of the Association regarding the Federalists taken with the assent of O'Connell. He wrote to O'Brien, who was in the country at the moment :—

"When you write to Richmond notice the fact that Mr. O'Connell's son moved a vote of thanks to Mr. Dillon Browne without the consent of the committee, and did so because of Mr. Browne's opposition to the Charities Bill, which in its present form a majority of the committee approved. What is worse, he did so after Mr. Browne had made a speech adverse to our whole policy, attacking the Federalists, calling on the people to turn them out, and this because they did not aid his opposition to a useful measure. I have made up my mind if such conduct be repeated to withdraw silently from the Association. . . There are higher things than politics, and I never will sacrifice my self-respect to them."

The *Pilot*, which was the organ of the O'Connell family for any action or advice which it might be convenient to disavow, followed up the move in the Association by a direct attack on the policy which was giving it dignity and power. I find among Davis's papers a note of this date :—

"There was a disgusting article in the *Pilot* last night; one which, I think, Barrett would never have dared to write without the knowledge of his masters. It must be dealt with one way or the other; and I wish you would come out as early as you can in the morning to talk over it. I think it desirable to have O'Connell discountenance, or countenance it (whichever he chooses), that we may deal with it accordingly. The gist of it is an attempt to stop the Repeal Reading-rooms." *

Before these troubles became dangerous they were forgotten in the tumult of unsuspected events. It is held as an axiom in Ireland that no concession was ever won except when England was in some imminent difficulty, and it was naturally regarded as good news that troubles with France suddenly broke out in two hemispheres. King Louis Philippe had a quarrel with Morocco, and threatened to bombard the capital if his demands were not satisfied; England interposed in defence of the Dey, whose territory supplied Gibraltar with necessary provisions; and one of the king's sons rejoined by the publication of a pamphlet insisting that the navy of France was now a match for the navy of England, and not indisposed to try issue with it on the earliest opportunity. The other trouble arose in the South Pacific. Pritchard, the English consul at Tahiti,

* Duffy to Davis, Richmond Prison.

attempted to influence the Queen after she had placed her territory under the protection of France, and was rudely repulsed by a French official. In the language of Sir Robert Peel, he was subject to "a gross outrage accompanied by a gross indignity." Here were good grounds of quarrel, and it was admitted on both sides of the channel that, before fighting France, Peel must conciliate Ireland, and, as a first step, set free the prisoners at Richmond. O'Connell and Lord Palmerston were equally of this opinion ;* which was naturally shared by multitudes of enthusiastic people, who already saw the door of Richmond opened. The Queen, it was rumoured, would be sent over to perform the task graciously.

The deliverance could come in no way more satisfactory to Davis, who desired that the country should have relations with France and America amounting to a definitive foreign policy. At an earlier period he wrote his matured thoughts on this subject :—

"Ever since those distant ages when Europe rang with the praise of Irish scholarship, we have been too secluded. Yet something remained besides English intercourse. During the long struggle with England the sons of the Irish chiefs were commonly brought up at the Spanish or Roman Courts, and during the wars of the sixteenth and seventeenth centuries there was constant commercial, military, and diplomatic intercourse between Ireland and the Continent. We made treaties with France, Lorraine, Spain, and the Ecclesiastical States ; we exchanged our fabrics for theirs ; we received assistance in arms and men from them all. Still there was not enough of this. There was enough to make Irish parties occasionally the tools and victims of foreign ministers ; not enough to secure help when and how 'twas required ; not enough to obtain habitual recognition of our nationality, which would have awed down Italian intriguers and English tyrants.

* See " Young Ireland," chap. ii.

In the eighteenth century there was still some intercourse, but it was by stealth, and existed only to procure soldiers for the continental armies, and maintain certain religious connections. Our foreign relations, restored for a moment during the existence of the French Republic, perished with the Union, and it was not till the crisis of the Catholic agitation, in 1827, that we again established them.

"How great an influence our American and French connections exercised on our oppressor need hardly be repeated. We had aided America during her struggle with 16,000 soldiers and her best general—Montgomery. Grateful for our help, and filled with our exiles, she was ready to return the service. Fearful lest the veterans of Valley Forge should come eastward, or France spare Lafayette for a campaign, England grew pale and conceded free trade in 1779, and legislative independence in 1782. Not that England feared France or America; but she feared Ireland, when aided by them. It has been often said that Dumourier helped to carry the Toleration Act of 1793; but his victory of Jemappe derived half of its persuasive power from the intimacy of Ireland with France, amounting to fraternity in the case of the Ulster Protestants. For Belfast boasted a brotherhood with Paris, and Irish addresses were seen on the table of the Convention. In 1828, the letters, money, and miscellaneous hints from America, the instructive voice of the Parisian press, and the minute inquiries made by the French Cabinet into certain branches of Irish statistics, hastened emancipation. . . . Foreign alliances have ever stood among the pillars of national power, along with virtue, wise laws, settled customs, military organization, and naval position. Advice, countenance, direct help, are secured by old and generous alliances. Thus, the alliance of Prussia carried England through the wars of the eighteenth century ; the alliance of France rescued the wavering fortunes of America; the alliance of Austria maintains Turkey against Russia; and so in a thousand instances besides.*

Dillon, who was in the country, took a more sober view of the situation. In a note to Davis, he wrote :—

"What do you think this African business will come to? I cannot believe that it will terminate in anything serious for the present. The old black rascal will concede anything the French please to demand, and they have no notion of anything more than

---

* "Voice of the Nation."

compelling him to let them alone. As for Pritchard, I agree with the sage of the *Evening Post* that the knowing ones at both sides have no notion of fighting about such a paltry business. . . . Say in your answer how Duffy is, what he is doing, and do not omit to remember me to him."

The action of the French fleet on the African coast did not release the State prisoners; but that event came about in a way nearly as unexpected.* When sentence was pronounced, notice, as we have seen, was given of a writ of error before the House of Lords, and when the prisoners were nearly three months in Richmond, a day was fixed for taking into consideration the question whether they were legally convicted. This appeal excited but languid interest in Ireland. Justice from such a Court seemed hopeless, and the preliminary stages of the inquiry strengthened this distrust. The English judges, according to practice, were called upon to advise the Lords on the legal bearing of the questions at issue, and a large majority of them advised that the conviction at Dublin was a good one. There was still a chance of success, however, for which it was right to be prepared, and Davis wrote to John O'Connell, suggesting

---

* What ultimately came of French enterprise in Africa, Davis sang later:—

"The Frenchman sailed in Freedom's name to smite the Algerine,
The strife was short, the crescent sunk, and then his guile was seen;
For, nestling in the pirate's hold—a fiercer pirate far—
He bade the tribes yield up their flocks, the towns their gates unbar.
Right on he pressed with freemen's hands to subjugate the free,
The Berber in old Atlas glens, the Moor in Titteri;
And wider had his *razzias* spread, his cruel conquests broader,
But God sent down, to face his frown, the gallant Abdel-Kader—
The faithful Abdel-Kader! unconquered Abdel-Kader.
                    Like falling rock,
                    Or fierce siroc—
                    No savage or marauder—
                        Son of a slave!
                        First of the brave!
                    Hurrah for Abdel-Kader!

R

that his father ought to be ready, in case of his deliverance, with a plan for carrying the cause the next stage towards success. O'Connell, who, as it proved in the end, had now no plan, and no longer believed that any plan would succeed in his lifetime, could only send a placebo of general assurances.

"The agitation, when he gets out, will be active, you may be sure; but as to the precise steps, he is meditating on that point, and says nothing definite upon it yet. I think, however, all are agreed to have no more monster meetings—at least, designedly so." *

When the writ was heard, Lord Lyndhurst (Lord Chancellor) and his friend Lord Brougham sustained the judgment of the Irish Court, and Lord Cottenham (the Whig Ex-Chancellor), Lord Denman, and Lord Campbell (Whig Law Lords) reversed it, with grave censure of the Irish Chief Justice and the system of jury-packing which he had upheld. Davis, in a letter to Pigot, announced the reception of the news in Ireland, and the surprise it produced :—

"Thursday night.†

"You may guess our wonder when in committee to-day the news came in that judgment was reversed; it literally rang through Dublin, strangers stopping each other to tell it. 'Tis a great and useful triumph ; would it had not come from a triumvirate of English Whigs !

"We have arranged a procession for Saturday to bring our friends from prison, and carry them by the Four Courts, Castle, Parliament House, with bands and banners, and *a review* of the trades at Richmond ; but don't suppose we're off our legs. O'Brien and I have just parted after grave speculations as to the future, and I, as usual after success, am in low spirits." ‡

* John O'Connell to Davis, Richmond Prison, August 26, 1844.
† August 27, 1844.
‡ The day before, Davis wrote to Webb :—
"I cannot go to you on Monday nor any day next week ; but the coming decision on the writ of error and the threatened visit of the Queen will oblige me to stay in town till both are over. I shall go to you for a day or two before I take to the hills. O'Brien's conduct pleased every one except the

O'Connell's victory over the Government gave the national cause an immense impetus. It was a great opportunity, but he was in a condition of mind and body when opportunities come in vain. Physically he was in the preliminary stage of a mortal disease, and morally he had fallen under the influence of his incapable son, and thought only how best to retreat from a position which he considered untenable. The circumstances of the hour were peculiarly favourable to a steady advance on the lines occupied by the recent policy of the Association, of resolute, practical, unboasting but unshrinking nationality.

At the first meeting Davis produced a pamphlet in favour of a Federal Union, just published by Mr. Grey Porter, the High Sheriff of the peculiarly Protestant county of Fermanagh, himself the grandson of a bishop. Henry Grattan proposed Captain Mockler, the representative of a noted Orange family, as a member; and Smith O'Brien announced the adhesion of Hely Hutchinson, brother of the Earl of Donoughmore. O'Connell's speech, however, was what men awaited with strained attention, as the fingers of the barometer which announced the coming weather. It predicted uncertain times. He noticed in succession various pleas for advancing the cause, only to reject them ; and reserved his favour for the preposterous design of appealing to the English constituencies, to require their members in the House of Commons (where Irish nationality was in a minority of about two in the hundred), to impeach

Tory bigots, who found he had worsted their representative, Lord Erne. Lord H—— has done nothing. His policy is stagnation till the Queen comes, as she will unless new events interfere. I trust I have taken pledges enough for Irish dignity should she come; '21 shall not occur again [the period of George IV.'s visit to Ireland]. Rumours we have enough, but none worth troubling you with. The facts are in the *Nation*."

the Government for misfeasance in the late State trial,
before the House of Lords, where our cause had not
so much as one solitary representative. It is scarcely
necessary to add that impeachment was a process as
obsolete as trial by combat. He talked in private
of letting the Federalists show their hand, and, after
a few feeble speeches in public, retired to Darrynane
to take his annual holiday. At the same time,
O'Brien, who had been overworked during the three
months of the imprisonment, went to his country-
seat, for a short recess, and John O'Connell reigned
at Conciliation Hall.

Davis urged me also to make holiday after my
temporary imprisonment, and volunteered to take
charge of the *Nation* during my absence. If rest be
the legitimate requital of work, he had more claim
to a holiday than any of us, but he would not hear of
beginning it till after my return.

I had accepted an invitation from O'Connell, to
visit him in his mountain home in Kerry; two of my
friends, John O'Hagan and D. F. McCarthy, accompanied me, and there are frequent allusions to this
excursion in Davis's letters at this time. To Pigot
he wrote :—

"O'C. left yesterday for Darrynane. He is wisely playing a
slow game to let the Federalists and travelling Parliament men
[the supporters of Dr. Maunsell's project of a Parliament sitting
alternately in London and Dublin] show themselves, as they are
about to do.

"He expects you to Darrynane. You will meet Duffy, etc.,
there, and would greatly like it. . . . Hudson is in Wales, and
sent me a trumpet call, a quick step, and an air from it. Also an
essay on the language which, after all, he seems to think is Celtic.
Hurrah for my ancestors, and for yours, and you, and myself, and,
as poor Tone I think says, hurrah generally."*

* 67, Bagot Street, September 29, 1844.

His constant engagements at the *Nation* office did not slacken his correspondence. He announced to Wallis Maddyn's final decision not to take part in any device for reviving the dead *Dublin Magazine,* and Wallis replied in a singularly characteristic letter. The man who did nothing but lecture those who worked, naturally remonstrated with the man of action for his languor and indecision, and pronounced the world in general out of joint :—

"I am no way surprised at what you tell me relative to Maddyn. I could have set your mind at rest on that subject six months ago, had I understood how much depended on it, and had you been content to take my word for it. But I think it a great pity the project should end in nothing on any such account; and you must not be angry with me for saying that Maddyn's conduct and your discomfiture at it, both bear too much the stain of that caprice and irresolution which will, I fear, despite all our efforts at amendment, continue long, alike individually and collectively, our besetting and betraying sins. Because a particular man will not guide the plough, or a particular horse draw in it, the field is not to be tilled at all! I can well understand that James Duffy would be better inclined to risk his capital with a man of Maddyn's now established reputation. Not but that I fear he would find himself out in his reckoning. In fact, I must say that, as regards writing, I know no two men so little suited to serve a popular periodical of the kind proposed as Maddyn and myself. And for management and editorship surely a dozen men might be found possessing in a greater degree than either of us the requisite steadiness and discretion. As to the ever-increasing want of such an organ, there can surely be no second opinion. Does not every political vacillation, every incoherent pamphlet, every applauded gasconade, every new rampancy of ignorance and intolerance, every mock miracle,* and still baser mock belief in it, demonstrate alike to friends and foes our lack of all manly discipline? Have not even the chattering chimpanzees of Paris learned to scoff and scorn us? For it is not that our people do not think for themselves, but, properly speaking, they do not think at all. Neither do they read, God help them, anything that can be called reading."

* Some orator at Conciliation Hall has spoken of O'Connell's deliverance from the House of Lords as a manifest miracle.

After three weeks spent among the noble scenery of Waterford, Cork, and Kerry, as Davis's touring friends approached Darrynane, I announced my intention of returning immediately to town, and setting him free for an autumn excursion, but he declined the proposal.

"My DEAR D.,

"You *must* not come back here till the middle of October. I cannot leave town, as one of my brothers is going to be married about the middle of next month. I will then go to Belfast to meet Thomas O'Hagan. The *Nation* is easy to me, and will grow easier. Send 'Laurence O'Toole' within a week, or leave it to number six of the revised 'Spirit of the Nation.' I am proud of my own dear, dear Munster having pleased you so much. I love it almost to tears at the thought. Maddyn has puffed me frightfully in the third part [of "Ireland and its Rulers"]. You forgot the literary materials [materials for the literary page of the *Nation*]. O'Connell holds out against any rule on the reading-rooms [a rule to grant a subsidy on certain conditions], but is practically liberal in voting money for them, so we must make the best of it. I wrote to William Griffin [brother of Gerald Griffin, author of the "Collegians"], he will gladly guide you [in Limerick]. Tell McCarthy to write words to McCarthy's march in the *Citizen*. Give him my respects, and my best regards to John O'Hagan. E. B. Roche * wants much to meet you and to get you to Trabolgan.

"Tell O'Connell that the first news Robert Tighe [an Irish barrister] had of the liberation was from the shouting of the Frankfort mob! What other man since Napoleon could have produced such an effect? Present my respects to the O'Connells, and believe me as busy as a swallow."

A couple of days later there came another hasty note :—

"DEAR D.,

"Here are some letters which you can leisurely answer at Darrynane. I reviewed the 'Memorandum on Irish Matters' on September 14th. Got John Pigot to play the 'Boucleen

* Then M.P. for Cork County, afterwards Lord Fermoy.

Buidhe' and 'The Marriage' for you [airs to which Davis had recently written songs]. 'Tis as sweet as your 'Mina Mumhain.'

"For God's sake get O'Connell to undertake, or to allow others to undertake, a plenipotentiary mission to establish Repeal Reading-rooms, and give them books and good advice. Damn the ignorance of the people—but for that we should be lords of our own future; without that, much is insecure."

O'Connell, in his pleasant home fast by the Atlantic, was a patriarchal chief. His talk was of rural sports for the most part, and the duties of a country gentleman. He wrote to his most confidential correspondent, as he talked, of what was uppermost in his mind.

"I found everything in the best order here. I am, in truth, a great farmer, and have certainly the best crop of hay in proportion of extent of ground or beyond it of any farmer in the province. The potato crop in this vicinage is excellent—considerably beyond the consumption of the growers, and on that account a very probable source of wealth, as the inhabitants of other districts are deficient in that necessary article of Irish food. I found my pack in the high pride of beauty. It would delight any being capable of delight to see them and hear them *trail*. I had a splendid hunt yesterday." *

The third part of " Ireland and its Rulers," which appeared at this time, contained a sketch of Davis under the name of Dormer, in strong contrast to the bulk of the book, which was hostile to nationality.

"Dormer," he wrote, "brought to the service of the Irish masses an amount of natural ability and acquired talent, rarely, indeed, to be found in the cause of the Irish multitude. Of acquirements vast in extent, though perhaps too miscellaneous in their character; of an intellectual suppleness that allowed him to manifest the powers of a poet of high promise, while he was immersed in the details of political life; learned profoundly in the history of his own country, and well acquainted with that of other nations, and with philosophical capacity of considerable original grasp—he pos-

* O'Connell to P. V. FitzPatrick, October 3, 1844.

sessed a mind and accomplishments which of themselves would be
sufficient to secure for him the respect of all those who admire
genius and knowledge.   But when it is added that his fine and
valuable mental gifts are conjoined with an unsullied character,
remarkable not only for the noble disregard of self but for its love
of fair play, while dealing with an avowed opponent, how much
ought such a man to be admired while developing his activity and
working out his energy in a gangrened state of political society
like that of Ireland?   For though Dormer could with eminent
power lash the passions of his party into phrensy, not even in his
most excited hours would he be guilty of the characteristic faults
of the Corn Exchange.   An Irish patriot, without the taint of
vanity; an Irish democrat loathing those vile arts which have
made the word 'agitator' synonymous with much of what is
abominable; an Irish popular leader without hypocrisy, servility,
or meanness—such is the spirited and generous Dormer." *

The criticism on O'Connell was often harsh and
unjust, but the volume contained practical suggestions and historic warnings of great value.   O'Brien
was much pleased with it, and seemed to regard its
bitters as wholesome and tonic.

"O'Brien," Davis wrote to the author, "is in delight with your
book.   He says not three men in the empire could write so well,
and hopes and expects you to be yet with us and for us.   God
grant it."

Respecting the sketch of himself, he added :—

"It would be folly to say that I do not see you *meant* to
describe me in one of its chapters.   I am warmly grateful for the
affection that misled you into it.   I am but one of many, as
resolved as a river is to descend, to lift the English rule from off
Ireland and give our country a career of action and thought.   For
this purpose much action and thought through a series of years
must be used by us.   Action, even in a military sense, is not mere
cutting, firing, and charging.   Organization, education, leadership,
obedience, union, are all action, too—the best and most mature
action in some cases—in ours, I think, for instance.   There is as
much action in the depôt as in the service companies, as any soldier

* "Ireland and its Rulers," pt. iii., p. 252.

can tell you. Again, I believe your conclusion, that success is impossible save by war, to be wrong in part. Well, no matter now—time will judge us, and, if we fail, will be justly as strong against our policy as you, while it will have none of the apologies for our difficulties, the respect for our intentions, nor the tenderness which so overpraises, as you have. I do not pale at such censure, but trust and try to overcome it by success. Our work is only beginning. This is all about myself, and you are to blame. . . . I have thought it better, considering the bitterness of your attacks on O'Connell, not to write an analysis of your third part. Do you mean to write a fourth part? I advise you *not*. Indeed I go further, and recommend you to avoid touching your Irish political contemporaries for some years to come."

The opinion of Davis's closest friends on the sketch was probably expressed with sufficient accuracy in a note I sent him from Darrynane.

"We got the *Tablet* at Father Mathew's, and read 'Dormer' there, which we thought clever and generous, but not graphic. As O'H. says, an acquaintance recognizes its truth, but it would give a stranger no clear notion of the original. It is a sin to complain, however, where there was so much good feeling and manliness.

"From Darrynane we will go to Limerick; where I will call on your friend Griffin, and home *immediately*, making a month in all—the pleasantest I can recall, always excepting my honeymoon. Apropos of honeymoons, I wish it was your brother's brother that was getting married—I fancy it would promote his happiness, and put a strait waistcoat upon discontents which shake the peace of Jupiter in his seclusion."

The object of the northern journey, where he proposed to meet Thomas O'Hagan, was one of grave import. Mr. O'Hagan had joined the Repeal Association as a Federalist, and many of the more liberal and enlightened Whigs came to share his belief that Federation would furnish a solution of the national difficulty. Sharman Crawford openly declared for it; and Mr. Ross, the member for Belfast; Colonel Caulfield, brother of the Earl of Charlemont; Mr.

Thomas Hutton, formerly member for Dublin city; and a number of barristers of good standing in their profession, were in general agreement with him. It was proposed to hold a private consultation at Belfast, the cradle of the greatest national movements in the last century. Hudson and Davis, who were ready to go all lengths for unmitigated nationality, promoted this conference, and would have accepted Federalism, and given it a fair trial. From his correspondence at this time, we may infer that the design of a conference originated with Davis. Mr. Ross wrote to him in October :—

" I should be very happy to meet you and Mr. Hudson, and talk over the Federal scheme ; and, if it were possible, I would go to Belfast on the 19th for the express purpose. . . . You won't find much interest in Federalism or any other 'ism' among the flax-spinners and linen-merchants of the north. They are driving a good trade and making money fast ; you well know how people thus circumstanced are distrustful of experiments of a political nature : not that they are indifferent to politics, far from it ; if any existing right were in jeopardy they would be up in arms in a moment."

And again, a fortnight later :—

" We are both surprised and vexed " [he is speaking for Sharman Crawford and himself] " at the hesitation of parties who, till lately, seemed all eagerness to take the initiative in a Federal movement ; but we are ready to adopt any modification of our manifesto which may render it generally acceptable—provided the change proposed shall not affect its essential character. . . . Either the control of national ecclesiastical property must be given to a national representative body, or, as Mr. Caulfield suggests, the whole question of the Irish Church Establishment must be settled, as a preliminary step to the organic change we have in view. Mr. Caulfield's plans do not admit of his going to Dublin immediately ; neither do mine : but if you and Sharman Crawford would meet Hutton, J. Perry, O'Hagan, Murphy and the rest, ascertain our real position before the country, and come to some general understanding among yourselves, neither Mr. Caulfield nor I would find much difficulty in joining you afterwards. From all that I can gather of public opinion, it appears to me that Cork is our only stronghold at present; and certainly, if we cannot find cordial support from a pretty numerous body of influential men in Dublin and in the north, it would be worse than idle, as far as the cause is concerned, and exceedingly detrimental to ourselves as public men, to make a fruitless parade of our opinion before the world."

One of the projects which occupied this period of inaction at Conciliation Hall was a National Club, with a high subscription, a handsome uniform, and a close ballot to propitiate the fastidious. It originated among the Richmond prisoners—with Dr. Gray, I think,—and was taken up warmly by Davis. He believed such a body would win recruits who would never join the Repeal Association. He ventured even to hope that it might become a substitute for the Council of Three Hundred.

He wrote to Maddyn :—

"We are getting up a 1782 club here. You must join it; for, with God's blessing, Ireland will take you back some day and nurse you tenderly after your exile."

And to Denny Lane :—

"You ought to get your uniform at once, and at any inconvenience attend the opening day. You should send us more members. Cork has more men fit for the club, and fewer in it, than most of our provincial cities. This club can do all we want, if it be resolutely and earnestly supported. I entreat of you to work for it, and that without delay. Send us candidates, make members, get them dresses, push its reputation everywhere. I'd like to have a talk with you on this. Barry is well and idle; Dillon ditto. Poor Duffy has lost his eldest child, and his wife is dying. John Pigot in London, preparing himself for the Bar. T. MacNevin is working like an enthusiast. S. O'Brien is and does all we could desire. We are making great way with the educated Conservatives; but do not talk of this."

But to win those who held aloof from the Association, the club must exclude the men who made the Association odious, and this was an experiment of a character which cost Vergniaud and Madame Roland their heads. Carlyle scoffs at the futility of attempting to make a revolution by excluding the ruffians, and, if the ruffians are strong and malignant, it is never likely to prove an agreeable task. Lane, in reply, opened up this objection and others, which proved to be well founded :—

"I'm sorry that I can't have a talk with you on the subject, as I confess I do not at all understand the 'Eighty-Two Club. I fancied at first that I had some glimmering of its meaning, but I thought that the means adopted were altogether inadequate and inappropriate to secure the end in view. I fancied it was to make Repeal genteel—which I do not consider of any value, even if it were possible,—to turn Hercules into an Antinous, and teach him to wield his club gracefully, is, I think, an idle task. Let Repealers be strong and earnest and they may be as ungraceful as they will—it is better have them clench their teeth and knit their brows than smile with elegance. It would be impossible to form a large body of Repealers who have what may be called 'position in society.' If you can form a star of them so much the better, but where do you draw the line of distinction between the nucleus of aristocracy and the nebulous mass of shabby gentility which surrounds it? Begin with Lord French, Sir Richard Musgrave, Smith O'Brien, and the members of Parliament,—exclude M. N.— he is indignant,—admit him—well, exclude O. P. and he is outrageous; or admit him and you must admit X. Y. Z.,* and so on, until you include every man who can borrow a guinea and get tick from his tailor—or else you cause dissension. You must either miss your proposed object, or do worse, divide your party. No! You should have got up a good club, like the Kildare-street, where a man could not complain if he were rejected; or you should have had a society of some sort like what you once proposed to Lefanu for the Young Ireland of both parties, into which men of all opinions would be admitted; or you should deluge Royal Irish Academies, and Royal Dublin Societies, and every old institution with Repealers. You may make the great body of the Protestants

---

* The original letter contains the names of the persons indicated above by the letters of the alphabet.

at present swallow Nationality, but you cannot make them gulp down Repeal, or, as they believe it to be, O'Connellism. If they become national 'tis all we want; the rest will follow as sure as the fruit follows the flower—you must have a spring and a summer before you have an autumn.

"I had another idea about the 'Eighty-Two Club, that it might be turned into a National Convention,—the method in which the men were admitted at the first ballot puts this out of the question. It was very injudicious to have such a flourish of trumpets at its foundation, and such trivial rules coming immediately after. [Rules as to uniform, entrance fee, etc.] There was a good deal of the old Irish fanfaronade about it which I hoped was dying out amongst us. In Cork the people in general have a great hatred of uniforms; the town councillors and aldermen here could not be got to wear robes. This I think principally arises from the morbidly keen sense of the ludicrous which Cork men generally possess. Tom Steele could not live a week in Cork."

We shall see later that these predictions were bitterly verified.

At this time Maddyn announced a project he had in hand, which greatly interested his friend :—

"I have been collecting a few books for a life of Flood, to be published in England. It would state his merits clearly, intelligibly, and with fairness. The worst thing I know about Flood was his hinting that he was Junius! When I was in Dublin last there was an anti-Grattanite set amongst your party—a set which cried up Flood. His anxiety to get into the English House of Commons, while there was a Parliament in Ireland, shows that, after all, his views on 'Nationalism' were very equivocal, and certainly were inferior to those of Grattan. The first twenty years of his life were the best. His influence upon Grattan was very decided : 'He persuaded the old, he inspired the young' is a half confession of that influence. He was a man of great power of mind, but 'there was a screw loose' somewhere in his character or in his body, that prevented him from a harmonious development of his nature. . . . With my life of vexation and annoyance, I deliberately read the books in which joy and the good of life and the world are depicted by genius. I have found Molière an admirable adviser and companion—he beats any author I know for imparting a sense of cheerfulness, and for sharpening our perception of the joyous and the gay."

Davis wished the book to become part of a series of Irish orators then in course of publication, and his friend seemed not unwilling. In his reply he discussed the rival orators of 1782 with discrimination and sympathy :—

"In the foreign politics of Ireland Henry Flood was the true statesman, but in the domestic politics, Grattan had the larger, more generous, and more enduring views. Flood's nationality was entirely too Northern for a whole Irishman—it had no dash of the Milesian in it; but there was merit in Grattan's feelings for the Catholics that all true Munster men would deeply sympathize with. Admitting that Flood was right on the 'simple Repeal,' yet we are not to forget all Grattan's other illustrious services. In talent for statesmanship, and capacity for calculating occurrences, and the means of bringing them about, it strikes me that Wolfe Tone was much abler (albeit that he failed) than either Flood or Grattan. Had he been in the shoes of either, had he had the rank, fortune, family, and authority of Flood, or had he had the stirring power and electrical eloquence of Grattan, he would have created more of an era than both of his predecessors did. His design of 'The United Irishmen' showed more political thought of a masterly and comprehensive kind than anything I know in Grattan or Flood."

MacNevin had already taken up the same subject, and when Davis wished to transfer it to a man whom he esteemed a better historical critic, and a more experienced writer, MacNevin petulantly refused to give way. But after a little his better nature prevailed, and he consented to do whatever Davis thought most useful.

"I do *not* feel inclined," he wrote at first, "to accede to your unreasonable request that I should give up my intention to write a memoir of Flood, the materials of which I had half collected, and the subject of which I like exceedingly, for some great unknown of yours that is to be brought into light by the patronage of Anglesea Street. James Duffy asked me to do it. I wrote to Dillon to incite him to do it; he declined, and wished me to do it; and, unless I can see some better reason than you have yet given,

I will do it. I have no notion of relinquishing what pleases me, for the peculiar behoof and benefit of some nest-egg of yours. . . . If this hidden great man wishes to become a writer to my inconvenience and annoyance, let him take Sheil. I prefer Flood."

But after a little time he felt he could not resist Davis.

"If you have any peculiar desire to take Flood, do it. It would be a great disappointment to me, for I expended time and money in collecting materials, and I like the subject much more—infinitely more—than Sheil. I have opinions of my own upon that era, and I wish to write them, but I don't wish to annoy you by a refusal. So act as you please."

The result was not fortunate; Maddyn finally shrunk from the enterprise, and, after half a century, Flood's speeches have not yet been collected. But MacNevin, with effective assistance from the great rhetorician himself, made an excellent collection of the speeches of Richard Sheil.

CHAPTER VII.

CONFLICTS WITH O'CONNELL.　1845.

WE have seen that the Federalists, consisting mainly of Whigs, but with some notable sympathizers among the Tories, were beginning to move. There was no public muster-roll of the party, but a memorandum found among Davis's manuscripts indicates how widely he believed the desire for a Federal Union had spread.

"The wealthiest citizens of Dublin, Cork, and Belfast, many of the leading Whig gentry and barristers, and not a few Conservatives of rank, hold Federalist opinions. They include Episcopalians, Presbyterians, and Roman Catholics, Repealers and Anti-Repealers."

Hudson, at the same time, prepared and sent to his friend a list of actual or probable recruits, which will give at least the measure of their hopes.

Peers.

Arran.	Fingal.	Charlemont.
Miltown.	Howth.	Listowel.
Lismore.	Cloncurry.	Netterville.
Cremorne.	Meath.	Talbot de Malahide.
Kenmare.	Stuart de Decies.	Mount Morris.
Southwell.	Rossmore.	Carew.

Ulster.

Sharman Crawford.　D. R. Ross, M.P.　Lord Achison.
　　Colonel Rawdon, M.P.　　Saunderson (Cavan).

Connaught.

Lord Clements.   Col. Samuel White.   Sir Valentine Blake.
Thomas Martin.   The O'Connor Don.

Leinster.

Lord Brabazon.   Chapman.
Colonel White.   Boyce of Bannow.
William Murphy (Smithfield).   Luke White.
James Grattan.   Thomas Hutton.
Torrens McCullagh.   J. Perry.
Archbold (Kildare).   Sir Wm. Somerville.
Charles Walker.   Colonel Butler.
J. H. Talbot, and   Sir Rd. Nagle.
J. Maher (Wexford).   Farrell (Athlone).
Hugh Morgan Tuite.

Munster.

Colonel Macnamara.   Thomas Wyse.
William Fagan, M.P.   Hayes, Cork.
Colonel Beamish.   Richard Dowden (ditto).
Sir Richard Musgrave.   G. S. Barry.
Sir William Beecher.   Sir J. Power (Kilfane).
Sir Denham Norreys.   Sir R. Keane (Cappoquin).
Morgan John O'Connell, M.P.   Sir David Roche, M.P.
Power of Gurteen.   John O'Brien.

The theory of the party was that the Union had been effected by corruption and force, that it had worked ruinously for Ireland, and that a new international treaty with juster provisions ought to be substituted for it. Davis, under the title of a Federalist, in an anonymous letter to the Duke of Wellington (already cited), formulated their principles, and it is curious to note that public opinion in the two islands, after nearly half a century, is running abreast with their theories :—

"I do not seek a raw Repeal of the Act of Union. I want you to retain the Imperial Parliament with its imperial powers. I ask you only to disencumber it of those cares which exhaust its patience and embarrass its attention. I ask you to give to Ireland a Senate

s

of some sort, selected by the people, in part or in whole; levying their customs and excise, and other taxes; making their roads, harbours, railways, canals, and bridges; encouraging their manufactures, commerce, agriculture, and fisheries; settling their poor-laws, their tithes, tenures, grand juries, and franchises; giving a vent to ambition, an opportunity for knowledge, restoring the absentees, securing work, and diminishing poverty, crime, ignorance, and discontent. This, were I an Englishman, I should ask for England, besides the Imperial Parliament. So I would for Wales, were I a Welshman, and for Scotland were I a Scotchman; this I ask for Ireland.

"It is not impossible to combine an Irish legislature for local purposes with the integrity and foreign importance of the empire. A local parliament granted soon, and in a kindly and candid spirit, would be fairly worked, and would conciliate that large and varied body, which, from wisdom, or want, or patriotism, or ambition, are intolerant of having their local laws made, and their local offices filled, by Englishmen. Allow them to try their hands and heads at self-government; it will consume their passions, and, unless they are blockheads, will diminish their sufferings. Aid them by advice. You are an Irishman and a consummate genius —you might have been a hero. Do not lose your last opportunity. Believe me, my lord, if you and half a dozen men of business— Imperialists, Federalists, and Repealers—were to sit down in earnest to devise a plan for satisfying the wants and calls of Ireland for local government, while you guaranteed the integrity of the empire, you would accomplish your object without much difficulty, and disappoint the foreign foes of that empire who justly regard Ireland as an ally."

Davis's relation to Federalism is not difficult to understand; after the Clontarf surrender, he looked upon it as a possible and honourable compromise. Shortly after that event he wrote to a correspondent in England: * "So strong is the desire for a quiet and friendly resumption of nationality, that if England offered us a federal connection to-morrow it would have the support of even the ultra men."

In a review of Sismondi's "Italian Republics,"

* R. R. Moore, of the Anti-Corn Law League.

he painted with evident sympathy the public spirit,
local patriotism, and indestructible vitality of small
states federated together, as contrasted with the
internal weakness of great unwieldy empires, often
overthrown in a single battle. In fact, the existing
condition was intolerable, the end most desired was
impossible for the present, but here was a *tertium
quid.*

The best thing that could befall O'Connell after
his imprisonment was that the Liberal party should
take up Federalism. It would increase prodigiously
the chance of a speedy settlement, whether on his
lines or theirs. He strove to persuade Crawford and
others that their proper course was to join the Association, not as Repealers but as Federalists, as Mr.
O'Hagan and the Bishop of Killaloe had done; but
they would not listen to this proposal. Some of them
disliked and distrusted him personally, and they all
knew that no one could induce a tithe of the party
to enter Conciliation Hall on any pretence. But
the objection to his scheme lay deeper; if the proposal was to be listened to in England, and accepted
as an alternative to Repeal, it was plain that it must
not originate with the Repealers. When it became
certain that the Federalists would not join him,
O'Connell was seized with the fatal idea of joining
them, by declaring himself a convert to their opinions.
He had left prison with the determination of retreating definitively from the position of the Mallow
defiance, and here, unfortunately, he perceived a
favourable opportunity. He privately urged two
Federalists who were among his personal friends,
William Murphy, a Smithfield salesman of great
wealth, and Thomas O'Hagan, to ascertain the wishes

and intentions of their Federal associates. They tried doubtless to comply with his wishes, but without much success. From Darrynane he wrote to Vincent FitzPatrick, the most trusted of his confidential agents :—

"I am becoming very impatient to hear *authentically* from the Federalists. Are they at work? . . . O'Hagan will do well to ascertain, *and in writing*, the views of as many as possible, but he ought to be cautious as to publication. I am writing a letter that will contain the *principles* of federation, leaving the details for future consideration." *

His impatience overcame him, and, while the Belfast consultation was in progress, he wrote a letter to the Association announcing this change of opinion. In the midst of a long political disquisition there was this pregnant sentence :—

"For my own part," he said, "I will own that since I have come to contemplate the specific differences, such as they are, between simple Repeal and Federalism, I do at present feel a preference for the Federative plan, as tending more to the utility of Ireland and the maintenance of the connection with England than the proposal of simple Repeal. But I must either deliberately propose or deliberately adopt from some other person a plan of Federative Union before I bind myself to the opinion I now entertain."

The Duke of Wellington's conversion to Catholic Emancipation, Peel's to Free Trade, Disraeli's to Household Suffrage, or Lord John Russell's to religious intolerance in 1851, did not take his party by more complete surprise that this startling declaration. The time was when it would have been received without criticism in the press, as it was actually received in the Association, or with only a subterranean murmur of dissent, but that time was passed. It was felt instinctively that this sudden surrender

* "Private Correspondence of O'Connell."

might be fatal to the national cause by killing
popular confidence, and that even as a stroke of
policy it was a mistake. If there had not been
a national movement, strong and triumphant, Federalism would never have been heard of; if the national
movement was transformed into Federalism the
existing party would probably disappear, for Sharman
Crawford and his friends would never serve under
O'Connell. Davis was at Belfast, Dillon in Mayo,
and all the men with whom I was accustomed
to consult gone on their autumn holiday. The course
the *Nation* would take was of supreme inportance,
for if *it* was silent no national journal in the island
could be counted on to face the wrath of O'Connell.
But Davis was actually engaged in Federal negotiations at the moment, and to denounce Federalism in
the *Nation* would be to put him in a false position.
On the other hand, to acquiesce after the people had
been pledged in twenty monster meetings to unlimited nationality would shame us before our allies
in America and France, and humiliate us before our
opponents in England, and would infallibly drive the
best men out of an association which did not know
its own mind on the most momentous question. It
was not Federalism that was objectionable, but
putting the livery of the party on the shoulders
of Nationalists.

I solved the difficulty by writing as the leading
article in the *Nation* a letter to O'Connell in my
own name, and speaking only for myself. I objected
to the change he proposed, contending that it would
not serve Federalism and might ruin Repeal, and
insisting courteously that the Association had no
more right to alter the constitution upon which its

members were recruited than the Irish Parliament
had to surrender its own functions without consulting its constituents.   The letter was reproduced
extensively by the newspapers, and the controversy
spread to nearly every journal in the empire, and
finally to those of France and the United States.
It was generally predicted that the *Nation* and the
party it immediately represented would be destroyed,
but that, though O'Connell would conquer them, his
new profession of faith might be regarded as the
funeral oration of Repeal.   Neither prediction was
verified, both the *Nation* and the public cause outlived the difficulty.   The story has been told in detail
elsewhere,* and we have to do with it here only as it
concerns Thomas Davis.

Before O'Connell's letter appeared he wrote. to
me from Belfast : " Our mission here has prospered
beyond hope, but if Dublin holds back all may yet
fail."   When it appeared he received the first
announcement with singular self-control.

" O'Connell's letter," he wrote to Smith O'Brien, " is very able
of its kind, but it is bad policy, if not worse, to suddenly read his
recantation.   He insulted the Federalists, then patronized them,
then refused to tolerate them in Parliament unless they joined the
Association, and now he discovers they are right all out, and of
course were right all through.   My opinion is, you know, what
I have always avowed in the *Nation*—namely, that Federalism
is not, and cannot be, a final settlement, though it deserves a fair
trial and perfect toleration.   I believe there would be no limit
to our nationality in twenty years whether we pass through Federalism or—[a blank in the original letter].   I write by this post
to John O'Connell, urging his father not to repeat his opinions,
at least till Federalists do something."

I wrote to Davis describing the stress of circumstances under which I had acted, and inviting him

* See " Young Ireland," book iii., chap. 3.

if he agreed with me, to take part in the controversy. He replied :—

> "Monaghan, Thursday morning.
>
> "MY DEAR D.,
>
> "On reflecting that other events may have happened since I left, and regarding the policy of pressing the discussion further at this moment as doubtful, I have concluded not to write on our relations to Federalism, and to ask you to weigh the propriety of letting it be for a week. I shall be in town on the 1st."

During the week's truce of silence which I adopted on Davis's suggestion, O'Connell's personal enemies in the press yelled forth that the Young Irelanders were manifestly conquered in the first skirmish ; were dumb, and swallowed their leek in silence, and so forth.

Davis returned to town immediately, and associated himself with the course taken by the *Nation.*

> " We shall rejoice," he wrote, " at the progress of the Federalists, because they advocate national principles and local government. Compared with Unionists they deserve our warm support; but not an inch further shall we go; principle and policy alike forbid it. Let who will taunt or succumb, we will hold our course. No anti-Irish organ shall stimulate us into a quarrel with any national party; no popular man or influence shall carry us into a compromise. Let the Federalists be an independent and respected party ; the Repealers an unbroken league—our stand is with the latter."

And on my behalf I added, in relation to the storm of menace with which we were assailed,—

> " The legitimate leader of the movement was not more willing to lead than we to follow; we proclaimed strict obedience and discipline as essential to success, and we practised them ; for where there are many captains the ship sinks. But at all times, and now not less than any other time, we stood prepared to hold our own opinion against him upon a vital question (such as the present) as freely as against the meanest man of the party. We

do not run all risks with a hostile Government, in proclaiming day by day weighty and dangerous truths, to abandon the same right under any other apprehension."

The Federal cause, Davis assumed, was completely ruined by this unexpected *coup* of the leader. To O'Brien, he wrote :—

" All chance of a Federal movement is gone at. present, and mainly because of O'Connell's public and private letters; yet I am still doing all in my power to procure it, for I wish to cover O'Connell's retreat. He is too closely bound up with Ireland for me ever to feel less than the deepest concern for his welfare and reputation." *

The Federalists were naturally discouraged and angry. " O'Connell," said Deasy, " has jumped into our boat and swamped it." Sharman Crawford was deeply indignant, and complained privately to O'Brien that O'Connell had first attempted to wheedle the Federalists, and then betrayed them.

" He wants," he said, referring to a former transaction,—" he wants to take the same undignified course, humbugging both Repealers and Federalists; trying to make the Repealers believe they are Federalists and the Federalists that they are Repealers; and keeping a joint delusive agitation, knowing right well that whenever particulars came to be discussed they would split up like a rope of sand."

But he had inflicted a worse injury on himself

---

* O'Connell had not consulted O'Brien on this new movement; but when the controversy sprung up in the press he wrote him a private note, suggesting how much might come out of it:—

"'The principal actor in Dublin," he said, "in the arrangement is William Murphy, called 'of Smithfield.' He is a man who has acquired enormous wealth, and has long been a principal 'brains carrier' of the Irish Whigs. A most shrewd sensible man, Thomas Hutton, the very wealthy coachmaker, has assisted and is assisting. I could mention other influential—highly influential—men. There is to be a Federalist meeting at Belfast on the 26th. Caulfield, brother of Lord Charlemont, leads or presides. Sharman Crawford, Ross, the member for Belfast, and other notabilities attend. Hutton, who is a Presbyterian, goes there, and passes through Armagh, to muster as many important Presbyterians as he can, or at least to procure their signatures. O'Hagan, the barrister, attends the registry, and will be at the meeting on the 26th."

than on any one else. The tone of the national press
and of conspicuous Nationalists was so hostile to his
new opinions that he had to renounce them with
something like contempt. While he still lingered
in the country, he began to note painful evidence
that his old popularity had received a dangerous
check, owing, it may be confidently surmised, to his
Federal escapade. At the beginning of November
he wrote to the Secretary of the O'Connell Tribute:

"Do you know that I have a feeling of despondency creeping
over me on the subject of this year's tribute. It seems almost to
have dropped still-born from the press. In former years, when
the announcement appeared it was immediately followed by
crowded advertisements in the Dublin papers to meet and arrange
the collection. The Cork, Waterford, Limerick, etc., newspapers
followed, but there is not one spark alight." *

Doheny, who encountered him at a public dinner
at Limerick on his way to town, thought he was
ruffled by a similar feeling among his audience, and
he arrived in Dublin in no pleasant mood.†

He returned to the Association at the end of
November, and broke contemptuously with allies
he had so recently sought.

"They were bound," he said, "to declare their plan, and he
had conjectured that there was something advantageous in it, but
he did not go any further; he expressly said he would not bind
himself to any plan. Yet a cry was raised, a shout was sent forth,
by men who doubtless thought themselves fitter to be leaders than
he was, and several young gentlemen began to exclaim against

* O'Connell to P. V. FitzPatrick, Nov. 2, 1844, " Private Correspondence
of O'Connell."
† "Your name was received with the loudest cheers; to such a degree
indeed as, in my mind, to rouse the great man's wrath. But although the
reception was most flattering, still there is a strong feeling that the *Nation*
was wrong in intimating that Dan had abandoned the cause. To be sure
most men who entertain that feeling have not inquired into the justice or the
value of the argument in the *Nation:* they content themselves with saying
that it is necessary to preserve the inviolability of his character" (Doheny
to Duffy.)

him instead of reading his letter for explanation. It was not that
they read his letter and made a mistake, but they made the mistake and did not read the letter. He had expected the assistance
of the Federalists, and opened the door as wide as he could without
letting out Irish liberty. But," he continued, "let me tell you a
secret:—Federalism is not worth that"—snapping his fingers.
"Federalists, I am told, are still talking and meeting—much good
may it do them; I wish them all manner of happiness: but I don't
expect any good from it. I saw a little trickery on the part of
their 'aide-de-camp,' but I don't care for that; I have a great
respect for them. I wish them well. Let them work as well as
they can, but they are none of my children; I have nothing to do
with them."

The risk of the Association being suddenly transformed was at an end, but his northern allies were
disgusted and alienated, and cynical politicians declared that the punishment of the *Nation* was only
postponed to a favourable opportunity. Davis did
not allow himself to be moved either by the vacillation or the menace, but pressed on towards his life's
purpose with unfaltering step.

"Disunion," he wrote, "has ceased among your leaders—let
energy revive amongst you. The parties of England scoff at your
complaints and jest at your sufferings. Poor millions of Irish,
half-clad, half-housed, half-fed, England jests at you; middle
classes of Ireland, men full of ambition and genius, robbed of your
commercial gains and your political rights, England spurns your
prayer as the writhing of helpless worms. Are you helpless,
millions of Ireland? Strong hands, brave hearts, growing minds,
owners of the kingdom of Ireland, are you poor imbeciles? Have
you blood, and strength, and manhood? And if you have, what
will you do? Will you burst into an unskilled insurrection and
feed your foes with your ruin? Will you drop your heads and
sob like overworked horses, and let these despots drive you as
they like? Will you take to the miserable resources of the
drunken Ribbon Lodge or the blind fury of assassination? We, who
are ready for anything, so that it give good hope of your success,
we answer for you—we answer thus: We will teach and avow
Repeal more openly and boldly than ever; we will establish
people's courts, people's bands, people's reading-rooms; we will

be more earnest of conciliation, more tolerant to the errors of all who are for independence; and now, coming on this winter, we pledge ourselves to each other and to the teeth of our tyrants— that we will carry the Repeal organization into every parish, and wait until our leaders tell us we are organized enough, united enough, and educated enough to use the first opportunity."

The press of all parties made itself busy with the controversy and its abrupt conclusion. *Tait's Magazine* summed up the situation in terms which represented adequately the verdict of independent spectators :—

"The Agitator has ceased to be master of the agitation. The magician is impotent to exorcise—has only a qualified and conditional power to command—the spirit that his spells have evoked. He cannot now do what he will with his own; there is a power in the Loyal National Repeal Association, behind the chair, and greater than the chair. Why did Mr. O'Connell take the first opportunity he could find to snap his fingers at Federalism, so soon after having deliberately and elaborately avowed a preference for it? Not merely because Federalists stood aloof, and did not seem to feel flattered by his preference, but chiefly because Mr. Duffy wrote a certain letter in the *Nation*—a letter, we may say in passing, which more than confirms the sense we have long entertained of this gentleman's, and his coadjutors', talent, sincerity, and mental independence—refusing, in pretty flat terms, to be marched to or through the Coventry of Federalism. Mr. O'Connell has since, not in the best taste or feeling, sneered at 'the young gentlemen who thought themselves fitter leaders than he was;' but the young gentlemen carried the day, nevertheless, against the old gentlemen. We see in this, that there is a limit to the supremacy of this extraordinary man over the movement which his own genius originated; what he has done he is quite unable to undo; Repeal has a life of its own, independent of his influence or control; his leadership is gladly accepted and submitted to, but always under condition, that he leads the right way."

The genuine disposition of the party to avoid any quarrel with O'Connell, compatible with the maintenance of their integrity, is evidenced by con-

temporary correspondence. I found among Davis's
papers a note I wrote to him at this time, before
leaving for London to keep my terms.

"Dillon and J. O'H. have been here to counsel two things, the
suppression of MacNevin's letter (on Young Ireland) as a pamphlet,
and the receiving of O'Connell's last letter as a full declaration for
Repeal, as the *Freeman* has done. Dillon, who is anxious, will
speak to you about this himself. I am inclined to agree with him.
All we can hope from O'Connell is a *practical* return to Repeal, a
verbal confession of error is out of the question. Dillon justly
argues, that if we treat him captiously, we will have no sympathy
from the people, who want to see him right, but don't want to see
him scolded."

During this visit to London we made an unsuc-
cessful attempt to carry our opinions into the House
of Commons. Mr. R——, afterwards Lord ——, was
in personal and political sympathy with us, and one
of us wrote a speech which he undertook to deliver
in that assembly. Pigot, in a note to Davis, announced the result of the experiment.

"Saw Duffy on the evening before. He looks somewhat torn
down, but better than I expected. We went to the House last
night to hear R——, who stammered and spoke so badly that we
ran away before seeing him after the debate. It is true he said
the words that contained an idea of our party's policy, but he did
it so badly that they fell dead. The House was very kind, and
showed him more favour than he deserved."

The punishment of the *Nation* was indeed only
postponed. I have heard an experienced statesman declare that the hardest penalties he suffered in public life were penalties for doing some
manifest duty, and the young men were destined to
pay for their success in this unsought contest by a
long conflict with O'Connell, which proved disastrous
to them, and in the end fatal to him.

We have seen what Davis and his comrades were

doing for the Irish cause, and how forbearing was their judgment of O'Connell. They had won a right to his absolute confidence, and the generous interpretation which confidence begets; but strong men are rarely magnanimous, and political leaders, like kings, come to regard independence as incipient treason. There is now no doubt that the leader determined to break with the young men, and, if he could not reduce them to unquestioning submission, to reduce them at any rate to political impotence. Paragraphs began to appear in provincial papers charging Davis with anti-Catholic sentiments. They might as reasonably have charged him with anti-Irish prejudices. He was a Protestant with the most generous and considerate indulgence for the opinions of the bulk of his countrymen. But it was a point on which the people were naturally sensitive and ready to take alarm. The first name which came to light in connection with this detraction was a singularly unexpected one. Edward Walsh, a National schoolmaster, contributed some sweet simple verses to the *Nation*, and having afterwards fallen under the censure of the Board of Education and got dismissed, supposed that his connection with the *Nation* had done him a disservice. I accepted this view of the situation, and obtained other employment for him from Mr. Coffey, proprietor of the *Monitor*. The close work of a newspaper office galled him, and Davis, who sympathized with the poet harnessed to unaccustomed work, got him transferred to the staff of Conciliation Hall, and after a little time procured him shorter hours and better pay. These circumstances naturally increased our surprise on reading, in a county paper, a letter from Mr. Walsh, stating that Davis, during my absence on the excursion to Darrynane, had rejected one of his poems on account of the Catholic sentiments it contained.* Making the largest allowance for the sensitiveness of the poetic temperament, this imputation was little short of an act of baseness, for nothing can be more certain than that such a motive did not operate at all.

An attack of a much graver character came from another quarter. The *Dublin Review*, in noticing Maddyn's recent book, pointed out that the assailant of O'Connell was a man who had once been a Catholic but had abandoned his creed for a more prosperous one, and it treated the criticism of such a person with contempt. The reviewer was a professor of dogmatic theology, writing in a religious periodical, and no one will wonder that he insisted on this view of the transaction. But Davis, who was jealous for his friend, and still more for religious liberty, censured the spirit of the reviewer as destructive of Irish union.

"If this be, as it seems, a threat, all we can say is, it shall be met. The Repeal Association, under O'Connell's advice, censured most severely those in Cork who hissed a convert to Protestantism. Neither he nor we nor any of our party will stand tamely by and see any man threatened or struck by hand or word for holding or changing his creed. If this were allowed (we say it in warning), events would ensue that would indeed change the destinies of Ireland."

The reviewer, who was a strong, passionate, but perfectly honourable man, turned fiercely on his critic, and, in a letter to the *Weekly Register*,† denounced the *Nation* as teaching anti-Catholic doc-

---

* The letter appeared in the *Wexford Independent*.

† *The Weekly Register* (which had outlived the *Morning Register*, of which it was an offshoot). He wrote under the signature of "An Irish Priest."

trines. Several instances were cited which it was perfectly possible for a teacher of dogmatic theology to consider dangerous, but which were innocent in design, and if they appeared in any Irish journal of to-day, would not attract the slightest censure. The reviewer would have scorned to make any charge which he did not believe to be substantially true, but he was in a passion, and he was fighting for his individual will as vehemently as for his convictions.

These events gave a convenient text to Mr. John O'Connell, and we found after a little time that it was circulated among the priests south and north, that there was a dangerous spirit in the *Nation*, hostile to religion. It is needless to give any answer at present to these accusations. The writers of the *Nation* have lived their lives and for the most part died their deaths, and the question is disposed of on the best evidence. But it is certain that a serious impression was produced at the moment, and carefully worked up by the industry of the " Young Liberator " with at least the tacit sanction of his father. Davis was seriously moved by the fear that, after all that had been done and suffered, the national cause might be again ruined by bigotry and hypocrisy. He was still in Ulster when the letters of " An Irish Priest " were published, and he wrote to me from Belfast :—

"I have written to J. O'Connell, O'Brien, etc., by this post, to stop the lies of the bigot journals. I have done so less even on account of the *Nation* (which can be steered out of the difficulty in three weeks without any concession) than to ascertain whether the Catholics can and will prevent bigots from interfering with religious liberty. If they cannot, or will not, I shall withdraw from politics; as I am determined not to be the tool of a Catholic ascendancy, while apparently the enemy of British domination. . . . The last *Nation* is excellent, and is another proof that, after March next, you will be able to let me retreat for a year on my history [of Ireland]. I have given up verses since I left Dublin, and feel as if I could not write them again; so leave plenty (for publication in the *Nation*) when you are going to London. I shall be up by the end of the week. Hudson and I took a sly trip through Monaghan, Leitrim, Roscommon, etc. I am tolerably well in body, and in good spirits."

On the same day, he wrote to Smith O'Brien :—

" I entreat of you," he said, " to write to O'Connell requiring some disavowal, or at least a stop to the bigoted attacks on the *Nation*. I wrote that a man had as good a right to change from Catholicity to Protestantism as from Protestantism to Catholicity, and called the State trial miracle ' mock,' and censured the Italian censorship. I shall do so again; and I shall never act with a party that quarrels with such opinions. I will not be the conscious tool of bigots. I will not strive to beat down political, in order to set up religious, ascendancy. You, unless I have much mistaken you, will subscribe to what I now say. The Federalist leaders here go entirely with me, and, in fact, now or never, we Protestants must ascertain whether we are to have religious liberty. I have written to J. O'C. on this. My defence of D. O. Maddyn (' Ireland and its Rulers,' part iii.) against the *Dublin Review* seems to have called out this attack. Is this to be endured? Is it even politic to endure it?"

O'Brien's reply exhibits the just and considerate character of the man. He put himself in the place of his opponents in the controversy, and suggested how much they might urge in support of their views.

" In compliance with your request," he said, " I have written to O'Connell requesting his intervention to put a stop to the discussions arising amongst the national party. I have read the letter of ' An Irish Priest.' It is very clever, very Catholic, and, if unity were not essential, it would be a fair manifestation of opinion adverse to those promulgated by the *Nation*. I need not say I agree much more with the opinions of the writer in the *Nation* than with those of the Irish Priest; but, then, you and I should remember that we are Protestants, and that the bulk of the Irish are Catholics. I foresee, however, that unless O'Connell is able and willing to act as a mediator on the present occasion, we shall have a PRIEST and an ANTI-PRIEST party among the Catholics of Ireland. This I should much deplore. Unity is essential to our success, and therefore division at present would be madness; but even if Repeal were won, I should deeply regret such encroachments on the part of the clergy as would justify organized resistance, or, what is quite as bad, infidel hostility to all those feelings and opinions upon which religion rests. I make these observations without professing any sort of propagandism in regard of the matter of Faith, and as an uncompromising advocate of civil and religious liberty in its most unlimited sense."

I wrote a specific reply to the Irish Priest in the journal where his letter had appeared,* and Davis, who maintained friendly relations with the proprietor since his brief connection with the *Register*, remonstrated with him personally on the injury he was inflicting on the public cause.

"[Strictly private and confidential.]

"MY DEAR STAUNTON,

"You are a patriot, and you are not a bigot, and therefore I am at a loss to account for your having published an anonymous letter full of illiberal principles and malicious hints. Nothing would have tempted me to do so towards you. But, laying that question aside, I seriously wish you to reflect, ere you publish another of these documents, where this quarrel may end. A man professing himself a Priest advocates a censorship, advocates social persecution of converts from his creed; is indignant at praise of the greatest Irish writer of fiction alive [Wm. Carleton], because he wrote anti-Catholic stories years ago, decries the superstition of some of the Irish leaders of both sides; and finally cries out 'Infidels' against those who are opposed to his intolerant opinions. If his opinions be patronized by the Irish Catholics, the Irish Protestants must feel that religious liberty is in danger,

---

* As respects the journal publishing the imputation, I reminded the editor that there was not one of us now charged with anti-Catholic designs who had not frequently written in his own paper, before the *Nation* came into existence, and I invited him to account for the metamorphoses we must have undergone, if the imputation were well founded, in passing from Elephant Lane to D'Olier Street. As regards Davis, whose very name was unknown to the bulk of the National party, I said, "I am ashamed that any Catholic should make a defence necessary in the case of a Protestant who, I believe in my soul, has done more for the nationality of Ireland than any man living but O'Connell—a man whose labours are traceable through all the counsels and all the publications of the association, and in a new and healthy influence on the art and literature of the country."

T

and will take measures to preserve it. Such, I assure you, is the
feeling amongst the members of my Church, strongly so among
the Repealers, and still more strongly among the Federalists. Of
course the least continuance of such a quarrel will be regarded by
the Conservatives as putting an end to all hope of compromise.
I am resolved not to yield one of the points in dispute, nor to
submit for an hour to such an Inquisition. You must now see
that the very existence of a Repeal party is perilled, and I trust
that *solely on public grounds* you will put an end to so hazardous a
quarrel.

" Truly and friendly yours,

" THOMAS DAVIS.*

" To M. Staunton, Esq."

John O'Connell replied to Davis's remonstrances
in vague generalities, with a significant allusion to
the Federal controversy;† but his father joined
issue in an able and trenchant letter, which treated
the remonstrances with scorn, thinly veiled within
irony.

" Darrynane, October 30, 1844.

" My DEAR DAVIS,

" My son John has given me to read your Protestant
philippic from Belfast. I have undertaken to answer it, because
your writing to my son seems to bespeak a foregone conclusion in
your mind, that we are in some way connected with the attacks
upon the *Nation*. Now, I most solemnly declare that you are most
entirely mistaken—none of us has the slightest inclination to do
anything that could in anywise injure that paper or its estimable
proprietor, and certainly we are not directly or indirectly impli-
cated in the attacks upon it.

" With respect to the ' Italian Censorship,' the *Nation* ought to

---

* 67, Bagot Street, November 6, 1844.

† " I need not in any way discuss the question of the letters of the ' Irish
Priest,' as my father has written to you on that subject, and I think I had
better not interfere; neither will I discuss the Federalist affair. My father
has gone to town to show what his ideas, plans, and hopes are ; and you have
there the opportunity of discussing· them with him, while I, in these remote
parts, remain in waiting for his words to influence my opinions and acts. I
am very sorry indeed to gather from your letter that neither your bodily
health nor spirits are what I sincerely wish them. Take care you do not
overwork both, as I strongly think you have done, especially the physical
vigour. To judge from your sweet poetry, the powers of the mind in no
way fail under their fatigue " (John O'Connell to Davis).

be at the fullest liberty to abuse it; and, as regards the 'State Trial Miracle,' the *Nation* should be at liberty to abuse, not only that, but every other miracle, from the days of the Apostles to the present.

"But we Catholics, on the other hand, may be permitted to believe as many of these miracles as we may adopt, either from credulity or convincing proofs. At the same time, I see no objection to a Catholic priest arguing any of these points, or censuring, in suitable and civil terms, opinions contrary to his own.

"As to the Cork attack upon a Protestant proselyte, you know that I publicly and most emphatically condemned it, as did the Catholic press of Cork.

"With respect to the *Dublin Review*, the word 'insolence' appears to me to be totally inapplicable. All the *Review* did (and I have examined it again deliberately) was to insist that a man who, from being a Catholic, became a Protestant, was not a faithworthy witness in his attacks upon the Catholic clergy. Now, independent of that man's religion, of which I care nothing, there never lived a more odious or disgusting public writer, with one single exception, and that is the passage in which he praises you.

"The 'insolence' of the *Dublin Review* consisted, as I have said, of merely stating that a pervert from Catholicity, who abused the Catholic clergy, was a suspicious witness in declaring their guilt. Would you not have a right, if a person who from being a Protestant became a Catholic and abused the Protestant clergy, to state that his evidence against them ought to be considered as suspicious or even unworthy of belief? Yet, for no greater offence than that, the *Review* is attacked, and a high and a haughty tone of threatening assumed in speaking of it.

"I really think you might have spared the insinuation that you and other Protestants were 'pioneering the way to power' for men who would establish any sort of Catholic ascendancy. I know this, and I declare it most solemnly, that in the forty years I have been labouring for the public I never heard one bigoted expression, not only in our public meetings, but in our committees and private discussions, from a Catholic; but I have often felt, amongst some of the Liberal Protestants I have met with, that there was not the same soundness of generous liberality amongst them as amongst the Catholics.

"I hate bigotry of every kind—Catholic, Protestant, or Dissent—but I do not think there is any room for my interfering by any public declaration at present. I cannot join in the exaltation of Presbyterian purity or brightness of faith; at the same time that I assert for everybody a perfect right to praise both the one and the other, liable to be assailed in argument by those who choose to enter into the controversy at the other side. But, with respect to the *Dublin Review*, I am perfectly convinced the *Nation* was in the wrong. However, I take no part either one way or the other in the subject. As to my using my influence to prevent this newspaper war, I have no such influence that I could bring to bear. You really can much better influence the continuance or termination of this by battle than I can. All I am anxious about is the property in the *Nation*; I am most anxious that it should be a lucrative and profitable concern. My desire is to promote its prosperity in every way I could. I am, besides, proud as an Irishman of the talent displayed in it, and by no one more than by yourself. It is really an honour to the country, and if you would lessen a little of your Protestant zeal, and not be angry when you 'play at bowls in meeting rubbers,' I should hope that, this skirmish being at an end, the writers for the *Nation* will continue their soul-stirring, spirit-enlivening strains, and will continue to 'pioneer the way' to genuine liberty, to perfect liberality, and entire political equality for all religious persuasions.

"If I did not believe that the Catholic religion *could* compete upon equal and free terms with any other religion, I would not continue a Catholic for one hour.

"You have vexed me a little by the insinuations which your letter necessarily contains, but I heartily forgive you. You are an exceedingly clever fellow, and I should most bitterly regret that we lost you by reason of any Protestant monomania.

"We Papists *require* co-operation, support, combination, but we do not *want* protection or patronage.

"I beg of you, my dear Davis, to believe, as you may do in the fullest confidence, that I am most sincerely

"Your attached friend,
"DANIEL O'CONNELL."

Some of the Protestant repealers shared Davis's apprehension. Hely Hutchinson remonstrated with Maurice O'Connell on the danger to the cause, and Burke Roche, afterwards Lord Fermoy, threatened, a little too boisterously perhaps, the measures of defence he meditated.

"If I hear much more of this damned outlandish bigotry in

Conciliation Hall," he wrote to Davis, "I will go over and give you all a piece of my mind, which will be more useful than palatable."

Dr. Cane, one of our most notable adherents among the professional class, treated the move as a pure party trick to be evaded, not a sincere sentiment before which it might be necessary to give way.

"You told me," he wrote to Davis, "if such a view spread itself, you and a large number of Protestants would retire from the present movement. Now, am I safe of not offending you if I say, If you have a statesman's eye, you must have seen how natural and how likely was such a move; and, if you are of the fit material for a leader, that move could neither surprise nor affright you from the national field. It would be but the arising of a new difficulty, which would be removed, not by the man who blindly dashed his shoulder against it, but by him who slowly, steadily, cautiously placed the lever under it, and with imperceptible moves overcame it and cleared the way."

In the beginning of November Davis again wrote to O'Brien, sending him country journals in which the attack had been reiterated, and others in which it was rebutted.

While Davis was thinking only of the public cause, his associates were thinking of him; they determined to stake all they were or might become in his defence. He was right, and grandly and heroically right, and they would stand by him whoever might be his assailants. He must not be singled out or isolated; they were all his comrades, and it was a common cause. The prevailing sentiment was not alarm but bitter indignation. It seemed to them manifest perfidy to the cause to assail the man who had served it with most conspicuous genius and a patient assiduity and self-negation without parallel. O'Connell was receiving a princely income from the people; his son was candidate for the succession to the popular tribunate; but Davis sought or accepted no reward for his labours, beyond the scanty income of a journalist, and was unwilling that his name should be ever heard in public places or seen in the newspapers.

MacNevin was among the first to give expression to this feeling. In a letter to a Belfast newspaper he vindicated his friend.

"Woe," he said, "to the country wherein could be found a single tongue to slander so pure and earnest a man; one whose indomitable labour, whose wonderful information and enthusiasm are devoted, without one thought of ambition or self, to the arduous task of raising up our country."

But his generous indignation carried him further. Davis had friends, he declared, who would not permit him to be sacrificed. They repudiated the somewhat fantastic name of "Young Ireland" which had been bestowed upon them, but they admitted and proclaimed the fact of their friendship and union. They were members for the most part of the professions, or artists or writers, of competent means and liberal education; and a habit of consulting together and of meeting in social intercourse gave them the appearance of a party, without any desire or design on their part. Why were these men suddenly assailed in national journals? Were they tainted in morals, dishonest in their dealings with the world, or disreputable in their conduct? A charge had never been made against any man supposed to belong to their obnoxious school of any crime, vice, immorality, or dishonesty, and they might at least ask that unblemished lives and unimpeached honour should raise the prejudice in their favour of strong religious convictions. Most of the prominent men, he went on to say, were Catholics—neither cold, indifferent, nor anti-Catholic. There were undoubtedly anti-Catholic Catholics, but they were usually crawlers at the Castle gate—wretches who traffic on the sale of the little bit of religion which they have left; men, whose servility extends even to the prostitution of their souls, and whose black and bitter bread was earned by the barter of their faith. But it was not men who joined the popular party, who worked in its ranks with disinterested zeal, who toiled in its committees, and who exposed themselves to want of patronage at their profession, and to all the assaults of an adverse and an angry press;—it was not these men who are usually found anti-Catholic, or infidel, or indifferent. The enthusiasm which led them into action would preserve them from the withering tenets of the sceptic or the infidel. They adopted a respectful and conciliatory tone towards their Protestant fellow-countrymen; they abstained from scornful and angry controversy, and they would continue to do so. They would prefer to endure the low and ignorant abuse to which they have been lately exposed, rather than to give the Protestants and Presbyterians of Ireland any reason to suppose that they sought to entrap them into a struggle for independence only to make them the victims of sectarian bigotry and ambition.

"And what was there that was new and fresh in the agitation in which this party did not participate—nay, I fear not to say it, which they did not devise and originate? Their object was, not to supersede the wholesome excitement of public meetings—the ancient and venerable routine of prescriptive agitation,—but to add to the stimulant of public talking the quiet teaching of the press, the instruction to be derived from books, the more refined excitement of bold and vigorous poetry. Their songs are sung in Protestant drawing-rooms, and their poets have received the unbought approval of the greatest critics of England—poets, let me add with pride, in some instances members of that Catholic priesthood whose teaching we are slanderously represented to disregard, and whose character and sacred profession we are, with audacious falsehood, said to despise."

Character, he said in conclusion, was dear to all honourable men, and, as it was all the reward they sought, they would not permit it to be filched away in silence or with impunity.

The systematic design to defame Davis produced a reaction which first taught the young men their power. Hitherto they had never aimed at any other result than to work silently in the national cause. They were not popular in the sense of being familiar and favourite names with the people, for to win popularity there must be much self-display and self-assertion, and most of them shrunk from exhibiting themselves. Davis's position in the Irish movement was not unlike Alexander Hamilton's in the American Revolution, and Dillon was in some points akin to Franklin. How obscure these founders of the United States were in their day beside Patrick Henry or Thomas Jefferson, yet without Franklin and Hamilton the revolution would have probably been abortive. Dillon, like Franklin, loved to reduce his opinions to axioms which lodged themselves in the mind. He was fond of quoting Franklin's maxim, that justice is as strictly due between neighbouring nations as between neighbouring citizens, as a man is not less a robber if he plunders in a gang than if he robs for his own hand. And Davis, like Hamilton, silently and in the shade was shaping the policy which other men carried to council chambers and platforms.

Frederick Lucas, who in the present controversy and in many which succeeded it, sympathized with Conciliation Hall rather than with them, estimated the position of the young men fairly and liberally.

"They have been rapidly rising," he said, "into notice, and into power. They are indeed subordinate to O'Connell, but they openly avow that they belong to another school of doctrine; they have grown up under the shadow of his wings. They have fought cheerfully and loyally under his banners; and, so far as we can judge, they have never exhibited any symptom of a mean, stupid, or illiberal jealousy of his extraordinary and overwhelming authority. But, though they have displayed this free-will docility, 'this proud submission,' 'this dignified obedience,' they have never concealed the fact that they have marked out a clear and distinct course for themselves; that they are not the mere echoes of Mr. O'Connell's sentiments; that they are not the slaves or the servants of any man."

While this controversy was still running its course it was checked by a counter-current. It became known that the English Government, which had long maintained occult relations with the Court of Rome, had recently sent a gentleman of an old English Catholic family to the Pope to induce him to forbid Catholic bishops taking part in the Repeal movement. A letter had arrived from the Propaganda bearing this character, and the question how it would be received was anxiously debated among Protestant Nationalists. The jealousy of foreign interference, which Irishmen have always felt and still feel, burst out like a volcano. All sections of the National party, O'Connell, the Young Irelanders, and the National Whigs took a decided stand against any interference by Rome in our secular affairs, and it became quite plain that fears in this direction were altogether groundless. The bulk of the Irish bishops interpreted the Roman letter as not interfering with their liberty, and continued to act with the Repeal Association.

Other events ensued which made any open attack on the young men impossible at the moment. Grey Porter, of whom I have already spoken, joined the Association on the specific condition that its accounts should be audited and published. Lord Cloncurry, who could not be induced to enter Conciliation Hall, justified the hopes of the founders of the 'Eighty-two Club by becoming a member of it. Neither of them would have remained a moment if the bigotry privately fomented made itself heard on the platform. The Dublin Library, an old popular institution, elected the principal Young Irelanders [*] and some of their friends on its managing committee, and Davis was admitted a member of the Royal Irish Academy. The Art Union of Dublin, under peculiarly Conservative management, offered for the first time prizes for the best works by resident painters and sculptors on Irish subjects.

Carleton, who had long and justly been regarded as an opponent by the people, wrote at the instigation of the young men a powerful novel, exposing the iniquities of the Irish land system. "Valentine McClutchy" was originally intended as a feuilleton for the *Nation*, but in process of construction had swollen to a three-volume novel. Isaac Butt and Joseph Lefanu, the political and literary leaders of the young Conservatives, were engaged writing historical novels, treating the wars of the seventeenth and eighteenth centuries with generous fairness, and a flood of Irish books poured out equally

[*] Davis, MacNevin, John O'Hagan, Richard O'Gorman, Gavan Duffy, and their friends Smith O'Brien and Sir Colman O'Loghlin, were among the number.

from the Conservative and Nationalist press. A translation by John O'Donovan of the "Annals of the Four Masters," the great storehouse of Celtic history, was produced in handsome and costly volumes, at the risk of the University. A popular edition translated by Mr. Geraghty, a good Irish scholar to whom English was somewhat a foreign tongue, was announced, and Clarence Mangan undertook to turn it into presentable English. The competition was not desirable in the interest of Irish literature, but it could not be prevented without doing more harm than good. O'Connor's "Military History of Ireland," revised by Samuel Ferguson,* was also in preparation. The work done and influenced by the young men made it a dangerous as well as a wicked folly to disparage them.

O'Brien made a point that Davis should take the chair at Conciliation Hall,† and a little later moved

---

* Afterwards Sir Samuel Ferguson, President of the Royal Irish Academy, and author of "Lays of the Western Gael," etc.

† "I must positively insist upon your taking the chair next Monday. The time is come when you ought to act a prominent part in Irish affairs. O'Connell will attend the meeting after next (Jan. 20th), and there are many reasons why it is better that you should make your appearance during his absence."

The language Davis held in the chair was characteristic. He spoke the simple truth, without a touch of exaggeration, when he said, from the chair of the Association, "I thank you for your cheers; but it would not be candid in me to let you conceive that it was for them I laboured. I and others work not for popular applause—if your shouts were given to our enemies and your curses to us, we would work exactly as we are doing." And on another occasion, "Trust me that no men in the country have more clearly considered the greatness of English power and the animosity of English feeling towards Ireland than the men who are now in that box (the box reserved for the Committee), and who in the Committee-room upstairs laboured day after day to remove English rule from Ireland. Have you, before embarking in this great contest, looked to the magnitude of it? Have you clearly weighed that this power which you seek to get rid of has now ruled your country for six centuries; that it is an empire with hundreds of thousands of soldiers in India, and with an extent of Canadian territory so large that from its face the whole surface of England and Ireland would not be missed; or are you men who have rashly entered into perchance a quarrel—certainly a serious moral struggle—with such a power as this? If you are, and you are now looking upon these things for the first time, you will be a vote of thanks to him for his valuable reports, constituting the best part of the work done by the Parliamentary Committee.

I have noticed how a quarrel with France during O'Connell's imprisonment stimulated Irish hopes. Since the imprisonment troubles with the United States arose, which promised to have a still more significant result on the policy of the country. England had certain claims on the Oregon territory, and the language used by the Prime Minister in Parliament implied that she would support them by force. At the opening of the session of 1845, Peel recurred to the subject, and frankly declared that he desired to make peace with Ireland before engaging in a foreign contest. There was a dangerous conspiracy in that country against the authority of Parliament which could not be broken up by force; but he was persuaded that it might be broken up by a spirit of forbearance and generosity. And he was about to make the experiment forthwith.

His first proposal was to increase the grant to Maynooth College, and make it a permanent appropriation, instead of a vote on the estimates, which provoked an annual faction fight. The Maynooth Bill was fiercely resisted in England as " an endowment of Popery; " there was a stormy protest in the House of Commons, and a hurricane of petitions against it from the country. In Ireland the Nationalists received it thankfully, but the party who were

beaten, and will deserve to be beaten ; you will be trampled on by the British Minister. If you are cowards—if you are rash—if you are capricious men who shrink from long labour—I tell you, you will be beaten and put down amidst the scorn of Europe, and you will deserve it. But if you have clearly considered the cost of what you are doing, if you are resolved that you will succeed—from this spot, in the name of my friends--in your name—I may tell the British Minister to give up this idle contest in which he must eventually be beaten."

in tranquil possession of a profusely endowed Church
and a wealthy University, opposed it tooth and nail.
The Evening Mail warned the Government that
resisting the bigots was a dangerous game. "The
Union was carried by a rebellion in which the then
Government was more than suspected of being a
party. Let Sir Robert Peel take care that it be not repealed by a similar process." This was a threat, which
has since grown somewhat stale, that the Orangemen
would rebel if they did not get their own way.

After Peel's policy was announced, Davis wrote to
Denny Lane :—

> "I am weary wishing you here. The events as to Maynooth
> will greatly weaken our enemies; and Oregon promises well,
> though I trust nothing to it. For our hopes' sake do not let Cork
> be guilty of any meanness should the Queen come. This should
> be easy in Cork; here it will be harder. But we are resolute and
> timely, and cannot fail; so her coming shall be turned to good.
> Why don't you write more songs? Your last, to the air of 'The
> Foggy Dew,' was beautiful, and comes constantly on my recollec-
> tion like a southern twilight. I have nearly recovered the cold,
> winter, and Repeal essays [he was one of the judges whose duty it
> was to read a long series of prize essays on Repeal], but have too
> many things to do, and so my life is a string of epigrams which
> displeases me. I am left too much without affections; but I am
> coldly happy and dutiful. . . . Duffy is well as a man can be who
> sees his young wife dying by inches. Barry and the rest of the
> set well, and more serious than they used to be."

Peel's second proposal was to found an adequate
system of middle-class education. Colleges would
be established in Cork, Belfast, and Galway, liberally
endowed by the State to provide a purely secular
education. To this scheme the bulk of the Liberal
Irish members, led on this question by Thomas
Wyse, gave a cordial welcome. A majority of the
Catholic bishops approved of the general design,

objecting to certain details. All the barristers and
country gentlemen in the Association, and the
middle-class generally, supported it. To Davis it
was like the unhoped for realization of a dream. To
educate the young men of the middle class and of
both races, and to educate them together, that prejudice and bigotry might be killed in the bud, was
one of the projects nearest to his heart. It would
strengthen the soul of Ireland with knowledge, he
said, and knit the creeds in liberal and trusting
friendship. He threw all the vigour of his nature
into the task of getting this measure unanimously
and thankfully accepted. The plan needed amendment in essential points, but those who designed it
would not, it might be safely assumed, permit it to
be spoilt for want of reasonable amendments. The
students were to be non-resident, and there was not
adequate security provided for their good conduct
and moral discipline out of class. The appointment
of professors was retained in the hands of Government—a method which tended to destroy academic
independence. But if these defects were removed,
the colleges would be an inestimable gain. There
was no people on the earth among whom systematic
education was so grossly neglected; we sent out our
young men habitually to fight the battle of life without the arms of defence or offence possessed by all
their competitors, and they commonly paid the
penalty in laborious and unprosperous lives.

The first note of dissension came from the mar-
plot of the National party. Mr. John O'Connell, in
the committee of the Association, denounced the
measure as a plot against the faith and morals of
the Irish people. This criticism would have been

treated with contempt but that his father unexpectedly came to his assistance. O'Connell during
his public life had repeatedly advocated the education
of our young men in mixed schools and colleges for
the same motives which influenced Davis, but he
now renounced this opinion as unexpectedly as he
had renounced Nationality for Federalism a few
months before, and, echoing the language of a Tory
bigot in the House of Commons, declared the
measure to be a huge scheme of godless education.
Davis besought him to keep the question out of the
Association, whose sole object was to repeal the
Union, and where angry debate was sure to follow
on such a collateral question. This truce O'Connell
positively declined, and at the first meeting in Conciliation Hall he proclaimed his fierce antipathy to
the scheme. He was willing, he said, to leave the
question to the bishops; if they accepted the
measure he would feel bound to do so, but meantime
his opinion was that it was hopelessly vicious. Mr.
John O'Connell followed. He denounced the Irish
members who had presumed to sanction this abominable scheme in Parliament. The laity ought to leave
the question to the bishops, but, though willing to
do so, he could not altogether suppress the feelings
of abomination and execration at so infamous a proposal. While the heir-presumptive employed this
language he was well aware that the best men in the
Association approved of the measure, but he probably
hoped that they would be silent to avoid dissension.
Peace may be bought at too high a price, however,
and Davis immediately followed him, analyzing and
vindicating the plan. O'Connell interposed to
declare that debate was premature, as they had not

seen the measure. He could not blame Mr. Davis, as the question had been opened by himself, but it would be more judicious to wait till the bill was printed.

Next day a renewed attempt to keep the question out of the Association was made. A memorial, signed by forty members of the general committee, was privately presented to O'Connell supporting this proposal. The remonstrance was so formidable that he felt compelled to acquiesce. It was agreed that the question should be mentioned no more in the Association till the bishops had decided, but both parties were to be at liberty to push their opinions outside Conciliation Hall. Davis and all the writers of the *Nation* appealed successively to the people, and O'Connell wrote a series of leading articles in the *Freeman's Journal* to refute them. These proceedings were within the legitimate conditions of the truce, but Mr. John O'Connell considered himself at liberty to use the agency of the Association to send to the country for signature petitions praying for the utter rejection of the Bill. Among the men of mark in the movement there was not so much as one who sided with the O'Connells. But the men of. no mark, "the parasites and pickers up of crumbs," were very busy stimulating resistance. And John O'Connell, who had recently represented the Young Irelanders as indifferent to religion, found here a lucky opportunity of insisting that his suspicions were well founded. But his sagacious father began to discover a fact he had little suspected, that with the Young Irelanders had grown up a new class of politicians as different from his ordinary retinue as the teetotalers were from the sots.

Smith O'Brien, being in the country at the moment, wrote a letter supporting the colleges, which he wished to have read to the Association. When it was submitted to the general committee, according to practice, O'Connell opposed its being read while the question was temporarily withdrawn from debate. It was urged that O'Brien ought to have the same opportunity that other leaders had of putting his opinions on record, and that a letter from the country was not like a speech, a renewal of the debate. But O'Connell would not yield the point, and Sir Colman O'Loghlen and Davis, both friends of O'Brien who shared his opinion on the point at issue, consented to withdraw the letter for a time. There was no choice between doing so and breaking up the committee. But O'Brien was dissatisfied, and complained in terms which seem to me to exhibit a want of consideration unusual in him.

"Cahirmoyle, May 18, 1845.

" My dear Davis,

" Being inexpressibly annoyed by the suppression of my letter on the subject of academical education, I sat down and wrote a long letter to you on the subject, but fearing lest it might give you unnecessary pain, I have since burnt it. I now enclose a note for Mr. Ray, which I shall feel obliged by your transmitting to him as soon as you have read it. If my letter appear in Tuesday's *Evening Freeman*, or Wednesday's *Morning Freeman*, the object which I had in view in writing it will be partly attained. I am quite unable to understand why any except the ' Separatist ' of the committee should have consented to its suppression. Feeling that I have other duties to perform as well as this which belongs to me as a member of the Repeal Association, I cannot consent to withdraw it.

" I hope, therefore, that there will be no further postponement. It is quite impossible to conceal the differences which exist on the subject of academical education. It would be base and unmanly on my part to seek to conceal the strong opinion which I entertain respecting a question in reference to which I have already taken a

U

very prominent part. I have not the least objection that others should state their opinions with equal candour, and, indeed, they have done so already. There was nothing in my letter which could possibly offend any one.

"I shall probably be in Limerick on Monday, so please to direct thither. I shall not be able to attend the Navan dinner.

"Believe me, yours very truly,

"WILLIAM S. O'BRIEN.

"All well here. The country very charming."

Davis replied with a temper and forbearance which must have realized, to a just and reasonable man like O'Brien, how completely he was in the wrong.

"I should not have consented," he said, "to the holding over of your letter, but that had it been read yesterday it would have led to a violent debate which would almost necessarily have broken up the association. There was no second opinion as to the danger. Under such a peril I and others who concurred in your views acted as we did, though certainly I felt that our doing so might cause you much annoyance, and would be a very great liberty—one that I, at least, shall never take again." *

The meeting of the Catholic bishops resulted in a memorial to the Lord Lieutenant, professing their "readiness to co-operate with the Government on fair and reasonable terms, in establishing a system for the further extension of academical education," but not in the proposal as it stood, which they considered dangerous to faith and morals. The terms they proposed seem to me to fall within these lines,

* During the period of doubt, he wrote to Maddyn :—

"I long more and more for your coming soon. We are, of course, anxious about the academical question. Should the Catholic bishops go strongly against mixed education, or should Government persist in claiming the nomination and dismissal of the professors, the plan must fail. The latter danger is the greater, as, by what I hear, the best of the bishops are with us. Should the plan be freed from Government despotism and be carried out, we shall have : (1) a home provision for a literary and scientific class; (2) security for an educated middle and upper class in four or six years; (3) we shall have got over the last subject, short of fighting, which could break up the party. Our after-course will have only front foes, and I don't care for them." (May 18th.)

being essentially just and reasonable. They asked that a fair proportion of the professors and other office-bearers in the colleges should be Catholics, whose moral conduct had been certified by testimonials from their respective prelates ; that all appointments to office should be made by a board of trustees, of which the Catholic bishops of the province where the college was erected should be members ; that any officer convicted before the board of attempting to undermine the faith or injure the morals of any student should immediately be removed from office by the board ; that as the students were to be non-resident, there should be a chaplain appointed to superintend the moral and religious instruction of the Catholic students, to be appointed on the recommendation of the bishop of the diocese in which the college was situated, who should also have the power of removing him.

In a Catholic country, where a Protestant Church was profusely endowed out of the earnings of the people, and a Protestant university out of the confiscation of Catholic lands, and where education had been an agent for proselytism for two hundred years, these precautions were neither unreasonable nor excessive.

There was another concession demanded which might have been made the subject of a compromise. The bishops pointed out that Catholic students could not attend lectures on history, metaphysics, moral philosophy, geology, or anatomy, as they were taught by Protestant professors, without imminent danger to their faith and morals. But history might have been omitted from the course ; it is best studied in the closet ; and Protestants, it was suggested, would

not object to anatomy or geology being taught by
Catholic professors.   With respect to the few remaining subjects there might be two professors for each—
an expense and inconvenience worth encountering
for the inestimable advantage of rearing up a generation in habits of personal friendship.   But O'Connell
was determined there should be no agreement.   He
would defeat the Young Irelanders where they had
put forth all their strength; and it may be further
surmised that he was determined Peel should not rob
his late allies, the Whigs, of the credit of conciliating
Ireland.   At the meeting following the publication
of the bishops' memorial, he declared that they had
pronounced the nefarious scheme dangerous to faith
and morals, and affirmed that it must be rejected
utterly.   Let there be separate colleges in separate
cities for Catholics, Protestants, and Presbyterians,
and no education in common.   Mr. John O'Connell
followed, exaggerating the opinions of his father, and
denying that the bishops sanctioned mixed education.
Smith O'Brien, who had at length the opportunity of
being heard, declared that he honoured the solicitude
of Catholics for religious education, but he himself
thought a system of adequate precaution might be
engrafted on the Government scheme.

Among Davis's fellow-students in College was a
young man named Michael George Conway.   He was
gifted with prompt speech and unblushing effrontery.
In college his capacity was early recognized, and an
eminent man, who was a tutor when they were under-
graduates, assured me that a more successful career
was predicted for Conway than for Davis.   But he
wanted conduct and integrity, and had gradually
fallen out of men's esteem.   He was among the

candidates for the 'Eighty-two Club who had been recently blackballed, and he came down to the Association burning for revenge. He fell on a chance phrase of Barry's in the debate, misrepresented it outrageously, and declared that it was characteristic of his party and his principles—a party on which the strong hand of O'Connell must be laid.

"The sentiment triumphant in the meeting that day was a sentiment common to all Ireland. The Calvinist or Episcopalian of the North, the Unitarian, the Sectaries, every man who had any faith in Christianity, was resolved that it should neither be robbed nor thieved by a faction half acquainted with the principles they put forward, and not at all comprehending the Irish character or the Irish heart. Were his audience prepared to yield up old discord or sympathies to the theories of Young Ireland? As a Catholic and as an Irishman, while he was ready to meet his Protestant friends upon an equal platform, he would resent any attempt at ascendancy, whether it came from honest Protestants or honest professing Catholics."

During the delivery of this false and intemperate harangue O'Connell cheered every offensive sentence, and finally took off his cap and waved it over his head triumphantly. He knew, as all the intelligent spectators knew, that a man destitute of character and veracity was libelling men as pure and disinterested as any who had ever served a public cause, and he took part with the scoundrel. It was one of the weaknesses of his public life to prefer agents who dared not resist his will; but this open preference of evil to good was the most unlucky stroke of his life. Twelve months later he died, having lost his prodigious popularity and power; and of all the circumstances which produced that tragic result, the most operative was probably his conduct during this day.

Davis followed Mr. Conway. The feeling uppermost in his mind was probably suggested by the con-

trast between the life of the man and his new heroic
opinions; and it will help to put the reader in the
same standpoint if I inform him that the pious Mr.
Conway finally professed himself a convert to Protestantism to obtain the wages of a proselytizing
society.

Davis did not regard himself as a debater, but he
proved himself on this occasion to be a master of
debate.   Cool, resolute, good-humoured, he raised
and disposed of point after point with unbroken
suavity, in a manner I have never heard exceeded in
legislatures or party councils.   After a man has
served as a Cabinet Minister he speaks with more
confidence and decision; and it need not be doubted
that the large influence Davis had exercised during
the imprisonment, and the cordial acceptance of his
proposals in committee, brought the confidence
which only comes from success, and he treated with
O'Connell, modestly but firmly, as the representative
of opinions which could not be disregarded.

"'I have not,' Davis said on rising, 'more than a few words to
say in reply to the useful, judicious, and spirited speech of my old
college friend, my Catholic friend, my very Catholic friend, Mr.
Conway.'

"Mr. O'Connell: 'It is no crime to be a Catholic, I hope.'

"Mr. Davis: 'No, surely no, for——'

"Mr. O'Connell: 'The sneer with which you used the word
would lead to the inference.'

"Mr. Davis: 'No, sir; no. My best friends, my nearest friends,
my truest friends, are Catholics.   I was brought up in a mixed
seminary, where I learned to know, and, knowing, to love my countrymen, a love that shall not be disturbed by these casual and
unhappy dissensions.   Disunion, alas! destroyed our country for
centuries.   Men of Ireland, shall it destroy it again?'"

The reader knows in some degree what Thomas
Davis was, what were his life and services, what his

relations to his Catholic countrymen were; that he had left hereditary friends and kith and kin to act with O'Connell for Irish ends; and they may estimate the effect which the attempt to represent him as a bigot had upon the generous and upright among his audience. John Dillon ruptured a blood vessel (as we shall see later) with restrained wrath; others broke for ever the tie which had bound them to O'Connell. He was not worthy, they declared, of the service of men of honour, who used weapons so vile against a man of unquestioned honour. Davis took up the question of the colleges, and examined it with undisturbed temper and judgment. While he spoke, O'Connell, who sat near him, distracted him by constant observations in an undertone; but the young man proceeded with unruffled demeanour and calm mastery of his subject. He cordially approved of the memorial of the Catholic bishops, which declared for mixed education with certain necessary precautions. They asked for "a fair proportion" of the professors, meaning, beyond dispute, that the remainder should be Protestants—this was mixed instruction. They asked that the bishops of the province in which the college was situated should be members of the board —this was mixed management. They demanded that, in certain specified branches, Catholic students should be taught by Catholic professors—this was a just demand, but it implied a system of mixed education. They asked for Catholic chaplains to protect the faith and morals of the students—a perfectly just demand. He too denounced the Bill as containing no provision for the religious discipline of the boys taken away from the paternal shelter. And, beyond all, he denounced it for giving the Government a right to appoint and dismiss professors—which was a right to corrupt and intimidate.

O'Connell, who had already spoken for two hours, made a second speech in reply to Davis. His peroration was a memorable one. The venerated hierarchy, he insisted, had condemned the principle of the Bill as dangerous to the faith and morals of the Catholic people.

"But," he said in conclusion, "the principle of the bill has been supported by Mr. Davis, and was advocated in a newspaper professing to be the organ of the Roman Catholic people of this country, but which I emphatically pronounce to be no such thing. The section of politicians styling themselves the Young Ireland Party, anxious to rule the destinies of this country, start up and support this measure. There is no such party as that styled ' Young Ireland.' There may be a few individuals who take that denomination on themselves. I am for Old Ireland. 'Tis time that this delusion should be put an end to. ' Young Ireland' may play what pranks they please. I do not envy them the name they rejoice in. I shall stand by Old Ireland; and I have some slight notion that Old Ireland will stand by me."

I have elsewhere described the scene which ensued.*

" When O'Connell sat down consternation was universal; he had commenced a war in which either by success or failure he would bring ruin on the national cause. Smith O'Brien and Henry Grattan, who were sitting near him, probably remonstrated, for in a few minutes he rose again to withdraw the nickname of ' Young Ireland,' as he understood it was disclaimed by those to whom it was applied. Davis immediately rejoined that he was glad to get rid of the assumption that there were factions in the association. He never knew any other feeling among his friends, except in the momentary heat of passion, but that they were bound to work together for Irish nationality. They were bound, among other motives, by a strong affection towards Daniel O'Connell; a feeling which he himself had habitually expressed in his private correspondence with his dearest and closest friends.

* " Young Ireland," book iii., chap. 7, " The Provincial Colleges."

" At this point the strong self-restrained man paused from emotion, and broke into irrepressible tears. He was habitually neither emotional nor demonstrative, but he had been in a state of nervous anxiety for hours; the cause for which he had laboured so long and sacrificed so much was in peril on both hands. The association might be broken up by a conflict with O'Connell, or it might endure a worse fate if it became despicable by suppressing convictions of public duty at his dictation. With these fears were mixed the recollection of the generous forbearance from blame and the promptitude to praise which marked his own relations to O'Connell, and the painful contrast with these sentiments presented by the scene he had just witnessed. He shed tears from the strong passion of a strong man. The leaders of the Commons of England, the venerable Coke, John Pym, and Sir John Eliot, men of iron will, wept when Charles I. extinguished the hope of an understanding between the people and the Crown. Tears of wounded sensibility choked the utterance of Fox when Burke publicly renounced his friendship. Both the public and the private motives united to assail the sensibility of Davis.

" O'Connell, whose instincts were generous and cordial, and who was only suspicious from training and violent by set purpose, immediately interposed with warm expressions of goodwill. He had never felt more gratified than by this evidence of regard. If Mr. Davis were overcome, it overcame him also; he thanked him cordially, and tendered him his hand. The association applauded their reconciliation with enthusiasm. After this episode Davis resumed—

" ' He and his friends, in their anxiety to co-operate with O'Connell, had often sacrificed their own predilections, and never opposed him except when they were convinced in conscience that it was a duty to do so. He trusted their disagreement would leave no sting behind. If there had been any harshness of feeling, if any person had made use of private influence to foster dissension and to misrepresent them to each other, he would forgive it, if the offence were not repeated. He would sit down with a prayer to Almighty God that the people of this country, and the leaders of the people, might continue united in the pursuit of liberty in which they were so often defeated before at the moment of its apparent fruition; and with a supplication to God that they might not be defeated again.' "

Davis's friends were too angry at the injustice he had suffered to sympathize with his generous emotion,

and some of them remonstrated.* But he was determined to make nothing of the incident so far as it
concerned himself. He wrote to Pigot :—

"I send you the *Freeman* of to-day, by which you'll see that
O'Connell and I came to a blow-up in the association, but were
reconciled, and fancy ourselves better friends than ever. I hope so.

"I ought to have taken any other hour to write to you, for I
am out of spirits, having just come from seeing John Dillon, who
is ill, transiently I hope. Do not write to him of it, as he may
get nervous. He has had a cough all the winter, and got generally
excited at the meeting yesterday, and had last night a slight bleed-
ing in the lungs. Corrigan says it is a little delicacy and no more ;
but I shivered when I was walking home at the possibility of
danger to him ; but, again, do not write to him of his illness nor
mention it to *any one*.

"Some other persons for whom I am much concerned are ill,
and only for political vows and the ever-recurring destiny which
I feel not to let *this* effort of Ireland be vain, I should sink into
gloom.

"My own health is excellent. So, I'm told, is yours.

"You seem much pleased with Carlyle. Duffy and J. O'H.
told me some talk of his that I thought vicious, and affected to a
serious extent.

"In a fortnight I hope affairs here will be recovered from
several little ills."

And again, a few days later :—

"I am delighted to tell you that John Dillon is better, and
Corrigan thinks he can travel to the country at once. On Monday
night he had an alarming effusion of blood in the lungs, and consumption was feared. He had been subject to coughs all the
winter, used to sit in hot rooms, drink quantities of coarse tea, and
take little exercise. His chest is now relieved, his voice strong,
and his spirits up, but he must take the greatest care of himself
and live healthily. The excitement of Monday (for he was sitting

* "Your speech was admirable; your emotion to me unintelligible.
Was not John O'Connell, the Tanist that is not to be, present? Was not
Clements? Was not Hopkins? How the d—— could you *feel* amongst
them? The air is rarefied with rascality; how could you breathe in it? . . .
By the way, I hereby abdicate the title of 'the most eloquent member of
Young Ireland.' There is more real eloquence in your manly enthusiastic
truth than in all my tinselled antitheses. I am cured of my ambition "
(MacNevin to Davis).

behind me when I had the row with O'C.) seems to have caused
the rupture, and as he has got over it the alarm may be useful.

"I fancy O'C. wished to make it appear to those not present
that he had some triumph over me, for he was very wrath at the
tone of the *Nation* of Saturday, where I treated him as an equal;
but I believe we shall have no further fight on the subject. He
offered on Saturday to canvass Merrion Ward for me; but as I was
not on the Burgess Roll I could not stand.

"The report in the *Nation* is more correct than the *Freeman's*.
Conway caused the fight, designedly, because *we* refused his
alliance, and he was blackbeaned in the '82 Club. O'Connell
stood up cheering him after his most rabid sentences. From the
moment I rose, O'C., who was only separated from me by Henry
Grattan, maintained a running comment to disturb and frighten
me and to rouse the people—half his insolence is not given—but
he utterly failed. I spoke twice as well as if he had let me alone,
and I was listened to admirably. His reply was nonsense and
abuse. When he sat down, Steele rose so quickly as to prevent
me, and I said to O'C.: 'Mr. O'Connell, you are mistaken in supposing us a separate party, or that we ever called ourselves Young
Ireland. It was a nickname given and used in jest.' His apology
for the name gave me an opportunity, as I thought, of rescue. I
was much excited; I remembered how I used to regard him; one
letter (to a woman) crossed my mind, and so I found my tears, and
lost my voice, and sat down. O'C. appeared to every one affected,
and has spoken of me since as 'embedded in his heart,' but *that*
certainly is gammon. If this day go off well all will be well.

"I am glad the Bill is to go on, but I abhor the plan of Government appointments." *

He wrote in the same spirit to Denny Lane.
Lane's reply will enable a judicious reader to comprehend the motive-power of the party—the desire
to serve Ireland at whatever disadvantage, and the
total absence of personal aims. On one point I
believe Lane was ill-informed. I never observed
anything in the bearing of Davis towards O'Connell
which a just and honourable man would resent; it
was respectful but not obsequious, the natural de-

* 67, Bagot Street, Monday, June 2, 1845.

meanour of one gentleman to another. After the
public reconciliation, the *Pilot*, the confidential
organ of the O'Connells, continued to assail Davis
with coarse brutalities, and it was difficult to be
solaced by a harmony with an accompaniment like
this. His friend Lane, however, considered such an
antagonist, even with his semi-official character, as
of slight importance.

"I have read the article in the *Pilot* which you sent me, but do
not think it worth notice. You stand on too high ground to be
affected by such mean, unfair, and grovelling attacks. Moreover,
the article is so long, so illogical, so dislocated, and so indistinct,
that you need never fear the writer unless he mends his pen.
There is, as far as I can learn, only one opinion here about the
unjustifiableness and tyranny of 'O'Connell's attack on Davis.'
I cannot conceive that any man could entertain a doubt about the
character of Conway's attack on Barry. I quite agree in your
opinion of your own conduct; the being affected was certainly
unfortunate, as every one of the public will attribute it to weakness on the subject you were then engaged in, and cannot of course
guess that your feelings were excited by any other than present
causes. But you were certainly right in the main in the course which
you pursued, as no one could have anticipated what followed on
O'Connell's part—a line of conduct impossible to have been imagined .
by any reasonable being. There can be no doubt that the whole
proceeding was a heavy blow and great discouragement to Young
Ireland; but never mind—a man must expect those rebuffs, and
they ought only to incite him to work on, while they often give him
a useful lesson. . . . The first is that O'Connell is the most popular
man that ever lived, and will be implicitly obeyed by a great body
of the people whatever be the orders he gives them. Next, he is so
used to implicit obedience, and has so often been able to get on
after having cast off those who mutinied against his nod, that he
will think nothing of doing the same again. . . . Next, the man is
so thoroughly Irish and hearty, and so devoted to the religion to
which the people are devoted, that he is, without exaggeration,
loved by them as a father. Next, the Catholics are bound to him
by their gratitude for his achievement of Emancipation, and nine-
tenths of the priests throughout Ireland are his servants and the
people's masters. Well, what does all this come to? To this, that

his power is irresistible, and that the power of the people of Ireland is rendered ten times more effective that it would otherwise be, being concentrated in his person, so that, even if it could, it should not be resisted unless in extremities. Next, he does not bear control; you can give him no more than a hint of differing in opinion from him. If you have power, and differ from him, you cause a split and do serious mischief. Suppose you have no power besides your own, if you differ from him he cuts you off and destroys your usefulness to the cause. Division has been our bane, and is to be avoided by every means short of dishonour, or great or irreparable injury to the cause; if it becomes absolutely necessary to differ from O'Connell, you must get O'Brien, who is a sensible man, and who will do so only in an extreme case, to express in the most temperate manner your dissent. O'Connell would never have dared to treat him as he treated you. . . . I have heard people remark, what I never observed myself, that there is often in your manner something very dictatorial. I suppose that I am so used to your impertinence that I do not notice the fault, but I am sure it exists, and it is a very dangerous one; it frequently makes enemies, and always deters those who would otherwise become converts. Try and see yourself as others see you, and mend the fault. You must, in the first place, feign the modesty, which I believe you possess, and do not irritate a man like O'Connell; consider your own position relatively to his, and wear that deference of manner to him which you know he loves. You will thus make yourself as useful to the country as you possibly can, under present circumstances. . . . Do not overvalue any triumph in the committee; 'tis not the conversations of the actors behind the scenes that make the drama. Your committee is good for pointing out what is to be done in the association—a kind of undress rehearsal, but it is what is done in public that really produces the effect. I have more to say to you, but I am afraid you are tired already. I will write to you again to-morrow about the display here. Show this letter to Barry, and also, if you like, to Duffy." *

It was not Davis's habit to justify himself; he had entire reliance in the good faith of his friend, and he accepted the censure on his demeanour in committee without protest.

* Lane to Davis, Cork, June 11, 1845.

" In committee (in which I find myself more powerful than you suppose) J. O'C. has been lectured by O'Brien and reproved by all the Catholic bar. In truth, Clements, O'Dowd, Costello, Drs. Nagle and Murphy, are the only supporters of separate education among·us now, for Browne is on 'mission' and Conway is below par. What you say of my general manner is, I fear, quite true. I lose patience with the lying, ignorant, and lazy clan who surround O'C. Indeed I have to maintain a perpetual struggle to prevent myself from quitting politics in absolute scorn ; ·but my heart melts, when I think it possible for a union of brave, patient men to lift up the country, in more ways than politics. But till the 'scene' in Conciliation Hall, O'C. and I were most courteous in manner to each other, though frequently opposed in opinion.

" By the way, O'C. is not sincere for separate education. In the absence of the O'C.s last autumn, O'Neill Daunt and I prepared by order of the committee resolutions positively for mixed education. They were passed unanimously by both committees, O'Brien in the chair. On Johnny's first appearance in the committee they were read to him, and he gave them a flat negative, saying he wished Roman Catholic education to be under the Jesuits. In half an hour afterwards O'Connell came in, heard them, and said, ' I have been for years and still am an advocate for mixed education.' He then went on to say that it would be right to consult the bishops. In a few days after he recanted this opinion, under (we have no doubt) Johnny's influence.

" I never intended to notice the attack in the *Pilot*, though it . and the *Newry Examiner* [edited by M. J. Conway] keep constantly at me and the *Nation*. The regard for O'B. is all assumed, as I could prove to you. He was within an ace of leaving the Hall on Monday, during Johnny's speech."

The motive and animus of the young men in maintaining this contest for the education and discipline of their own class, will be best understood by the utterance of one of them at this time in impassioned verse—

" How sorrowful the useless powers our glorious Island yields—
Our countless havens desolate, our waste of barren fields,
The all unused mechanic might our rushing streams afford,
The buried treasures of our mines, our sea's unvalued hoard !

But, oh, there is one piteous waste whence all the rest have
  grown;
One worst neglect—the mind of man left desert and unsown.
Send Knowledge forth to scatter wide, and deep to cast its seeds,
The nurse of energy and hope, of manly thoughts and deeds.
Let it go forth; right soon will spring those forces in its train
That vanquish Nature's stubborn strength, that rifle earth and
  main—
Itself a nobler harvest far than Autumn tints with gold,
A higher wealth, a surer gain than wave and mine enfold.
Let it go forth unstained, and purged from Pride's unholy leaven,
With fearless forehead raised to Man, but humbly bent to Heaven.

" Let it go forth—a mightier foe to England's power than all
The rifles of America—the armaments of Gaul!
It *shall* go forth, and woe to them that bar or thwart its way;
'Tis God's own light—all heavenly bright—we care not who
  says nay." *

Davis was not turned aside a moment from his
task. He prepared a petition asking amendments
in the Bill, which was signed by leading citizens
of Dublin, the flower of the Liberal bar, and every
man of weight or character connected with the
Repeal Association outside O'Connell's family. The
petitioners declared that provincial colleges were
necessary in Ireland, and if judiciously managed
would be a public blessing, and they recognized the
policy of establishing them as wise and conciliatory. They pointed out the necessity for providing
religious instruction for students, separated in many
cases from their parents or guardians, and they
contended that it would not be found impracticable,
without omitting necessary branches of knowledge,
to guard on one hand against doctrines subversive

* Mr. Justice O'Hagan, the writer of the above verses, wishes me to say
that, while retaining to the full the strong desire for education, as one of
the supreme wants of Ireland, he felt and feels that the Irish bishops were
entirely in the right in not accepting the Queen's Colleges.

of revealed religion, and on the other against
tampering with the religious tenets of any class
of students.   They also prayed for the opening of
Trinity College and the establishment of a system
of practical and industrial education there.   As
respects the appointment of professors they suggested
that they might be chosen in the first instance by
a board of examiners named in the Bill, and afterwards by the governing body of each College.   To
Lane, Davis wrote :—

> "I am glad you like my petition.   If anything could change
> my mixed feeling of admiration and censure of O'Connell into
> genuine hostility, it would be the vicious adulation and lying
> incentives proffered to him by the little, stupid, mercenary devils
> about him, and his patronage of the vilest and weakest of them.
> They are trying to drive O'Brien, myself, and others to secession,
> hoping to have the uncensured handling of public money with
> their gluey claws; but they shall be disappointed and beaten." *

Dr. Cooke Taylor, who was in communication
with the Liberal leaders, assured Davis that most or
all of the points insisted upon in the petition would
be conceded.

> "Under the seal of secrecy I can give you some information

---

* The political lackeys of O'Connell felt free to be insolent to a person
out of favour, and one of them—Captain Broderick, I think—demeaned
himself in such a manner that Davis referred to a friend the question whether
he ought not to hold him responsible for his conduct in the manner then
usual.   This note, from M. J. Barry, says all that is needful on the point:—
"The gentleman whom I consulted is advanced in life, was formerly in
the army, has been engaged in several affairs of honour, and would, I am
satisfied, recommend no course which was not strictly in accordance with the
most rigid demands of self-respect.   I stated to him as fully as I could
remember all that occurred, omitting nothing that could be considered to
constitute an affront, either in manner or language, and his distinct opinion
was that there was no ground for demanding an explanation, but that the
best course was to let the matter rest.   Under these circumstances I could
not feel justified in advising you to any other course, and I am quite satisfied
to take on myself the full responsibility of recommending you to take no
further steps in the transaction.
"Show this letter to no one but Duffy or O'Brien; but show it to these,
if you choose."

respecting the leading points in your petition. The appointment to professorships will depend on some kind of examination, either of testimonials or of candidates themselves, and will not be a mere piece of ministerial patronage. The Government is disposed to open Trinity College, but hopes to effect this object by a proposal emanating from the college itself; the recent decision in Heron's case is deemed likely to remove many difficulties. Deans such as you recommend will certainly be appointed, and I believe that every suggestion your petition contains will be acted upon to the full extent. The only question will be as to the mode of attaining; there is pretty close agreement about the end to be attained."

It was determined in the committee of the Association that the Irish members should attend Parliament for a short time, and strive to effect amendments in the Bill. To O'Brien, who arrived first in London, Davis wrote :—

"O'Connell goes over [to London] to-night, and so much the better. The effort of the Repeal members [to amend the Bill] should be made with all their force. It is also desirable that he should be removed for a while from the persons who suggest suspicions, alarm his Catholic feelings, and stimulate his large but vehement soul. 'Tis marvellous what evil influence such little creatures can exercise over so great a mind. We had a most serious affair in committee yesterday, in which all Protestants who interfered in the education question were denounced in the strongest courteous language by O'Connell and his son, and by other parties in a rougher fashion. O'Connell seemed anxious that the supporters of mixed education should secede from the association; but none of us did so, nor ought we under *any* circumstances short of impending expulsion. We have the same right to be in the association as any others, and no person ought, on the principles of the association, to force on any question, except Repeal, against the will of any considerable body of active members. However, if there is to be a break-up, the longer 'tis postponed the better; and you should on no account be absent whenever O'Connell brings the question to such an issue, as he threatens to do on his return from London. In such a case, dignified, cool, firm, combined action may enable us to avert disaster from our cause and country. The subject is not to be raised

x

in the association till O'Connell's return. He or his son has forwarded petitions plump against the Bill to the country."

Pigot reported the arrival of the Irish members at the scene of action :—

" Last night I went to the House to see O'Brien. His motion was on, so he could not come out to me. John O'Connell did, to my great surprise. It was an unexpected pleasure to find he had not been left at home in Ireland to ruin matters while O'B. was away. Maurice will be easier to deal with. O'C. himself came up to the gallery to see me, but we had no word of politics, of course, in such a place. I hope, from his manner last night, that there is some chance of his being mild and reasonable in committee."

Sir Robert Peel held out hopes that he would modify the method of appointing professors, and he promised to add clauses facilitating the endowment by private benevolence of divinity lectures and the erection of halls for their delivery. He was eager to make the measure a practical success, but he had the bigotry of England in revolt against him, and O'Connell, whom he was accustomed to regard as the legitimate spokesman of Irish opinion, showed no disposition to be contented with any amendments. He wrote repeatedly private notes to the Archbishop of Tuam that the bishops had the game in their hands, and would get all they wished if they only stood firm.* The result proved to be very different; the Bill was read a third time without serious modification, and two generations of young Irishmen have paid the penalty of mistakes on both sides which rendered futile a beneficent design.†

---

* " Private Correspondence of O'Connell " (John Murray, 1888).

† Some hopes were entertained that the Liberal members would succeed without O'Connell, but they came to nothing. Pigot wrote to Davis:—

"I agree in your wish for success through Wyse and company, and perhaps it may be the result, too; yet 'tis not that we ought to prepare for. One great advantage is that good preparation for one implies and leads to the best preparation for the other. The moment I am well enough I will

In view of O'Connell's return to Dublin, the project of breaking with the friends of mixed education was eagerly debated among the partisans of the "Young Liberator." A barrister without practice, capacity, or conduct, who had been blackballed with Mr. Conway in the club, publicly resigned his connection with the Association as he could not act there with men who expressed their want of confidence in him elsewhere. Others who feared the same discipline made his grievance their own, and called on O'Connell to defend his true friends. Some of the young men were disposed to end the contest by quitting the Association, but O'Brien, to whom the design was reported, was against secession.

"I hope," he wrote to Davis, "no one will dream of resigning. The association is formed for national objects, and not to promote the views of any one or more individuals. I trust, however, that all the momentary difficulties which embarrass us will be removed, and that we shall advance forward with increased rapidity. . . . You ought to arrange that two or three of our young speakers should take a part on each Monday during O'Connell's absence. It is of the utmost importance that the country should be made to feel that Repeal does not depend upon A or B or C, but will always have champions bold, yet discreet, until the end shall be attained."

Davis reassured him :—

"O'Loghlen [Sir Colman] and all whom I have consulted are firm against secession. O'Loghlen proposes, and I agree with him fully, that if O'Connell on his return should force the question on Conciliation Hall, an amendment should be moved that the introduction of such a question, against the wish of a numerous and respectable portion of the committee, is contrary to the principles of the association and likely to injure the cause of Repeal. A steady elaborate discussion for a number of days would end in the withdrawal of the motion and amendment, or in rendering the

begin my share again. Did you get the books as well as maps? I have made an abstract into a MS. book, after the manner of the 'Maximes,' and with a view to publication."

motion, if carried, powerless. An explanation would follow, and
—the cause would still be safe. Secession would give Ireland up
without a contest to the bigots ; it would, besides, be criminal and
hardly honourable to secede, as if, forsooth, we had joined a retinue,
not a free league, and could take up our hats and abandon the
cause on receiving offence or injustice. . . . Once this peril is over,
all will be safe."

A few days later he says :—

"I have been, and am, doing all in my power to prevent the
injurious results of the differences on the Colleges Bill, and have
been fortunate enough to put an end to a discussion in committee
which was tending fast to mischief. In my mind any advantages
to be derived from the Bill are not worth even a moment's division
amongst us."

To this opinion O'Brien cordially adhered ; he
was not prepared to sacrifice the greater cause to
the lesser :—

"I feel entirely the importance to the cause of Repeal of my
maintaining sincere, unreserved, and friendly co-operation with
O'Connell; but I am bound also to add that, under the present
circumstances of our relative positions, I would prefer to withdraw
for a time from active efforts in the association, rather than
appear there as an adversary to his policy." *

All these proceedings, threatening, as he believed,
religious liberty, deeply moved Wallis, and he un-
bosomed himself in a letter to Davis :—

"'Tis a crushing blow, at the back of all other public and
private discomfitures, to behold, in the sixteenth year after Emancipation, a deliberate and almost undisguised demand for the
establishment of an Inquisition in Ireland—not as bad as the old
inquisition of Spain and Portugal, but far worse—an inquisition
not expending its chief solicitude about the *lana caprina* of doctrines and ceremonies, or wielded as an engine of state by super-
annuated despotisms,—not such—not an inquisition of *autos da fe*
—but a far sleeker and subtler practitioner of moral infanticide,
and procurer of mental abortion, providing for the perpetual falsi-
fication of history, and menacing with extreme penalties all honest

* O'Brien to Davis, Limerick, December 1, 1844.

interpretation of the works of God; whether it be the Earth which is His footstool, or Heaven which is His throne, or the body of man which is His image, or the mind of man which is deemed to be a quenchless spark of Himself. Talk of penal laws against certain modes of worship! What are these to penal discourage-ments of all that does honour to human nature, of those who are the very salt of the earth; the miners and inventors, the essayers and utterers of truth? And then, to see, in Ireland, the more honest portion of the National party taking refuge under those very resolutions of the bishops, from the still more revolting extravagancies of a ferocious demagogue; and, in England, not one word of honest rebuke from any representative of any party—in Parliament, I mean, where it was most imperatively called for;—I cannot digest it; it literally chokes me to think of it."

Here was a contest in which men of liberal instincts outside Ireland could scarcely hesitate in choosing sides. But so perverse and intractable are national prejudices, that his most bitter assailants were some of the leaders of liberal opinion in Eng-land. In an article written by Thackeray, which took the form of a letter from "Mr. Punch (of *Punch*) to Mr. Davis (of the *Nation*)," Davis was turned into contemptuous ridicule, for presuming to maintain his opinions against O'Connell, and assured that, since Marat a more disagreeable demagogue had not appeared than himself.

At the instance of Davis and O'Loghlen it was determined to hold a national levee on the anniversary of the O'Connell imprisonment, where a public pledge might be renewed that corruption should not seduce, nor deceit cajole, nor intimidation deter the Irish people from seeking self-government. It was held in the historic Round Room of the Rotunda, and was attended by the municipal authorities and the Repeal leaders from all the great centres in Ireland. Some of the deputations urged upon both parties in the late contest that further division would be fatal, and would not be supported or sanctioned by the country.

Davis in a note to Maddyn described the impression the national levee made upon him :—

"The most impressive scene I ever witnessed in a popular assembly was when O'Brien proposed the pledge. He shook like an oak in storm with excitement, and his voice was like the wind through its boughs.

"If I had to deal only with O'Connell we never would fall out; but he is surrounded by sycophants who lie away against every man whose honesty they fear. However, we are good friends now, and if the Catholic laity are *bold* and *firm*, the only question likely to endanger our confederacy will be happily solved."

And to Pigot he wrote on the same subject :—

"Friday brought the most imposing scene I ever witnessed. When O'Brien came to propose the pledge, the corporations were seated in order down the side of the pillar-room, the club and others on the floor, an oval space was in the centre with O'Brien at one end and the Chair at the other; I was close to O'B., and his breast heaved and his eyes clouded, and his voice gurgled with passions. The assembly was as solemn, and the pledge was taken in earnest. The 'martyrs' [the late Repeal prisoners] were present, and they signed the parchment afterwards. The round-room was really a noble sight, and our club curved round the seven oligarchs, and, stretching into the passages, gave it a military air. The procession was immense, and spectators up to the chimney-tops. Among the lookers-on was the Lord Lieutenant. He was in a room in Sackville Street. The day was really great, and the effects will be serious."

But the contest, of which the college question was only the outward sign, was suspended, not composed. To O'Brien Davis wrote confidentially his impression of the actual position of affairs :—

"I will not interfere again till an attempt be made to pledge the association to evil resolutions. If the O'Connells wish, they can ruin the agitation (not the country) in spite of any one.

Between unaccounted-for funds, bigotry, billingsgate, Tom Steele missions, crude and contradictory dogmas, and unrelieved stupidity, any cause and any system could be ruined. America, too, from whence arose 'the cloud in the west' which alarmed Peel, has been deeply offended, and but for the *Nation* there would not now be one Repeal club in America. Still we have a sincere and numerous people, a rising literature, an increasing staff of young, honest, trained men. Peel's splitting policy [a policy which split up the Tories], the chance of war, the chance of the Orangemen, and a great, though now misused, organization; and perhaps next autumn a rally may be made. It will require forethought, close union, indifference to personal attack, and firm measures. At this moment the attempt would utterly fail; but parties may be brought down to reason by the next four months. Again, I tell you, you have no notion of the loss sustained by John O'Connell's course. A dogged temper and a point of honour induce me to remain in the association at every sacrifice, and will keep me there while there is a chance, even a remote one, of doing good in it."

This was O'Brien's reply :—

"It is quite true that the tone taken by John O'Connell has done infinite mischief, and upon this point I have not concealed my opinion from him. But I am not disposed, on that account, to despond. The care which ought to be taken by the friends of mixed education with regard to the matter should not be less firm because we do not agree with the sentiments which he has put forward. We have declared that we would repudiate the College Scheme unless it gave security to religious men of all parties, that religion should not be excluded wholly from these institutions— and unless public liberty should be protected from the corrupt influences of such extensive Government patronage. Whilst therefore no practical difference now arises between us and the separate educationists, we are, in my opinion, bound to sustain them in their opposition on those grounds on which we have ourselves (whether wisely or not is not now the question) proclaimed our opposition to the measure."

Davis's friends were determined that he should no longer shelter himself from the public recognition of his services. Invitations came to him from the provinces to various public entertainments. But this was not enough. For three years he had given all his time and thought to the public cause, and men to whom it was a profitable trade to undertake missions and other temporary employments for the Repeal Association scoffed at him as a briefless barrister. He was briefless because he declined to hold briefs, but he was competent to be a great lawyer, and some of his friends urged him to go circuit, and establish habitual relations with his profession. The project did not receive the universal assent of his comrades. Dillon wrote to me :—

"If Davis will not attend two public dinners, I would much rather he would select Sligo than Galway. Tell him I will write to him from Sligo, and, as I would say the same things to both of you, that letter will do for you, and you can shew him this. I was greatly annoyed at hearing a report that he was going circuit. That, I think, would be altogether ruinous. Every one would say that he was driven out of politics. I have been thinking that he and you ought to start a penny magazine, and conduct it yourselves, making use of James Duffy to circulate it. If you would join in the speculation I am certain it should necessarily succeed, and it would be a powerful engine. 'It stands upon you' to work against the powerful confederacy that has been formed to crush you, and in your persons everything that is upright and independent in the country. May God defend the right."

On the other hand Denny Lane approved of the design on public grounds :—

"I am very glad," he wrote to Davis, "to hear that you are coming down to the Assizes. The going circuit, I think, more than anything else, can make a man acquainted with the provincial mind of Ireland, which is really of much greater proportionate power than the ex-metropolitan mind of any other country. In fact we have no metropolis—neither the court of claret-coloured coats nor that of wigs and gowns is enough to make Dublin anything but a country town. We have no theatre, no periodical literature, no gathering of artists, no great merchants, above all, no legislative assembly collecting into a focus every ray of intellect and enterprise in the country. In fact we have nothing of what makes Paris or other capitals the 'governor' of the great engine of a nation."

From this time forth till the day of his death Davis was habitually slandered in private gossip by a herd of blockheads who thought abuse of him a sure road to favour with Mr. John O'Connell, who now posed as the victor in the late contest.

When the autumn approached, the leaders of the Association scattered for their usual holiday, and this feeble, barren young man was placed by his father in supreme control of the great popular organization. It is still a point in controversy whether the disastrous use he made of this opportunity was the result of simple incapacity, or of that malicious spirit which the Americans call "cussedness." It is certain that he wished to rehearse the part of dictator, and was not indisposed to do whatever the Young Irelanders wished to be left undone. Week after week new outrages were committed against the fundamental principles on which the national confederacy rested. It was open to Irishmen of all political opinions who desired the repeal of the Union; but it was suddenly pledged to a Whig-Radical programme of measures to be obtained at Westminster. It was bound to cultivate the goodwill of friendly nations, as an important moral auxiliary; but the two most friendly nations in the world, the only two which took any genuine interest in our affairs, were wantonly insulted. O'Connell himself declared that he would not accept repeal if it were to be obtained with the assistance of such a people as the French, and he proffered England Irish assistance in the Oregon controversy, to pluck down the stripes and stars. That the Association should be free from sectarian controversy was a condition of its existence; but week after week harangues were delivered on the German Catholic Church, and the holy coat of Treves. One of the most respectable men in the movement, an adherent of O'Connell from the Clare election down to that day, was asked by the Young Liberator how he dared to come to the Association to remonstrate against the attacks on America as unwise and unnecessary. The evil wrought only concerns us here from the necessity of explaining allusions in Davis's correspondence, which might otherwise be unintelligible.

The move towards Whig-Radicalism greatly alarmed Smith O'Brien, who counted on Tory adhesions. He wrote to Davis :—

"I much regret to find that O'Connell has given notice of some resolutions which commit the association to the adoption of an opinion in favour of household suffrage, vote by ballot, the voluntary principle, the abolition of the poor-law. Nothing can be more injurious than this plan of giving notice without consulting the committee. Nothing can be more fatal to the success of the cause than that it should be promulgated that those who wish to give to Ireland a domestic legislature must consider themselves pledged to measures of so extreme a character as those involved in these resolutions. . . . Having received lately intimations of support of the Repeal cause from quarters in which I did not in the least expect to find it, I am doubly disappointed in finding that the policy about to be adopted by the leaders of the association is such as to destroy all my hopes of immediate progress. We shall succeed in the end, but it is too bad that we should so often spoil our own game and raise up difficulties and delays." *

Of the attack on America, Dillon wrote to Davis :—

"Everybody is indignant at O'Connell meddling in the business. His talk about bringing down the pride of the American Eagle, if

* July 23, 1845.

England would pay us sufficiently, is not merely foolish, but false and base.   Such talk must be supremely disgusting to the Americans, and to every man of honour and spirit.   He lectures the *Spectator* for saying that the 'loyalty' of the Irish may be secured for a 'consideration,' and he says the same himself the next moment.   The plain policy of the party now is to assume a menacing attitude, for either there will be a war or England will be obliged to shrink."

The effect of the mispolicy was speedy and signal in America.   The Repeal Associations in Baltimore, New Orleans, and other cities were dissolved, and the native press was furious against our ingratitude. But the attack on individual liberty outraged Dillon more than the blunders in public policy.

"I have just read," he wrote to Davis, "with inexpressible disgust, the speech of John O'Connell, and the scene which followed between himself and Scott.   It behoves you to consider very seriously whether the *Nation* is not bound to notice this matter. I feel very desirous that you personally should avoid any further encounter with the O'Connells for some time. . . .   In truth, from the turn matters are now taking, a decent man cannot frequent the public meetings; for he must either create dissension or have his reputation damaged by silently listening to the absurd and mischievous stuff that is talked there.   But I doubt much whether a newspaper can, without compromising its character, allow these proceedings to pass unnoticed.   My notion is that Scott has a right to protection, and that the public will, or ought to, feel indignant if this protection be withheld.   The *Nation* could not possibly get a better opportunity of reading a long required lecture to Johnny.   The immediate topic is one on which public opinion is universally against him. . . .   [Mr. Scott, who was an old man long associated with O'Connell, and having no relations with the Young Irelanders, made a slight effort to pacify America by excluding from Conciliation Hall Negro slavery, Texas, Oregon, and the whole range of Transatlantic questions upon which O'Connell and Mr. John O'Connell had been haranguing.]   Can anything be more evident than the puerile folly of it?   When the Americans were engaged in their own struggle only fancy one of their orators coming down to the Congress with a violent invective against the abuses of the French Government of the day.   Any

man who is thoroughly in earnest about one thing cannot allow
his mind to wander in pursuit of things not merely unconnected
but inconsistent with that thing. It is impossible latterly to bear
with the insolence of this little frog. There is no man or country
safe from his venom. If there be not some protest against him, he
will set the whole world against us."

Somewhat later he wrote, "In this county [Mayo],
as far as I can see, Repeal is all but extinct."

But the public blunders of the maladroit tribune
did not exhaust his energies; he found time to
stimulate the calumnies on Davis and his friends.
From Tipperary, Doheny wrote to Davis :—

"It [the *Nation*] is in great disrepute among the priests. I met
a Doctor at Nenagh who lost two subscribers to a dispensary for
refusing to give it up. . . . I was thinking of writing an article
on the subject. If you and Duffy don't approve of it when you see
it, it can be left out. O'Connell's *hints* are taken to be corrobora-
tive of the ruffianism of others."

MacNevin's impetuous nature could not silently
wait events. He wrote to me at this time :—

"Dillon is sick of the abomination of desolation on Burghquay.
It never opens its sooty mouth on the subject of Repeal now. By
the way, where *is* the Repeal Agitation? Is it hunting at Darrynane? . . . My parliamentary mania is cured; I would not accept
the representation of any constituency at the beck of such a body.
I will work with you and Davis, but no more with the base
melange of tyranny and mendicancy. I am glad that Davis does
not go to the association; I shall not go when I return."

When the people despair of political success,
disorder is sure to ensue, and the national cause
began to be stained with crimes.

"Can nothing be done," Smith O'Brien wrote to Davis, "to
stop the agrarian outrages in Tipperary? They are most injurious
to us, to the population, and to the country—to say nothing of the
horrors attendant on a system of private murder."

The most respectable of the recent recruits

began to waver. Grey Porter had retired, and Hely Hutchinson declined to enter Parliament, though a southern county was offered to him. This was the condition of public affairs a few weeks after the question of the provincial colleges was forced upon the Repeal Association.

I have not tacked to any transaction in this narrative the moral which it suggests; the thoughtful reader prefers to draw his own conclusions. But for once I ask those to whom this book is dedicated, to note the conduct of Catholic young men in a mortal contest. The hereditary leader of the people, sure to be backed by the whole force of the unreflecting masses, and supported on this occasion by the bulk of the national clergy—a man of genius, an historic man wielding an authority made august by a life's services, a solemn moral authority with which it is ridiculous to compare the purely political influence of any one who has succeeded him as tribune of the people—was against Thomas Davis, and able, no one doubted, to overwhelm him and his sympathizers in political ruin. A public career might be closed for all of us; our journal might be extinguished; we were already denounced as intriguers and infidels; it was quite certain that by-and-by, we would be described as hirelings of the Castle. But Davis was right; and of all his associates, not one man flinched from his side,—not one man. A crisis bringing character to a sharper test has never arisen in our history, nor can ever arise; and the conduct of these men, it seems to me, is some guarantee how their successors would act in any similar emergency.

CHAPTER VIII.

A NEW DEPARTURE. 1845.

UNDER these checks and discouragements Davis did not fall back, but pressed forward. When the sky was clear he would gladly have retired for a time, but when the wind was high, and the horizon dark, retirement was impossible. To attend Conciliation Hall was indeed a waste of life, but the special work of the *Nation*, "mind-making," as he named it, remained, and he threw himself into it with admirable industry. It is necessary for parties to cast the lead from time to time, and take an observation in order to know their actual progress, and the late controversy enabled him to measure the great gain in self-reliance and independent opinion which the middle-class had attained, and taught him to set his hopes on a sure but distant future. It is pathetic, almost tragic, to note the use he made of what proved to be the last months of his life.

Only the work of a Minister of State, controlling a great department, can equal the variety of interests on which he had to issue instructions, tender advice, or call for information. He sat in his little book-lined den in Bagot Street, or in his bureau at the *Nation* office, and moved a hundred minds to furnish the data on which conclusions are founded, or to carry out suggestions for promoting his main design.

I found among his papers a list of agenda, probably prepared about this time. Some of the work has been since done, but whatever remains incomplete has a valid claim upon the young men of to-day :—

1. Maps of Ireland (historical, and for practical use). A large map; and little guide-book plans with sketches of every ruin.

2. Historical Buildings, Pictures, Busts, Statues, etc., in our Towns.

3. Irish Almanacs (Irish letter-paper, with music, landscapes, emblems, historical designs, etc.).

4. A Musical Circulating Library (established by a club, and allowing counties to subscribe).

5. Irish Biographical Dictionary.

6. Absentee List [a roll of the owners of Irish estates who were non-resident].

7. History of the War from 1641 to 1652.

8. Military History of 1798.

9. Former Commerce with Denmark and Spain.

10. Irish Statistics (each county separately, as in Scotland).

11. An Illustrated History.

12. Restoration of Churches, etc.

13. Reprint of Historical Pamphlets.

14. Lives of Illustrious Irishmen—Brian Boru, Dathi, Nial, Columba, Columbkille, Malachi, Duns Scotus, St. Lawrence, Cathal, Donald O'Brien, McCarthy (with family notes and antiquarian authorities, Lodge, Cambrensis, Lynch, O'Donovan (Annals of the Four Masters, Hallam, Keating, O'Halloran, O'Flaherty), Byrne), Art O'Kavanagh (see Irish annals), Kildare, Shane O'Neil, Hugh O'Donnell, Tirone, Settlement of Ulster, Roger O'More, Owen Roe and his brothers, etc., Ormond, Tirconnell, Sarsfield, Molyneux, Swift, Lucas, Flood, Grattan, Tone.

The once simple programme of the National party had become a tangled skein, but he pushed controversy aside, and applied all his strength to the purpose of training the people for freer lives and higher duties hereafter.

The young men of the middle-class were his special pupils, and pleasant evidence came to him how cheerfully they followed his counsels. Horace Fitzgerald, a young Munster gentleman afterwards member for Tipperary, utilized a visit to Paris by searching for papers concerning the Irish Brigade, and reported the result of his inquiries to Davis :—

"I applied to an old acquaintance, General de la Hite, who has taken a great deal of trouble to obtain for me permission from the Minister of War to inspect the documents regarding the old Brigade. They wish, however, to know what particular period I mean to inquire into, and they would then facilitate any research, but it is absolutely necessary I must designate a particular epoch and a person connected with the subject."

From Rome came the pleasant news that the inscription on the tombs of the Irish princes buried in the church of St. Pietro de Montorio, which time had greatly effaced, had been revived by the care of one of the noble house of Caulfield who was a descendant of the princes of Tyrconnel.

Mr. Kingsley, a student at Highbury College, preparing for the ministry of the Congregational Church, wrote :—

"Your articles thrill my heart with fire and fury. I am ready for any work that may be required of a southern patriot."

And again :—

"A friend of mine, Mr. Gibson of Mallow, an Independent minister there, is the proprietor of a printing establishment, and has been for some time anxious to give whatever assistance he could to the Repeal cause. It has occurred to him that the people are not yet sufficiently educated to understand fully all the able articles in the *Nation* and the other Repeal papers, and that there is room for a cheap publication, written in a style more suited to the people's capacity. He has requested me to ascertain whether it was likely that such a thing would 'take.' . . . A circulation of two thousand copies per week would yield him a clear profit of three hundred pounds a year. So he calculates, and he seems quite up to all the expense of printing, etc. Of this he would give me one hundred pounds if I undertook the editorship. My heart is in the cause, and it would gladden it to be employed in its advancement."

The two new recruits asked guidance how to make themselves good and serviceable Irishmen.

"Neither Gibson nor I," Mr. Kingsley wrote, "know anything of the Irish language, nor, indeed, much of Irish antiquities. We are, notwithstanding, Irish all out. Will you recommend me some books to get on Irish history, etc."

Davis wished his correspondent and young men generally to study Gaelic.

"The native language," he insisted, "should be cherished, not only because it was the necessary instrument of all original research in our early history, but because without it the geography, music, and nomenclature of the country would be unintelligible.

. "The hills, and lakes, and rivers, the forts and castles, the churches and parishes, the baronies and counties had Irish names—names which describe the nature of the scenery or ground, the name of founder, or chief, or priest, or the leading fact in the history of the place. Meath tells its flatness, Clonmel the abundant riches of its valley, Fermanagh is the land of the lakes, Tyrone the country of Owen, Kilkenny the Church of St. Canice, Dunmore the great fort, Athenry the Ford of the Kings, Dunleary the Fort of the Sea; and the Phœnix Park, instead of taking its name from a fable, recognizes as christener, the 'sweet water' which yet springs near the East-gate."

From his native town one of his political pupils * sent him a report on the progress of mind-making there, but it is to be feared that his geese were too habitually swans to please a man of Davis's rigid accuracy.

"In this town there are several young men of good talents, chiefly among the working classes; one of our best Repeal wardens, J. T. Collins, is a specimen, and one whose talents, if properly

* R. B. Barry, Mallow, March, 1845.

cultivated, would add another to the school of Canova. His Execution of Momus, in stucco, would not dishonour Hogan or McDowel,
and yet this honest-hearted young fellow is more than half his
time out of employment, although he brings himself to work on
the roof of a house at 2*s.* 6*d.* per diem. Another of our townsmen,
Hickey, when a mere boy, a few years ago, got a prize in Dublin
for, I believe, a colossal figure of Homer: he is the son of a black-
smith. O'Donoghue, a lad of fifteen years old, and, walking our
streets literally clad in rags, possesses gifts that remind one of
Maclise. William Kent, a drunken (alas!) shoemaker, who is only
just returned from Wales, where he had been, by special invitation,
for the last two months, making a cork leg for a gentleman, possesses a natural talent which, if improved by study, would enable
him to rank with the Hunters in anatomy. In the school of design
we have Donovan, a common wood-turner, living in a back lane,
who was more than once the recipient of our gracious Queen's
Bounty for some curiously constructed miniature models of spinning wheels, etc., which he sent to the royal children. Robert
Winn, a house-painter—a modest Mozart—is the leader of an
amateur band, second to none even in her Majesty's service. We
can also claim as a townsman Mr. Thomas Nagle, at present master
of Earl Listowel's—that excellent nobleman—private band; he is
self-taught, and a composer of no mean pretensions.

"The morality of war articles taught us self-restraint, while
they also taught us self-reliance, and made us look the enemy
more boldly in the face, not eager for an attack, yet not skulking
from an encounter; and, my dear sir, with such men as Davis,
Duffy, and Co., working in the same ranks with our well-beloved
O'Connell (during whose life, which may God prolong, no other
leader shall usurp our affections), I fear not for the liberties of old
Ireland, were they even to be battled for on the 'tented field.' . . .
Mr. Callaghan, Repeal M.P., sports two Repeal buttons, but does
not subscribe a farthing to the association."

Dillon sent him some useful suggestions from
his retreat in the West:—

"If you could do something towards supplying the country
bands with teaching and music, you would be doing a great
service. This always strikes me when I come to the country. I
spent the greater part of yesterday in the National school here,
and I was quite astounded at the quantity of information the
little fellows displayed. Their knowledge of geography in par-

ticular is most surprising. I think we must wait for these fellows.
I intend to get up a public examination in this school next summer,
and to give prizes. This will have the double effect of stimulating
their ambition and of putting some good books into the hands of
the best of them. Would it not be well to suggest a general
project of this kind in the *Nation ?* "

John Daly, a humble but zealous antiquary,
projected a society for publishing Irish airs, gathered
in remote places, and asked Davis's assistance,
which was promptly granted :—

"I shall," he wrote, "gladly subscribe to, and, so far as my
scanty leisure and miserably deficient knowledge admit, shall
willingly act with your society; but I recommend you not to
issue your prospectus till after Dr. Cane's visit to Dublin."

And again :—

"I can, I fear, only give you my name and subscription, for
my time is already over-taxed. If you will send the corrected
prospectus to Mr. Bindon, with this note, he may, perhaps, join
your committee, and he would be of real service to you.

"Also, perhaps Dr. H. Hudson, of Stephen's Green North,
would do so, and would be a most valuable auxiliary. His brother
is on the continent, or I should propose it to him. Your committee is not large enough, and has too few Dublin men on it. . . .

"The only volumes of Danish history to which I can refer
you are Laing's ' Sea Kings of Norway,' recently published in
three volumes, and of the highest authority; Johnston's ' Guide,
etc.,' easily procured; and a large folio, by a Copenhagen Society,
which is in the Queen's Inns Library, and, I suppose, in Trinity
College."

Daly explained his project, which he afterwards
to a considerable extent carried into effect.

"Ireland, indeed, stands indebted to Mr. Hardiman for rescuing
very many of her songs from oblivion; but Mr. Hardiman's collection was published in such a manner as to put it entirely out of
the reach of the parties for whom such a work should be intended
—I mean the Irish peasantry. The plan which I intend pursuing
will be this: the work will be printed in numbers, containing

eight octavo pages, good paper, and beautifully clear type, at the price of two-pence each."

At the same time, the intellectual movement in the provinces was fed from headquarters. Dr. Scott, an industrious antiquary in Kilkenny, wrote to Davis of the re-edification of a mediæval church in that city, for the *Nation* was the zealous guardian of our historical and ecclesiastical remains :—

" The whitewash has at length been removed from the pillars and the arches in the aisles of St. Francis' Cathedral; the wall which divides the chancel from the aisles is to be taken down, and a handsome open-work screen put in its place, on which is to stand an organ with a double face—one looking into the aisles, the other into the chancel. By this the whole length of the church, in all the beauty of its elegant proportions, can be seen at a glance. The windows over the grand entrance have been restored to their original length; all the windows are to undergo the same change. The aisle is vastly improved by these changes; the mouldings of the arches between the pillars in the aisle are not all of marble, some are a kind of rich-coloured sandstone. The variety is pleasing; all the pillars are of the one material— marble. . . . The tomb of the Roman merchant (Banim Story) was discovered the other day: ' Simon Carlovitchi, A.D. 1728.' "

Pigot, from London, reported the success of an Irish artist in whom we were all interested :—

" Maclise has again this year painted the best picture in the Exhibition. It is from ' Comus.' I think he improves much, though he has done sublimer things before. McDowell [sculptor] has one piece, but the drapery is very poor, and the merit most in the idea only."

Maddyn projected a study of Burke for the *Nation*, which he desired should be a searching and exhaustive estimate :—

" Of all the numerous commentators on Burke," he wrote, " Mackintosh understood him best. Mackintosh's idea of Burke, you recollect, was, ' that he was the greatest philosopher in action that the world ever saw.' But clear as were Mackintosh's ideas

of him, he lost sight of the zeal and amazing personal ardour of
Burke. From what Mackintosh has written of him, no one could
imagine the fervour of Hasting's prosecutor, or the blazing passion
of the old man roused on the brink of the grave by the French
Revolution. The idea of ' philosopher in action ' was Burke's own
view of a true politician, whether he be democrat or royalist. . . .
I have given much consideration to your proposal of the History
of Ireland since 1688. It is a book I would be enchanted to set to
work upon. But long before you proposed it, I was thinking of
the ' Statesmanship of Ireland since 1688,' with these materials.
It would be a work partly critical and partly illustrative, consisting of chapters on ' Molyneux and his Book,' ' Swift, his Influence
on Ireland,' ' Lucas,' ' Flood, and how much he did in Ireland,'
' Henry Grattan,' ' William Pitt's Influence on Ireland,' ' Wolfe
Tone,' ' Clare,' and ' Castlereagh.' These are the men who ruled
the Ireland of the last century. Molyneux and Lucas are the
smallest of them, but nevertheless they would be missed out of
the working of the century. I regard Lucas as an excellent specimen of a workmanlike tribune—a man more anxious to produce
results than most popular leaders generally are. Pitt had more
influence in Ireland than any Englishman or Saxon since Cromwell. The other English ministers had very secondary influence
on our destinies, and the other Irishmen (besides those I have
named) were more illustrative than active, more subsidiary to
their contemporary parties than substantially necessary to the
actual politics of the times. . . . I would therefore prefer to write
a *bonâ fide* History of Ireland since 1688 to 1829. It would be
virtually a history of Irish Protestant Nationality, and I would
strongly sympathize with its local feeling, though, from my natural
prejudices as one born a Catholic, I would not feel with much of
its purposes. There would be plenty of Irish spirit in the book,
and I would labour to make it creditable to my name."

Davis replied :—

" Your plan about the ' Burke,' " he wrote, " is excellent, but
I think even with intervals in their publication the articles ought
not to exceed three.

" When you were here I think we all overrated Flood, and
upon childish grounds enough—' the Renunciation Act.' Both
Flood and Grattan were wrong in trusting the rights of a newly
emancipated province to the pledges of its old ruler. Might could
alone make such rights last. . . .

"Nothing has been settled about the history, as I am too anxious for the arrangements to precipitate it.

"Pope was, in all his works, an intimate and favourite of mine; but I condemn him now on principle. Didactic writing for the sake of action may well be in verse, but not mere criticism or analysis.

"Have you ever tried dramatic writing? Do you know Taylor's 'Philip van Artevelde,' and Griffin's 'Gisippus?' I think them the two best serious dramas written in English since Shakespeare's time. A drama equal to either of them on an Irish subject would be useful and popular to an extent you can hardly suppose. . . . Ireland is really ripening, that is my chief pleasure. I have too many pursuits to enjoy any of them very keenly, save for an hour of exultation now and then.

"I cannot be convinced that your frame is sickly. It is sensitive, and your mind still more so. You have not attended to your physical education, and London is unfit for you; but more of this some other time." *

The Repeal Essays for which the Association had granted prizes, were now selected by O'Brien, Davis, and John O'Connell. Davis announced the result to Pigot.

"M. J. Barry got the 1st prize, Staunton the 2nd, for a great reply to Rice and Martin ; and a Presbyterian clergyman (nameless to the public) the 3rd. We are also going to print a short Federalist Essay as an Appendix. Barry's will do great good, it is so clear and manly.

"Repeal is bettering every day, and, thank God, is less windy than it was.

* When the paper arrived he wrote again to Maddyn :—
"I am delighted to find you think of coming here. The offence you gave by the book ['Ireland and its Rulers'] will never pass from the minds of certain persons here, but any more general irritation has passed, and, though I say it who should not, our immediate party is too strong to allow of your being annoyed unless you sought (what you would avoid most) the society of the persons to whom I have referred ; so come in May, and while you are here other things will grow up and you will become native again, and we'll solemnly exorcise sad demons from each other. J. D. told me a few days ago that he did not like to begin the history (it is to be in parts) till January, 1846 ; but as to you, he consented to your taking my place, and right glad he ought to be at the exchange. Of that, too, shall we talk in the bright coming May." (February 6, 1845.)

" We had no opportunity of dealing with B. [Barret], as he was an original member [of the 'Eighty-two Club]. The uniform is strictly civilian, except the foraging cap.

" We are devoting much real thought to the Land Question, so that we may be unanimous and practical. If we succeed in being so, everything else will be easier.

" Cultivate acquaintance with any of the Young England, or of the genuinely literary men, you can; it will be most useful by-and-by.

" Do not be impatient (as is your fault) with Wyse; he is better than his manner. His book on Education is admirable; though, like all books on the subject I ever saw, not sounding the depths of humanity.

" We shall have one hundred uniforms at the club on the 16th. Lord Cloncurry cannot come to it, but it is otherwise all right. We have had some blackbeaning and disputes, but things are square enough now.

" Grey Porter's junction will secure the publication for which he stipulated [the publication of the accounts of the Repeal Association]. He is manly, forcible, has seen the politics of Italy, Hungary, Norway, etc., is no Quaker, but a little raw.

" Either Peel must finally break with his old friends or lose the trivial profits of his concessions.

" We shall have a flood of Irish publications this coming season. Curry has books forward. Hodges and Smith have Mat O'Connor's 'Irish Brigade,' and two other most important but unnamable books advanced. Petrie's book out; Lefanu's 'Cock and Anchor,' an Irish novel; the Repeal Essays in one vol. Various Parliamentary Committee Reports forward. MacNevin's 'Sheil' printed. My 'Curran' partly in type and *carefully* edited. 'Flood,' etc., under the tools. MacNevin's 'Volunteers' (the first of the shilling volumes) partly in type. Duffy's collection of 'Ballads' ready. My 'Tone,' and Barry's collection of 'Irish Songs' to be specially attacked. Henry Grattan's fifth volume just ready for the press. Dr. R. R. Madden's third series sold to James Duffy per my agency, and many other things. Other literary progress in 1845 promises to be real."

The Protestant clergyman who wrote the Repeal Essay was Rev. James Godkin, an Independent Minister. When his name became public with his own consent, he was dismissed from his missionary duties, but Davis procured him employment in the *Freeman's Journal* office, and hoped to get him appointed a professor in the new colleges. From that time forth he acted with the National party, through many struggles and troubles, up to his death.

During this work Davis's correspondence with private friends did not slacken, but it was directed chiefly to stimulate them to work. To politicians, literary men, artists, booksellers, and Repeal Wardens, he wrote a weekly shoal of letters enough to make a *dilettante* stare. And all this without fussiness, self-importance, ill-humour, or any of the vices by which over-worked men avenge themselves on the world. He wrote to Maddyn :—

"You promised once to write on the Irishmen in England— pray do so, and fully; we want them home. Classifying them into artists, lawyers, writers, and politicians would be, I think, the best plan; but you can judge. In about a week I'll answer anent the History; for to accomplish the end sought, it should be a history, not a series of sketches.

"When writing the notice of Burke for the *Nation*, you could, without much additional trouble, prepare the selection of his speeches, putting parts of the pamphlets in an Appendix. It may be wanted sooner than was expected. I think the 'Grattan' gravely and gracefully written, without a wrong sentence; but I wished for more. His conduct from 1784 up is too lightly glanced at. I write to you freely. Willis's 'Forde' will be in the *University* next month." *

To Pigot he reported progress generally :—

"Maddyn's 'Grattan' is out, and is the best specimen of printing ever seen in Dublin. Half of the 'Sheil' is in type. 'Curran' will be third. The intervals will be two months.

"We have agreed to give £100 prize for a School History of Ireland, to be given in by January 1, 1846.

"The Land Question is now everything, and O'C. and I very cordial on it and on most things. So far so good. Our power is getting genuine at last.

* Feb. 2, 1845.

"Our '82 uniforms look admirably, and, were we rid of some scamps, the club would be all right. As it is, we are in high spirits, though somewhat at a loss for non-indictable songs. Duffy's wife is still holding out. May I put you down for a copy of Mangan's 'Poems,' price 10s. 6d.? Helen Faucet is very admirable in every way, and your story a calumny. I met her at Stokes's, but only dreamt once of her since, and that was last night when she seemed strangely combined with a Repeal Essay! Burton has been picturing her, and a body of '*us Academicians!*' addressing her. [The members of the Royal Irish Academy, of whom Davis was now one, presented Miss Faucet with an address.] . . . Dillon *has* drafted a report and swears to edit some speeches. [Dillon's philosophic indolence was a common subject of banter among his friends.]

"I am *equally* glad of your health and your hard reading. Vigorous habits, power equal to your need and position, and something over for adornment and benevolence, are the conditions of happiness. I sometimes, when I see fine spirits, like rudderless ships, drifting to ruin, think to be a preacher and to guide individual minds, but end by returning to my public mission. Ever toil at your sober duties. If great opportunities, lightening inspirations come, be the man of the hour and act and create, but never *toil* for these things. Emerson's best critical thought is that Nature does not endure a spy."

He knew that an historical romance would greatly move and instruct the popular mind, but he deluded himself with the hope that such a work of art could be had to order. He wrote to Maddyn :—

"'The Boyne Water,' a novel by Banim, has excellent things, such as the scenery at the Boyne and Fairhead, and the starvation of Derry, which he exaggerates; but upon the great political elements then at work he looked casually and unwisely. I wish to heaven some one would attempt Irish historical fiction! Griffin's 'Invasion' and some of his short tales were excellent; there is a novel, too, called 'The Adventurers,' written by I know not whom, upon the wars of Hugh O'Neil in Elizabeth's time; but besides these and the 'Boyne Water,' I know nothing readable of the class. There is a thought in the letter of Griffin, published in the *Nation*, that to paint Ireland struggling incessantly and unsuccessfully, now beaming with hope, now crouching in despair, still never crushed and never quite triumphant, would suit some masterpainter of history. Fiction could not deal with such a long period

of this Enceladus history ; but it could take Ireland between two
crises, palpitating between the sorrows of some defeat and beginning to be prepared for another strife. The characters on whose
loves and hates the plot rested should not be historical, for such
a work should not reach any decisive time in our history. It
should wind up with private fortunes, leaving the public and such
public men as were introduced still under the mountain. This,
you'll say, is to paint despair—say, rather, perseverance, for those
who struggled unsuccessfully did not struggle in vain ; they lived
vigorously and died well ; and at all events this *is* our history for
three hundred years past, and must be told. The weight of that
past is upon us now, and, sanguine as I am that this country
could be rescued, I often doubt if it will, for history casts shadows
on my hopes."

With leisure he would perhaps himself have
written historical romance, as he wrote historical
ballads, from the inspiration of a great purpose and
passionate love of the task ; but Maddyn was a
critic, not a creator.

Davis still hankered after a monthly magazine.
He knew that the organ we possessed had such access
to the popular mind as an academic periodical could
never attain, and that the minority whom he especially desired to reach read it in a way they had
never read the *Citizen* ; but there are historical
subjects which need a large canvas, and his deeply
pondered scheme of a revived nation which had to
be poured out in driblets in a weekly journal, might
be deliberately formulated in magazine papers. There
was probably another motive. Shut out as he was
by his own choice from the popular tribune, he
wanted the instrument which Burke wielded with
such effect—the political pamphlet in the only shape
in which it survived in his generation. He applied
to his closest friends for advice and co-operation.
Wallis, who had a natural preference for his own

method, gave a prompt assent, and pointed out
dangers ahead which were not yet visible to many
eyes :—

"The matter you mention does not require any deliberation.
I say at once, that, should God spare me health, strength, and eye-
sight, all of which of late have threatened to be somewhat pre-
carious with me, nothing would give me greater pleasure than to
co-operate cordially and effectively in such a project as you speak
of; that is, of course, supposing a reasonable provision made—
which there ought not to be much difficulty in making—for the
exclusion of sectarian and other deleterious influences. . . . And
'Catholicus's' attack on the *Citizen*, a couple of years ago, was but
a late outbreak of the grudge long nourished against that journal
for its moderate and unsectarian character. Again, you may not
be aware that O'Connell several times tried to get hold of the
Citizen and make of it an incense-altar for himself; and in the
perplexities now before him, and which threaten to accumulate in
every shape the further he pursues his blind career, it is hard to
say what he may not do, or what he may not lay hold of in his
desperation. Faith, contrary as it would be to the tenour of his
whole life, and of the achievements which do him most honour,
I, for my part, should not be surprised to see him, some of these
days, making a new breach between Catholic and Protestant, and
playing the part of a Popish Tresham Gregg, on a very gigantic
scale ! Well, these portents and any such are no reason for our
not doing what we can, but rather a reason the more for working
harder and for being wary into the bargain. As to what department I could best serve a journal of the sort you mention, it is
matter for after discussion. As far as I am concerned, what I
would be inclined chiefly to stipulate for, would be as follows :—
(1) A full cognizance of all preliminary arrangements; (2) a
thorough knowledge of the men I am to work with ; (3) a lion's
share in the management of my own department, whatever that
might be; (4) a virtual control over the escapades of too zealous
coadjutors; (5) some check over [James] Duffy himself, in the
existence of a Proprietary or Committee, or some such body.
There may be objections to Duffy, but to have succeeded as he has
done implies the possession of many counterbalancing merits.
And then, he is the only man who could try the experiment with
any chance of success. I have at different times during the last
couple of years lamented the want of some such organ, and see

innumerable things to be effected, that could be done in no other way."

I also assented cordially on one condition—that he would take the project into his own hands: a method which would not only give his friends a special interest in its success, but raise the periodical to immediate importance as a younger brother of the journal which had prospered so marvellously.

"Since I saw you I have been thinking of the magazine, and I am convinced if you retain the proprietorship it may be made successful and profitable. If I had no *Nation* to attend to, I believe I might undertake to make it succeed. . . . Let it be a novelty; not a humdrum imitation of this or that existing periodical, but a new creation, and the six or seven thousand persons who give sixpence a week for the *Nation* will give a shilling a month for the *National Magazine.* It will effect great good if it becomes popular, as it may and must. Carleton's story of 'Willy Reilly' [a story Carleton had written for the *Nation*] would be a good one to open with—it would probably attract an English and Scotch circulation. Your *Nation* reputation will sell it in Dublin, and perhaps throughout Ireland. The work is of a kind you would do with more satisfaction to yourself than the drudgery of the law. Don't say no.

"Always yours,
"C. G. D."

Davis replied, without deciding either way for the moment:—

"August 5th.

"My dear Friend,
"Thanks very many for your note.
"Ever yours,
"T. D."

Maddyn pleaded that his hands were already too full:—

"With respect to the magazine, it would be impossible for me to join in it; I cannot accept, for the present, more engagements than I am under. I am very, very weary of writing for my bread.

It is a wretched existence. I am going into a novel as soon as I can get some ease and quiet."

And he informed his friend that he had undertaken duties in connection with *Hood's Magazine*, and that he, too, was in search of recruits :—

"Hood's lamented illness has kept them back, but it will go on, and no mistake, for Spottiswoode, the great printer, is the capitalist of the magazine. It will, I think, merge into a Liberal organ before long, as the editor of it is biassed that way. Have you anything that you would give them? Turn it over in your mind. The magazine sells three thousand a month, and your writings would certainly be seen. Do you think Duffy could be got to give some of his poems for it—even one short paper would be of value ?" *

His friend William Eliot Hudson, on whom the burthen of the *Citizen* had fallen, was willing to try again, but only after a carefully considered plan had been accepted by a number of writers able to carry it to success. The capitalists were forthcoming— Colonel Caulfield, Thomas Hutton, and himself; but, without turning into a new channel the stream which kept the *Nation* at work, where were such writers to be found ?

"As to the Mag. or Quarterly Review, my conclusion is that nothing of the kind can be done—can succeed—by mere dint of money. Of course, a *quantum suff.* of that ingredient is necessary. But it is intellect of the proper order alone that can insure success. A few active minds—spirits of energy, united and glued to the undertaking,—ready pens, determined that it shall succeed—stored with information and thought, and prepared to consider it their own creation,—two, three, or four such would do it. Maddyn,

---

* It is noteworthy that in the midst of a hundred engagements Davis found time to send to Maddyn's magazine the contribution he asked. "Here is a non-political ballad of the Irish Pale. If you like it, toss it into your magazine ; if not, send it back with the scribblement I sent before. I suppose there is no hope of seeing you here. *You* ought to rule the new Irish Society [in London] ; you and it would gain by the relation, and it could be made very useful " (July 17, 1844).

clearly, is one such. We want more. Two or three must make it their principal object—others aiding may have primary objects, and assist in this as secondary—but the two or three must be ready to make all other projects secondary to this.

"That is, I consider, the *conditio sine quâ non.* What could T. H., Col. C., and I, with three or six or nine others such as we do? Not the essential thing. We could not *be* the *matériel.*

"To say it should be done in November is idle. It ought not to be started without a strong organization and abundant preparation. I am sick of failures—attempts—raw and imperfect plans.

"Wallis's case is a deplorable one. I find the same complaint as you make of T. M. 'Nothing is right.' Indeed that unhappily applies to both the above. It was all very well for a few years. There is so much worry in the world that it is good to find it pulled to pieces—but to be always pulling to pieces!

"What you write about 'Irish airs' is connected with something I before hinted I should want to talk to you upon—but let this and all the rest keep till we 'collogue.'"

Davis could have satisfied all his friend's reasonable demands; for, not only the best of the declared Nationalists, but some undeclared ones, like Fergusson and Lefanu, would probably have aided him; but the magazine project never came to anything. It was replaced, however, by a serial which proved of permanent value.

It is a natural tendency to attribute to a notable man whatever belongs to his era. Swift is the hero of a hundred adventures of which he knew nothing. Curran is made to father the *bon-mots* of a whole generation. O'Connell not only represented his own prodigious work, but the far-seeing policy of John Keogh which dictated the election of a Catholic for Clare, the movement of Pat Lalor which kindled three provinces against tithe, and even the brilliant *mots* of Dominick Ronayne; and I have heard a hundred times attributed to Davis work which was not his but that of some of the friends around him,

though his own store was so full and overflowing
that it need not be supplemented from any source.

The new project—the latest in which he had
a share—the Library of Ireland — Davis did not
originate, but accepted from me ; but he threw all
his prodigious energy into it for the limited time
that remained, and though he only saw two volumes
issued, his own writings, collected after his death,
have added immensely to its popularity and usefulness.   The design was to publish a monthly volume
of history, poetry, or fiction, calculated to feed the
national spirit or discipline the national morals ; and
millions of these books have since been printed and
are in the hands of Irishmen all over the world.
Early in autumn Davis wrote to Pigot that the
project was launched :—

"Your brother David was with a large party of us whom
James Duffy entertained yesterday at Bray, [to celebrate the first
issue of the Library of Ireland], and I was delighted to find his
strength and spirits excellent.   He is a very noble, thoughtful,
warm fellow.

" Our Library of Ireland promises better than any other undertaking of our party, and, what is better still, is likely to be aided
by Whigs and Tories.

" The American hurrah for us, and against O'C.'s speech [on
Federalism], was a useful diversion.

". . . Johnny has thrown the agitation two years back.   John
Dillon doing well.   C. G. D. better than ever in his life.   Myself
in good health of body and in a *calm* mood—after a storm; you
know the proverb."

Shortly after, he wrote to the same correspondent:—

"August 5, 1845.

" C. G. D.'s ballad volume is at its third edition, really *bonâ
fide*, and will, I am sure, sell 10,000 copies.

" He and every one gone to the country, and I am alone, anxious
for various reasons ; but in work, and that is a shield from most
assaults on the mind.

"I am very glad you are becoming a lawyer in more than name.

"I have just this minute been looking at my niece who is two hours old, and a very pretty little Irishwoman. Do you or don't you mean to marry young? If I'm ever married, which is not likely, our wives will, I suppose, be inseparable gossips, and with that interesting prophecy,

"I am, as ever, yours,
" T. D."

In July he wrote to Lane :—

"My delight at finding you once more in health and spirits makes me forgive your insolence, more especially as age and weariness are creeping over me (I am twenty-nine, and can only walk thirty miles), and I know no one qualified to succeed me, being such as you describe, except Denny Lane.

"I have not yet seen your letter,* but shall get it to-night. I think you are *quite right* in requiring Callaghan to attend Parliament or Conciliation Hall; this is a fair and proper demand, and a politic one. It totally differs from the attempt to bully men into a Repeal pledge, or a resignation, who entered Parliament unpledged, legislative trustees during the Parliament to which they were elected, trustees for the whole country not the electing constituency. Such is the constitution and such is the doctrine politic for those who do not seek the turbulence of democracy. I for one desire *representative rule*, and never will be a party to a *system* of pledges, though I may, and in the case of a domestic legislation pledge at next election will, consent to aid a revolutionary exception.

"Thanks for 'Ariadne.' Keep Barry to songs. He writes them incomparably better than any one else in Ireland, but I do not like his political didactics."

Samuel Forde, who died of consumption in Cork at three and twenty, was, in Davis's opinion, the greatest artistic genius that Ireland ever produced. Daniel Maclise, who was his fellow-student, declared that his drawings were as vigorous and correct as Michael Angelo's. Davis himself says of him :—

---

* Alluding to a letter Lane wrote under the signature of "An Elector," calling on D. Callaghan, M.P. for Cork, to attend the meetings of the Repeal Association.

" We have seen on wrapping-paper, and on all manner of little slips, pen-drawings by him of Irish draperies and figures, in which the tall, vehement men and dear loving girls—the ample cotamores and voluptuous cloaks of Munster, were as noble as anything in classic sculpture, yet as real as you'd meet in a Bantry or a Mallow market."

The young artist and his brother were sons of a Cork artisan whom poverty and discontent drove to America, leaving his family young and unprovided. The elder brother became a composer, and a collector of Irish airs, and Maddyn introduced him to Davis with warm commendation. He sent, at the same time, a paper on Samuel Forde, by another Cork man, Mr. Willis, then a successful barrister, afterwards an eminent judge, which he designed for the *Dublin University Magazine*, if it should be acceptable in that quarter. Maddyn complained with just indignation how habitually the Celtic capital had neglected its young men of genius.

" There has been no monument—not even a tombstone—erected to Forde's memory in Cork. Even his name is not cut on the flag beneath which he lies interred at St. Finn Barrs. There are several of us here who wish to make some stir about it; the publication of this sketch of his life would help it very much. . . . He was not unlike Griffin in his reach of imagination, but far more bold and original; but, like Griffin, he was exquisitely tender and gentle. He was not, however, sorrowful or querulous, and, though intensely religious, there was nothing dismal about Forde."

By the intervention of Davis the sketch was published in the *University Magazine*.

John Mitchel was engaged on a life of Hugh O'Neil for the Library, and, being in doubt on the subject of Irish standards and armorial bearings, Davis asked light from the great antiquaries. John O'Donovan wrote him :—

z

"Some short time since Mr. Petrie showed me a letter of yours, making certain inquiries about the *arms* (not weapons) of Ireland, and desired me to let him have anything I might have gleaned on the subject for you. I thought I had some notices of the ancient arms of Ireland, which I copied from a MS. in the Lambeth Library, but I could not find it at the time. I spent all this day looking for 'rags and rhymes of history' relating to Ireland, and found in the third *stratum* of my papers the following notice of the Irish Arms copied from a MS. about 150 years old, formerly in the possession of Mr. Hardiman, author of the 'History of Galway,' and now—God knows where! Perhaps you will allow me to copy it for your inspection, though I fear it is too late.

"'*The Armes of Ireland.* Reward and Revenge. The first coate th'one side charged with a demi-Eagle on a field argent of the right side signifies reward, for that bird is the most noble and princely of all birds, and the Irish are verie gratefull and loyall. The hand of the left side with a naked sword signifies force and revenge. Y⁰ 2 coloures, black and white, signifie constancie and honestie. The seconde coate three crownes; the third, to witt, the Lyon, denotes courage and strengthe, is the same with that of Scotland thither introduced by the oulde Scottes of Irelande (which untill the tenth century of Christianity was absolutelie Scotteland, and the inhabitants *Scottes*, and thenceforthe for some ages called *Scotia Major*, to distinguish it from *Scotia Minor*), for the double × × counterflowered with which the Scotche Lyon is now invironed, is but a late addition on their league with France. The fourth coate, to witt the harp, TO which Instrument the Irish above all other nacions are much addicted TO, and pfect players thereat, is the Common Arms now borne for all Irelande in the ENGLISH KING OF ENGLAND'S ARMES.'

"My 'Irish Grammar' is at last printed, but it is so big that nobody well ever think of reading it. We are too English at the present day to throw away any time upon languages that have died a natural death (for languages die while the people remain). The vigour of the Saxons is admirable, and they must be considered a superior race, as they have extended their language not only over the three Islands of Great Britain, Mann, and Ireland, but also over the United States of America, and over a considerable portion of Africa and Hindostan. They are indeed a great race, and though they commenced their career in Britain by hellish treachery, which would impress the conviction that they are descended, as Professor B····ᵈ makes all mankind ᵇᵉ from serpents (of the Ichthyosaurus and Pleiosaurus class), still they have latterly

exhibited such noble qualities as would induce one to be of opinion
that they are descended from bull-dogs of the best breed.

> " Believe me to be,
> " Yours very sincerely,
> " JOHN O'DONOVAN.

" I have been a good deal amused at finding you set down as
Thomas O'Davis in the list of subscribers to a work by Colonel
Patrick O'Kelly ! You are Cymbric and of Alchuth, not Gaelic."

Another eminent antiquary helped him respecting a difficulty in the " Ballad Poetry of Ireland,"
the second volume in the new monthly series.

" I cannot understand what meaning was intended for some of
the words in 'Shule aroon,' nor do I think the song, in its present
form, original or old. . . . The talented editor of this volume
leans heavily on translators from the Irish, in the opening of his
beautiful introduction. He is, certainly, right, though I think he
uses the word 'translator' rather arbitrarily. If I understand him
correctly, the person who turns the substance of an Irish poem into
English verse, whether he does so directly or through the medium
of an interpreter, is the translator. And, according to this rule,
I find Mr. Mangan put forth as the best of all translators from the
Irish. Now, it so happens that Mr. Mangan has no knowledge of
the Irish language, nor do I think he regrets that either, but any
one reading this introduction must believe that he is deeply versed
in Irish, and that he has translated directly from the originals the
three pieces which appear with his name in this volume. . . . It
was I that translated these poems (the three of them) from the
originals—that is, I turned the Irish words into English words;
and Mr. Mangan put those English words, beautifully and faithfully, as well as I can judge, into English rhyme. If I have not
made a faithful translation, then the versification is not correct,
for it contains nothing but what is found in the translation, nor
does it contain a single idea that is not found, and as well expressed,
in the original." *

Professor Anster, the translator of "Faust," sent
him a note respecting the same volume :—

" I find my name in the advertisements of the 'Library of
Ireland.' I trust that publication may do. It looks well. I

* E. Curry, August 29, 1845.

suppose the accident of my having written 'A Little Fairy Ballad'
is my best claim for the promised immortality. I hope the date
of that ballad is preserved, as Banim and Lover have both imitated
it; and, if reprinted in such good company, I should be glad that,
whatever may be thought of it, it should be known that it was
written ever so long before either of theirs. It was printed in
the Edinburgh edition of my poems in 1819, and written three
or four years before." *

Mr. Michael Banim, brother of John, and his
collaborateur in the "Tales of the O'Hara Family,"
had a memoir of his brother in preparation, and
Davis asked him to give it to the new series. This
was his reply :—

"The memoir, I grieve to say, lies yet unfinished. You are
not unaware that my occupation is that of a man in trade, and
it requires almost constant personal attention to watch the business I am engaged in. Since I called on you in Dublin, I have,
of necessity, devoted but little time to my desk, and, therefore, the
memoir is backward. If my more pressing occupations permit,
I intend sitting down to it shortly; but I adhere to the resolution
of making it introductory to the republication of selected portions
of the 'O'Harra Tales.' Business is with me anterior, literary occupation secondary; and it would be making an engagement which
circumstances might prevent me from fulfilling, were I to say I
would perfect my yet crude notions for publication as part of the
'Library of Ireland.'" †

Davis urged John O'Donovan to collect a volume
of his historical miscellanies for the same series :—

"I fear," O'Donovan replied, "that my papers on the Irish
family names would not be worth reprinting in their present form,
and I have been thinking of compiling a larger work on the subject. This, however, I cannot do until the 'Annals' are printed, and
if you think those little articles worth reprinting, I would have no
objection to see them out again, with a few corrections, which I
could easily make. From the Carew collection of manuscripts, in
the library at Lambeth, I have learned many new facts relating

---

* John Auster, LL.D., June 29, 1845.
† Mich. Banim, July 5, 1845.

to the Anglo-Irish families of Munster, which I should like to insert; but I have little or no time to spare at present. . . . We, Irish Shanachies, are beginning to dissipate the halo of national enthusiasm which encircled our organs of veneration and self-esteem, and are likely, in a few generations more, to settle down to Saxon coolness. Then, however, we shall be more unmanageable to our penal-law makers than were our more enthusiastic predecessors, who excited their countrymen to deeds of desperate bravery by describing to them the glorious deeds of Milesius, King of Spain, 1300 before Christ. What astonishes me is, that our ancestors, when they set about fabricating a national pedigree, did not trace themselves to Hercules, Hector, or Achilles. The translations and forged documents—I allude to what has been done in Ireland for the last fifty years, for we have had a *collectanea de rebus Hibernicis*, nearly all worse than forgeries; the 'Chronicles of Eri,' a barefaced and silly forgery; an essay on the 'Round Towers of Ireland,' by a Turlough O'Brien, who, out of vanity, changed his baptism name from Terry to Henry. This last work is a disgrace to the human intellect; but the author, I am glad, for the sake of our literature, to say, was a madman, and died mad in London. And in our own good times we have seen 'Etruria Celtica' ushered into light under the name of 'The Ulster King at Arms,' who is believed in England to be at the head of the literature of Ireland. This last work, though not what could be properly called a *forgery*, is still in its conclusions worse than any that preceded it in silly audacities and childish conceits, which a schoolboy could refute. . . . My eldest brother removed to America, where he is beginning to acquire some of the original courage of the mountaineers of Carbery! Nothing could recover me! I have ascended the highest mountains of Ireland, and viewed all her most enchanting scenery, but still I never was cheered by them. And, moreover, I have not yet learned to walk like a freeman! I was born a slave, and the impression stamped on the human soul and impressed on the nerve by the consideration of having been so born cannot be removed for life. This is a fact which political philosophers do not take into consideration. . . ."

He ends an elaborate pedigree of the O'Donovans with this sketch of himself:—

"John, born August 3, 1809, and still living. He is of a ^mixed_mongrel race, and is beginning to think that he has derived more of the elements of common sense from the Burkes, Archdeacons, and Puritans than from the Kavanaghs and O'Donovans of the great race Olioll Olum." *

The success of the library was an infinite pleasure to Davis, and he reported it exultingly to his friends. To O'Brien he wrote :—

"What of Sarsfield's statue? I think Moore would like to do it [Christopher Moore, who had made effective busts of Curran and Plunket, but proved on trial to be unequal to statues]. Kirk is not competent. The 'Ballad Poetry' [second volume of the new "Library of Ireland"] has reached a third edition, and cannot be printed fast enough for the sale. It is every way good. Not an Irish Conservative of education but will read it, and be brought nearer to Ireland by it. That is a propagandism worth a thousand harangues such as you ask me to make. We are going to print [Torrens] M'Cullagh's 'Lecture on History' and O'Donovan's 'Essays on Irish Names and Families' in the series. Hugh O'Neill's life is written, and is admirably done. One of the volumes will be ' Thomond and the O'Briens,' dedicated to a living member of that clan, written by a Clare man of Conservative family; but this is a secret known only to you, to the author, and to myself. I have little chance of getting from town. Still I am in iron health. Many thanks for your kind invitation to Cahirmoyle. Grey Porter is here; he is unchanged."

To the first note O'Brien replied :—

"I cannot but hope that the publication of the monthly volume will be of infinite value to the national cause, if the intellectual and moral standard of the work can be kept as high as it ought to be. I like the two first numbers very much—I could not lay down the 'Ballads' until I had read the whole volume. I am delighted with the article in yesterday's *Nation* respecting the prospect of a union between Orange and Green. It makes me for a moment believe that the dream of my life is about to be realized. I know that I could not recommend [in the Association] that a few hundred copies of this number of the *Nation* should be sent into the Orange districts, without awakening jealousies which it is very unadvisable to raise; but I think it worth while the consideration of you and Duffy, whether it would not be well to print this article on separate slips of paper, and send them by post into

* John O'Donovan, July 28, 1845.

the heart of Fermanagh. Glorious, indeed, would be the spectacle of a union of the two great contending Irish parties, who have been taught to hate each other." *

The paralysis of the Repeal Association led Davis to renew the attempt to organize the Federalists. At least, they might make their authentic opinions known, and this could only be done effectually through a journal. The first idea, as we have seen, was a quarterly review, under the editorship of Maddyn. Early in the year he wrote to him, again urging him to accept this position.

Maddyn replied promptly :—

"There is nothing I would desire more than to be of use to Ireland, but the deuce of it is I have strong doubts about the right of joining your party, which is the only one with ideas in it. O'Connellism I dislike; there is so much public humbug in it, and make-belief, etc., and yet I frankly confess that Nationalism has fearful fascinations to my mind."

But Davis came gradually to see, what was plain enough to some of his friends from the outset, that a quarterly journal would reach so small a minority of the people as to be nearly worthless, and in mid-summer he informed Maddyn that it was proposed to buy the *Monitor*, a three-day evening paper, and again invited him to take the editorship :—

"It is discussed among some Federalist friends of mine whether they shall not buy the *Monitor* newspaper. It is a Whig paper, has several times avowed Federalism, has the character of independence and honour, but is much damaged by a bitter, hard, narrow editor. The parties thinking of its purchase are men of property, virtue, and education. They would seek in it an organ for independent national opinion, irrespective of parties or sects, fostering an Irish literature, softening asperities, sustaining free thought. Ultimately, if an opportunity came, they would like ·

* Further correspondence respecting the "Library of Ireland," between the editor of the series and literary allies, will be found in "Young Ireland," book iii., c. 6.

to direct their influence to the carrying of a Federal arrangement between the two islands. The paper is published on Mondays, Wednesdays, Fridays. The *Nation* is printed with its types, and uses some of its news; so is and does the *Railway Gazette*.

"But the whole project depends on getting as editor a man to whose honour, patriotism, taste, education, and genius the proprietors could commit the whole affair. I do not think there is any one here or in London fit for it but yourself. It would give you the opportunity I know you always desired, of raising the moral and intellectual character of your country. Your income would certainly be good, and would increase; the men you would have to deal with all you could wish; your position quite independent, alike of Castle and Conciliation Hall.

"Though I am certainly anxious, from personal feeling, that you should be here, I would not advise you to this course if I foresaw the least likelihood of annoyance to you in *any* stage of it. Should you, as I trust and hope you will, approve of the design, pray let me know quickly, as the whole project is unsettled, but would, I am sure, be defined rapidly if you could be looked to with certainty."

Maddyn had grave objections to the projects submitted to him :—

" I would not accept the *Monitor* under the party that owned the *Citizen*. I believe in their virtue and patriotism, but I have not the least confidence in their literary or political capacity. They might have done great things in the year 1843 and subsequently, but they had not the stamina in them. Their pretensions were immense, but their performances with pen or tongue did not justify their claims to eminence of any kind. The kind of persons that I would like to look to as my employers would be a set of business men, of capital and social ambition (even of a coarse kind). The kind of men I would like are those of vulgar sense and strong hearty purpose. I could manage matters for them better than if they were an ambitious junto of small politicians craving mere personal notoriety. . . . The arrogance of a millionnaire or the pompous airs of a real Milesian never could have matter of offence for me. But there is one thing towards which I am cynical, and that is the manner of a man like M——. Superciliousness without substantial power is very hard to bear, and the affected condescension of the diminutive great still harder to endure. Now, if M—— was to be an owner of the *Monitor*, I would have nothing to say to it. . . . I should like to go to Dublin, but, at the same time, the town life of London has a great deal to amuse and interest a Gil Blas like myself; I would have more friends in Dublin and less amusements. I would have a certainty of being useful there; I would have a better chance of being honourably known here. It would be easy for me to go on with a balance of advantages *ad infinitum;* but I will sum up by saying that a good salary and moderate work would induce me to give up London, but not literature." *

This was Davis's rejoinder :—

" The *Monitor* was suddenly stopped, so nothing will now be done about a Federalist organ till November. If you come here then I do not doubt that an arrangement quite satisfactory to you can be made.

" Are your health and spirits good ? Tell me. In haste,

" Yours,

" T. D.

" He of whom you spoke unfavourably had nothing to do with the project."

The disappearance of the *Monitor* did not terminate the negotiation. I find among Davis's papers a note of mine furnishing the data for a new paper in lieu of the *Monitor*.

" I send you the calculation (for a thrice-a-week paper) as exact as I can make it. It can scarcely be a pound wrong.

" A twice-a-week paper will cost a third less and be equally effective. The price will suit the public better, and it is a happy compromise between a weekly which comes too seldom, you think, and a three-day one which is too dear for a large circulation. Don't suppose that it will make no difference to a wealthy party whether the subscription is £2 or £3. Trust me it will. Besides, it will make a serious difference to the proprietors, while they are waiting for success, whether they have to pay £36 a week or £47. For propagandism twice a week is as good as twice a day, or better, for men must have time to digest new opinions.

" Unless an unprecedented advertising connection can be secured, there will, either way, be a considerable loss. They must be prepared for this. A circulation of less than a thousand would

* July 3rd.

not pay, and such a circulation, I suspect, for a Federalist paper is out of the question."

But the tragic event recorded in the next chapter brought this and a hundred other beneficent projects to an abrupt end.

As July approached, the era of party celebrations in Ulster, Davis addressed to the Catholics and Protestants respectively words of advice which they may still read with advantage and with reverence, as the latest counsel of a tried friend :—

" To the Catholics of Ireland, with great sincerity we would say, Respect the foolish enthusiasm of your brother. You have no right to dictate to him what course he shall pursue. Strive with him in kindness; win him to your convictions by the silent eloquence of your conduct. If he forgets the courtesies which Christianity should have taught him, and insults your pride by the celebration of your defeat,—pardon and pity him. You can effect nothing by vulgar brawls but to render inveterate the passions which offend you. Cultivate an honest pride which can look down on these mean aggressors, and a forgiving nature which will conciliate towards you the hearts of your erring countrymen."

And he reminded the Protestants how little they had gained by the triumphs over their own countrymen, of which they were so proud :—

" The men who defended Derry and Enniskillen gained nothing. Their lands were ravaged by the war, and, as appears from the evidence of the Williamite, Dr. George, more by the English than by the Irish army. They carried their complaints, these stout old militiamen, to London; they printed their ' deplorable cases ' by the hundred; they first got soft and then hard words; they were left to rot in the alleys of the English capital, never relieved by a sixpence from king, nobles, or Parliament." *

The larger work on which Davis and his friends were employed will be best understood by examples. The Royal Dublin Society asked for an increased

* *Nation*, July 12, 1845.

grant from Parliament, and it was proposed to invite
the Irish members whom the Association could influence to support the claim. At the same time, the
society was requested, through Smith O'Brien, now
one of its members, to make some useful changes in
its administration. There were admirable lectures
delivered by eminent professors on industrial knowledge and the economy of manufactures; but they
were delivered at an hour when the artisans for
whose benefit they were intended could not be present. It was proposed to substitute evening lectures.
The society had also exhibitions of Irish manufacture,
but they were not well attended; it was suggested
that the increased grant might enable the society
to open them gratuitously. The society acquiesced
in both suggestions, and showed a cordial willingness
to accept the popular initiative in practical questions.

The early death of John Banim, a national novelist, who shared the political hopes of his race, left
his widow ill provided. As the executive had the
disposal of an annual grant for literary pensions
derived in part from Irish taxes, it was resolved to
claim a provision for her from that source. A committee was organized by the writers of the *Nation*,
and it was considered at the time a note of progress
that the men who composed it should have consented to act together for any purpose. They were :
—Daniel O'Connell, M.P., John Anster, LL.D. (the
translator of "Faust"), Smith O'Brien, M.P., Isaac
Butt, LL.D. (then leader of the extreme Conservatives), Dr. Kane (since Sir Robert Kane), John O'Connell, M.P., Charles Lever (the author of "Harry
Lorrequer"), Torrens McCullagh, LL.B. (now Mc-
Cullagh Torrens), Thomas Davis, Samuel Ferguson

(the late Sir Samuel Ferguson, Deputy Keeper of the Records in Ireland), Thomas O'Hagan (since Lord O'Hagan), William Carleton (author of " Traits and Stories of the Irish Peasantry "), E. B. Roche, M.P. (since Lord Fermoy), Joseph Le Fanu (author of "The House by the Churchyard," etc.), Charles Gavan Duffy, Hubert Smith, M.R.I.A., Thomas MacNevin, Dr. Maunsell (editor of the *Evening Mail*), Grey Porter (still assiduous in Irish affairs half a century later), James M'Glashan (proprietor of the *Dublin University Magazine*), and M. J. Barry.

The committee succeeded, through the agency of A. B. Roche mainly, in inducing Sir Robert Peel to grant a small pension to Mrs. Banim.*

We made a determined effort to get popular education organized and endowed by associating it with the temperance movement. Before the establishment of the *Nation*, Father Mathew accepted, and published broadcast, a proposal of mine, that he should substitute moral stimulants for the sensual stimulant which he had taken away—that the Teetotal Societies should become *Élysées* for cultivating the understanding and improving the morals of the people. In time it seemed that every town in the island would have its temperance hall, and every

---

* The surviving author of the " Tales of the O'Hara Family," who, in politics, was an unswerving adherent of O'Connell, acknowledged that this service to his brother's widow was attributable to the new men.

" DEAR SIR,

"I beg to return you my very sincere thanks for the very effectual performance of your promise to me, in my sister-in-law's business. However others may have worked in the matter, I impute it solely to your kindness that such success has been the result; and I will always regard you as the person to whom my brother's widow is really indebted.

"I am, dear sir, your obliged servant,

" M. BANIM.

" Kilkenny, May 10, 1845.
"Chas. Gavan Duffy, Esq."

hall, we insisted, ought to have its lecture-room, where the artisan might be taught the principles of mechanics, the farmer the latest improvements in agriculture, and every one something that would make him a better man and a better citizen. There was a movement on foot to create some permanent memorial to commemorate Father Mathew's services, and we thought that such a system of adult education would be a nobler monument than any carved in marble or cast in bronze. Davis and I wrote repeatedly in this sense, but in the end there were no funds available. A long array of dukes, marquises, earls, baronets, privy councillors, and members of Parliament, ecclesiastics of both Churches, and the leaders of the bench, bar, and magistracy served on the preliminary committee; but the treasurer, Mr. Peter Purcell, assured me that one half of these personages never paid their subscriptions, and a sum sufficient to defray debts, which Father Mathew had incurred to medal makers and printers on behalf of the Temperance Societies, was all that could be obtained.

Wallis, who was as morbid and almost as suspicious as Rousseau, was discontented that his methods and theories of public action were not accepted by his friends, and that they did not do for his private comfort and prosperity what every man in the end must do for himself, or find left undone. He announced to Davis his intention of going to London and living there by journalism.

" I have," he wrote, " a deep sense of your kindness, not alone in affording me pecuniary aid; but still more in the trouble you have taken to find me occupation, and to procure and bring me books to enable me to accomplish it. It is the more to be regretted that we should take such opposite views, both of the work in question and of many higher and more serious matters. But the fault is in our stars, and not ourselves; though it is strange that men in a good many respects similar in temperament, and both notable for a tardy development of such powers as they possess, should prove, alike in theory and practice, in aims, and in the choice of means to attain them, so different, if not antagonistic. . . . National liberty is a grand and a very precious thing, worth paying a very high price for; but it is not worth the sacrifice of every other liberty. For me, in my humble sphere, liberty of opinion and speculation, freedom of thought and freedom of speech, were ever the noblest of all rights and aims. For them I sacrificed, as the event has proved, every element of well-being that my position and character endowed me with. Every blossom of enjoyment, every fruit of memory, every seed of hope I offered up on that altar. . . . The heartless apathy evinced towards me by some of my oldest and most intimate associates, and the studied contumely with which they have chosen to demonstrate it, at a time when my ill-health and other circumstances might have suggested a little forbearance, have already greatly loosened the few remaining ties I had to kind or country. If, at the present stage of the matter, I find myself flung thus abruptly to rot or ripen on the London dunghill, the severance will be complete. I shall never return to Ireland again, or take any step to identify myself with a land from which those who ought to have known me best have so deliberately and scornfully ejected me. I shall deem myself as virtually transported as if I had been dragged on a cart from Kilmainham to the hulks. In which case, you will perceive my undertaking as to Flood must fall to the ground." [*]

Samuel Ferguson, who was gradually approaching nearer to Davis in opinion, acknowledged a copy of the quarto " Spirit of the Nation " in terms which must have been very gratifying to his correspondent.

" Accept my best thanks for the ' Spirit of the Nation ' which I will preserve as a memorial of your friendship and an incitement

---

[*] Wallis did not carry out his intentions quite as he had projected them. After a short visit to London, he returned to Dublin, and became a contributor to the *Nation*. But his morbid temper was a torture to himself and others, and he finally returned to London, where he became a writer in the *Morning Chronicle*, in some sense its foreign editor I believe, and died in 1865, in a similar employment.

to my own love of song and country. When I see how we are all
working, I hope soon to see Dublin at least a better Edinburgh. A
sentence of Bishop Parry's, addressed to Sir James Ware, is perpetually sounding in my ears: *Diu nimis obscurata tenebris deliluit
Hibernia, nec sibi prorsus cognita nec aliis. Diu satis eclipsim passa
est, rudis admodum et indigesta; filiisque suis peregrina, se ne fuisse
Lucus-que dubitavit. Tandem vero, tanquam vero ad augendam Caroli
gloriam, calamique vestri in honorem reservata, novos induit spiritus
formamque venustiorem.* The contribution to Charles's or Victoria's
glory is a secondary matter. These efforts are serviceable to ourselves, and will redound to the service of those who come after us.
God knows our self-reliance is all in all; and, with the growing
self-reliance of the young men, wider prospects may open. In the
mean time I am satisfied with the progress we are making, even
though it aim at no greater result than literary and intellectual
supremacy."

Among the latest difficulties sent to Davis for
solution, was one which required peculiarly delicate
handling. O'Connell was a Celtic chief accustomed
to defend his clan in all emergencies, and some
of them were very trying. There were two hundred
and fifty Repeal wardens in London, industrious
artisans for the most part, who, after their day's
labour was closed, undertook new work for the love
of Ireland. An inspector-general was appointed over
them, with so liberal a salary that it sometimes
amounted to a lion's share of the weekly receipts.
The office was conferred on a dissolute poor relation
of O'Connell's, called in derision ' Lord Kilmallock,'
—the identical person from whom Thackeray, as we
learn from his correspondence, studied his Captain
Costigan and Mulligan of Ballymulligan. The
inspector-general got into debt, could only make his
appearance at Repeal meetings on Sunday, and,
to avoid arrest, lived the remainder of the week under
a feigned name in some inscrutable hiding-place.
The Repeal wardens complained that regular work

was rendered impossible under this system, and they were threatened from head-quarters with immediate dismissal from their honorary employment. O'Connell proposed to meet the difficulty by increasing Mr. William John O'Connell's salary. Davis and a minority of the general committee stubbornly resisted this waste of public money, and insisted that the honest wardens should not be molested for a just and necessary remonstrance; but their resistance was made in vain.

Thomas Meagher, who never saw Davis in the flesh, saw him in the mirror of imagination. In a lecture delivered in America he pictures him as he was in the period at which we have now arrived :—

"Follow him, and you will visit the workshop of the artisan, where he talked of Irish oak for furniture—the studio of the artist, to whom he has rapidly and brilliantly suggested and grouped a picture from Irish history—the Galleries of the Royal Hibernian Academy, where he has discovered new beauties in the lurid fancies of Danby, or the portraits of Burton—the Library of Trinity College, where he has consulted an old manuscript and fixed a date—the Museum of the Irish Academy, where he has met Doctor Petrie and with him inspected some newly dug up Danish or ancient Irish relic—the Committee Room of the Repeal Association, where he threw new and friendly light upon some subject of angry debate. Probably he has led you to the *Nation* office, where he has corrected a handful of proof-sheets—visited half a dozen booksellers' shops, and called on William Eliot Hudson, to hear him play over an arrangement of some glorious old Irish airs, which he had recovered from a blind piper in the wilds of Connemara or the glens of Munster."

But it must be confessed much of this incessant labour yielded results which were only temporary or illusory. He set an undue value, I think, on mere social sympathy and the dilettante nationality which grew enthusiastic over the Cross of Cong, or a Jacobite song of the later bards, but was indifferent to the present sufferings or hopes of the people. One of his friends, who spoke in parables, told him the story of a chemist who took infinite credit for a discovery by which he could extract fire from snow, till some realistic person requested him to specify how many snowballs would boil his tea-kettle? He desired to make Conservatives Nationalists like Addis Emmett or Whitley Stokes; but he rarely succeeded in doing more than making them Nationalists like Walter Scott or John Wilson, devoted to the literature and antiquities of their native country, but content with its subjection to England. In Ireland Nationality meant admitting the whole nation to a platform where a single class had long exercised exclusive authority—a voluntary sacrifice of old possession to abstract justice which individuals will sometimes make, but which it is visionary to expect of any large class of mankind.

The last volumes on which Davis was engaged were a new edition of Curran's speeches, and a memoir of Wolfe Tone, which was to appear as the third volume of the " Library of Ireland." Of the latter the printer wrote to him at the end of August, reporting progress, and answering inquiries which he had undertaken to make.

"50, Capel Street, August 20, 1845.
"Dear Sir,
" I send you a proof of your manuscript.
" Mrs. Moru Chandler, 148, Abbey Street, has the portraits of Wolfe Tone, and you can see them whenever you call.
" Mr. Scott has built on the site of Wolfe Tone's house—the number is 44. He says that Mr. Thomas Jervis White, 4, Lower Gloucester Street, who is agent for the property, is a very communicative old gentleman, and that he would feel a pleasure in giving you all the information you desire.
" Dear sir, yours truly,
" T. Caldwell."
2 A

The last letter Davis received from his friend
Maddyn announced two projects which he had in
hand, only one of which was ever realized.

"Sevenoaks, Kent, September 3, 1845.

"I have been working very hard upon a new book, the first
volume of which must be out in October. It is a large work, three
volumes—to be called ' The Age of Pitt and Fox ; ' it is to be printed
with my name. When I get back to town I will send your contribution to the *Nation.* I came here to see Knole Manor, the
family seat of the Dorsets. I saw there the original portrait of
Goldsmith by Sir Joshua. I was sadly disappointed. The size
is kitcat, and the forehead wants the grandeur given it in the
engravings.

"I am meditating a series of papers for the *Nation,* to be called
the ' Who-can-he-be Papers.' Their idea is this :—

"I stumble, in England, upon a gentleman whom the narrator
knows at once to be Irish, but he can't make out his name, or anything about him. The stranger tells all manner of singular
anecdotes, sketches characters in a few sentences, describes men
and things with much spirit and freshness. All the subject-matter
of his discourses and anecdotes is Irish. I meet this Irish gentleman in London, I meet him at Windsor, in Devonshire, everywhere
I go ; other people also meet him, but none can tell who he is.
Through the papers a dramatic interest is kept up as to who he is.
His conversation and remarks are curious, interesting, and quaint ;
occasionally showing research and reflective spirit, always exhibiting facility of reference. But his matter is entertaining and
readable. Such is the loose idea of the thing I propose. It would
be a novel feature in the *Nation,* and both you and Duffy could
write any papers in it, once the thing was set in motion. We
could try the effect of three or four. If the authorship could be
concealed from the public it would be a point in its favour. A
couple of papers relative to Ulster and Belfast would remove
suspicion from me.

"The ' Ballad Poetry of Ireland ' is admirable. It is all
to nothing the best edited collection I ever saw. The introduction
is a choice specimen of writing.; it merits what the *Spectator* said
of it—and what more could be desired ? It reflects immense credit
on Duffy."

As the autumn approached, Davis wrote a note to
Maddyn, which, like all his correspondence with that

bosom friend, disclosed the deepest feeling of the
hour :—

"As Duffy, and indeed every one who at all contributes to the
Nation (save myself), will be out of town for five or six weeks,
your sending me the 'Burke' and, if possible, one or two other
papers, would be a great—a very great—convenience to me. I
would not ordinarily mind having the entire of the paper thrown
on me; but I have been for some time, and am likely to continue
for a while, in a state of feverish anxiety on a subject purely
personal, and which I hope I may yet be able to talk of to you.
There is hardly any one I shall so rejoice on every ground to see in
October or November; now I am too much troubled in mind to be
worth your society. Won't you come in the autumn? We will
have delightful projects, and gossips, and expeditions, and I trust
some good to our common principles and country may follow too.
You don't know the *men* here; the autumn is by far the best season
for that." *

Maddyn in his reply glances at Davis's personal
trouble, of which it will be now necessary to speak,
but he obviously misunderstood its nature.

"I am the more sorry for whatever is troubling you, as I
cannot be of assistance, but I hope that, whatever it is, it will
soon be over, and that you will not be disappointed. We Irish
often get too excited in difficulties; be calmly ready to bear the
worst, and, if it comes, indifference will be a shield—if the best,
you will have so much the more cause for joy." †

The personal trouble was one which is rarely
wanting as a motor in the lives of young men. He
was in love. When he began to write verse, one of
his friends who thought a Laura was an essential part
of the equipment of a Petrarch, asked him if he had
ever been in love. "I have never been out of it,"
was his laughing reply. But these amourettes were
passing fancies, and his profound nature craved a
great and permanent passion. At length he encoun-

---

* Davis to Maddyn, July 31, 1845.
† Maddyn to Davis, August 4, 1845.

tered the girl who was to rule his life. In September, 1844, during the Richmond imprisonment, while he was engaged in his most exacting work, the first reference to the lady crops up in his correspondence, though he had known and loved her months earlier.

"You have Hibernicized the Huttons so much," he wrote to Pigot, "that they have borrowed a lot of my collection of Irish airs, and the lady whose name you write so flippantly sings the 'Bonny Cuckoo.' Are you very vain for all this?"

Pigot, who was not slow to comprehend the state of the case, replied:—

"You are amusing about the Huttons, but your coquetry is all fair when you can get that graceful wild girl to sing 'Bonny Cuckoo' and 'Annie Dear' for you. 'Tis very pleasant, too, to have collections of music-books for such disinterested proselytism. . ." *

A couple of months later he wrote to the same friend, projecting for him a destiny which he now dreamed of for himself:—

"I am much grieved at your illness of mind and body; take care that you are not trying to live too much without personal attachments. I wish you were married to a soft generous Irish girl who would worship and nurse you." †

Annie Hutton was the only daughter of Thomas Hutton, whom we have already heard of as a leading Federalist—an opulent and honourable citizen who had sat in the House of Commons for a time as member for Dublin, and still took a lively interest in public affairs. When Davis met her she was barely twenty years of age, a slender, graceful girl with features of classic contour and marble hue. He has left a charming portrait of her in a little poem written when she was about to visit Killarney, from whose Elysian fields the imagery is all gathered.

* September 13, 1844.   † November 10, 1844.

" Her eyes are darker than Dunloe,
Her soul is whiter than the snow,
Her tresses like arbutus flow,
    Her step like frighted deer :
Then, still thy waves, capricious lake !
And ceaseless, soft winds, round her wake.
Yet never bring a cloud to break
    The smile of Fanny dear !

" Old Mangerton ! thine eagles plume—
Dear Innisfallen ! brighter bloom—
And Mucruss ! whisper through the gloom
    Quaint legends to her ear ;
Till strong as ash-tree in its pride,
And gay as sunbeam on the tide,
We welcome back to Liffey's side,
    Our brightest, Fanny dear."

For " Fanny " the sympathetic reader will now read
" Annie." The love-songs of that era are less natural
and spontaneous, I think, than the love-songs of his
peasants and peasant girls. They are less the first
passionate ardour of a youth for a maiden, than the
lofty devotion of a minstrel or cavalier for a gracious
lady. For example :—

" Oh, fairer than the dawn of day
    On Erne's islands !
Oh, purer than the thorn spray
    In Bantry's highlands !
In sleep such visions crossed my view,
    And when I woke the phantom faded ;
But now I find the fancy true,
    And fairer than the vision made it."

Or this :—

" Methinks that there are passions
    Within that heaving breast
To scorn their heartless fashions,
    And wed whom you love best.

> Methinks you would be prouder
> As the struggling patriot's bride,
> Than if rank your home should crowd, or
> Cold riches round you glide."

The proverbial impediments which bar the course
of true love did not spring in this case from the
coldness of the lady. His songs are those of a
happy lover. But at thirty years of age, when the
responsibilities of manhood awaited him, it was too
plain that he had sacrificed professional advancement,
and all that is vulgarly called success, to public duty.
He was a perfect publicist, but in Ireland the
national journalist carried on his work under the
constant risk of ruinous State prosecution. Quite
recently the Lord Chief Justice, who under his
ermine cope carried the heart of a malignant partisan,
had directed a jury to find the *Nation* guilty of libel
for having repudiated a quack advertisement announcing pills which cured consumption in its last
stages. And while his acquaintance with Miss
Hutton was still young there broke out, on the other
hand, as we have seen, a storm of bigotry which
threatened to drive him from public life. If a prudent
father consented to overlook the insecurity of his
worldly position, a generous lover could not shut his
own eyes to it. Here was a source of grave and constant anxiety, and of the low spirits already noted
in his correspondence with Maddyn. Pigot, too,
recognized the change of mood, though he does not
seem to have conjectured the cause of it.

" Your bad spirits," he wrote, " fret me a great deal, and I
would waste a long sheet, rating you, but that it is just post time
here. For Ireland, with God's blessing, you will ever work as
now; but your hopelessness, or heartlessness, or something worse
—listlessness, is noways true—and I confess you put me in low
spirits that you should so yield to morbidness."

It is a conjecture merely that a verse in one of his ballads suggested an alternative which must sometimes have arisen in his mind—the picture of a young energetic settler in a new country :—

> " There are lands where manly toil
> 　Surely reaps the crop it sows,
> Glorious woods and teeming soil,
> 　Where the broad Missouri flows ;
> Through the trees the smoke shall rise,
> 　From our hearth with *maith go leór*,
> There shall shine the happy eyes
> 　Of my *Máire bhán a stóir.*
> 　　Mild is *Máire bhán a stóir*,
> 　　Mine is *Máire bhán a stóir*,
> 　　Saints will watch about the door
> 　　Of my *Máire bhán a stóir.*"

It is good and pleasant to know that no impediment finally separated the noblest heart beating in Ireland at that hour from the woman he loved. During the most stringent labours of the period just past in review, he became the affianced lover of Miss Hutton. A single note from the lady will sufficiently indicate the frank and chivalrous relations established between them. The love of Davis raises his promised bride far above the region of conventionality, and makes whatever concerns her of an interest like that which kindles for the Beatrice of Dante, or the heroic wife of Garibaldi the sympathy and solicitude of a nation.

"How shall I tell you how happy I was to get your dear, dear letter, for which I love you twenty times better than before, for now you are treating me with confidence, not like a child whom it pleases you to play with. Do you know that was (but it is nearly gone) the one fear I had, that you would think of me as a plaything, more than as a friend ; but I don't think you will since last night. There now, dearest, you have all that is on my mind. I would have told you the last day you were here, only I did not know exactly how to say it, and thought it might be said better in a letter. Why do you say you wish I was oftener kind to you? And why do you think me cold sometimes?—indeed, I don't intend it, love. You say you are 'lazy,'—I *don't* believe it; 'desultory,'—I *won't* believe it; 'of selfish habits,'—I *can't* believe it;—there now, 'thim's my sintiments!' as our friend Dr. S. would say. I'll tell you what, you must not write such nice letters to me, because it makes me slightly insane, as you may perceive. Oh! I forgot I intended to begin this with a profound scolding; I am really very angry with you for writing my unworthy name in that beautiful book of 'Melodies.' Indeed, you must not, dearest, be giving me so many books; besides, I like better to have them when they are yours.

"I had such a lovely drive all round Howth yesterday, and at the most beautiful part was alone, which I was very sorry for; I like to have some one to enjoy beauty with me, not to talk about it, but just quietly to enjoy. It was very beautiful, Killiney all brilliant in the sunlight, with white-sailed boats dancing merrily over the water, and then the Dublin and Wicklow Mountains behind frowning blackly, as if jealous that they had no sun, and Bray Head; the Grey Stones, and Wicklow Head stretching out farther and still farther away. And there wasn't a sound to be heard—so different from the other busy side of Howth that we had just come from. I had a pleasant companion in the 'German Anthology' [Clarence Mangan's Translations]."

Miss Hutton's mother, who was a woman of notable capacity and accomplishments, one of the gifted circle whom Miss Mitford called her friends, valued and esteemed Davis, understood the nobility of his character and the vigour of his intellect, but was far from being in sympathy with the main purpose of his life. This was a trouble he had long encountered in his own family, among those whom he loved best, and who loved him best; and here is evidence that difference of conviction would not prevent the lady from being a gracious and considerate *belle-mère* :—

" DEAR MR. DAVIS,

"Many thanks for the tickets. One of my family will avail himself of your kindness, but this morning I have only my Annie at home; but some friends will be glad to go. I sent you a note yesterday before I received yours. I am truly sorry you should be out of spirits, but would prescribe a walk to the country as a good restorative; you may guess the direction. The spring is lovely; would that the living works of God were as perfect, and then our spirits would not flag nor faint, and our eyes would be open to the beauty that surrounds us in every form, marred only by ourselves. Shall I be very angry or not with your insulting phrase of my ' chance patriotism'? Oh that such spirits as yours would see that no good can come through bad means! and then you would mourn as I do, heart and soul, that the character of our brave, noble, generous countrymen is debased and deteriorated, not by their oppressors, but by their friends. Now, don't smile in scorn at my patriotism. I am afraid I have secured myself against another attack by this infliction—a subject that awakens such deep feelings and emotions; I ought not to have touched upon where I cannot with any sense of mercy for your valuable time even enter upon it properly. So farewell. Don't believe I love my country less because, with all true and deep acknowledgment of Mr. O'Connell's early services, I abhor his late and present courses, and fervently wish such minds and souls as yours and a few others were exorcised of this evil spirit and its influence.

" Yours very sincerely,
" M. HUTTON.

" Elm Park, Friday morning."

During these crowded months, the period of his hardest work and most exulting happiness, he ripened notably in health, spirits, and self-confidence. " All who remember him during that time," says one of his friends, " can testify to the wonderful change he underwent even in appearance. His form dilated, his eyes got a new fire, his step was firmer, and the look of a proud purpose sat on him." *

When autumn arrived, he declined to share the

* Mr. Justice O'Hagan.

excursions of his comrades, having more attractive engagements at home. But he insisted on my going to the country, and volunteered to take charge of the *Nation*. All the contributors were holiday-making; and the entire work of the journal became oppressive to a man transported for a time into a region where it is always holiday, and work is interdicted. But in lieu of becoming querulous under the burthen, he contented himself with a friendly remonstrance to the malefactors through the " Answers to Correspondents." * At the beginning of September I returned to Dublin, and found him in vigorous health and exuberant spirits, except when the talk fell on the calamities at Conciliation Hall. For a week or ten days things went on in their usual course. He came daily to the *Nation* office to consult on current topics, and was still full of projects for the far future.†

* " Most of our poetical contributors seem to have glutted themselves with summer fruits, and gone to sleep. Of course they will waken 'refreshed giants.' Meantime we shall despatch a fairy to trouble their dreams with the old tune of 'get up early.' Waiving ceremony, we think the conduct of half a dozen of our best friends vile in the extreme. We wish we could make the hills wetter, and the inns dirtier, their talk dull, and their tea indigestible for such treachery " (*Nation*, August 30, 1845).

† I find among his papers letters from Colonel Thompson, who represented generous and cultivated Radicalism; Sharman Crawford, a Federalist and a friend to the tenant farmer; and James Hardiman, who cultivated Irish antiquities and Celtic literature with steady enthusiasm, but only to a limited audience: but none of them are of permanent interest.

CHAPTER IX.

In the midst of this generous and fruitful work,—on the threshold, as it seemed, of a long and happy career,—when his power to stimulate and control his generation was greatest and most stringently needed, —from the midst of a crowd of loyal friends, and from the side of the woman he had wooed and won for his bride, Thomas Davis, by God's inscrutable judgment, received the summons which none can resist—the strong no more than the weak. On the 9th of September, 1845, he did not appear at the *Nation* office as usual, but a note came from him announcing what he believed to be a slight stomachic derangement :—

> "Tuesday morning.
>
> "MY DEAR D.,
>
> "I have had an attack of some sort of cholera, and *perhaps* have slight scarlatina. I cannot see any one, and am in bed. Don't be alarmed about me; but don't rely on my being able to write.
>
> "Ever yours,
> "T. D."

The lines were somewhat tremulous, but as I learned from his servant that the note was written in bed, the change from his usual clear and vigorous

handwriting excited no suspicion.   A note from
MacNevin, written to him in a tone of banter, intended to amuse a sick chamber, will sufficiently
indicate the entire absence of alarm among his
friends :—

> "I regret very much to hear that you have been unwell, the
> more especially as your ailment took so unpatriotic a turn as
> 'English' cholera.   The unfortunate disease won't remain long in
> your Celtic constitution.   I suppose you are quite well by this
> time. . . . Will you write me (and pray do it at once if you are
> well) a list of places and books to find all about the Ulster
> Plantation in, as I have, greatly to my pleasure, been awarded
> that subject by Charles Duffy [for a volume of the " Library of
> Ireland "].   It is not too antiquarian ; and I am quite sick of
> modern patriotism. . . . Pray do now write me one line from your
> couch, where 'Tityre tu recubans sub tegmine— quilti.'"

The brave young man, tossing in feverish pain,
was thinking chiefly of duties necessarily neglected
for a time, and of the risk that news of his condition
in some alarming shape should reach the heart which
it would wound the sorest.   After a couple of days he
wrote to me again :—

> "Dear D.,
>   "I have had a bad attack of scarlatina, with a horrid
> sore throat; don't mention this to *any* one, for a very delicate
> reason I have ; but pray get the Curran speeches read, except the
> Newry election.   Have Conway's *Post* of 1812 sent back to him,
> and read and correct yourself so much of the memoir as I sent.
> In four days I hope to be able to look at light business for a short
> time.
>   "Ever yours,
>   "T. D."

The handwriting in this note was still more
blurred and tremulous than in the first, but the tone
was so confident, and the reliance of his comrades
on the vigour of his constitution, which seemed safe

against all the mischances of life, was so complete, that they banished all apprehension. His mother and sister, whom he tenderly loved, and who loved him with passionate affection, were at his bedside. Dr. Stokes, a physician in the first rank of his profession, was in attendance; and no one doubted that in a week or so he would be at his post again. I replied to his second note as one does to a friend absent for a day or two, by some casual mischance:—

> " MY DEAR DAVIS,
>
>   " I will do all you desire forthwith. When may I hope to see you? Leave word with your servant when you are well enough to be seen. I cannot now keep your illness a secret, because I told John O'Hagan and M'Carthy yesterday; but I will prevent them going to see you. John says you have an opportunity of rivalling Mirabeau, by dying at this minute; but he begs you won't be tempted by the inviting opportunity.
>
>   " Always yours,
>   " C. G. D."

Towards the end of the week he improved greatly; so greatly that he insisted on driving out for an hour for a purpose which may be conjectured with considerable confidence. A relapse followed this imprudence, but not a whisper of danger was heard. On Tuesday morning, September 15th, I was summoned to his mother's house to see his dead body. Never in a long life has a stroke so wholly unexpected fallen on me. There lay the man whom I loved beyond any on the earth, a pallid corpse. His face still wore the character of sweet silent strength which marked it when he lived, and it was hard to believe that I should never more feel his cordial clasping hand, or see his eyes beaming with affection and sincerity. He had grown rapidly worse during the night time, but was confident of recovery until almost the end, and spoke impatiently of interrupted work. At dawn he died in the arms of Neville, a faithful servant, who had been in constant attendance on him.

I immediately communicated the tragic news to his closest friends who were absent from Dublin. It was received with wails of pain and dismay.*

* "Your letter," Dillon wrote me, "was like a thrust from a dagger. I had not even heard that he was unwell. This calamity makes the world look black. God knows I am tempted to wish myself well out of it. I am doing you a grievous wrong to leave you alone at this melancholy time. I was preparing to be off by the post-car, but my friends have one and all protested against it, and I verily believe that they would keep me by force if nothing else would. God help us, my dear fellow; I don't know how we can look at one another when we meet."

"I have been," wrote MacNevin, "in a state of the greatest agony since I got your letter last evening. I could have lost nearer than he with less anguish;—he was such a noble, gentle creature. And to me always exaggerating my good qualities, never finding fault, and never, never with an angry look or word. He was more than a brother; and I loved him better than all the brothers I have. Our bond of union is broken; what mournful meetings ours will be in future. . . . My God, how horror-struck will be Dillon and Smith O'Brien! I never closed my eyes since I got the fatal news."

A few days later he wrote: "I feel so lonely and bereaved, the soul has gone out of all my hopes for the future, and even the conviction of the dear friends I have still goes but a short way to reconcile me to a loss that I know is irreparable. I had a mournful satisfaction in reading the beautiful tribute in the *Nation* to his extraordinary virtues."

Maddyn wrote in a more subdued tone of affection, which men of his opinions, for he was a Unionist, may still read with profit :—

"I need not say how your letter stunned me. I can hardly credit the intelligence still. With no one in this world did I more sympathise. I never loved any man so much, and I respected him just as much. But we all felt the same way towards him : let us see what we can do to honour his memory and to preserve his fame. The man Thomas Davis ought to be exhibited in as strong colours as consist with truth, not only to his countrymen but to the citizens of this empire. The world must be told what his nature was, how large and patriotic were his designs, and how truly pure were his purposes. For he was one of those spirits who quicken others by communication with them. For the purpose of recording his career in a literary shape, I venture to suggest that his personal friends should meet and determine that his life should be given to the public, and that all of them should contribute whatever materials they could to such a work. You ought to be the recorder of his life ; for that office you of all his friends are the most fitted, not alone by talents and literary power, but by thoroughly close and catholic sympathy with the noble Davis in all things. There was more of the *idem velle* and *idem nolle* between him and you than between any other of that large circle who admired him living and lament him dead. Your close intimacy and identification for the last three memorable years, your agreement with him on all practical and speculative questions of Irish politics, your

Not one of them, it may be confidently surmised, had conceived the possibility that the strong man might disappear without a moment's notice, and carry with him much that was most precious in their lives. One of the most gifted of his friends wrote, with scarcely a note of exaggeration: "The sun shines and we note it not; but let the eclipse come, and we fear and tremble. Over his glory has come the eclipse of death, and we fear, and tremble, and weep." I have already written what I saw and felt on that occasion, and I prefer borrowing the narrative to telling the same tale in other words.

"Though it was the season when Dublin was emptiest of the cultivated class, a public funeral was immediately determined upon by a few leading men, and the assent of his family obtained. But it was no cold funereal pageantry that accompanied him to the grave. In all the years of my life, before and since, I have not seen so many grown men weep bitter tears as on that September day. The members of the 'Eighty-two Club, the Corporation of Dublin, and the Committee of the Repeal Association took their place in the procession as a matter of course; but it would have soothed the spirit of Davis to see mixed with the green uniforms and scarlet gowns men of culture and intellect without distinction of party and outside of all political ·parties. The antiquaries and scholars of the Royal Irish Academy, the Councils of the Archæological and Celtic Societies, the artists of the Royal Hibernian Academy, the committee of the Dublin Library, sent deputations,

personal cognizance of the extent of his unseen labours to serve the country he loved—these things seem to command that you honour yourself and your friend by taking charge of his memory. Let me entreat of you to resolve upon doing so."

and the names best known in Irish literature and art
might be read next day in the long list of mourners.
He was buried in Mount Jerome Cemetery, in latter
years the burying-place of the Protestant community,
but once the pleasure-grounds of the suburban villa
where John Keogh the Catholic leader took counsel
with Wolfe Tone, the young Protestant patriot, how
to unite the jarring creeds in a common struggle for
Ireland. The Whig and Conservative Press did him
generous justice. They recognized in him a man
unbiassed by personal ambition and untainted by the
rancour of faction, who loved but never flattered his
countrymen; and who, still in the very prime of
manhood, was regarded not only with affection and
confidence, but with veneration, by his associates.
The first proposal for a monument came from a Tory;
and Whigs and Tories rivalled his political friends
in carrying the project to completion. To the next
meeting of the Association, O'Connell wrote: ' I
solemnly declare that I never knew any man who
could be so useful to Ireland in the present stage
of the struggle.' O'Brien on the same occasion
described him as one who ' united a woman's tenderness with the soul of a hero.' Even Mr. John
O'Connell discovered, somewhat late in the day, that
' if there did exist differences of opinion (between
Davis and other Nationalists) they were differences
of honest and sincere conviction.' But the bulk of
the people throughout the island little knew the
calamity that had befallen them. A writer of the
period compared them to children who had lost their
father, and were unconscious of all the danger and
trouble such a fact implied. In Dublin it was necessarily different; many of the industrious classes

knew and loved him; and it was noted as a strange instance of unsought popularity that the ballad-singers of the Liberties, who had no longer, as of old, a Swift or a Goldsmith for their poet, sang a lament for Davis to street audiences in the traditional tropes and jingles which he had so long laboured to supersede by poetry and sense. 'Each brave Milesian, of Erin's blessed nation (was invoked by the poets of Meath-street) to join in the mournful theme for the brave son of Granu, young Davis the hero, who never knew terror or shame.'

" Judging him now, a generation after his death, when years and communion with the world have tempered the exaggerations of youthful friendship, I can confidently say that I have not known a man so nobly gifted as Thomas Davis. If his articles had been spoken speeches his reputation as an orator would have rivalled Grattan's, and the beauty and vigour of his style were never employed for mere show, as they sometimes were by Grattan; he fired not rockets, but salvos of artillery. If his programmes and reports, which were the plans and specifications of much of the best work done in his day, had been habitually associated with his name, his practical genius would have ranked as high as O'Connell's. Among his comrades who were poets he would have been chosen Laureate, though poetry was only his pastime. And these gifts leave his rarest qualities untold. What he was as a friend, so tender, so helpful, so steadfast, no description will paint. His comrades had the same careless confidence in him men have in the operations of nature, where irregularity and aberration do not exist. Like Burke and Berkeley, he inspired and controlled all

2 B

who came within the range of his influence, without
aiming to lead or dominate. He was singularly
modest and unselfish. In a long life I have never
known any man remotely resemble him in these
qualities. The chief motive-power of a party and
a cause, labouring for them as a man of exemplary
industry labours in his calling, he not only never
claimed any recognition or reward, but discouraged
allusion to his services by those who knew them best.
Passionate enthusiasm is apt to become prejudice,
but in Davis it was controlled not only by a disciplined judgment but by a fixed determination to be
just. He brought to political controversy a fairness
previously unexampled in Ireland. In all his writings
there will not be found a single sentence reflecting
ungenerously on any human being. He had set
himself the task of building up a nation, a task not
beyond his strength had fortune been kind. Now
that the transactions of that day have fallen into
their natural perspective, now that we know what
has perished and what survives of its conflicting
opinions, we may plainly see, that, imperfectly as
they knew him, the Irish race—the grown men of
1845—in the highest diapason of their passions, in
the widest range of their capacity for action or
endurance, were represented and embodied in Thomas
Davis better than in any man then living. He had
predicted a revolution; and if fundamental change
in the ideas which move and control a people be
a revolution, then his prediction was already accomplished. In conflicts of opinion near at hand a
prodigious change made itself manifest, traceable to
teaching of which he was the chief exponent. During
his brief career, scarcely exceeding three years, he

had administered no office of authority, mounted no
tribune, published no books, or next to none, and
marshalled no following; but with the simplest
agencies, in the columns of a newspaper, in casual
communication with his friends and contemporaries,
he made a name which, after a generation, is still
recalled with enthusiasm or tears, and will be dear
to students and patriots while there is an Irish
people." *

From the death-bed of my friend, I passed at a
stride to the death-bed of my young wife, and was
for a moment unfit for work. But my absence proved
a gain. The article in the *Nation* announcing Davis's
death and burial, which attracted much attention at
the time, was written by one who did not share his
opinions or mine, but who honoured Davis's great
gifts, and was never more at home than when coming
to the aid of a friend in a critical emergency. The
late Lord O'Hagan, then a young barrister, every
moment of whose time was bespoken for professional
business, did me this essential service. His opinion
of Davis corresponds with the opinion of all men of
judgment and sympathy who encountered him, and
is a necessary part of the contemporary verdict of his
intellectual peers.

"Of his acquirements," he said, "it were almost as vain to
speak, as of his genius. They ranged through all the walks of
human thought and speculation, and they were profound as they
were various. But of his own people, of their annals, their
statistics, their literature, no man of his years, no man of his
generation, we believe, had so full an insight."

But rating his intellectual gifts so highly, he

* "Young Ireland," bk. iii., chap. x.

regarded his faculty of conciliating opponents as his most marvellous endowment.

"Rare qualities," he said, "must be his who, without compromise of his own opinions, nay, while he asserts them with peculiar strength and boldness, can soften bitter asperities, conquer ancient prejudices, and command the love and confidence of his political foes. . . . Rare qualities are needed in him who would bring those who have held themselves apart in mutual distrust, because in mutual ignorance, to look each other kindly in the face, to know they have common thoughts and wishes, to recollect that they are not only members of the brotherhood of humanity, but men who have a common country to love, to serve, and to be proud of. What he did," he added, "was but a mere promise of the things to come, had he been spared to form the mind, and lift up the spirit of his countrymen."

His friends determined to make him known to the world for what he truly was. A committee of leading men of the metropolis, without distinction of party, commissioned John Hogan to carve his statue in white marble. Mr. Burton,* who knew and loved him without sharing his political opinions, painted his portrait. A memoir of him was published in the *Nation.* A selection was made from his historical and antiquarian essays, and his poems were collected and carefully edited.† Elegies were written on his memory by his most distinguished contemporaries. A verse from Ferguson's elegy will adequately represent them all :—

> "I walked through Ballinderry in the springtime,
>   When the bud was on the tree;
> And I said, in every fresh-ploughed field beholding
>   The sowers striding free,
> Scattering broadcast forth the corn in golden plenty,
>   On the quick seed-clasping soil,
> Even such, this day, among the fresh-stirred hearts of Erin,
>   Thomas Davis, is thy toil."

* The present Sir Frederic Burton.
† The poems were edited by Thomas Wallis, the essays by Gavan Duffy.

And the people to whom he was but a name began to understand what an immeasurable calamity had befallen them. As the biographies and correspondence of the era get published, a new generation will find data on which to judge what he was to his contemporaries. Among the distinguished men who have acknowledged their obligation in youth to the school of which Davis was the chief, it is pleasant to recognize Professor Tyndall in his Presbyterian seminary in the north, Father Burke, the greatest pulpit orator of his generation and perhaps of his race, in his Catholic school at Galway, Mr. Lecky in his English University, and Carleton when he had reached ripe manhood.

"I was but a boy at the time," said the great Dominican, "but I remember with what startled enthusiasm I would arise from 'Davis's Poems,' and it would seem to me that before my young eyes I saw the dash of the Brigade at Fontenoy. . . . He and the men of the *Nation* did what the men of this world have never seen done in the same space of time, by the sheer power of Irish genius; by the sheer strength of Young Ireland's intellect the *Nation* of 1843 created a national poetry, a national literature, which no other country can equal. Under the magic voices and pens of these men every ancient glory of Ireland stood forth again."

"In my experience of society, in my knowledge of life, and, I think I may add, with some little insight into human nature," says the greatest Irish novelist of latter days, "I feel bound to declare, that no individual at all bearing any resemblance to Thomas Davis ever came in my way. A character so full and complete, a mind so large and comprehensive, is one which does not appear for centuries."

Miss Mitford in her lettered leisure grows enthusiastic over his latest poem.

"The more we study this ballad * the more extraordinary does it appear. Not only is it full of spirit and of melody, but the artistic merit is so great. Picture succeeds to picture, each perfect

* "Sack of Baltimore."

in itself, and each conducing to the effect of the whole.   There is
no careless line or a word out of place; and how the epithets paint—
'fibrous sod,' 'heavy balm,' 'shearing sword.' It is something that
he should have left a poem like this, altogether untinged by party
politics, for the pride and admiration of all who share a common
language, whether Celt or Saxon."

Jeffrey, no longer editor of the *Edinburgh Review*,
but always a lover of letters, exhorts his wife to read
and enjoy a collection of Irish ballads which he
supposes to have been made by the young writer in
the *Nation* who had just died so prematurely, but
whom he still knows so vaguely that he confounds
him, name and book, with one of his surviving
comrades.*

W. E. Forster tells, in a diary published since
his death,† of meeting a young parson in Ireland who
was an enthusiastic lover of Davis; and in England, France, and Australia I myself have had
kindred experiences.

Shortly after his death Samuel Ferguson estimated his labours in the *Dublin University Magazine*,
the mouthpiece of the Conservative majority, more
generously than would have been possible while he
was still an active combatant in pendent politics.
After speaking of the Repeal Association before the
rise of the Young Irelanders, in terms of inordinate
contempt, he says :—

---

* Lord Jeffrey wrote to his daughter at this time—"Granny (Lady
Jeffrey) went to church, and I read a very interesting little volume of 'Irish
Ballad Poetry,' published by that poor Duffy, of the *Nation*, who died so
prematurely the other day.   There are some most pathetic and many most
spirited pieces, and all, with scarcely an exception, so entirely *National*.   Do
get the book and read it.   I am most struck with 'Soggarth Aroon,' after
the first two stanzas; and a long, racy, authentic, sounding dirge for the
Tyrconnel Princes.   But you had better begin with 'The Irish Emigrant,'
and 'The Girl of Loch Dan,' which immediately follows, which will break
you in more gently to the wilder and more impassioned parts. . . . God bless
all poets! and you will not grudge them a share even of your Sunday bene-
dictions." (Lord Cockburn's " Life of Lord Jeffrey," vol. ii., p. 405.)

† " Life of Hon. W. E. Forster," by Mr. Wemyss Reid.

"But, in the latter end of 1842, the agitation assumed quite a new character; and it became apparent that repeal had been taken up by men who, believing the measure desirable and practicable, agitated it for its own sake, and were evidently ready to make great sacrifices for its attainment. The first fruits of sincerity were respect and attention."

It soon became plain, he adds, that the new teachers were bent on preaching generosity and justice to the whole people,—

"and on stimulating in their hearts the noble sentiments of self-respect and self-reliance, without which the liberty they demanded would amount to no more than a license to put themselves into the hands of new masters. They also observed, concurrently with these manifestations of a lofty and sincere morality, in the organ through which the leaders of the new school expressed themselves, a surprising development of intellectual vigour in almost all departments of literature, and a keen and generous appreciation of genius, from whatever quarter it might present itself."

Thomas Davis, as a Protestant like themselves, first became known to the Conservatives of the capital, and, says Ferguson—

"when they found him a gentleman of most unaffected, charming deportment, a poet, a judge and lover of art and elegant literature, exceedingly well read, and of a character and temper the most genial and humane, it is not surprising that affection for the individual supervened on respect for the politician, and admiration for the man of genius; and that he speedily became the friend and favourite of the *élite* of the intellectual world of Dublin."

The effect which the writings in the *Nation* produced, and the generous competition which Davis's genius called forth to rival his own work, greatly impressed Ferguson.

"The young mind of the country," he says, "starting as from a trance—or from that fabulous spell which our legends tell us keeps Finn's mighty youths asleep under the green hills, waiting the advent of an Irish Arthur—came out from its forgotten recesses, strong and eager for any achievement to which he might desire to guide it. Song, the instinctive expression of generous emotion, gave the first indication of reviving power. He had sounded the intellectual *reveillé* of a whole people; and, if they had slept long, they awoke refreshed. Strains as bold as his own replied to him on every side. The sternest opponents were captivated; and all parts of the United Kingdom yielded a generous applause."

Ferguson bears testimony to the use which Davis and his friends made of the influence they won.

"They sought," he says, "to teach the people justice, manliness, and reliance on themselves; to supplant vanity on the one hand, and servility on the other, by a just self-appreciation and proper pride; to make them sensible that nothing could be had without labour, and nothing enjoyed without prudence; to teach them to scorn the baseness of foul play, and that if they were to fight, they should fight like men and soldiers—these were the lessons which he now appeared a chosen instrument for imparting; and in fulfilling this mission, while Providence left him with us, he did toil with faithful and unremitting energy."

The influence extended from literature to art, and exercised a strong and beneficial sway over public taste :—

"Some of the most beautiful of both Petrie's and Burton's pictures have been executed within the last year, but the poetic sentiment which pervades them we cannot help claiming as in some measure a tribute to the memory of him by whom so many minds were opened to all poetic influence."

Even Davis's appeals to the military spirit of the country were preferable, he conceived, to the incredible dictum that no political amelioration was worth one drop of blood :—

"The Irish Protestants, who created, at the cannon's mouth, the only real Parliament this country ever possessed, have not hitherto felt themselves so defrauded by its transfer, as to make it their duty or interest to demand its restitution. If they did make such a demand, it would be with the cannon in the background, and that behind no masked battery."

And he adds later, in allusion to English criticism on Irish nationality,—

"If the Conservative gentry of Ireland thought fit to invite their friends and tenants to meet them at a new Dungannon, there is no power in Britain which could prevent the severance of the two islands. And there can be no more fatal delusion than to suppose that Irish gentlemen, because they do not profess the Roman Catholic religion, are insensible to contemptuous language against their country ; or that they are disposed to rest satisfied under any social inferiority whatever to the rest of the United Kingdom."

The sympathetic reader has now seen what was the life of Thomas Davis. At the outset he had the choice to accept the estimate of the biographer, or to reject it as incredible. Now he can judge for himself. He has seen what the young man of one and thirty did and projected, what impression he made on those who surrounded him, and those who only saw him from afar off. How many loved him without sharing his opinions! They saw, in the language of one of them, " a bubble where he saw a star ; " but, whatever were his opinions, they recognized in the man himself one " whose daily bread had been heroic thought." It is the sure fate of a feeble fire to go out and be forgotten. But Davis's reputation has gone on gathering increased light and heat for nearly half a century.* Comparing him and one of his associates, a keen observer once said, " That dandified young cynic chills me like the east wind,

---

* A Welsh bishop was good enough to call my attention to a periodical, published in the Principality, called *The Red Dragon*, which contained a memoir of Thomas Davis among a series of the notable men of Wales. The memoir was just and cordial, but it was accompanied by a portrait posed and costumed like a German student, but scarcely more like Davis than I to Hercules. And while this book is passing through the press, a volume of Thomas Davis's Prose Writings, edited with complete sympathy and appreciation by Mr. T. W. Rolleston, has appeared in the popular Camelot series, and will help to make him known to Englishmen and Scotchmen.

but Davis, though he is sometimes abrupt and dogmatic, warms my whole being with a sense of sincerity
and friendliness." And this love of race and kind
still radiates out of his memory, as it radiated out of
his life. A young Celtic poetess who only became
acquainted with his writings after his death, exclaimed, " Might not one such Protestant make us
forget the Penal Laws ? "

A man may be as surely known by the character
of his enemies as by the character of his friends. To
the chorus of praise and blessings, there were natural
exceptions. Mr. Kenealy, known at a later date as
leading counsel for the claimant of the Tichborne
estates, was at this time a contributor of sensational
papers to the *Dublin University Magazine,* where he
took occasion to deplore the folly of a country which
neglected the genius of Sheridan Knowles and set up
altars to the memory of a " dogfaced demagogue of
two and thirty." An experienced statesman has
bequeathed us the warning that when a publicist is
bitterly slandered the chances are that he provoked
the slander by doing some essential duty. And this
was Davis's case. A year earlier Mr. Kenealy wrote
in the same periodical a paper on Thomas Campbell,
in which he declared that the Scottish poet was a
creature as unpoetical as a dry old mummy disen-
tombed from an Egyptian catacomb; and that it
would be just as possible to create a sympathetic
interest for one as for the other. He retailed at the
same time some criticism imputed by him to Campbell on his peers, the poets of England, a specimen of
which is worth reprinting.

" ' Swift,' says Campbell, ' was an abominable ruffian, though a
shrewd knowing knave, and I am glad Jeffrey always goes out of

his way to attack him in the *Edinburgh.* Swift had absolutely no
one good quality, and in this he differs from nearly all other literary men. Byron was a blackguard and a liar, but he had a lurk-
ing love for liberty, which redeemed some of his errors—indeed, I
should say a great many. Shelley was a filthy atheist, but the
most sincere of men. Pope was a knave and slanderer, but he was
occasionally charitable. Gray was a selfish scoundrel, but he had
at least the merit of being inoffensive ; as we say of a sloth or a
sow, he was a harmless, dirty beast. Johnson was a coarse brute
and a tyrant, but then he was a good Protestant. Milton, a savage-
minded wretch, but he did one good act—he defended the execution of Charles the First. I might go through the list for ever.
Swift had not a single good quality, from the first moment of his
rascally birth to the last minute of his miserable death."

Davis rebuked this savage scurrility in the *Nation,*
not fiercely, but with sweet serene counsel, which
seems to have stung the critic to a blind rage.
Punishment was due, he said, to great criminals
living or dead,—

" but the reputation of a struggling man of genius—of a man
who had intellect enough to illuminate his age, but not craft
enough to conceal his own weaknesses—the reputation of such a
man is a tender and delicate thing with persons of generous
natures and high feelings. Nay, the weaknesses, the vacillations,
the inconstancies, the anger, the furious passion, the hasty revenge,
the broken promise, the abandoned friendship—all these things
are not to be marshalled and recorded against a heart that, after a
life of care and agony, lies cold and pulseless—against a reputation
that is part of the intellectual history of a nation."

Another assailant was Mr. John O'Connell.
When Davis was nearly three years in his grave he
moaned out his regret that a brother member of Parliament had made him acquainted with a cowardly
piece of treachery of which Thomas Davis had been
guilty ! When an explanation was insisted on, the
brother member turned out to be the worthy Mr.
Dillon Browne, and the cowardice was Davis's hiding
away in Connaught after the Clontarf Proclamation,

when he had gone to Mayo to consult with John Dillon. Dillon, in a few contemptuous sentences, blew the calumny out of the region of controversy.*

A word must be said of his literary remains. The unpublished writings found among his papers consist of two or three reviews, a lecture on the study of Irish history, and verses addressed to the lady whom he loved which were withheld from publication for obvious reasons. They were written in the last few months of his life, and are of unequal merit, but those who love him will rejoice to see them all.

Here is one, painting his new happiness :—

" I.

"Refreshened and uncloyed
They are springing out again,
The passions of my boyhood,
Like lions from a den :

---

* " To the Editor of the ' Nation.'

" 20, Great Charles Street, March 17, 1848.

" My dear Duffy,

"The last number of your journal contained an address from Mr. John O'Connell, in which he repeated a very scandalous and malignant calumny against the memory of our late lamented friend, Thomas Davis. . . . The facts connected with Davis's absence from Dublin at the period of the arrests, are shortly these. About a month before the time fixed for the meeting at Clontarf, when no person dreamed of arrests, he left Dublin, intending to make a tour of the south and west of Ireland. . . . At the time the arrests took place he had reached Castlebar, and in a few days after he paid me a visit, where I was then staying, in the country. I need hardly state (the supposition is ludicrously inconsistent with his character) that he took no steps to conceal himself from the local authorities ; and, after remaining two days with me, he started for Dublin, alleging as a reason for his departure the necessity of being present at head-quarters at such a crisis. I cannot refrain from observing, that this accusation might have come with better grace from any other quarter. Considering that Mr. John O'Connell professed to be the friend of Davis to the hour of his death, and bearing in mind the tears which he and his father shed over his grave, it might have been expected that he would have left this calumny to the vile or malignant slanderers who originated it.

" I am, my dear Duffy,
" Yours faithfully,
" John B. Dillon."

See note on Maurice O'Connell, p. 388.

There are crowns upon the bramble,
And angels among men,
And triumph in each ramble,
And fairies in the glen.

" II.

" I rush across the mountain
Twice wilder than the wind,
I squander without counting
The money of my mind.
All hands have pleasant pressure,
All voices sing a song,
'The world was made for pleasure,
And it cannot last too long.'

" III.

" And what has changed my being,
And what baptized my heart,
That, 'mid old sorrows fleeing,
My lightning spirits dart?
And why this cherub chorus?
And why this hov'ring dove;
Peace round, within, and o'er us?—
Sweet sweetheart, it is love."

There is another of the same period, and the same exultant spirit :—

" I.

" I used to sing of war and peace,
Of heroes dead and buried;
Of Ireland's wrongs forbade to cease
Until her sons were serried.
But now I've not a fiery thought,
Nor rhymes, who had so many:
My soul is soft; my heart is caught;
I only sing of Annie.

" II.

" Now, if I read of ancient days,
Or search through storied regions,
'Tis but to swell romantic lays,
Or mould beguiling legends.

Nay! if I sit and hear the wind
    Pour through a castle's cranny,
I only seek sweet sounds to find
    And weave in songs for Annie.

" III.

" Or if at times I lift my hand
    In warning or in anger,
Or blow a blast across the land
    To startle coward languor;
And if at times I toil to shield
    The wronged and hapless many,
It is to have a blither field
    To sing my songs for Annie.

" IV.

" And yet, Machree, were we not fond
    Of Freedom and Old Erin;
Were we not fretted by each bond
    Our countrymen are wearing;
Were we not full of hope to see
    Our country great as any,
Methinks the power would pass from me
    To sing for even Annie."

His Annie made a visit to the South, and he
pursued her with sympathy and fond wishes.

" I.

" Would I were now thy guide,
        Annie dear,
Where across Munster wide,
        Annie dear,
Cliff-guarded rivers glide,
Lakes in the mountains hide,
Towers topple o'er the tide,
        Annie dear.

" II.

" Glance down the silver Nore,
        Annie dear,
Whisper till day was o'er,
        Annie dear

Tenderly lead thee through
Soft winding Avondhu,
Softer 'twould seem for you,
              Annie dear.

" III.

" Fairest I'd show you there,
              Annie dear,—
Brave men and maidens fair,
              Annie dear ;
Never a nobler race,
Sweet tongue and gentle grace,
Often how sad the face,
              Annie dear.

" IV.

" Then, would you list me tell,
              Annie dear,
How their sad fate befell,
              Annie dear,
Faith to a foreign king,
Feuds thick as leaves in spring ;
Oh, 'twould your bosom ring,
              Annie dear !

" V.

" No, we would haste away,
              Annie dear,
Off to Cuman Eigh,
              Annie dear ;
Wander in Finbar's isle,—
Was it a maiden's wile
Drove him to that defile,
              Annie dear ?

" VI.

" Lone in some gliding boat,
              Annie dear,
Oft from Glengariff float,
              Annie dear ;
List to the ocean's sighs,
Look in the purple skies,
Look in each other's eyes,
              Annie dear.

" VII.

" Holding your bridle rein,
            Annie dear,
Arran's steep ridge we'd gain,
            Annie dear;
Never was view so fair,
Island, lake, hill, and air,
Dream a long day-dream there,
            Annie dear.

" VIII.

" Long silent echoes wake,
            Annie dear,
Circle round Killarney Lake,
            Annie dear;
Mingling wild minstrelsy,
Legend, and history,
Pondering love's mystery,
            Annie dear.

" IX.

" Oh ! that it ne'er would end,
            Annie dear;
Sweet 'twere such life to spend,
            Annie dear;
Then, like an angel's dance,
Ending in a holy trance,—
Ah ! 'tis a wild romance !
            Annie dear."

" ANNIE AWAY.

" AIR—' *Mary Neill.*'

" I.

*   *   *   *

" II.

" Her hair it is the trees at night;
Her forehead is the moon;
Her eyes they are a nameless sight;
Her heart a tender tune.

We told each other to forget,
　　As if we thought we should;
'Twas said we might not wed, and yet
　　We kissed as if we could.

" III.

-　" They said 'twas good for us to part,
　　Nor, maybe, meet again;
Or, if we met, her callow heart,
　　Might well be changed ere then.
They knew not Annie as I knew,
　　For all their kindly fear;
For all our sad and strange adieu,
　　You'll wed me, Annie dear."

"MY ANNIE.

" So gentle and joyous—the cloud floating by
Doesn't sail half so gracefully over the sky;
And the sun in the flower-bedded dewdrop that lies
Is common and cold to the love in her eyes.

" Oh heaven, such a heart! and to think that it's mine!
To think, when I'm absent, that sweet heart would pine;
To think that she pants when my footstep is near,
　And dreams of my breast as a refuge from fear.

" My God, look upon her! how good and how fair!
And charge the good angels to make her their care;
And grant that our grey hairs may mingle below,
Ere our souls close together to Paradise go."

Two or three ballads on other subjects, which he
left ready for publication, will be found in the Appendix, and must find a place in all future editions
of his poems — a book which will not disappear,
methinks, while any Irish literature remains. I have
omitted to note one of its most significant characteristics; his verses are not only as natural, as
buoyant, and as full of the spirit of the country as
the best of her sons, but as pure as her daughters.

Moore has left behind him youthful erotics, for which in his old age he not only blushed but wept. It needs a large charity towards the sins of genius to pardon the loose life and vagrant muse of Burns. The noble, personal independence of Béranger, who would not accept fee or favour from any party; who refused to be presented to the Citizen King, to sit in the Republican Assembly, or to touch the gifts of the Bonapartes, cannot make us forget that his *chansons graveleuses* have, perhaps, corrupted the morals of France as decisively as his patriotic songs fortified its public spirit. But there is not one impure thought in the poetry or prose of Davis.

The grievous blow which so suddenly destroyed Miss Hutton's happiness had such an effect on her health that her mother hurried her abroad in the hope that the distraction of foreign travel might divert her thoughts from her sorrow. A letter written to a sympathetic friend at this time is all the more touching from the fact that the death-stroke which struck down Davis struck down as surely her who was to have been his wife :—

"In the midst of all my sorrow the thought flashes through me, What pride, what glory to have been the chosen one of such a heart! Oh, if I were to live through an eternity of grief I would not give up that short month of happiness, that little time of communion with all that was most pure, most holy on earth. . . . I try to think of all he has been spared; no woman's love could have saved him from bitter disappointment; no care of mine could have prevented his glorious spirit being bruised, crushed by the unworthiness of those he had to deal with. . . . No ideal I could form could be brighter, purer than he was. . . . One little short month it was, and yet a whole existence of love, which I pray will purify and raise my whole soul till it be worthy to join that bright one gone before."

" She faded away," says a friend who knew her

well, "from the hour of his death." One task alone
interested her: he had asked her to translate from
the Italian, "The Embassy in Ireland of Monsignor
Rinuccini," which lights up a period of profound
historical interest. But the task was beyond her
strength, and the book was only completed and
published by her mother twenty years after her
death. She died on the 7th of June, 1853, in the
twenty-eighth year of her age, and will live long in
the memory of those who love and honour Thomas
Davis. None of us can escape the question she
raises in her letter, What would have befallen if
Davis had not died? Our history, like all histories,
is full of problems like this. If Swift had accepted
the Captain's commission which William III. offered
him? If Phelim O'Neill had been captured with Lord
Maguire? If Tone had been permitted to colonize
his island in the Pacific? If Hoche had landed in
Munster? If a mitigation of the penal laws had not
opened the bar to O'Connell? Any one of these
casual circumstances would have turned backward
the current of our history. If Davis had not died,
he would probably have been driven out of the Repeal
Association, with Smith O'Brien, when the new
Whig compact was completed, and he would have
brought to Munster in '48 the foresight, will, and
resources of a born soldier. He would not have
succeeded, for the time for success was past, but
he would have failed gloriously. As it is, has he
not succeeded gloriously? His spirit has palpably
animated whatever generous work was undertaken
for Ireland from the day of his death to this hour.
His comrades, while they survived, carried the
opinions which they shared with him into literature

and public life, into confederacies and parliaments, into prison and exile, and never failed to take up the Irish question again and again while life remained. A new generation, scattered over three continents, has found inspiration in his writings, even when they have sometimes wandered aside from the broad and noble highway which he traced out for Irish liberty. It is easy enough now to see that the work for which he was fittest was to be a teacher, and he is still one of the most persuasive and beloved teachers of his race; but beyond the pregnant thoughts he uttered, and the noble strains he sang, the life he led was the greatest lesson he has bequeathed to them.

MAURICE O'CONNELL ON DAVIS.

It is right to state that Maurice O'Connell, who had a gallant and generous nature, clouded by personal troubles, distinguished himself from his brother by a genuine appreciation of Davis. He wrote a touching monody on his death, and it came in a note which did not exaggerate his sentiments towards the dead patriot :—

"Darrynane Abbey, October 14, 1845.

"MY DEAR DUFFY,

　"I have not addressed you since the death of our beloved friend, because the crowd of condolers would give the air of conventional compliment even to an expression of sincere sorrow; and next, though not least, that I grieved to know that you had other and more sacred matters of sorrow. May the Giver of all things console you in that bitterest of afflictions. I enclose a few verses framed, I think, in a tone which poor Davis himself would approve of—as my offering to his memory.*

"Amidst this wilderness of song and testimonial, surely the most effectual tribute to his memory will not be neglected. His writings should be collected and published as soon as possible. They were his offerings to his country, and should be perpetuated. It will be an interesting study to trace the workings of his mind, and to point out to the future men of Ireland how much he did to advance her literature and her liberty, and in how short a space, by strenuous unremitting devotion to her cause.

"Yours, my dear Duffy, most truly,
"MAURICE O'CONNELL.

"Chas. Gavan Duffy, Esq."

---

* The verses will be found in the *Nation* of November 8, 1845.

APPENDIX.

UNPUBLISHED VERSES.

HERE is a street ballad, written with something of the plainness and vigour of Swift, which he probably intended for an experiment often debated, and made by some of his friends after his death, of substituting sense and spirit for the incoherent nonsense which made up the bulk of ballads sung to the people.

"OUR PARLIAMENT—A STREET BALLAD.

"AIR—'*Faga an belac.*'

"I.

" 'TWAS once in College Green, boys,
    Our parliament, our parliament,
But its blessings might be seen, boys,
    Where'er you went, where'er you went.
'Twas won by armèd men, boys,
    The Volunteers, the Volunteers;
We were united then, boys,
    And had no fears, and had no fears.
But England sowed dissensions,
    And reaped 'em, too, and reaped 'em, too:
From Ireland's " mad contentions "
    The Union grew, the Union grew.

" II.

" The arms that won our right, boys,
  Were crossed in wrath, were crossed in wrath ;
And England urged the fight, boys,
  To weaken both, to ruin both.
And some were English slaves, boys,
  Who bent, alas ! who bent, alas !
And some were greedy knaves, boys,
  Who sold the pass, who sold the pass ;
And thus they took away, boys,
  Our parliament, our parliament :
God's curse upon the day, boys,
  When off it went, when off it went.

"III.

" But as our fathers did, boys,
  In 'eighty-two, in 'eighty-two,
And Right and Honour bid, boys,
  Their sons can do, their sons can do.
Let Protestant unite, boys,
  With Catholic, with Catholic,
And we'd this very night, boys,
  The English lick, the English lick.
'Twas once in College Green, boys,
  Our parliament, our parliament,
And there it shall be seen, boys,
  Or they'll repent, or they'll repent."

"AN IRISH NAVY.

" I.

" Oh, 'tis a sight to heal the blind
    And make the cripple leap,
  Our banner romping with the wind,
    Our navy on the deep,
    Our navy on the deep ;
  And our batteries roar,
    As the Irish vessels sweep
    From our shore.

"II.

" Was ever land so marked by God
To rule upon the waves?
The surges come to court her sod
And own themselves her slaves,
And own themselves her slaves.
Oh no, her subjects ever true,
Whatever Erin craves
They will do.

"III.

" That navy goes in Indian seas,
To guard our merchant's barque,
To tell on every breeze
How well our cannon bark,
How well our cannon bark;
And oh ! how bitterly they bite,
When Ireland's foes they mark
In the fight ! "

"ROUGH DRAFT OF A SONG FOR THE 'EIGHTY-TWO CLUB.

" OH ! when their ancient rights our buried fathers won,
It was with drum, and cannon, sword, flag, and gun.
Then, ye gallant 'Eighty-Two—
With your green coats, ready leaders—
Where are your swords?

"II.

" The lion, ere he springs, may be stopped by word or eye ;
But when once he is blooded—slay him or die!
Oh ! when in that hour of need,
Be your stroke quick and steady—
Waste not your words!

"III.

" Th' avalanche that stops, can't resume its fatal might ;
If the hawk paused in swooping, who'd heed his flight?
Oh, a people's hopes set loose,
They must triumph soon, or perish !—
Which shall it be ? "

Here are a couple of fragments worth preserving :—

" I.

" HER cheeks are fresh as April showers,
Her step would hardly bruise the flowers,
Her heart is gay as summer hours,
    When on a May eve stealing
To meet the lad she loves so well
And hear him how he loves her tell—
His own dear girl, his dark-eyed Nell,
    Sweet Eily of Lough Greeling!

" II.

" She hastens down the thorn brake,
And reaches soon the whispering lake ;
'Tis ever bright, yet for her sake
    She thinks it now looks brighter.
And Hugh O'Reilly waits her there,
And sad his eye and wild his air,
Oh, does he strive with deadly care,
    Or does he wish to spite her?

" III.

Not he, but Tyranny's hard hand ;
For alien law his life has banned,
And he must leave his native land,
And but for his ——— "

———

" My love is gay and tender,
    His coat is Irish green,
He is a brave Defender
    As ever yet was seen.
Oh, many are in prison,
    And many more are dead,
Had Ireland sooner risen,
    The green had beat the red."

Here is a hymn which I found in his handwriting, unlike in
many respects anything else he has written. It is, perhaps, a
translation, or, possibly, a copy of verses which pleased him. I
feel a doubt whether it be his :—

"PILGRIM'S HYMN.

" FADING, still fading, the last beam is shining;
Ave Maria, day is declining.
Safety and innocence fly with the light,
Temptation and danger walk forth with the night;
From the fall of the shade till the matin shall chime :
Shield us from danger and save us from crime,
Ave Maria, audi nos.

" Ave Maria, hear when we call,
Mother of Him who is brother to all;
Feeble and failing we trust in thy might,
In doubting and darkness thy love be our light;
Let us sleep on thy breast while the night taper burns,
And wake in thine arms when the morning returns :
Ave Maria, audi nos."

IRISH HISTORY.

The sympathetic student will be glad to have the hints which
Davis wrote on a single sheet of letter paper for his proposed
history.

POLITICAL, SOCIAL, AND MILITARY HISTORY, FROM 1692 TO 1829.

Books, &c. | College Library | Marsh's Library | 22 pts. | Rolls office.
| British Museum | Paris |
Governors of Ireland | Plowden | Thorpe papers | Ormond.
Write to priests for anecdotes of Penal laws.
Statutes | Journals of Commons | Walker's Magazine.
Cox's Magazine | Dalrymple | Swift's Works | Mason's State P^{hs} to
   W. W.'s, Dublin | King & Harris MS.
Tone's life | Madden | Lucas' Works | Flood's Life and Letters.
Grattan's Memoir & Speeches | Curran's | Pamphlets.
Baratiana | Travels in Ireland, see College Library.
Edgeworth, Morgan, Griffin, Banim, Campbell's L. of Ireland.
Arthur Young on Manners.
Dublin Society's Labours | Wyse and reports.
Curry's Life, Parnell's, O'Connor's, Howard's, Scully's.
MS. notes on Penal laws.   Sir J. Frd the fair of Cashell, Pipers
   | Sheeby | fee simples O'Sull^n (Thierry as a model) recruit-
   ing for the Brigade (see papers).

Music, Bunting, Squire Jones | Dr. M'Donnell.
Local Hist^{ries} Hardiman, Macgregor, Smith, Mason, Windele Dutton,
(Rowley Lascelles) Au^m Hy., Wilson's Volunteers | Teeling,
Hay, Graham, Musgrave, Holt, Lord E. Fit^d diff^t States in
diff^t Provinces.

Chr^l table.	Financial tables.
Catalogue of Pamphlets, books, etc., used, & criticisms on them & papers.	Pop$^{tion.}$
	Surface & dis$^{ons.}$
	Tables of gov$^{rs.}$
———	Ch^{rmn} Ministers.
Arts & lit^{re} during this time, costume. ———	Arch. bps. & bps.
	Provosts.
Society, arch$^{re.}$	Parliaments.
Trade (Spain, Engl.)	Lists of Absentees.

He estimated, at the same time, the space the separate periods
would occupy.

Intro^n & Rev^n	50	— to Cath^c Com^e	30	
(clear and highly wrought.)		Lord Fitz^m	20	.
First effect of Rev^n	20	U. I.	30	
Molyneux	5	Insur^{tn}	50	
— to Swift	15	Union	50	
Swift	50	To 1812	30	
Lucas	30	To 1817	20	
Flood	50	To 1823	30	
Grattan	50	To 1829	50	
			———	
			580	

INDEX.

PRINTED BY WILLIAM CLOWES AND SONS, LIMITED, LONDON AND BECCLES.